T
DEM
AND THE
LIGHT

Also by Axie Oh

The Girl Who Fell Beneath the Sea

XOXO

ASAP

Rebel Seoul

Rogue Heart

The Floating World

Content Warnings: *Violence/death, needles/syringes, child soldiers, child abuse, and brief mention of suicidal ideation*

THE DEMON AND THE LIGHT

AXIE OH

HODDERSCAPE

First published in Great Britain in 2025 by Hodderscape
An imprint of Hodder & Stoughton Limited
An Hachette UK company

The authorised representative in the EEA is Hachette Ireland, 8 Castlecourt Centre, Dublin 15, D15 XTP3, Ireland (email: info@hbgi.ie)

1

Map illustrations by Virginia Allyn

A CIP catalogue record for this title is available from the British Library

Hardback ISBN 978 1 399 71878 3
Trade Paperback ISBN 978 1 399 71879 0
ebook ISBN 978 1 399 71880 6

Typeset in Adobe Garamond Pro

Printed and bound in Great Britain by Clays Ltd, Elcograf S.p.A.

Hodder & Stoughton policy is to use papers that are natural, renewable and recyclable products and made from wood grown in sustainable forests. The logging and manufacturing processes are expected to conform to the environmental regulations of the country of origin.

Hodder & Stoughton Limited
Carmelite House
50 Victoria Embankment
London EC4Y 0DZ

www.hodderscape.co.uk

For my brother, Jason,
who first introduced me to Final Fantasy

VOLMARIA
VOLMAR
HAEBAEK MOUNTAINS
THE NAKJIN
GAYA PASS
CHEONGDEOK MOUNTAINS
SEORAWON
OCCUPIED TERRITORIES
GORYE VILLAG
SARENIYA
THE COTTAGE
THE VALLEY
THE FLOATING WORLD
HAEBAEK MOUNTAINS
THE UNDER WORLD
TAMA ISLANDS

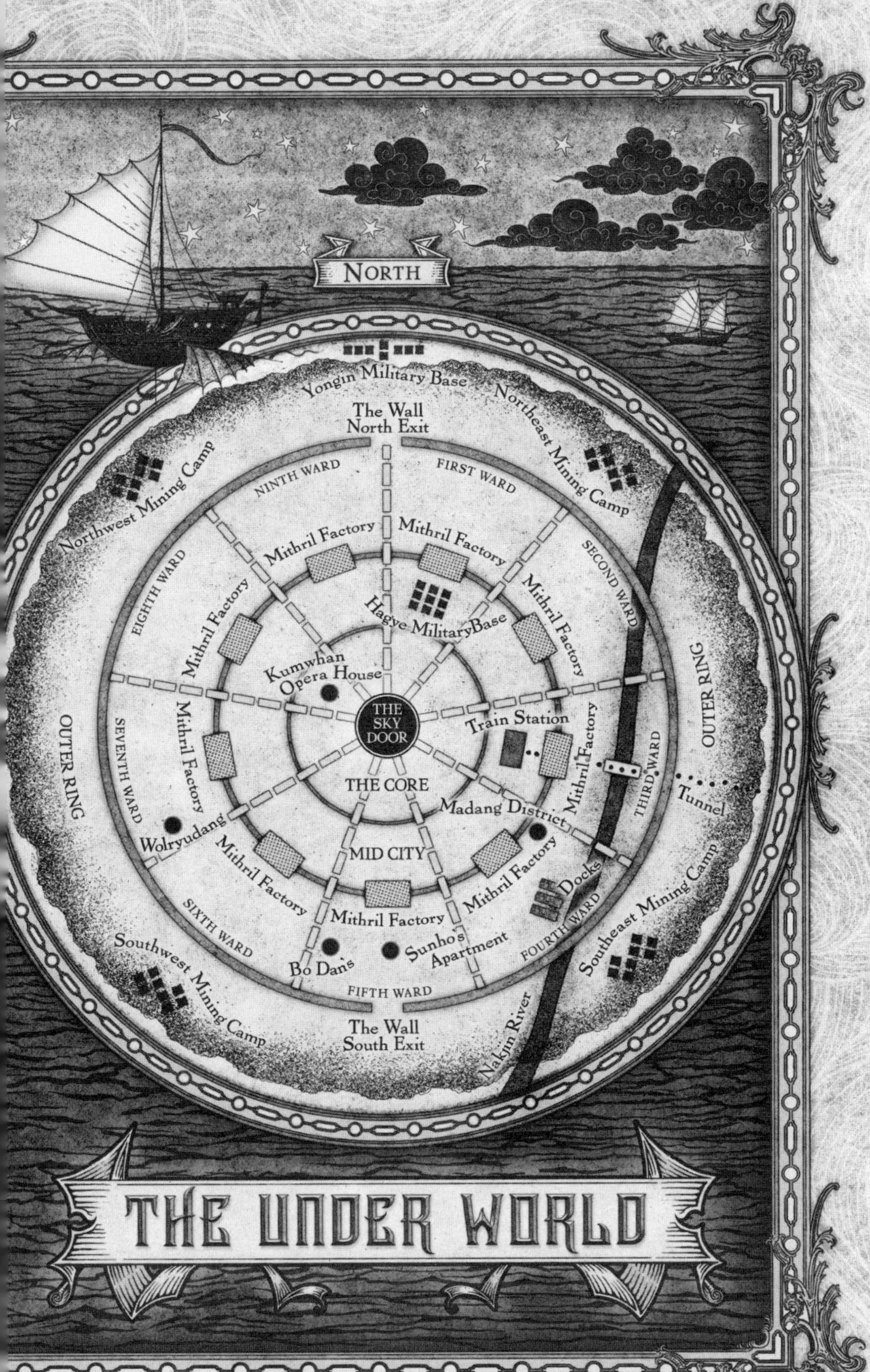

NORTH
Yongin Military Base
The Wall North Exit
Northeast Mining Camp
Northwest Mining Camp
NINTH WARD
FIRST WARD
SECOND WARD
EIGHTH WARD
Mithril Factory
Mithril Factory
Mithril Factory
Mithril Factory
Hagye MilitaryBase
Kumwhan Opera House
THE SKY DOOR
Train Station
OUTER RING
OUTER RING
SEVENTH WARD
Mithril Factory
Mithril Factory
THE CORE
Madang District
THIRD WARD
Tunnel
Wolryudang
MID CITY
Mithril Factory
Mithril Factory
Docks
Southeast Mining Camp
SIXTH WARD
Mithril Factory
Sunho's Apartment
FOURTH WARD
Southwest Mining Camp
Bo Dan's
FIFTH WARD
The Wall South Exit
Nakjin River
THE UNDER WORLD

ACT ONE
THE DEMON

CHAPTER 1

REN

East of the Haebaek Mountains
The Valley

REN TOSSED HER paper fan high into the sky, flipping backward onto her hands and landing just in time to pluck the hilt from the air. All around her the villagers erupted into cheers, and Ren imagined the jubilant sounds spreading like a chorus of wind chimes across the valley. Folding her fan across her arm, she winked at the children, who waved hands sticky from the sweet rice cakes they'd been gobbling up all evening.

The village was aglow with red and blue festival lanterns, and as her gaze swept the familiar sight, she felt a pang in her chest. Tomorrow she was leaving—she'd already informed Commander Su of her decision. Once she set foot onto the imperial barge, she'd no longer be Ren of the Valley, but someone whose destiny was much larger and more frightening.

The thought sent a shiver through her, and she quickly pushed it to the back of her mind. Worrying was for the morning. Tonight was for celebrating the recent harvest, and for honoring the spirits of those loved ones who had recently departed.

With a flick of her wrist, she spread her fan, swaying it side to side for balance as she extended one leg and began to spin. As she turned, her Light kindled to a flame within her. It emanated from her core outward, suffusing her with warmth.

The wind swirled around her. She spun faster. Her magic was still so new to her, raw and untrained. There was much for her to learn about how to control it and what she was capable of. She could manipulate wind, heal minor wounds, and wield silver Light, but what *else* could she do? Only recently she'd discovered she had wings. They'd manifested the morning of the Festival of Light, when she'd used them to save herself.

To save Sunho.

For a moment, it was as if he was beside her. She could see his handsome face, his eyes that shone brightest when gazing at her. She could feel his hand, warm and strong, gripping her own.

Then, just as the sensations arrived, they shifted, her mind flooding with images of teeth and claws. Her ears rang with the agonized roar of a soul being ripped in two.

Breaking from the spin, she stumbled and fell to the ground. Her heart pounded in her chest. She heard the children calling out to her as if from a great distance. Their cries were confused, fearful. She needed to reassure them, to get to her feet and finish the performance. She lifted her head and met Little Uncle's gaze in the crowd. A week ago, he'd had difficulty sitting upright; now he stood beside Hwi, his curly hair pulled back from his face in a loose topknot. His brow was furrowed, but he gave her a short, swift nod. *Go on, Ren,* his expression seemed to convey. *It'll be all right—you only need finish what you started.*

She rose to her feet. Then, with a flying leap, she flipped twice in the air before landing, breathless. Bending forward, she bowed to the audience. Immediately she was inundated with children, pouring over her like a school of minnows. She dropped to her knees, gathering as many of them as she could into her arms.

"Ren, you'll come back to visit, won't you?" Hwi's gap-toothed brother asked, his eyes bright with tears.

The headman's granddaughter tugged at Ren's sleeve. "You're not leaving *forever*, are you?"

"Please don't go," Hwi's little cousin cried, her cheeks red from the cold. "Who will play with us when you're gone?"

"You'll have Hwi," Ren consoled them. "And Little Uncle, of course."

As it had all week, her heart pinched at the thought of leaving them—especially Little Uncle. But she couldn't take him with her. Little Uncle was still recovering from the illness that had almost claimed his life. The same illness that had driven Auntie on a journey in search of a cure, from which she hadn't yet returned.

A few of the children had quivering lips, but they nodded bravely. "We'll miss you!"

"I'll miss you more!" Ren promised.

"Cheer up, Ren," Hwi's brother said solemnly, his expression serious for someone so young. "Everything will be all right."

Tears pricked the corners of her eyes, and she grabbed him in a fierce hug. "*Thank* you."

One by one, the children jumped to their feet. As Ren joined them, picking up her paper fan, she saw Commander Su approach from where he'd been speaking with the village headman, likely discussing tomorrow's early departure.

She'd only known the commander briefly before he'd pledged his support of her, yet in the past week she'd come to rely on the seasoned warrior, who despite his rough-hewn appearance harbored a soft heart.

As the commander lifted himself from a bow, Ren felt a rush of gratitude. Though likely burdened with an increasing number of responsibilities following the arrest of General Iljin, he'd accompanied her to the valley and had waited with patience and kindness until she was ready to leave. In their short time together, she'd learned that the commander had served the general for years, believing him when he said Ren's mother had jumped from the edge of the Floating World. In truth, the general had pushed her.

She'd also been surprised to learn that he'd acted as a mentor to the general's only son, Jaeil, who had remained on the Floating World under guard until the outcome of his father's trial, which Commander Su reassured her would take place soon after Ren's return.

She was certain of her feelings about General Iljin—he was hateful, a traitor and a criminal. But Jaeil . . .

She still didn't know what to think of the captain. When they'd been children, he'd been her friend. And though perhaps misguided in his methods, he had tried to help her once it was discovered she might be alive, going behind his father's back to do so.

Commander Su shifted his gaze west, to where the Haebaek Mountains loomed in the distance. "There's a storm gathering over the mountains," he said. Though it was evening, gray clouds hovered around the highest peaks. "If we leave before sunrise, we should be able to circumvent the worst of it."

Ren's smile was rueful. A month ago, she'd have been terrified of the prospect of boarding an airship that would take her into the sky, her fear of heights seemingly insurmountable. Now she felt only a slight shiver of anticipation.

"Whatever awaits us back on the Floating World," the commander said, "you'll have my full support."

"Thank you, Commander," she said.

A burst of laughter across the circle drew his attention. "Forgive me," he said. "You should be celebrating with your friends."

Ren shook her head. "It's better that I slip away now," she said. "I don't think I have the heart for lengthy goodbyes."

Commander Su bowed again before taking his leave. Ren stole one more glance around the circle, then ducked into an alley. She came out on the river path that ran beside the village. It was peaceful compared to the lively activity around the village center.

Across the river, the long grass rippled like waves in the ocean. A lone thrush called out to its mate, the clear, flutelike sound melancholy in the twilight.

Halfway up the path, her attention was caught by a dozen golden lanterns drifting toward her on the water. They'd come from the villages upriver. Messages of remembrance were written carefully in brushstrokes on the papered sides.

As she gazed at the lanterns, her eyes filled with tears. She also had loved ones who'd recently departed—her childhood nursemaid, Doona, and Big Uncle. She knew she shouldn't blame herself for their deaths; the demon that had attacked Gorye Village and the assassins sent to Bright Moon Temple were born of the evil decisions of others. But that didn't lessen her pain.

She didn't know for how long she stood by the water's edge, only that after a while the lanterns had disappeared; instead, fireflies appeared over the river. Her breath caught in surprise. It was winter, much too cold for fireflies, and yet she saw that they covered the area around the riverbank as well as the field beyond, winking in and out like tiny stars. She wiped the tears from her eyes and, with the fireflies for company, walked the long way home.

The wind chimes dangling from the eaves jingled as she pressed open the door to the cottage. For a moment, she stood upon the threshold, taking in the familiar sights. The hearth with the ashes raked neatly to the side. The low wooden table where her family had taken their meals together every morning and evening.

She'd packed a few belongings earlier that morning, so it was only a matter of fetching her pack from the room she shared with Little Uncle. Then she moved across the space to the only other room in the cottage, the one that belonged to Auntie and Big Uncle. Since returning, she hadn't stepped inside, wishing to respect Auntie's privacy.

Sliding open the door, she registered first the clutter. Most of the items from the traveling cart had been brought inside and pushed against the wall—the large chest where they kept their costumes, as well as Little Uncle's woodworking tools and Big Uncle's great barrel drum. She spotted what she was looking for perched atop a low cabinet—a small garment box.

The key was already inserted into the fish-shaped lock; she only had to wiggle it around before there was a *click* and the pieces fell apart. Slowly, she opened the lid.

The robe was as she remembered it, crimson in color, a red so dazzling it hurt to gaze upon. As she took it into her arms, she braced for a rush of images, but she remained steadfastly in the present. No awful memories of the night ten years ago arose to torment her.

She heard the door to the cottage open, only for Little Uncle to appear a few seconds later.

"I thought I saw you sneaking off," he groused. "You could have warned me." He held a brace of onions wrapped in twine in one hand and a satchel across his shoulder. "The matchmaker cornered me with a list, *a list*—" He broke off. "What's that?"

"A robe," Ren said, holding it up for him to see. "It belonged to my mother. She was wearing it the night she . . ." She'd rarely spoken of her past—Auntie had forbidden it, for her safety and theirs—but after Little Uncle had woken from his illness, she'd told him everything. Not just what had happened while he'd been asleep but also all that Ren had witnessed that night.

Little Uncle crouched in front of her, squinting as he examined the robe. "Then how did my sister get it?"

"I don't know . . ." Her mother had been *wearing* it when she fell. Later that night, Auntie had discovered Ren hiding in the hollow of a tree. Together they'd fled the Floating World. Had Auntie gone back to retrieve the robe? But when, and *why*?

"If only I could ask her," Ren said, gripping the fabric tightly between her fingers. She had hoped that Auntie might return within the week, but she was out of time. Sighing heavily, she released her fingers before placing the robe back into the chest, closing the lid and reattaching the lock.

"If you wanted to leave a message for my sister, I can help with that." Little Uncle removed the bag he'd been carrying from his shoulder, dropping it into her lap. She lifted the flap to find an inkwell, scroll, and brush tucked inside.

"The matchmaker cornered me by the ink trader's stall, if you must know," he grumbled.

Ren dropped the satchel to grab him in a hug. "Thank you! Was she very persistent, the matchmaker? I won't part with you for just anyone."

"That's a lie," he said loudly. "You're parting with me tomorrow." He'd been sulking ever since she'd told him two nights before that she was going on alone.

She studied his downturned face, memorizing his features, his slender eyes and rosy cheeks. She would safeguard this memory of him, for when she might need it most.

She closed her eyes, taking a deep breath. As she opened them, she pasted a smile on her face. "Should I not go back, then?" she asked, wrapping her arms around him tighter than before. "We could travel together in our own troupe, just the two of us. What do you think?"

"You don't mean that," he said, pushing her away gently and rising to his feet. "Write your letter. I'll see you off in the morning."

She waited until he'd left the room before she let her smile fall. It had been difficult the past week to pretend like she was fine. She didn't want him to know how fearful she truly was.

Reaching for the satchel, she removed the writing instruments, unraveling the scroll and laying it flat with the inkwell. She picked up the brush and dipped the tip into the ink. She'd made a fuss about asking Auntie about the robe, but as she placed the brush to the paper, it wasn't a question she had for her.

I went on a long journey, and I came home. But it's not over, she wrote, careful to keep her characters legible despite her shaking hand. *Ten years ago, you saved me. I've felt safe here, and happy. But in those years the Sareniyans have waged a war that has caused unimaginable suffering.*

A war in her name, even if it wasn't the name she'd claimed for herself.

I can't run away and hide any longer. There's a darkness in the world.

She thought of the demon that attacked Gorye Village, leaving Little Uncle gravely wounded. After he'd developed an illness that had turned his blood blue, she'd gone to the Floating World to find a cure for him, a journey that had taken her deep within the mithril mines.

When Ren closed her eyes, she could picture that strange laboratory, the site of horrible experimentation where humans were transformed into monsters, and the scientist she'd met there. He'd taken a vial of her blood in exchange for a supposed antidote—for what purpose, she didn't know.

And then there was the other darkness . . . the cruelty and corruption on the Floating World itself.

Ren's gaze traveled to the chest in the corner. In her mind's eye, she could see her mother standing at the edge of the cliff, but it wasn't the crimson robe that seized her attention. It was her mother's expression, as if all the light had left her eyes.

I'm afraid that going back might change me.

In the valley, she was Ren. A troupe performer. Auntie, Big Uncle, and Little Uncle's niece. On the Floating World, she'd be someone else entirely.

Princess. Queen. Celestial Maiden.

Those were the roles her mother had held, as had the women before her, all the way back to the original celestial maiden herself.

What does a legacy, *a heritage*, like that do to a person?

In going back to the Floating World, she was afraid of so many things. But what she was afraid of most was losing herself.

There was enough space on the paper to write a few last lines. If she was writing to Little Uncle, she would have written words of affection, but this was Auntie.

I'm sorry for leaving the first time without telling you, and I'm sorry for leaving now without waiting for you to come home. I'll try to remember everything you taught me.

Her brush hesitated over the paper. There was a sentiment she'd never expressed to Auntie before, but she was too cowardly to write the words, even now.

Thank you, she finished instead. *For everything. Your niece, Ren.*

REN WOKE THE next morning before sunrise. On the pallet beside hers, Little Uncle slept sprawled out with one leg thrown over a pillow. Lifting the blanket to his chin, she pressed her lips to his cheek. Then, grabbing her satchel, she fled the cottage.

He'd be upset that she left without saying goodbye, but she was afraid that if she did, she might never muster the courage to leave.

The Sareniyan aircraft were moored to the western pasture, each with dozens of ropes. As Ren walked over the rise, she lifted her gaze to the massive airships, hovering several feet above the ground. Their levitation capabilities came from the mithril embedded in chambers at their cores, and each was equipped with extendable rotors and sails to harness the wind. Squinting, she could make out a hazy blue glow surrounding all three of the ships. A cool breeze swept back the loose strands of her hair, and she wrapped her arms around herself.

She spotted Yurhee beside the loading dock of the nearest airship, where soldiers were directing wagons of goods up a long, flat ramp into the hold. She waved to the older girl, who jogged over.

Yurhee was dressed in tight-fitting breeches and a loose shirt, with a pair of goggles strapped to her forehead. As she approached, Ren was reminded of the first time she'd met the rebel, who was three years older than her. She'd thought Yurhee was beautiful; Ren could admit now that she'd been quite jealous of her at the time.

"Where's Tag?" Ren asked, hoping the brisk air would explain away her flushed cheeks.

Yurhee made a vague gesture behind her. "He's saying his goodbyes."

"Oh, I didn't know he'd made any friends in the village." Ren swept the field for Yurhee's silver-haired companion and found him standing by two sheep.

"We put the *Sparrow* in the hold, hope that's okay," Yurhee said, nodding at the *Blue Tortoise*, Commander Su's massive airship. After discovering that Sareniyans named their warships, Yurhee had decided that *their* aircraft—hers and Tag's—should have a name. "We'll travel with you as far as the Floating World, and then we'll go our separate ways. We'd have come with you—I, for one, would love to see a palace—but we've been away from Wolryudang long enough as it is."

Ren swallowed down a lump of disappointment. After much thought, she'd decided to return to the Floating World first before searching for Sunho. She didn't know where he was, or even how to go about looking for him. Yurhee and Tag had agreed to accompany her, but she couldn't keep them from their home and Wolryudang's proprietor, Grandma Jin, any longer. Still, she hadn't thought she'd have to part with them so soon.

"I'm glad," Ren said, "that for at least the first part, I won't be going back alone."

"Who says you're going back alone at all?"

Ren whirled around to see Little Uncle standing behind her. A conical straw hat sat crookedly atop his head, and he had a satchel thrown across his shoulder.

Ren gaped. "What are you—?

He lifted the brim of his hat to grin at her. "You didn't think I'd let you leave without me again, did you?"

"But you—you're ill!"

"I'm much better now, thanks to you!" As if to prove his words, he cartwheeled across the grass with one hand, holding on to his hat with the other.

Yurhee hollered and Ren laughed shakily. She knew she should refuse him, should insist he turn back, but she felt almost dizzy with relief.

"It'll be dangerous," she warned.

"I know," he said confidently.

"There will be demons."

"I know," he said, more soberly. He took a breath, then lifted his chin. "You're my niece. It's my responsibility to watch over you."

"You're only a year older than me!"

"Exactly. That's a whole year's worth of life experience."

There were probably a dozen reasons why Little Uncle shouldn't journey with her to the Floating World, but at this point, none of them mattered—she *wanted* him to go with her.

She must have still appeared unsure, though, because his smile gentled. "What will Auntie say if she comes back to discover that I let you go off alone?" He shuddered. "Honestly, I don't know what's more frightening—demons or my sister!"

A HALF HOUR later, all three of the airships that had accompanied Ren to the valley were ready for departure. Before Ren boarded the flagship, the *Blue Tortoise*, she and Little Uncle bid farewell to

Hwi. It was a difficult thing to manage—her friend had two little cousins clinging to each leg and a small ewe nestled by her feet.

"I'll look out for Auntie and tell her where you've gone," Hwi promised.

"Thank you," Ren said, taking her friend's hand and squeezing. "I'll miss you!"

As Ren and Little Uncle made their way up the ramp to the deck, Hwi waved vigorously, shouting, "Take care of each other!"

Ren caught the railing when the ropes anchoring the ships were cut, falling away as the airship began to lift into the sky.

Sunlight drew her gaze east to where the sun rose, spreading its golden rays over the valley. As she stared at her home for the past ten years, her heart swelled. These were the sights she would cherish most: the sheep roving over the fields like fluffy white clouds; the shining river that wound through the valley like the back of a silver dragon; and the villagers below, so distant now they appeared like small specks, indistinguishable from the flowers or the trees.

Then there was a *whoosh* as, above her, the sails caught wind, and the airship soared away toward the Floating World.

CHAPTER 2

REN

East of the Haebaek Mountains
The Blue Tortoise, *Sareniyan Imperial Barge*

COMMANDER SU REQUESTED Ren's presence on the bridge shortly after leaving the valley, and so she and Little Uncle left the main cabin where Ren's room was located to navigate the narrow halls. She was relieved that Little Uncle appeared to enjoy flying, effortlessly keeping his balance as the airship rose and fell, the sails and rotors working in tandem to move them speedily through the air. Pressing his face to a porthole, he pointed out a flock of birds flying beneath them.

As they walked, crew members stopped to bow to Ren, addressing her as "Princess" or "Your Highness." After the third occurrence, Little Uncle grinned. "That'll take some getting used to."

Ren sighed, then perked up. "Actually, I was thinking I shouldn't address *you* as 'Little Uncle' anymore, at least in front of others." "Little Uncle" was a name her family called him, as did the people of the valley. It was a term of endearment. But on the Floating World, he would act in a more official adviser role. "I want the Sareniyans to address you by name," she explained, "and with respect, and so I thought *I* should lead by example."

Little Uncle placed his hands behind his head, relaxing. "Well, try it out."

Ren pursed her lips. "Wook," she said, then wrinkled her nose.

"I guess *both* of us will need to get used to some things."

She grabbed his arm, pressing close to him. "I'm glad you're coming with me."

"Don't think I'm coming just for you," he teased with a wink. "The matchmaker's list was far too short. I wanted to expand my pool of candidates."

"I see . . ." Ren rested her head on his shoulder. "Anyone in particular catch your eye?"

He shook his head, heaving a dramatic sigh. "Too many soldiers. You know I don't want someone with a violent nature; I much prefer sweet-tempered men, like myself."

"You just prefer yourself."

He laughed, the joyous sound following them onto the bridge, where Commander Su bowed at their entrance, a warm smile softening his stern features. "Ah, what a pleasant sound. One doesn't often hear laughter on a battleship."

Ren released Little Uncle, and he stepped forward to bow. "I hope it's not an issue that I invited myself aboard."

The commander was already shaking his head. "Your presence here is more than welcome."

Shifting his attention to Ren, his expression turned grave. "I just received an urgent missive." It was then that Ren noticed a courier standing by the wall; her hair was damp, and flight goggles dangled from around her neck. "Volmaran battleships have been sighted near the Cheongdeok Mountains," Commander Su said, referencing the natural barrier that separated Volmar from the Occupied Territories under Sareniya's rule. "Once we reach the capital, it is paramount that I resupply the airships and leave to challenge them immediately."

Ren knew little about the war, only that it had started after her mother's death. General Iljin, backed by the Floating Council—Sareniya's governing body of nobles—had begun forcibly annexing the kingdoms that surrounded the Floating World. Once known as the One Hundred Kingdoms, they were now Sareniya's Occupied Territories. Though it wasn't until the general turned his eye to the great empire of Volmar to the north that the aggression escalated into a full-out war.

"Please accept my apologies, Princess," the commander said. "I had promised you my support when we returned to the Floating World, especially with regards to the council."

Ren grimaced. She had an inkling that Sareniya's nobles wouldn't take kindly to the opinions of an inexperienced young woman from a backwater village, even if she was their ruler by birthright.

"Though it reassures me," the commander continued, "that you'll have a companion you can rely on to give you sound counsel." He nodded to Little Uncle, who puffed out his chest.

Ren hid her disappointment with a faint smile. "I understand, Commander," she said. "Please stay safe, and hurry back as soon as you can. I have a feeling I'll need all the help I can get."

LATER THAT NIGHT, Ren and Little Uncle shared a meal with the commander in his quarters. Afterward, while Wook settled into his accommodations in the cabin beside hers, Ren ventured above deck. The air was thick with moisture, cool and brisk. Breathing in deeply, she picked up a heavy scent, a sign that a storm approached.

A few crew members were on the deck, adjusting the rigs for the sails. They bowed when she neared, but otherwise gave her a wide berth. Perhaps they believed she sought privacy, though it was more likely they avoided her for another reason. To the crew, she was a Sareniyan princess—not an equal, but *above* them. She wondered if this treatment was an indication of how it would be on the Floating World. If she would be held apart from the rest, like a star that was too far to reach.

The thought conjured memories of her mother—not as she was that last night at the edge of the cliff, but in other moments. In every single one of her memories, her mother was alone.

With a sigh, Ren moved to the railing, peering past it to see the other two airships trailing behind, one a little below to the left, the other on the starboard side.

In the distance, the Haebaek Mountains loomed closer than before. A storm had gathered around the highest peak, which was encased entirely in a colossal black cloud. The commander had assured her that as long as they stayed their course, they should bypass it. A spray of cool droplets misted Ren's face and she shivered.

Turning from the railing, she spotted a familiar figure standing farther down the deck, his hair bright against the night. She'd never spoken more than a few words to Tag, who was a talented mechanic, though they were both seventeen. Still, she found herself walking toward him.

He glanced up at her approach, nodding to her briefly before returning his gaze to the sky. Neither spoke for several minutes. Normally she felt an urgency to fill silences with chatter, but she didn't feel such a compulsion with Tag.

Maybe it was because he reminded her of Sunho. The two boys

weren't physically alike—Sunho was taller and dark-haired whereas Tag had hair the color of starlight—but they both were quiet by nature and had a calming presence about them.

Though, with Sunho, it wasn't *always* calmness she felt.

A longing came over her so acute she winced from the pain. She curled her hands around the railing, letting the cold seep through her skin.

She knew it wasn't just the reminder of Sunho that drew her to Tag. It was that Tag *knew* him. He was perhaps the only friend Sunho had, besides her and Yurhee.

He was one of few people who might understand how she felt.

"Do you think he's out there?" she asked. Instinctively, she knew she didn't have to explain whom she meant. "When I think about how much pain he must be in . . ." Her breath caught in her chest; she felt an ache at the back of her throat. "Not just physical pain, but the guilt he must be feeling, knowing what happened to his brother, that he—"

She broke off. She'd already told Yurhee and Tag what had occurred in the meadow, the last place she'd seen Sunho. Her magic had unlocked a memory, one that he'd buried deep within himself—the truth about his brother. That he wasn't missing; Sunho had killed him.

"I'm afraid," Ren said, "of what the guilt must be doing to him." To his heart, *his soul.*

She couldn't make sense of what had happened next, only that after learning the truth, Sunho had transformed. The boy she'd traveled with to the Floating World, who had begun the journey a stranger to her but by the end had become someone she cared about deeply, had turned into a monster with claws and fangs and wings.

She closed her eyes tightly. It didn't matter. He was still Sunho. He was still *her friend.*

"What if I can't find him?" she whispered. "What if I never see him again?" Her chest tightened and tears pricked the corners of her eyes. She hastily brushed them away. "I'm sorry. I don't mean to burden you with this."

Tag shifted beside her. He withdrew a white handkerchief embroidered with small periwinkle flowers from his coat and held it out to her.

"Thank you," she said, taking it and wiping at her eyes, then blowing her nose into the cloth. When she moved to give it back, Tag shook his head.

"Keep it." His voice was soft, slightly muffled by the collar of his coat.

Ren gripped the handkerchief in her hand.

"Sunho climbed a world to reach you," Tag said, and Ren looked up to see he'd lifted his face. He met her gaze. "I don't think anything could stop him from coming back to you."

A flush crept up Ren's neck. Tag looked away, and she noted with amusement that his ears had turned red.

After a brief silence, she cleared her throat. "Yurhee told me of your plans, that you'll return to Wolryudang."

Tag nodded. "Both of us have things we need to take care of," he said. "And . . . I want to check on Haru." Sunho's young neighbor, whom Sunho and Tag had saved from a fighting ring. Grandma Jin was watching the boy until Yurhee could return and locate his mother.

"Sunho would be relieved to know you're looking after him," Ren said, smiling warmly at Tag, who ducked his face back into his collar.

They stood a while longer at the railing. It had grown darker since she'd come outside. She shivered. The darkness appeared unending, abyss-like. Up and down the deck, crew members lit torches, their flames flickering sharply in the wind.

She winced as a strong gust of wind swept over her, whipping her hair back.

"Sareniya . . ."

"Did you hear that?" she said. It had sounded like a woman's voice. Ren turned toward the bow of the ship, where the voice had come from.

Tag frowned. "I didn't hear anything."

The sails fluttered wildly. It must have been the wind. They were approaching the storm now. In the next few minutes, they'd pass right beside the black cloud. A shudder swept through her body.

"Are you all right?" Tag asked, his brow furrowed in concern.

"I'm fine." He looked doubtful, so she smiled to reassure him. "I'm just cold."

"You should head inside."

"I will," she said. "Soon. I just want to think through a few things first. You go on ahead."

Tag appeared hesitant, but then he nodded.

She felt more than heard him leave; the wind felt sharper with his absence.

She wondered if she should have asked him and Yurhee for help once more in searching for Sunho, as she had before. The *Sparrow* was in the hold; they could leave tonight.

"Sareniya . . ."

She whirled around. She hadn't mistaken the voice.

Ren raced toward the front of the ship. The wind picked up,

blasting in and around her on all sides, strong enough to send her skidding backward. She heard the warning shouts of crew members, but she ignored them, forging ahead, raising her arm to shield her face.

The rain grew fiercer, battering the deck. Her hair came loose, lashing her cheeks. She was almost there, a few more steps. She dropped her arm.

A woman stood at the prow of the ship, her back to Ren, wearing a diaphanous black robe that tumbled from her shoulders onto the deck like spilled ink.

Not a hair on the woman's head moved. Her robe was still, without even a fluttering of the sleeve.

Raindrops struck Ren's skin like shards of ice.

"Sareniya."

She went still. It had been ten years, but she would never forget the sound of her mother's voice.

Ren stumbled toward the robed figure, reaching out her hand.

A boom shattered the night. She staggered and fell as the airship rocked to the side.

When she looked up, the figure no longer stood at the prow.

She leaped to her feet and raced to the railing, banging her knee against its side. She hardly felt the pain, searching the sky for a glimpse of the figure.

Instead, she saw a light in the darkness. She frowned as she spotted another, then another, hundreds of them, flickering like candles.

The ship jolted again. Ren pitched back from the railing, falling to the deck, as a loud cracking sound came from the starboard side. The sound was unmistakable: Something had rammed into them.

She looked upward to see the black cloud. It towered above her, lit up from within by the same lights as below.

Her stomach dropped as she recognized what they were. Torches, blazing all along the deck of a Volmaran battleship.

They were under attack.

CHAPTER 3

REN

The Haebaek Mountains
The Blue Tortoise, *Sareniyan Imperial Barge*

REN SCRAMBLED TO her feet, struggling to see through the pelting rain. She jumped as an arrow lodged into the wooden deck with a loud *thunk*. A whistling wall of sound drew her gaze skyward to where a cascade of arrows plummeted toward the ship.

She didn't think, holding up her hand and reaching for her magic. Light erupted from her palm, incinerating the nearest and scattering the rest harmlessly across the deck.

The illumination from her Light lasted for several seconds. When it dissipated, shouts arose from the enemy airship.

If the Volmarans hadn't known her location before, they did now.

She rose to her feet only to stumble, catching herself on the railing as the *Blue Tortoise* was hit broadside. The resounding crash reverberated in her bones. With a groan, the ship began to list to the side. The Volmarans were forcing them *into* the storm.

Within seconds the sky grew darker, the rain falling in thick, heavy sheets.

Below in the darkness, she caught sight of one of the Sareniyan airships, alight with flames.

A great shadow fell over the barge, and Ren jerked her head upward. Above the *Blue Tortoise* loomed a Volmaran battleship, a hulking vessel with black sails, flying so close above them that she could hear the ghostly creaking of its hull.

Rope ladders dropped over the side, their bottommost rungs clattering onto the deck.

The first Volmaran to board the *Blue Tortoise* took an arrow to the shoulder. He snapped the shaft, roaring as he rushed forward to grapple with a Sareniyan. Ren soon lost track of the battle as more Volmarans flooded the ship, garbed in black armor, their noses and mouths concealed by face coverings. Up and down the deck, they clashed with the commander's soldiers. Screams were ripped from throats as both Sareniyans and Volmarans were thrown overboard, their bodies hurtling into the night.

Staggering backward, Ren turned and raced toward the nearest stairwell. Rainwater gushed over the slick wood. Her boots squelched as she stepped in trails running scarlet with blood.

She was almost at the entrance when she tripped, hitting the deck hard and crying out at the sharp pain. Drawing her knee to her chest, she saw that she'd snagged her foot on the leg of a wounded soldier.

He was breathing heavily, his back against the foremast. An arrow had pierced his chest, narrowly missing his heart. His armor was black, a silver filigree tiger on his left shoulder. The symbol of the Volmaran empress.

He'd removed his nose and mouth covering. His eyes were young and fearful as they met hers. "Please," he croaked. He was barely older than Wook.

She looked toward the stairwell. She was so close, a few steps away.

Turning, she crawled to the soldier's side. As she knelt beside him, he coughed, choking as blood spilled from his lips.

The arrow had perforated his lungs. An inevitably fatal wound, and yet . . .

"Forgive me," Ren said, then ripped the arrow from his chest. He screamed as hot, viscous blood poured over her fingers. She'd only attempted healing a wound of this severity once before, when she'd first met Sunho. Like then, she let her instincts guide her, drawing on the Light, letting it seep into him. When he slumped back, unconscious, she pressed her fingers to his throat, relieved to find a faint pulse.

Shakily, she stood. That was the most she could do for him. It was up to Fate now whether he survived.

Stumbling toward the stairwell, she collided with a body. Another Volmaran. He whipped out a hand and snatched her wrist.

"So the rumors are true," he growled, his eyes narrowing. "The empress will reward me handsomely for a prize such as you."

He dragged her toward the ladders. She tried to wrench free, but his grip only tightened.

Suddenly the warrior jerked, letting go of her. He fell forward, a crossbow bolt lodged in his back.

"Are you all right?" Tag called out, gentle even amid the rage of battle. She twisted around to see him lowering his weapon.

"I'm okay," she said, rubbing her wrist.

He frowned at the movement but nodded toward the stairwell. "This way."

She followed behind him. "Let's find the others and then figure out a plan," Tag said hurriedly. "I don't know how much damage the *Tortoise* can take. If it gets any worse, we might have to abandon ship." Reaching the end of a corridor, he pressed his back against the wall, checking around the corner before proceeding forward.

The ceiling let out an unsettling groan. Tag picked up his speed, moving south toward the sleeping quarters.

As they turned down a hall, she heard sounds of a struggle, muffled kicks and cries. A Volmaran emerged from a room, carrying a young woman over his shoulder, flight goggles dangling from around her neck. Ren recognized the courier from earlier, kicking ferociously at her abductor.

Tag lowered his crossbow. He met Ren's gaze, signaling her with an infinitesimal shake of his head. He couldn't shoot the soldier, not without risking hitting the girl.

Ren racked her brain. Scouring the hall, she spotted a lantern in a sconce opposite the room. She reached for her magic and sent a gust of wind toward it. The flame surged, burning through the lantern and blazing across the soldier. Screaming, he dropped the girl to cover his face. With a shout, Ren raced down the hall, Tag in pursuit. Together, they rammed the Volmaran, throwing him into the cabin. Ren slammed the door shut as Tag grabbed a plank of wood, jamming it under the knob.

She quickly untied the courier's hands. "I'm so sorry," Ren said. The Volmaran had likely mistaken the young woman for Ren, as they were the same height and build. Ren felt sick with the knowledge that the courier had been targeted because of *her*.

The girl leaped to her feet, kicking the door. "That bastard! You should have waited. I would have gotten him."

Ren stood gaping at her, then choked back a laugh.

"They're here," Tag said.

The floorboards rumbled as soldiers with drawn swords thronged the hall.

"Princess!" the courier shouted, panic in her voice. Ren whirled around to see fire licking up the walls.

The flames were growing stronger by the second. Between the fire and the soldiers, they were trapped. Ren reached for her Light, only to feel a flicker of its presence. She must have overexerted herself—she'd never used her magic with such varying degrees in quick succession before. She wanted to scream in frustration at how little she knew of her own powers.

The Volmarans began to press their advantage, easing down the passage. The courier stepped in front of Ren, brandishing a short dagger. Tag lifted his crossbow, his finger primed on the trigger.

A mighty crash came from above.

The Volmarans stopped their advance, lifting their gazes toward the ceiling. A loud groan reverberated up and down its length as pieces of wood and dust fell to the floor. Then, with a resounding crack, it shattered and something large came crashing through.

As the courier leaped to the side, Tag threw himself over Ren, shielding her from the shower of splinters. A large chunk of the ceiling fell across his back, and he collapsed atop her.

"Tag!" Ren shouted.

Scrambling from beneath him, she pulled him, with the courier's help, out from under the wood.

"He's breathing," the girl said.

Ren sighed in relief, only for her eyes to catch on something drifting in the air before her.

A feather, black as night.

The ceiling had collapsed entirely. Rain slanted across the hall, dousing the flames. She'd seen feathers like this a few times before—in the middle of the bridge at Seorawon, in a secret laboratory deep within the mithril mines, and in a sunlit meadow on the Floating World.

She lifted her gaze. On the other side of the hall, the Volmarans groaned in pain, but she ignored them, her entire being focused on the Demon thrashing in the middle.

Sunho.

His feathers were like knives, slicing through the walls, the floorboards.

Ren took a step toward him. She heard the courier call out to her, but she didn't turn.

"Sunho," she whispered. Any fear she might have felt vanished beneath a longing so strong it left her breathless. She realized her yearning for him had been like an improperly dressed wound. And now that he was before her, it had reopened, bleeding without end.

She approached him slowly. He would recognize her. If not with his mind or his body, then with his *soul.* He *had* to.

He twisted around, lashing out with clawed fingers. Ren leaped back in time, but just barely—blood flowed freely from a gash in her shoulder.

Sunho roared, his wings banging the walls. He rose to his full height, towering over her. She pressed her hand against her wound, straining to see his face through the feathers that covered his body. A few swept past her, and she winced as they sliced at her skin.

"Sunho, please," she begged. "It's me, Ren. I'm—" She hesitated. What *was* she to him? They were travel companions. On their journey, neither of them would have survived without the other. She'd healed him, and he'd protected her. They'd fought side by side, teased one another. They'd comforted each other when they'd needed it the most. Her body trembled, remembering the way he'd touched her on their last morning in the meadow, his hands gentle on her waist, then firmer, his lips sweet like nectar.

"I'm your friend," she said softly. "Don't you remember me?"

She was enfolded completely in his shadow. He could crush her at any moment, yet she had to try to make him remember, to bring him back. She reached out her hand, not caring that her shoulder was on fire, that if she didn't heal herself soon, she'd likely faint from blood loss. If she could only see his eyes . . .

A bolt lodged in Sunho's shoulder and he jerked back with a scream.

"No!" Ren shouted.

Tag stood behind her, bleeding from his head.

"Don't shoot!" she yelled. "It's Sunho!"

With a roar, Sunho lunged forward. Tag released his last bolt and it struck Sunho in the wing. With a howl, he tore back up through the hole and into the storm.

Ren didn't pause to think, leaping over the Volmarans and rushing toward the stairs.

On the deck, the enemy soldiers had been pushed back to their rope ladders. Commander Su stood near the mainmast, directing his soldiers in pursuit.

"Ren!" She turned to find Little Uncle racing toward her. He swept her up in an embrace. "Thank the gods you're all right," he said, his heart thundering against her own.

She squeezed him tight, then stepped back. "Sunho was here. Did you see where he went?"

A clanging bell went off in the distance. Her heart lurched as she raced to the railing. In the sky below, Sunho had landed on a Volmaran airship. He was digging into the wood of the deck, ignoring the arrows that pierced his wings and back. Then he disappeared into the ship, reemerging a few seconds later holding a blue object. *Mithril.* The blue stone shone brightly in his claws before he opened his mouth, fangs gleaming, and consumed it whole.

Immediately the ship began to fall without the power of mithril to keep it afloat. As it plummeted, Sunho took to the sky.

"What's that?" Tag said, having come after her onto the deck. He was pointing to another vessel, smaller than the others. She hadn't noticed it before; its torches were extinguished. Unlike the others, it held only a single large catapult on its deck, manned by three people wearing voluminous black robes.

Ren squinted past the onslaught of rain. "What are they doing?" They'd maneuvered the catapult so that it was aimed at Sunho.

"I think they're trying to shoot him down," Wook said grimly.

"Sunho!" Ren screamed as the catapult released a projectile. It broke apart into a net, catching Sunho in the air. He roared, slashing at the ropes, but they only tightened around him. The aircraft then swiftly darted into the storm, dragging Sunho behind it by a cable.

They'd *captured* him. But why? Where were they taking him?

"Princess," Commander Su said, approaching her, flanked by two of his soldiers. "We've secured the ship, but the Volmarans might resume their attack. Please take shelter in the bridge for your safety."

Ren nodded dully, her mind in a haze. But as they moved toward the bridge, she tore away, running belowdecks.

She found Yurhee in the quarters reserved for the crew, shoring up the walls with pieces of broken furniture. Ren didn't waste time explaining. "Sunho was captured. We have to go after him. Please, Yurhee."

Yurhee frowned, taking in Wook and Tag, who'd followed. "The *Sparrow* won't fit everyone."

Little Uncle pushed Ren gently forward. "Go on."

Ren's heart sank. She was leaving him behind *again*.

"I'll wait for you on the Floating World," Wook reassured her. "You *and* Sunho."

Together they hurried to the hangar where the rebels had stored their aircraft. It was tinier than Ren remembered, built to carry only a single passenger, let alone two more. Tag settled in the back, roping himself to the side, as Ren crouched behind Yurhee.

The older girl lowered her goggles. "This is going to be rough." She signaled to Wook, who pulled a winch to lower the hatch. "Hold on tight!" Yurhee shouted as wind flooded the hold before dropping them directly into the middle of the storm.

CHAPTER 4

REN

The Haebaek Mountains
The Sparrow

THE *SPARROW* PLUNGED downward from the hatch for several heart-stopping seconds before the mithril kicked in, and Yurhee grabbed the yoke, pulling back hard. The small aircraft leveled, teetering in the wind.

Yurhee laughed. "Well, that was exciting!"

A lightning bolt speared the air, close enough that Ren felt its searing heat.

In the flash, Ren spotted the Volmaran aircraft, headed north. "There it is!" she shouted, pointing into the darkness.

"Hang on!" Yurhee jerked the steering gear, and their smaller vessel darted in pursuit.

They burst out of the storm cloud. Immediately the winds died down and the rain lessened to a drizzle. The night sky was clear ahead. In the distance, the Volmaran aircraft bobbed in the wind. It had relit its torches, a point of light in the vast darkness.

Yurhee flipped a switch and the headlights on the *Sparrow* flickered before shutting off completely.

"I saw three people on the deck earlier," she said, nodding toward the Volmaran aircraft. "But that doesn't mean there aren't more below."

The vessel was smaller than a battleship but twice the size of the *Sparrow* and had a lower deck.

"We'll follow them to wherever they're taking Sunho," Yurhee reassured her, "then sneak in and break him out. Until then, see if you can manage some rest."

Ren nodded, prying her hand from the side. Pressing her back to the wall, she slid to the floor. She winced as a searing pain radiated down her arm from her shoulder. The whole left side of her body was covered in blood; Sunho's claws must have punctured deeper than she'd thought.

Moving quickly, she untucked her blouse from her trousers, ripping off strips that she then wrapped tightly around her shoulder, gripping one end with her teeth and pulling. When she was finished, she collapsed against the wall, breathing heavily.

She knew that she should heal the wound, that she would only grow weaker from blood loss, but she wanted to conserve her remaining magic. She sat up to see Tag observing her with a furrowed brow. He was hunkered opposite her, cradling his crossbow in his lap. If he had thoughts on the state of her injury, or how she'd chosen to deal with it, he didn't voice them.

He couldn't have helped her regardless, not without unbalancing the ship. The vessel was so small that any slight shift in weight could send it toppling from the sky.

A memory arose of the last time she'd flown with Yurhee and Tag, when they'd rescued her from Hagye Military Base in the Under World. Then, every crevice of the vessel had been covered with crates filled with explosives. The aircraft was empty now, but it didn't feel any bigger.

That night, she'd also suffered a grievous wound, though she hadn't felt any fear. Sunho had been with her. Witnessing his worry over her had chased away the pain.

Sunho. She'd *found* him. Or, well, he'd found her. How did he come to be on the commander's ship? She wondered, in her heart of hearts, if he had sought her out, if his soul had longed for her, as hers did for him.

The people who'd kidnapped him, whoever they were, had come prepared, their ship equipped with a single device. Their intended goal was obvious: to capture Sunho. For what purpose? They hadn't been dressed like the Volmaran soldiers. They'd worn black robes, the details of which were indiscernible in the storm.

She pressed her hand to her arm, the wrappings already soaked with blood. Sunho would never have hurt her, but the Demon was different. Sunho had once described it as a darkness inside him.

What if he was lost to her? The thought was unendurable.

Overwhelmed with exhaustion, her eyelids fluttered closed, and she fell into a fitful sleep.

SOMETIME LATER, SHE woke. It was still night, the moon hidden behind a bank of clouds.

Yurhee glanced over her shoulder. "Oh good, you're awake." The older girl had lifted her goggles to see better in the darkness. "The Volmaran ship changed course a few minutes ago. It appears to be descending."

Ren sat up, ignoring the dull throbbing of her shoulder. "Where are we?"

"Based on our direction and current speed," Yurhee said, raising her voice to be heard over the wind, "I'd say somewhere near the border of Volmar. There aren't any major towns or settlements here. If I'm remembering correctly, Volmaria, the capital, is farther north."

Ren gritted her teeth, watching as the Volmaran aircraft veered to the right. Yurhee quickly directed the *Sparrow* to follow, dipping low over a pine forest. Soon, lights appeared, flickering faintly from beneath the thick canopy. Sunho must have passed out because he'd stopped struggling, motionless inside the net. The Volmarans flew toward the lights before touching down over a clearing. Ren glimpsed several wooden structures hidden among the surrounding trees.

"It looks like a compound of sorts," Tag said as Yurhee directed the *Sparrow* west, away from the clearing—they couldn't risk being spotted from below. "It's too small to be a military outpost, and I didn't see any watchtowers for a garrison."

"Don't tell me it's a secret facility." Yurhee shuddered. "One was enough."

After rescuing Ren from Hagye Military Base, Yurhee and Tag had brought Ren and Sunho to the mithril labs, navigating the treacherous mines beneath the Floating World. It was in those labs where Sunho had learned the truth about his past—that he'd been part of an experiment to enhance the scope of human capability using mithril.

"I'm going to land us out of sight," Yurhee said, maneuvering the *Sparrow* into a small ravine. She guided the aircraft smoothly over the tall grass before releasing the landing gear. It dug into the ground, slowing their momentum until the aircraft stopped entirely on a rocky riverbank.

Tag disembarked first, jumping off the back before helping Ren down by her good arm. Then he reached for the crossbow he'd set aside and pulled on a rope that opened a hatch in the hull. Ren's eyes widened at the sight of a small compartment filled with weapons. Tag reached for a prepacked satchel, slinging it over his shoulder. Grabbing a utility belt, he tossed it to Yurhee. For Ren, he plucked a sheathed dagger from a chest, holding it out to her.

She took the weapon, hefting it in her hand—it was the length of her forearm and weighed about the same as her bamboo flute—before tying the band it was attached to around her waist.

"Let's go," Yurhee said, tightening the strap of her utility belt as she walked swiftly toward the trees. "We only have a few more hours before sunrise."

Ren followed quickly behind her, Tag taking up the rear.

She was careful to keep her footsteps light, stepping over withered leaves and avoiding branches that might snap beneath her boots. A shiver racked her body, and she wrapped her arms around herself, ignoring the stab of pain in her shoulder. Her clothing hadn't fully dried from the storm, and parts of it clung to her skin like ice.

Yurhee set a brisk pace and they reached the compound in under ten minutes. It was surrounded by a wall, at least fifteen feet high. She gestured for them to wait while she approached it, disappearing around the corner and returning a few minutes later.

"It doesn't look as if they have guard patrols," she said. "They likely aren't expecting any trouble. This compound is well hidden." She turned back toward the wall, lifting her gaze. "This is as good a place as any to climb over."

She reached into her satchel and pulled out a grappling gun. "Grab on to me. We've only got one of these, so all three of us will have to go up at once."

Ren nodded, gripping Yurhee's waist while Tag wrapped his arms around the both of them. Raising her arm, Yurhee aimed the hook toward the top of the wall, then pressed the trigger. The hook—attached to a thin wire—catapulted into the air, piercing the stone. With a jerk, all three of them were launched upward, swinging over the top of the wall to land in an ungainly heap on the other side, their fall broken by a large, opportunely placed bush.

"Not exactly elegant," Yurhee said, brushing leaves off her sleeve, "but it gets the job done."

They'd landed behind a cookhouse. Large earthenware containers filled with the compound's winter rations were lined in neat rows against the wall.

"Follow me," Yurhee said, moving cautiously down a short alley.

Tag joined Yurhee at the front, checking around a corner before signaling her forward.

"Doesn't this remind you of when we broke into the ninth ward mithril factory?" Yurhee said to Tag as she pressed her back against the wall. "What fond memories. But now Sunho's a damsel in distress, and what a pretty damsel he makes."

"He's a giant feathered demon with wings and claws," Tag said dryly.

"Shh, we don't talk about that." Yurhee tilted her head meaningfully in Ren's direction. "Really, Tag, you're so insensitive sometimes."

As they walked, it occurred to Ren that they were *in* Volmar, a country she'd never been to, though there was nothing to indicate they'd left Sareniyan territory at all. The buildings were architecturally similar, each consisting of a single story with a curved rooftop.

She realized that though Sareniya had been at war with Volmar for ten years, she knew little of the country itself.

A memory from her childhood arose, from a time before the war.

The delegation from Volmar had arrived on the Floating World to celebrate her mother's birthday. They'd brought her gifts: a celadon bowl, the crimson pelt of a tiger, and a dagger embedded with white jade from the heart of their tallest mountain.

Ren had watched the procession from the side of the main throne hall, holding on to the hand of her nursemaid, Doona. The Volmarans shared the same features and language, and she remembered thinking, They're no different from us.

If anything, it was her mother who had appeared distant, standing alone on the dais. Sunlight had pierced the great windows behind her, blinding those assembled in the hall. They'd cast their eyes away.

But not Ren. Her gaze sought out the celestial maiden.

For a brief moment, without the eyes of the assembly upon her, the indifferent mask her mother always wore had dropped, revealing an expression of immense sorrow.

"There's where they landed." Ren looked up to see Tag assessing the clearing they'd noticed from above. The aircraft they'd followed sat in the middle of the field, abandoned. On the other side was a building that stood taller than the others. "They must have brought Sunho inside."

Ren felt her stomach flutter with anticipation. Sunho was *close*.

"What's your plan?" Yurhee whispered. "I have a feeling Sunho won't exactly cooperate with his own rescue."

"Just take me to him," Ren replied, her brow knitted. "I'll take care of the rest."

Yurhee nodded. "You got it, Princess."

Ren hadn't exactly formed a plan yet, but she had an idea. When the demon that attacked Gorye Village had wounded Wook, it had poisoned his blood. She'd gone to the Floating World to find a cure, and though she'd returned with an antidote, the elixir wasn't what had cured him. *She* had. With her magic.

An idea had planted itself in her mind soon after Wook's recovery. What if she could *heal* Sunho?

She hadn't told anyone about it—the risk to herself was great, and it was just a theory—and yet she knew the moment Sunho had crashed through the ceiling that she would try whatever it took to bring him back. She just hoped she had enough magic left.

Voices approached from behind them. Together, the three of them hurried across the clearing. Crouching outside a window on the far side, Tag took out a pry bar from his bag and handed it off to Yurhee, who jimmied open a window. They took turns slipping through, Tag closing the window behind them.

Ren stepped down from a low worktable scattered with glass vials and bottles. They were in a small room illuminated by several dim lanterns throughout. As Ren gazed around the room, dread pooled in her stomach. The sharp and unusual instruments on the tables. The gurneys equipped with metal restraints. They were the same as the ones she'd seen in the mithril laboratory.

"What is this place?" Tag shuddered, stepping back from examining an unidentifiable specimen suspended in a jar of liquid.

He and Yurhee hadn't gone with Ren and Sunho into the labs. They hadn't seen the evidence of experiments on animals, on humans. Two years ago, Sunho had been brought to a facility like this one, along with his two best friends, Rohoon and Heetae. That night, something terrible had happened. Afterward, Rohoon and Sunho had changed, and Heetae—

"Come take a look at this," Yurhee said. She was standing beside a large board hanging on the back wall. Tacked to it were dozens of notes and drawings.

"I've seen this symbol before." Yurhee pointed at a drawing of a single black wing. "It was on a map we stole from the ninth ward mithril factory. This facility must have been where the mithril was taken."

Ren's gaze snagged upon another illustration tucked behind it. She lifted the paper to find a rendering of a feather. She knew immediately that it wasn't one of hers, though the illustration was drawn in ink—it was too long, and narrow—nor was it a symbolic depiction, like that of the black wing.

Except that, the longer she stared, she felt as if it *was* hers; even with only ink, the artist had made it appear as if it were shining. Though that didn't make sense. The paper the feather had been drawn onto had warped with age. Whoever had drawn it had done so a long time ago.

"There's a door here," Tag called out, and she dropped her hand from the drawing. Joining Yurhee, she hurried across the room to where Tag had shifted open the door to reveal a staircase leading down.

"Oh good," Yurhee said. "Stairs that lead into unknown darkness, exactly what I'd hoped we'd find."

"After you," Tag said.

Yurhee sauntered forward, and Ren followed after her. The stairs ended at a metal walkway that looked down into a large chamber.

Sunho was chained to the floor at the center of it.

Ren lunged to the railing only for Yurhee to grab her arm.

"Wait," the older girl whispered. "Someone's coming."

Loud footsteps echoed from below as a figure dressed in black robes entered the chamber through a door beneath the walkway. From their vantage, they could only see his back. He approached Sunho, who appeared to be unconscious, a heaving mass of feathers, his face and body hidden by his wings.

In a way, the man's black robes mirrored Sunho's appearance, covering him from his head to his feet. A fleeting image of the sickly scientist she'd met in the mithril laboratory, dressed in the same robes, entered Ren's mind.

The stranger in the chamber below was tall and broad-shouldered. He pulled back his hood to reveal long black hair that fell past his shoulders. Tag shifted beside her, pulling his crossbow from his back. As he did, one of the bolts slipped from the quiver, falling to the floor.

Ren quickly reached out to catch it, but not before the tip hit the metal walkway with a clang. She whipped her head around to find the stranger staring up at them. She held in a gasp.

Black, red-rimmed eyes. Thick, protruding horns. Large, gaping fangs.

The face of a demon.

CHAPTER 5

REN

The Haebaek Mountains
Across the Volmaran Border

STARING INTO THE demon's visage, Ren's breaths grew shallow, her heartbeat quickening. It was like she was back on the cliff outside Gorye Village, facing the demon that had killed Big Uncle. Just as then, she felt as if a weight were pressing down on her, fear like a vise tightening around her limbs.

And yet, the longer she stared into the demon's face, the more its expression appeared motionless, almost . . . wooden. Its black eyes were pools of ink. Its elongated fangs were carved, exquisitely so, painted with bright crimson dye.

It was a mask.

Ren could have laughed. How had she not realized? She'd worn masks infinitely more grotesque, seen them on Little Uncle's face from across the players' circle hundreds of times.

Tag aimed his crossbow. At the same time, the stranger turned from the balcony. His movements were slow, unhurried for someone with an arrow pointed at his back. Ren exchanged a glance with Yurhee, who shook her head slightly. It was possible he might not have seen them—the walkway was shrouded in shadows while he stood in the light.

The stranger drew closer to where Sunho lay in a heap at the center of the floor. The only indication Sunho was alive was the slight rise and fall of his chest.

For several long seconds, the stranger loomed over him. Ren pressed closer to the railing, not caring that it brought her farther into the light. What was he doing? If he hurt Sunho, if he injured him in the slightest . . .

Slowly, he lowered himself to the floor.

Ren realized the stranger was *speaking* to Sunho, his voice a low murmur. But that didn't make sense. Sunho was unconscious; his breaths were even, uniform. She held her own breath in an attempt to hear what the stranger was saying, but it was difficult to decipher his words, his mask muffling them.

After a few moments, the stranger stood. But he didn't head back in the direction of the door he'd entered through. Instead, he began to climb the staircase that led to the laboratory.

Ren backed into Yurhee and Tag as they scurried farther down the walkway, relying on the shadows to cover them. She needn't have worried; the masked stranger continued up the stairs without glancing in their direction.

They listened for the soft click of the laboratory door closing behind him before Yurhee pressed Ren forward. "Hurry. He might be back soon."

Ren leaped past Tag, who was removing sticks of dynamite from his satchel, and hurried down the staircase. She realized the rebels meant to set off explosives, both destroying the laboratory and covering their escape.

"I'll unlock the manacles," Yurhee said, following her. "See if you can wake him up." She avoided the ones shackled directly to Sunho's limbs, instead racing toward where the chains were bolted to the floor.

Ren dropped to her knees in front of Sunho, in the same spot the stranger had occupied.

"Sunho." Her heart beat painfully in her chest. In his vulnerable state, he'd lifted his wings to cover himself. His breaths were labored; each ragged inhalation sent shudders through his body. "I'm sorry," she whispered. "I should have come faster. I should have searched for you sooner."

His wounds from where arrows had pierced his wings seeped blood. His feathers were slick with it. Ren held back a cry. He should have already begun to heal. It was one of his abilities, the mithril in his veins regenerating his body at a rate faster than normal. So why was he still bleeding?

She reached for him, plunging her hands into his feathers. She cried out as they sliced her skin. While some of the feathers were like a bird's, soft and pliant, others were like broken glass.

Grabbing the edge of his wing, she pushed it back with all her strength. She winced as a feather cut the delicate skin beneath her eye.

As the wing gave way, fear lurched in her stomach, knowing that she was about to meet him face-to-face. It wasn't that she feared him in the physical sense, though she was foolish not to—he could easily rip her to pieces. She was afraid that after coming all this way, she might fail. That she would look into his eyes and know, without a shadow of a doubt, that he was gone. Despair welled within her, filling her up until she thought she might drown from the pain.

No. She took a gasping breath. *No.* Even if he'd turned into the Demon, even if he no longer recognized who she was, he would *always* be her Sunho.

Sounds fell away—the low groans of the building, Yurhee's footfalls as she raced to unlock the final manacle. Even the sound of her own heartbeat faded to a muted, distant thumping.

Long, dark lashes swept across pale cheeks. Blue blood had dried at the corner of his full lips. He still possessed the body of the Demon, but his face had changed back.

Even monstrous and bloody, he was beautiful.

"Sunho, wake up." Ren pressed closer, heart aching that she had to wake him when in sleep there was no pain. "You're in danger. We need to leave. Please, Sunho."

His brow furrowed slightly, his eyes roving beneath his eyelids.

"Damn it," Yurhee cursed. "I can't get this last one loose. Tag, I need the pliers. Tag?"

Ren tore her gaze away to see that Tag had joined them on the chamber floor. The strap of his satchel hung from his shoulder. If he'd heard Yurhee, he gave no reaction. He was staring up at the balcony where the explosives he'd left were clearly visible beneath the railing.

Ren felt a sudden dizzying sensation. *The stranger had definitely seen them.* And yet . . . he hadn't raised the alarm. Otherwise, guards would have stormed the chamber. But she didn't have time to wonder about his motivations—they needed to leave.

She turned back to Sunho, lifting her hand to his face. His skin was icy beneath her touch.

She'd healed Wook from mithril poisoning. Sunho's affliction was different—if mithril had been poison to him before, when he was first injected as a child, he'd since adapted to its presence within him. But its influence had grown too strong, taking over; if she could hold the Demon back long enough, there was a possibility Sunho could regain control. She had to give him a chance to fight back. They could overcome the Demon together.

She took a deep breath, willing her magic, her Light, into him.

Heal, she thought. Warmth spread from her fingers. She could see it, a physical light, pouring into him.

The change in Sunho was immediate. His eyes snapped open, and he screamed. The sound was wretched, agonized. He sounded as if she was *burning* him.

She wrenched her hand away, heart pounding.

His face started to transform. His pupils blackened, spreading to fill the whites of his eyes. Fangs erupted from his mouth, weeping blue blood. He rose to his feet, his claws digging into the cement as his wings unfolded, his monstrous shadow spreading across the wall behind him.

"Ren, watch out!" Yurhee screamed.

Ren leaped backward just as Sunho lashed out, his claws slicing the air inches from her nose. Tripping over her feet in shock, she fell onto her backside. Sunho lunged at her but was restrained by the last shackle still affixed to the floor.

He raised his head and roared, the deafening sound echoing off the walls.

Ren stared up at him, the guilt overwhelming. She'd *hurt* him.

She knew so little about her powers, how they worked, how to control them. She'd destroyed the demon that had attacked Gorye Village with her Light—had she almost *killed* Sunho instead of healing him?

She felt helpless, foolish.

Banging and shouts erupted from behind the chamber door, where Tag and Yurhee had toppled over a stack of crates.

"Take cover!" Tag shouted, dragging Yurhee behind a stand of barrels.

A deafening boom shook the room as the explosives on the balcony detonated. Ren screamed, covering her head with her hands as the ceiling caved around her.

The roar seemed never-ending. When it was over, she lifted her face.

A great chunk of the ceiling had fallen inward, broken into two pieces on either side of her.

Sunho stood over her, his great wings coated with dust from the ceiling.

From his right wrist dangled the last shackle.

There was an explanation for what had happened—he'd broken free out of instinct, to shield himself from the roof caving in. She'd simply been close enough that his wings had also blocked her.

But she wanted to believe differently. That he'd done it on purpose to save her. To protect her.

Something wet and cool struck her cheek. Rain. Droplets fell through the great hole in the ceiling.

"Sunho," Ren whispered.

He shook his wings, shards of wood and dust falling from his feathers. With a great downward swoop, he leaped into the air toward the opening.

"Sunho!" Ren screamed.

Yurhee rushed over. "We have to get out of here!" She reached for Ren's hand, helping her to stand. "The building's coming down."

Ren shook her head. "I'm going after him. Will you be all right getting back to the ship?"

"What do you mean? What are you—" Yurhee broke off, her eyes widening when she realized what it was Ren intended to do.

"Don't worry about us," Tag said. He took Yurhee's hand, stepping back with her.

As before, Ren felt the Light within her pulse, radiating from within.

Sunho's transformation had been painful, but hers felt like slipping on a robe.

Silver-white light shone all around her. She arched her back, and wings of Light erupted from her shoulder blades. They settled against her back, corporealizing. A white feather floated in the air, brushing lightly against her cheek. The unfamiliar weight felt not like a burden but a strength.

She tested her wings, stretching the untried muscles. Then, lifting her gaze, she leaped into the sky. Up she flew, gasping at the coldness. Sparing a glance toward the compound, which had earlier appeared deserted, she saw a flood of robed figures racing toward the laboratory. Searching the ground, she spotted Yurhee and Tag sneaking out the back in the opposite direction.

Ren hurried to follow after Sunho, but she hadn't yet mastered the use of her wings, struggling against the wind that blew in all directions. She tumbled as a gust caught hold of her, flinging her toward the trees. She crashed into a tall pine, grabbing on to a swaying branch to keep from falling beneath the canopy.

When she recovered, she realized she'd lost sight of Sunho.

In her despair came an agonizing thought.

I should let him go.

He'd fled from her three times now. She'd thought it was because he'd transformed into the Demon, without conscience, without thought, but she couldn't believe that and also believe that he'd protected her.

It wasn't just her life that she risked in pursuing him, it was his soul. Because if he killed her, he could never return to his human self. He'd be lost to the Demon forever.

And yet . . .

Ren leaped from the branch, letting her wings catch her.

She felt like a broken thing, winging toward the one person who could make her whole again.

It was a simple desire that overshadowed all others.

She wanted to be where he was.

Sunho, I'm sorry. She would try one last time.

She would look for him in the place they'd promised to meet, all those weeks ago, on an aircraft beneath a mithril sky.

The house in the reed fields. I think of it, sometimes. At night, there are thousands of stars.

If you're there, I'd know where to find you.

It seemed impossible that he would remember, but she'd go there anyway. And she would face whatever outcome awaited her, whether she would succeed in bringing Sunho back to her side or lose him forever.

THE SUN HADN'T yet risen when Ren arrived, bobbing like a petal on the wind. She was exhausted, her wings barely keeping her afloat, but when she spotted the cottage peeking its head up from among the reeds, she found a last reserve of strength. She swept downward just as crows erupted from a nearby tree. They swarmed around her, plucking feathers from her wings.

“Stop that!” she shouted, waving her arms, but that seemed to only rile them up further.

She tumbled into the reeds, then stood up with a groan. Rubbing her backside, she scowled at the crows, who fled squawking back to the tree.

She let her wings drag behind her as she ran the last short distance to the cottage, pushing open the gate and stepping into the overgrown courtyard.

She knew immediately that Sunho had been here. Black feathers trailed to the door, which had been blown inward, as if a large creature had barreled through.

Ren raced across the courtyard. She hesitated at the threshold, her eyes adjusting to the darkness of the cottage.

It was as she remembered it, empty, with the hearth in the middle.

Sunho was in the corner, a seething mass of feathers. His breaths were ragged, each inhalation tortured, rattling.

His claws had gouged the floorboards; the remaining slats groaned beneath his weight.

She knew she should approach him with caution—he was wounded, likely terrified—yet she rushed to his side, throwing herself onto the floor. When he reared back, she reached up with her arms, wrapping them around his shoulders and pressing her face to his neck.

He roared, thrashing, but she held on to him. His feathers sliced her shoulders, her arms, opening new wounds, but she only clung to him tighter.

“I’m sorry,” she said over his bellowing cries. “I’m sorry for hurting you.”

She’d hurt him, more than any arrow or blade. The Volmarans

had wounded his body, but she had pierced his soul. She had tried to cure him, but the Demon wasn't an illness—it was a part of him.

She understood that now. She would never try to separate him from the Demon again. They were one and the same, and so she would embrace them both.

"Sunho," she gasped as he tried once more to dislodge her, his wings banging against the walls, his claws scratching at the floors. "Please, I can't do this alone."

She wanted to save him, for his sake, but also for herself. She was afraid of what awaited her on the Floating World—treacherous nobles, the threat of demons, a hateful war. And the legacy of the celestial maiden. A legacy that had destroyed her mother, that would destroy her if she let it.

"I need you." She needed his strength, his quick mind and gentle presence, his smile, and his laughter. With aching tenderness, she turned her face and kissed his cheek. "I love you."

She realized he'd stopped fighting, sitting so still it was as if he were made of glass. She let go of him, leaning back. His black eyes, which had appeared empty, held a glimmer of light. *Blue.*

Then Sunho winced, turning toward the door.

Sunlight poured through, spreading a gilded pathway across the floor. The sun was rising.

Sunho screamed, rage taking over him. Ren stood, stumbling backward. The light triggered something in him, a primal fear. Whatever bit of clarity he'd possessed had vanished. He rushed toward her, claws extended, teeth bared.

Ren closed her eyes and spread her wings.

She waited for a searing pain that never came.

Opening her eyes, she saw that Sunho had fallen to his knees before her.

He was gazing up at her, at the wings she'd spread on instinct, to shield him from the light.

Tears fell down her cheeks as slowly he began to change, his wings diminishing, his fangs and claws receding, his eyes turning from black to amber brown, and then finally the light in his eyes returned, that spark of blue.

"Ren?" he said, and his voice was *his*, tender and filled with wonder.

Trembling, she lifted her hand to his face. He bent forward and she felt the soft press of his cheek as he leaned into her palm, his eyes fluttering closed.

He was back. He was hers again. At last.

With a relieved sigh, she smiled. Then the exhaustion from the night overwhelmed her, and she collapsed.

CHAPTER 6

SUNHO

West of the Haebaek Mountains
Occupied Territories

SUNHO LEAPED FORWARD, catching Ren as she fell, her wings retracting until they disappeared altogether. His heart pounded in his chest, only easing when he saw that she slept peacefully, her breaths long and deep. She must have fainted from exhaustion. Cradling her to him, he bowed his head.

He knew he should be the one lending *her* strength—she'd endured much to save him—but he only tightened his hand around her shoulder. He drew her closer, his whole body trembling. *I'm sorry, Ren. Let me hold you like this a little longer.*

He felt as if he'd woken from a long dream in which he'd been the Demon, his existence one of pain, rage, and total loss of control. He'd been in agony for every second of it, as his soul fought for dominance within, the Demon's will like a dark and immeasurable tide.

Except it wasn't a dream. They were *his* wings that had jutted, heaving, from his back, *his* claws that had ripped into flesh, slashing and slicing.

Sunho's hand fumbled on Ren's shoulder, gripping her tighter, as if he could anchor himself to the present just by holding on to her.

His fingers traced something warm, slick. He lifted his hand to see that it was coated in red blood. Ren was bleeding; a bandage she'd wrapped around her shoulder had soaked through.

Memories from the night before flooded his mind. His reckless flight through the storm, plummeting into the middle of an airship battle. He'd crashed through the hull of the largest of the ships, thrashing his wings, tearing up the floorboards and walls. He'd been filled with confusion and rage, a feeling as if he were trapped. He'd sensed movement behind him. He'd whipped around, lashing out.

Ren.

She was so clear in his memory as she stood before him, gripping her shoulder where he'd slashed her.

The horror of what he'd done overwhelmed him. He'd hurt her, after promising that he never would. Sunho doubled over from the pain.

"I'm sorry," he whispered, pressing his lips to her hair. The soft strands were damp from his tears. "I'm so sorry."

A whirring sound from outside caught his ear. He turned toward the door, squinting against the sunlight that poured from the opening. The sound was unmistakable—aircraft rotors. Gently, he laid Ren on the floor.

Lifting his hand against the sunlight, he stepped past the threshold.

The reed field appeared undisturbed. The only sound came from the susurrus of the reeds as the wind swept by, rattling the stalks like feathery chimes.

The patch of reeds nearest the cottage began to rustle and a boy with silver hair stepped through, followed by a girl a few years older wearing flight goggles. They walked to the center of the courtyard. The girl lifted her goggles, perching them upon her brow.

"You look like shit," Yurhee declared cheerfully.

The last time Sunho had seen the rebels was at Wolryudang, a teahouse in the Under World. The last time he'd seen them as a *human*, he corrected himself. They'd been in the Volmaran laboratory with Ren, and on the airship, too.

His hand moved involuntarily to his shoulder, where the bolt of Tag's crossbow had struck him. His body had already closed over the wound, healing itself.

Tag's gaze followed Sunho's movements, though his expression remained carefully blank.

"How did you find us?" Sunho asked.

"We followed Ren," Yurhee said. "We knew the direction she'd gone, and Tag remembered overhearing a conversation you two had about this place. I told him there was no way we'd find you both, but Tag *begged* me to try and, well, here we are. Is Ren inside?"

Yurhee didn't wait for Sunho to answer, walking across the courtyard with long strides. He stepped aside for her.

Sunho's gaze returned to Tag, who'd remained quiet during their exchange.

"Are you all right?" Tag asked.

Sunho shook his head. "I'm fine. I'm not the one who's hurt."

Tag's only reaction was a slight crease between his brows. "Here." He thrust forward a wrapped bundle. "They're my clothes, so they'll be a little a small for you, but it's better than . . ."

Sunho peered down at himself. He was wearing the same clothing he'd worn the morning he'd transformed, which now hung in rags upon his body. Besides the numerous tears in his clothing, he had huge gaping holes in the back of his shirt where his wings had burst through. He was also filthy and covered in blood.

"Thanks," he said roughly, conscious now of not only his appearance but also likely his stench.

Tag's gaze shifted once again to Sunho's shoulder before he stepped back, allowing him to pass.

Sunho headed to the small stream that he remembered ran behind the cottage, this time following it farther into the reeds. It wasn't long before he emerged from the thicket to stand at the edge of the marsh. Before him was a wide lake. He watched as a crane flew low over the still water, the tips of its wings skimming the surface.

He unwrapped Tag's bundle to find clothing tucked inside, trousers and a shirt, as well as a pair of worn boots. It didn't take him long to undress, folding the remnants of his shirt and pants and leaving them on the bank. Shivering, he waded into the water, inhaling sharply as icy water sluiced over his ankles, then his stomach and chest.

He walked until his feet no longer touched the bottom. Submerging himself entirely, he sank into the darkness. As he floated, suspended in water, he thought of his final memory, the one he'd carried with him the longest, that had existed only in fragments until Ren's healing touch brought it together to reveal the horrible truth.

He'd killed his brother.

He hadn't meant to—it had been a mistake, an accident. When Teacher had injected him with mithril, it had triggered a transformation. He wasn't even aware what had happened until Junho had turned to him, blood spilling from his mouth, and choked out his name. His brother had a gaping hole in his chest, where Sunho's clawed hand had punched through.

What had happened afterward was a blur of pain and noise and horror. It had been a massacre. He'd killed everyone—the scientists as well as the other soldiers in his unit who'd been brought to the laboratory along with him. When it was over, he'd fled, his wings carrying him down to the Under World.

He didn't remember what had triggered his transformation back into a human, only that he'd awoken by the abandoned mithril factory in the first ward, without memories, except for the single one that existed in those shattered fragments. He wondered why he'd lost his memories—perhaps he'd wounded his head somehow. Or perhaps it was something else entirely, his mind's way of protecting his heart from breaking.

He sank farther into the water, the light that struck the surface of the lake growing paler with distance.

He'd forgotten so much, and still knew so little. Only one truth was clear to him: He couldn't control the Demon.

It didn't matter that he'd transformed back into a human; the monster still lurked within. Even now, he could feel its presence, like heavy wings beating against his heart.

A part of him longed to stay submerged beneath the lake, but he knew that soon he'd run out of air. There was also the part of him that was determined to go back, at least for a short while, to make certain Ren was safe. But afterward . . .

In the absolute darkness of the lake, he made an oath.

He would do everything in his power to protect the ones he loved. Even if what he protected them from was himself.

WHEN HE RETURNED to the cottage a half hour later, Tag had started a fire and was slicing potatoes and dropping them into an iron pot that he'd plopped onto the hearth. Yurhee sat opposite him, with her feet kicked up on a bundle of hay and a reed straw sticking out of her mouth.

Sunho checked on Ren first. She was asleep; wisps of hair had fallen from her braid to rest on her cheek. Yurhee had covered Ren with her jacket, and he carefully folded it back to see that either Yurhee or Tag had wrapped Ren's wounds with fresh bandages. Sunho carefully returned the jacket to its place, raising it to her chin. He hesitated, lingering, then gently tucked the strands of her hair behind her ear.

He would have stayed beside Ren longer, but he had questions for the others. Joining Tag and Yurhee by the hearth, he lowered himself to the floor.

Tag had finished slicing up the vegetables and was adding spices from a satchel slung across his waist. A heady aroma soon filled the cottage.

Yurhee sat up beside the fire. "So how much do you remember?"

"Most of it," he said grimly. After fleeing from Ren in the meadow, he'd flown recklessly, without care or direction. It wasn't until the third day that he became aware that he was being followed. The Volmaran vessel hunting him had kept its distance, fixing him within its sight but never approaching too close. It hadn't made its move until last night.

"Ren . . ." Sunho turned to Tag. "How is she? Her wounds . . ." Again, he felt the overwhelming pressure of guilt in his chest.

"Once she's regained enough energy, she'll heal on her own," Tag said. "She healed her uncle, you know. Whatever cure she obtained in the mithril labs didn't work. It was her magic that got rid of the poison."

Sunho felt some of the tension leave his body as relief swept through him. She'd managed to cure her uncle with her magic. The thought gave him pause, remembering how she'd tried to cure him, too.

"After Ren revealed she was the celestial maiden," Tag continued, "Commander Su arrested General Iljin, with the support of Ren's aunt. There's to be a trial once Ren returns to the Floating World. That's where we were headed when the Volmarans attacked."

So Ren had been on her way back to the Floating World. He wasn't surprised. She was a Sareniyan princess, their heir.

"What are you going to do?" Tag said.

Yurhee glanced up from where she'd been poking at a sweet potato roasting in the fire with a stick. "He'll go with her, of course."

When Sunho didn't immediately agree, she frowned. "What? You're not going to *leave* her, are you?"

Sunho winced. "I can't control the Demon. I could turn at any time."

"So what?" Yurhee scoffed. "It wasn't that bad."

Sunho stared at her.

"Okay, fine," she conceded, "it was awful. But it's not like Ren doesn't transform into her own winged form. It's poetic, really. You two are well-matched."

"Do you truly believe that?" Sunho asked skeptically.

"I don't know!" Yurhee threw her hands in the air. "All I know is that you shouldn't do anything rash until you speak with Ren. Promise me that, at least. I don't want her to wake up and have to explain that the person whom she quite literally risked life and limb to save decided to run off 'cause he's afraid."

Sunho winced, but Yurhee was right. "I won't leave," he said, "not without telling Ren first."

His words seemed to placate Yurhee because she gestured for him to help himself to the meal Tag had prepared.

Sunho ate a great deal, ravenous after his time as the Demon. When he was finished, he returned to Ren's side. She was shivering, her arms wrapped around her body as she trembled.

"What's wrong?" Sunho said, alarmed. "Does she have a fever?"

"I think she's just cold," Yurhee said. "It is winter, after all."

Winter. The word conjured memories of the frigid winters of the north, when the snowfall would sometimes reach as high as his chest.

"Lie next to her," Tag said. "She'll be warmer with your body heat."

"I don't want to hurt her," Sunho whispered.

"You won't," Tag promised. He stood, taking Yurhee's arm and pulling her toward the door—they'd replaced it after Sunho had thrown it into the wall. "Come on. Let's get more firewood."

"Wait, but *I'm* cold," Sunho heard Yurhee complaining loudly as it shut behind them.

Sunho shifted closer to Ren. He tentatively reached his hand toward her only to draw it back. There had to be another way to warm her. His eyes alighted on the hay pile Yurhee had been leaning against. He could weave a mat with the stalks; he'd seen Heetae do something similar. He moved to stand and was stopped by a soft pressure—Ren's hand slipping over his.

"Don't leave," she murmured.

His heart leaped at her voice, though he frowned at how fragile she sounded. He was used to its strong cadence, a result of the years she'd trained as a performer. Her voice was a song, his favorite one.

"I was going to get something to keep you warm," he explained.

"I'm not c-cold," she protested between chattering teeth.

His gaze softened.

"All right. You w-win. I am c-cold."

A shudder swept through her body and she whimpered.

He didn't hesitate after that, lifting the jacket and sliding in beside her. He felt awkward, unsure of himself, of his body that felt strange to him, as if the Demon was his true form and *he* was the imposter.

"Our roles have switched," Ren said, her voice weak yet teasing. "Last time, you were the one wounded, and I was the one caring for you."

"It's a little different this time," he said. Then they'd been strangers.

"That's true. Did you ever imagine that we'd end up like this?" He knew what she meant. Together.

"No." He'd thought he'd be alone, at least until he found his brother. "Did you?"

He felt the softness of her hair beneath his chin as she shook her head. She was the perfect size to press her face into the crook of his neck.

"Promise me you'll stay," she said, again in that small voice.

He gathered her close. He thought of the oath he'd made to himself in the depths of the lake. He could only keep one of those promises.

As he said the words he knew she wanted to hear, he was struck by despair, as if he was back in the lake again, sinking further into the darkness.

"I promise."

CHAPTER 7

REN

West of the Haebaek Mountains
Occupied Territories

REN WOKE TO a feather tickling her cheek; it was one of her own, white and shimmering in the sunlight that streamed through the open window. She sat up to see the whole room was covered with white and black feathers, as if a dove and a crow had battled.

A breeze through the window sent several of them up into the air. As they drifted downward, she lifted her palm to catch one of the black feathers. It was tinted blue at the edge, a deep cerulean. Gently, she traced her finger along the feather, finding it soft. It was only Sunho's outer feathers, then, that were sharp like knives—this one must have come from one of his inner feathers. Pulling back the collar of her jacket, she tucked it into her camisole.

As she looked up, she realized she was alone in the cottage. Her heart dropped into her stomach. Sunho couldn't have left. He'd *promised* her he'd stay.

She scrambled to her feet, grabbing the wall when she felt a rush of lightheadedness.

"Ren!" Yurhee appeared in the open doorway. She hurried over, followed by Tag, whose face was smudged with soot.

"Yurhee?" Ren said, her voice coming out as a croak. "How did you get here?" The older girl's cheeks were bright from the winter sun. She wore her hair in a high ponytail, and flyaway strands clung to the sweat glistening on her brow.

She had a vague recollection of Yurhee's cool hand on her forehead the night before, of the older girl removing her jacket and placing it around her shoulders.

"A combination of Tag's deduction skills, my speedy flying, and a whole lot of luck." Yurhee shrugged. "Basically, we followed you. The *Sparrow* took a bit of a beating on the way, but Tag should fix it right up in a day or two."

That explained the soot on Tag's cheeks. "Sunho," Ren began, searching behind them for his familiar figure. "Where is he?"

Yurhee held up her hands in a placating gesture. "Maybe you shouldn't be walking around just yet—"

"Did he leave?" Ren pressed.

"He's outside," Tag said. Yurhee shook her head, signaling for him to keep quiet, but he ignored her. "There's a lake behind the cottage—"

Ren took a stumbling step toward the doorway.

"Hey, slow down." Yurhee grabbed Ren's arm to keep her from toppling over. "Heal yourself first, at least."

"I *need* to see him," Ren said. She needed to know that what had happened the day before was real, that he had taken his body back from the Demon.

That he was himself again.

"I don't know. You really shouldn't—" Yurhee broke off, glancing at Tag, who'd placed a hand on her shoulder. He gave an infinitesimal shake of his head. With a sigh, Yurhee dropped Ren's arm. "Shout if you fall over or something."

"I'll go slow," Ren reassured her.

A few minutes later, she was hurtling through the tall grass.

She took the same path as Sunho, following his footprints in the mud. The crows were out in droves, winging about and cawing incessantly. A few swooped down, close enough that she could feel the buffeting of their wings.

"This again?" she shouted as one plunged toward her, and she had to duck to avoid its taloned feet.

She had the brief thought that perhaps they'd mistaken Sunho as one of their own—his black wings had given him the appearance of a crow, after all—and therefore identified *her*, the non-crow, as a threat. "I'm not going to hurt him!"

She raced forward, rushing the last few steps before breaking through the reeds. Immediately she spotted Sunho at the edge of the marsh.

He wore an unbuttoned shirt over a tattered undershirt, and trousers that barely reached his ankles. Tag's clothes, she assumed. He was gazing out at the lake, one foot in front of the other as if poised to take a step.

As he turned his gaze toward her, memories of the night rushed back, his body tense and anxious above hers; she remembered calling for him until he'd lain beside her, taking her in his arms.

"Ren," he said as she reached him. She saw his eyes flit to her shoulder before dropping to the ground.

She needed to show him that she was fine, that the wound looked worse than it felt, truly, otherwise he'd never forgive himself.

She took a deep breath, then let out a long, heavy sigh. His eyes tracked back to hers. "What's wrong?" he asked, his brow furrowed slightly.

"It's the crows," she said.

He lifted his gaze to where they'd hung back above the reeds. "What . . . ?"

"They've clearly taken a liking to you."

His attention turned curious, the tortured expression fading.

"I'm envious," Ren said, slumping her shoulders with a dramatic sigh.

"You're . . . envious," Sunho repeated carefully.

Ren nodded. "Because of the crows."

"Because . . ." She could see his thoughts working behind his dark eyes, which never left hers. "They prefer me, and not you?"

She pouted. "It's not fair. *I* have wings, too."

He was quiet for a long time.

She wondered what he was thinking, if he was pondering the absurdity of her words. Then he dropped his gaze. "I'm sorry," he said, his voice soft, consoling. Her pulse leaped. He was playing along with her. "We'll have to find you some doves. Or maybe a swan."

She wrinkled her nose. "Too mean." She and Wook had once been chased by a swan when the caravan had stopped by a pond on a hot summer's day. "A duck will do," she declared. "And then you can be one, too."

As she said the words, she blushed at their implied meaning. Wooden ducks were presented in pairs to couples at wedding ceremonies as a symbol of eternal love. The belief was that ducks mated for life.

The pained look in Sunho's eyes was now gone entirely. His gaze was intent as he held hers. The seriousness of his expression made Ren's stomach flutter.

"Okay," he said.

Ren blinked. Okay? Was he agreeing to be a duck with her, or was he agreeing to . . . more?

His gaze traveled once more toward the lake. From the darkness of the water, it was likely several hundred feet deep.

The anguish in his expression might have disappeared, but there was a melancholy about him that hadn't been there before his transformation. She knew it was because of his brother, and the final memory that had revealed to him the truth of what had happened that night, a truth so horrible it had turned him into a monster.

"When I was the Demon," Sunho said, "I couldn't remember my name, or where I'd come from. I couldn't remember who I was."

He turned to her. "But I remembered this place, the cottage in the reed fields. I didn't know what it was or why it mattered. I only knew that if I went there, I'd feel safe again."

"And did you?" Ren asked softly.

He shook his head. "Not at first, but then . . . you came. You brought me back."

"But how?" He'd been about to attack her, his claws poised to rip her apart.

"It was your wings." Sunho closed his eyes, as if the memory lingered just beneath the surface. "The light shining through them reminded me of the paper umbrella."

He opened his eyes. "I didn't . . . I *couldn't* recognize you, but I recognized that feeling of safety."

Ren reached for his hand. He didn't pull away but clung to her as she tightened her grip. "I'll *always* keep you safe." She didn't care that it was an impossible promise—in returning to the Floating World, she was leading them both into danger—but she knew that she would safeguard his heart, his body, his soul, as much as she was able.

"And I'll keep *you* safe," Sunho said. "Whatever it takes."

She might have felt reassured by his words but for the odd glint in his eye, as if there was something he was keeping from her.

IT WAS AGREED among all of them that they'd spend at least another two nights at the cottage. Tag had to make repairs on the *Sparrow*, and both Ren and Sunho needed time to heal from their various wounds.

Ren discovered that healing herself was more arduous a task than healing others; after mending her shoulder, she fell into a meditative sleep that lasted into the night.

The next morning, Tag and Sunho left to scavenge parts for the *Sparrow*. Tag thought he might be able to find some amid the wreckage of the train that had derailed, Sunho having apparently told him that the crash site wasn't far from the cottage.

From her spot on the small platform in the middle of the courtyard, Ren watched the boys disappear into the reeds. Flopping onto her back, she sighed loudly.

"That bad, huh?" Yurhee joined her, folding one leg beneath her and dangling the other off the platform edge.

"I'm worried about him." It made her feel uneasy, that glint she'd seen in his eye. As if there was a wall between them when there had never been one before.

"He's adjusting back into being a human after being a Demon for so long," Yurhee said. "Give him time."

"Doesn't he know that he can talk to me? That I accept every part of him?"

Yurhee sat back on her hands. A reed had appeared in her mouth, and she chewed thoughtfully on the stem. "I think . . . *he's* the one who has to accept himself."

Yurhee was right, of course, but that only made Ren feel more uncertain. What if Sunho *couldn't* accept that part of him?

"Come on." Yurhee jumped to her feet. "Let's go inside. It's getting chillier every day."

The boys returned early that evening, and by noon the next day, Tag had finished his repairs. Ren bid farewell to the cottage, placing a crown of reeds she'd woven by the door before joining the others on the aircraft. There was more room on the small flying machine than the last time all four of them had traveled together, though it was still very cramped. Ren rode at the front with Yurhee. Their ascent was smooth, if noisy—the crows sending off Sunho with squawking cheers—and a friendly, southwesterly wind sent them soaring in the right direction.

Ren had never approached the Floating World from above before. When she'd been taken there by Lady Maya, her aunt, they'd gone up through the Sky Door, the great crater at the center of the Floating World that opened once a year, during the Festival of Light.

As the *Sparrow* drew close to the landmass, the air became shrouded in a thick fog. Droplets of water clung to the hull: They'd flown into a cloud, one that stretched along the borders of the world.

From within the fog came the distant rumbling of a waterfall.

"Watch out!" Tag shouted. Ren grabbed on to the side of the aircraft as Yurhee jerked the steering gear, narrowly avoiding a large construct looming out of the mist.

Ren recognized the red and silver pennant flags of a watchtower. Shouts erupted from the parapet and an arrow whistled past. Yurhee swerved the craft to avoid it.

"Why are they shooting at us?" she shouted.

"I think it was a warning shot," Tag said.

"Damn it, we don't have a flag," Ren said, cursing herself for not remembering that detail from her extensive, albeit short-lived, diplomatic education as a child. "They'll shoot us down if we try to fly past without one."

Down below, a group of guards was maneuvering a massive arbalest toward the wall of the watchtower. It was armed with an iron spear that, if aimed properly, could cleave the *Sparrow* in two.

Reaching for her magic, Ren climbed atop the nose of the aircraft. She jumped, her Light forming into wings upon her back.

She could hear the shouts of surprise from the watchtower guards below as she swooped down toward them. As if startled, one of the archers released an arrow.

"Ren!" she heard Sunho shout, panicked, as she spun to avoid it.

The other guards quickly subdued the archer, and by the time she flew over the parapet, all five of them were crouched on their knees, foreheads pressed to the ground.

Ren flew back toward the *Sparrow*, alighting onto the deck.

"Well, that's one way to announce your arrival!" Yurhee whooped. "Or I guess it's your return, isn't it?"

Ren felt breathless; she'd summoned her wings and they'd come to her with ease. The arrow would have struck her if she hadn't avoided it, her wings reacting so seamlessly to her thoughts, as if they were an extension of her. She turned toward Sunho, wishing for him to share in her triumph, but he was hunched over, gripping the side of the aircraft. His expression was shadowed, as if he was fighting with something inside himself

She stepped toward him, but then Yurhee shouted, "There it is!"

They'd broken through the cloud, emerging from the other side.

Below them lay the celestial city, Sora, capital of the Floating World.

Elegant buildings with winged rooftops lined roads paved with beautiful white stone. Clear streams ran in rivulets throughout the city, the delicate waterways feeding into a slow-moving river. It grew more forceful as it approached the edge of the world, falling over the side in a great, thunderous waterfall.

Ren's gaze swept toward the farthest point of the city, where the Celestial Palace stood glittering against the horizon, its outer walls composed almost entirely of crystal and glass. A wide, silvery fountain pool burbled at the base of the alabaster steps.

The palace was even more dazzling than in her memories. Beyond its high walls she knew lay breathtaking gardens, with verdant lawns and crystalline lakes.

Yet, for all its magnificence, she knew that beneath lurked incredible danger.

She would never forget that this was the place where everything she had once loved had been destroyed.

As they descended, Ren made herself a promise: She would never let it destroy her.

ACT TWO

A World in the Sky

CHAPTER 8

REN

The Floating World
Sora, Capital of Sareniya

YURHEE MANEUVERED THE *Sparrow* low over the fountain—the tranquil waters rippled as the bottom skimmed the surface—before easing back on the control stick.

A small party of Sareniyans were waiting at the edge of the pool, on the white stone walkway that led up to the palace's steps.

She caught sight of a familiar head of curls among the crowd of strangers.

"Wook!" she shouted, alighting from the aircraft before it had fully stopped. She landed gracefully, her wings shimmering around her before dissolving into motes of light.

"Ren!" Little Uncle broke from the group, sweeping her into an embrace. "Thank the gods you're here," he said, letting go but then grabbing her hand. "You have to come quick."

Alarm shot through her as Little Uncle shouldered his way through the startled onlookers, pulling her up the steps toward the palace. She looked back, searching for Sunho, relieved when she spotted him following behind Yurhee and Tag.

"What's going on?" Ren asked. "Did the commander leave?" He'd informed her that he would, in order to challenge the Volmaran airships seen at the border.

"Yes," Little Uncle said, "shortly after we arrived. Which was wretched luck—he might have been able to stop them."

"Stop who?" They'd reached the top of the steps, racing across a massive courtyard paved with the same white stone as the city avenues.

Little Uncle spoke quickly. "Yesterday, the Floating Council went ahead with the general's trial. They passed a verdict just now. He was convicted of treason. He's to be executed immediately—him *and* Captain Jaeil."

Ren drew back, almost stopping Wook in his tracks. "Jaeil?"

Wook's eyes widened. "Yes," he said in a choked breath. "Hurry, Ren. You have to stop it."

She picked up her speed. Ren felt someone come up on her right and she turned to see Yurhee keeping pace with her.

"Did I hear that correctly?" the older girl asked. "Captain Jaeil, as in the one who kidnapped you and tore up Wolryudang?"

Ren winced. Jaeil *had* hurt her, and yet . . .

He'd been her closest friend once. Before Little Uncle and Hwi. Before Sunho.

She wasn't sure yet how she felt about Jaeil—his actions were confusing to her, his motivations unclear—but she certainly didn't want him to *die*.

Ren hurried up the stone steps leading to the main throne hall. The space was filled with people, their voices clamoring over one another as they faced the front of the hall. Seated behind a large bench presided three nobles, dressed in elaborate red-and-black robes. She recognized the woman who occupied the right seat—Lady Maya, her aunt. The woman on the left was unfamiliar to her. As for the man in the center, he sat in the largest of the chairs, which Ren recognized as her mother's throne.

This man was older even than Commander Su, perhaps in his late seventies. As she stared at him, a memory arose of a great shadow gazing down upon her, proclaiming her *small and weak, like her mother—*

"That's Lord Muyeol," Little Uncle said. "He's Lady Maya's father, your great-uncle."

Her mother's uncle, brother to a celestial maiden.

"We need to get closer," Ren said. They began pushing their way to the edge of the too-thick crowd. They'd almost reached the front when Ren caught sight of Jaeil.

He and his father were seated cross-legged on the floor directly in front of the dais. They were dressed entirely in white, their hands bound with rope behind their backs.

While the general appeared defeated, his face haggard—there was evidence of torture, his clothing bloodied and torn in places—Jaeil seemed composed, almost . . . detached. Like his father, it was clear he'd been tortured as well. His lip was split, and his left arm was twisted behind his back at an awkward angle.

In front of each prisoner was a small table, atop which sat a single teacup on a tray.

Ren jumped as Lord Muyeol's voice boomed across the hall. "You've been sentenced to death by poison. Do you choose to drink willingly, or would you dishonor yourself by refusing?"

General Iljin spat, his saliva landing near the silk slippers of the noble standing nearest. Jaeil, who'd been observing his father with a placid expression, turned to the dais.

"I would drink it gladly," Jaeil drawled, as if the lord had invited him to tea, and not to his own execution. "But even I can't drink poison with my hands tied."

Beside Ren, Wook visibly winced. Ren wondered if Jaeil had been this . . . difficult the entire duration of the trial.

"Cut his ropes," Lady Maya ordered the guards. "If he attempts to escape or fight back," she said, sneering at Jaeil, "he'll find himself the target of a dozen swift arrows."

"Rest assured, Lady," Jaeil intoned, "I am quite parched."

"He's an irreverent bastard, isn't he?" Yurhee said, a note of reluctant approval in her voice.

"He's going to get himself killed," Ren groaned. When Wook slid her a pained look, she added, "Well, more than he's already doomed himself."

She started forward. The nobles around her scowled, casting baleful glares her way. Without her wings, and dressed in a simple cotton jacket and trousers, she most likely appeared to them as an interloper.

The guards had finished sawing at the ropes that had bound Jaeil's wrists. In one swift motion, Jaeil reached for the teacup and lifted it to his mouth.

"Wait!" Ren shouted.

At the same time the general cried out, "My son!"

Light flared at Ren's fingertips. She summoned a gust of wind that swept across the room, knocking the cup out of Jaeil's hands. It arced through the air, end over end, and shattered into pieces at Lord Muyeol's feet.

Ren swayed, overwhelmed by the sudden release of power, only regaining her balance when she felt Sunho's steadying hand upon her shoulder.

"How dare you?" Lord Muyeol rose from his seat. With his

position on the dais, he towered over the assembly. "This is an official trial."

Ren squared her shoulders, stepping from the crowd. "Then, as heir, is it not my right to be present for it? After all, I was there the night General Iljin killed my mother."

Lady Maya's eyes met Ren's, though she gave no reaction except the lifting of a single brow.

Ren wasn't certain if it *was* her right. The general had many crimes to atone for; countless had suffered in the years he'd been in power. But this trial, she was starting to suspect, wasn't *just* about him. Her great-uncle and aunt had chosen to proceed without her, though the commander had assured her she'd oversee the trial herself.

They intended to make decisions on her behalf, like they had for her mother.

And the general wasn't alone in his crimes—most were sanctioned by the Floating Council, were *ordered* by them. He would take the blame, while they remained unscathed.

The chamber was silent as Lord Muyeol studied Ren.

There was a possibility that he and Lady Maya might denounce her. If they claimed Ren was an imposter, the nobles of the Floating Council were far more likely to support *them* than Ren.

It was Lady Maya who broke the silence, much to Ren's relief, shifting forward in her seat with a sigh. "I understand your agitation, niece. But even had you overseen the trial from the beginning, the outcome would have been the same. The penalty for treason is death."

"What about the captain?" Ren demanded. "What are his crimes?"

She could feel Jaeil's gaze on her where he kneeled behind her.

"Captain Jaeil is his father's only progeny," Lord Muyeol said. "As stated by the law, he is to be executed alongside him."

"That's ridiculous!" Ren protested. "You can't punish him for his father's crimes!"

"It is not *I* who am punishing him. These are laws that have been in place since the time of *your* ancestor, the first celestial maiden. To go against these rules is to go against generations of tradition."

An odd, tinny sound started to ring in her ear. *Was this her legacy?*

"Princess."

Was she part of something not magical and bright, but twisted and cruel?

"Ren."

It took Ren a few seconds to realize that it was Jaeil who'd spoken. He'd been kneeling on the floor, but slowly rose to his feet, cradling his broken arm with his other.

"I'm guilty of other crimes, more than just being my father's son," he said. "Insubordination, for one. Unauthorized use of military funds. Harboring a known fugitive."

Ren could have sworn that his lip quirked at this last confession, as if the reminder that he'd harbored *her*—when he'd attempted to smuggle her out of the Under World—amused him.

"None of those are crimes punishable by death," she argued.

"I've done worse," he countered darkly. "I'm just making it clear that I'm not without fault."

"No one would deny *that.*" She sighed. "I'm trying to save your life. You *could* help me out a bit and be more agreeable and a little less . . . you."

His eyes widened, as if he *hadn't* realized her intention. "Ah." He turned his face away from her. "I see."

Ren faced her aunt once more. "If it's a law ordained by my ancestors, then it seems only right that I be the one to break it."

The third noble seated at the bench shifted forward. "What do you suggest then, Princess?" she asked. "As punishment for the criminals."

Ren turned to the general, holding his gaze as she considered her verdict. It was the first time she'd looked him in the eye since announcing her presence to the assembly.

She remembered the fear she'd once felt when facing him, the monster that had haunted her dreams. Now she felt nothing, as if he were already fading from her mind.

"For the general, I demand imprisonment for the remainder of his life. And for the son . . ." She turned back to the dais. "I demand that he serve me as military counsel."

She needed to end the war with the Volmarans, and she couldn't do that on her own.

Commander Su would be an asset to her, but Jaeil—before his various injuries—had been on the front lines of the war. He would have invaluable knowledge. Commander Su had also warned her, after he'd first sworn his allegiance, that the two other commanders loyal to the general had broken off from the main branch following his arrest, taking their soldiers with them. It was possible that these warriors could be persuaded back into the fold to support his son.

The third noble nodded her approval. From the gavel resting on the bench before her, Ren deemed her to be a judge.

"Have you no desire for revenge?" Lady Maya asked, her voice carrying across the silent hall. "As you said, you were present the night *he* killed your mother."

Ren felt a heaviness in her limbs. "So I should kill him to lessen the pain of losing her?" she asked quietly. "There is no punishment that he can endure that would atone for her loss." At least imprisonment wouldn't burden her conscience; she would not immortalize him as a martyr, but forget him, as he lived.

"And . . ." Ren looked up, steeling her expression. "Even before he pushed her over the ledge, she was driven there by something." She met first Lady Maya's gaze, then Lord Muyeol's. "Or someone. I didn't understand then; I was too young. I'm not any longer. And I will not forgive the forces that made my mother feel as if she were dying years before she ever took her last breath."

She raised her voice so that it could be heard throughout the hall. "I might not seek revenge on her behalf, but I *will* seek justice. Jaeil is not his father, and *I* am not my mother."

Her message was clear: Ren would not be a puppet. She didn't return to give legitimacy to her aunt and great-uncle, or to the Floating Council. She had her own agenda, her own mind.

The judge cracked her gavel upon the podium. "The traitor Iljin, former commanding general of the Sareniyan armed forces, is condemned to life imprisonment. He is ordered to give a full accounting of his crimes, as well as all military endeavors conducted under his watch. In exchange for his son's freedom, he will abide by these conditions."

The general lowered himself in a bow, his forehead touching the floor. "Your grace is immeasurable."

"As for Captain Jaeil . . ." Lord Muyeol was the one who spoke, meeting Ren's gaze as he gave the decree, "he will be released immediately and pardoned of all crimes. However, if at any point he commits any further offense, the princess herself will be held responsible for his actions."

"I accept," Ren said.

The judge finished writing down the decree on a scroll and passed it to Lady Maya, who stamped it with a red seal.

"And so it is done," she announced, her strident voice carrying across the chamber. "The trial of the traitor Iljin has reached its conclusion."

The hall exploded into noise as people exclaimed over the dramatic outcome. Guards came to escort the general away, while Jaeil looked on, his face devoid of expression.

"Princess." Ren turned to see an elderly woman approaching her, bowing low. "I am Head Maid Eun. You must be weary from your travels. Please, allow me to escort you to your quarters."

"In a moment," Ren said. "I wish to speak with my companions first."

But as she peered into the crowd, panic set in. Nobles shouted for her attention. She searched for Sunho, spotting him at the center making his way back toward her. Her stomach sank when she realized there was no way for him to get to her, not without causing a scene.

He looked up, meeting her gaze.

"*Find Wook*," she mouthed. Her uncle was clever. Though he wasn't a noble, he'd playacted as one many times before. If someone could adapt to this world quickly, it would be him. He'd watch over Sunho, and she'd regroup with them both once she figured out her next steps.

Sunho must have understood her intent because he nodded.

"Princess?" Head Maid Eun was still waiting for her.

She tore her gaze away. "I'm ready."

They left the chamber through a door behind the dais, the clamor of voices cutting off as it shut behind them.

CHAPTER 9

REN

The Floating World
The Celestial Palace

REN STEELED HERSELF for a confrontation with her aunt, but when she gazed around the small chamber that Head Maid Eun had ushered her into, she found that it was empty.

She'd expected to feel relief, but an inkling of unease settled into her gut. No doubt she'd angered both Lady Maya and Lord Muyeol with her defiance.

The general might have pushed her mother over the edge, but someone had driven her to the precipice. If it had been her aunt and great-uncle, supported by the Floating Council, as she suspected, then she would need to proceed with caution.

She could never accuse them outright. If she wished to end the war with Volmar, she would need their support.

"This way, Princess," Head Maid Eun said.

Ren followed the woman through a door at the back of the chamber. It led to a covered walkway that bordered a courtyard smaller than the extravagant one outside the main hall.

The sun had set while they'd been inside, and servants holding candlelighters fluttered about. Ren watched as a young woman unlatched the latticed doors of a floor lantern, pressing the flame of her taper to the wick.

From the courtyard, Head Maid Eun took her through a gate into another, then another, each gate acting like a checkpoint overseen by at least two guards.

As they approached each gate, Head Maid Eun held up a wooden medallion for the guards to examine. Inspecting it closely, Ren could see that the medallion was carved with the symbol of Sareniya—wings, outspread—and stamped with a red seal, same as the one Lady Maya had used.

Continuing deeper into the palace, Ren started to recognize a few landmarks. The path lined with rhododendrons led to the western quadrant, where the servants' quarters and nursery were located. A large stone lantern marked the path to the eastern gardens, where she had often escaped her tutors to meet Jaeil in the meadow.

They entered a courtyard that was bare except for a single plum tree growing in the center. As she stared at the vibrant red blossoms, she felt the stirrings of a memory.

She had come from the meadow, where Jaeil had been reading to her from one of the books he liked so much. She'd only half been paying attention, as, for the better part of an hour, she'd been searching for a four-leaf clover. When she'd found one tucked in the bower of the zelkova tree, she'd leaped with joy. Immediately she'd gone looking for her mother. Not just to show it to her; she'd wanted to give *it to her. Maybe it was the influence of Jaeil's stories, but she'd believed rare objects were like talismans; they had the power to protect the person who possessed them.*

Entering the courtyard, she'd spotted her mother walking across. Ren had started to run. In her eagerness, she'd failed to notice the roots of the plum tree jutting out from the ground.

The pain had been sudden and fierce. Tears had sprang to her eyes, but she'd held them back. Tears were for moments of sadness. Her mother had enough of those.

She'd taken in a deep breath, covering her knee with one hand while opening the other. She sighed in relief when she saw the clover was still intact. She'd looked up, searching the courtyard, only to find it empty. Her mother had left her behind.

"Princess?"

They had reached the last gate; only one building lay ahead. The gate was unguarded, though Ren wondered if that would change soon. A small grove of pines lined a silvery path. Beyond it stretched a lake as still as glass, not even a bird to mar its serene perfection. Reflected upon its blue-black surface was a crescent moon.

Slowly, Ren raised her gaze to where a palace stood across the lake, like a star that had fallen from the sky.

While the Celestial Palace was made of crystal and glass, the Queen's Palace shone as white as the moon, as snow, as bone.

A shiver went through her, and she was unsure if it was from awe or fear.

She found herself walking toward it, along a path that wound around the edge of the lake.

Head Maid Eun joined her. "No one has occupied the Queen's Palace for ten years," she informed her, "ever since . . ."

Ren was surprised, only because she'd thought Lady Maya would have taken up residence within its alabaster walls. But perhaps even *she* hadn't dared.

"We've prepared the main rooms for your convenience—the

receiving room, kitchen, and bedchamber," Head Maid Eun continued, "but have yet to open the others. If there's one you'd like prepared, please inform either me or one of the palace staff. The entrance is this way."

Ren was relieved to find that the interior of the palace appeared more welcoming. The wooden walkways were smooth beneath her feet. Toward the northeastern corner of the palace, two attendants dressed in silver and pale blue were waiting outside the elegant doors of a bedchamber.

At Ren's approach, they reached their arms out, sliding the doors open on either side.

Ren held her breath as she entered, her gaze drawn to movement at the back where gauzy drapes fluttered in a slight breeze. She glimpsed greenery beyond.

"The queen's bedchamber faces the eastern gardens," Head Maid Eun explained, following behind Ren. "They connect to the main palace, though that part of the garden is enclosed for your privacy."

Ren had known the gardens were connected. Her mother had often traveled from this garden to the others.

"I will leave you to rest," Head Maid Eun said. "Should you wish to change your clothing, suitable garments have been provided." She nodded at several ornate chests against the far wall.

Lowering her head in a deep bow, the maidservant walked backward toward the threshold of the room. When she'd stepped far enough that she was in the hall, she continued to hold her position, until the attendants slid shut the door.

Ren was alone—or at least somewhat alone. The attendants would likely remain in the hall the entirety of the night.

She let her gaze wander, taking in the details of the room. Against the north wall was a massive bed, too large to be comfortable. All of her family could have fit atop it—Auntie, Big Uncle, and Little Uncle—with plenty of room to spare. In the far corner sat a large bathing tub behind a paper folding screen.

She walked over to the ornate chests, lifting the lid of the first. Her heart raced: The topmost robe was crimson.

Removing it, she held the garment up to her body. The robe fell to Ren's feet, hemmed perfectly to her height. Her mother had been taller, statuesque; it couldn't have belonged to her. Dropping the robe, Ren opened the next two chests to find more clothing fitted to her proportions. Head Maid Eun had said the garments had been provided, and yet, since this was the Queen's Palace, she'd thought . . .

She hurried toward the cabinets at the far side of the room, pulling open the doors by their brass handles. Empty. She tried another. Inside the third, she discovered a writing box, lacquered in mother-of-pearl. Eagerly she opened the lid, only to find that it contained nothing more than an inkpot and brush.

She slumped to the floor. Ren hadn't known what to expect in coming here. Only that this palace, this *room*, had belonged to her mother, yet there was no evidence to show that she'd *lived* here. Nothing to hint at what interests she might have had, no books or musical instruments or drawings. Not even a weapon, as Auntie might have had.

They'd *erased* her. Ren felt her Light flare within her, only to douse at her next thought. *Or maybe . . .*

Her mother hadn't left anything behind because there was nothing she had found worth keeping. The world had felt empty to her, and so she had kept her world empty.

Ren's gaze landed once more on the stationery box, noticing that it appeared rather bulky for the meager contents contained within.

Lifting the lid, she removed the inkpot and brush, then peeled back the bottom to reveal a hidden compartment. Inside was a small, stitch-bound book.

Ren picked it up with trembling fingers. She knew, even before she flipped to the first page, who the book had belonged to.

Written in elegant script on the back cover was the inscription: *For she who has wings will always be free. Aria, princess of Sareniya.*

Ren trailed her fingers reverently across the ink. This was her *mother's* diary. Like "Ren" was hers, "Aria" had been her mother's preferred name, a diminutive of "Sareniya."

She didn't flip to the next page but opened the book to the middle, reading the hastily written words.

Is this how the celestial maiden felt when she saw the face of the woodcutter for the first time, the heat of his eyes upon her? I think I might have understood, then, why she'd chosen to leave the sky.

For you, my love, I'd forsake Heaven.

Ren's hands were shaking so hard she almost dropped the book. These were her mother's words. But not about her father, whom she was rumored to have only felt indifference toward.

She recalled a recent memory, the night at Bright Moon Temple, before the assassins had attacked. Lady Maya had spoken of another man . . .

Your mother had a lover, before she married your esteemed father. A soldier. After their affair was discovered, he was killed.

"Sareniya . . ."

Ren felt an odd sensation at the back of her neck, as if someone had whispered into her ear. She twisted around, but no one was there, just the breeze sweeping through the open doors that led into the gardens.

"Sareniya . . ."

An odd, dreamlike haze fell over her. She dropped the diary with a muted thump, barely registering the sound.

Standing, she approached the doors. The trees loomed darkly before her. She stepped barefoot onto the deep, verdant lawn. The moon had risen higher, silvering the grass.

"Sareniya . . ."

She began to walk, following the voice that led her deeper and deeper into the gardens.

CHAPTER 10

JAEIL

The Floating World
The Eastern Gardens

JAEIL WAS ALIVE. Somehow, against all odds and his own lack of interest, he'd survived his execution.

It wasn't that he *wanted* to die, or didn't feel resentful at the court's decision, it was only that he didn't see how he could talk his way out of an outcome that had already seemed predetermined. He was his father's son. Nothing could change that, and there were rules in place to ensure no members of a traitor's family would retaliate years afterward: Eradicate the bloodline entirely.

It made sense to Jaeil. A son might seek revenge for his father's death.

He wouldn't, of course, but the members of the Floating Council wouldn't believe that.

Jaeil had been prepared to die in that hall. There'd been no one to take his side. Sana was in the Under World, recovering from the demon attack on the evening before the Festival of Light. His soldiers, those under his direct command, were stationed all over the place, with the majority at Yongin Military Base, outside the Wall. Commander Su, who might have spoken up on his behalf, had left the capital, with the assurance that the trial wouldn't commence without the presence of the princess.

Jaeil could admit that, beyond resentment, the other emotion he felt at the end was loneliness.

And then *she* appeared.

As Ren stood in front of him, defending him before the entire court, she was like a heroine from one the stories he used to read as a child. He'd sensed a stirring in his chest he hadn't experienced in a long time—hope.

After the trial was over, he'd watched as his father was led away in chains, and then he'd been set free. None of the guards had bothered to follow him outside the hall. It wasn't as if he had means to flee anyway—his private aircraft, taken into possession by the court following his arrest, was unlikely to be returned anytime soon.

From the hall, he walked without a destination in mind. Though he was born on the Floating World, he hadn't been back in years, not since joining the military.

He found himself treading a familiar path into the gardens that curved around the eastern half of the palace. They were expansive, filled with mazelike hedges, pavilions, lakes, and ponds. Jaeil was not sentimental, but even he could acknowledge the pleasing atmosphere.

Whenever he did come upon another soul taking in the sights of the garden, they gave him a wide berth. He was still wearing his prisoner's garb, the rough cloth of which chafed at his skin. He hadn't been supplied a sling, so he held his broken arm with the other—which perhaps made him a pitiable sight, but he found perverse pleasure in ruining the otherwise pristine views.

Over the mountains to the north, dark clouds gathered, and he wondered if it would snow overnight. He sucked in a breath of air, sharp from the cold.

A son might seek revenge for his father's death.

The law that punished entire bloodlines for the transgressions of one of its members had been overturned only once before, at least in recent memory.

Commander Su had been the one to first tell him of the incident; afterward, Jaeil had looked more into the story. A few years before Ren was born, her mother, the princess Aria, had an affair. Her lover was a soldier from the Under World who'd been invited to the palace on a goodwill mission. She was seventeen—the age Ren was now—and betrothed to another, someone chosen for her from one of the nine great clans. It was said that she and the soldier met in these same gardens, and in secret for months afterward before they were discovered.

As punishment for corrupting the princess, the soldier was executed. It didn't matter that Aria had begged Lord Muyeol, the head of the Floating Council at the time, to spare his life. It didn't matter that she'd loved him.

They say she watched him die, and not with the cool serenity that was expected of someone of her status, but sobbing the whole time. As if *she* was the one who'd been stabbed through the chest, bleeding out onto the stone.

The soldier's younger brother was also present at the execution, his only living family. Law dictated that he also should be executed, but he had a special talent, one prized by the Sareniyans: He had a unique understanding of mithril, had already begun developing a serum that could counteract its poisonous effects. It was because of this talent that the Sareniyans let him live. In exchange, he would conduct experiments on their behalf.

And for a time, he did—at least outwardly—appear to serve Sareniya, coming close to procuring a cure to mithril poisoning. He'd even, for a time, worked closely with the military on a secret project to create mithril-enhanced soldiers. It was after the project had failed that he'd disappeared.

Now he was back, harboring an abiding hatred for Sareniya, the place that had broken his heart so long ago. Jaeil had connected the pieces during the Festival of Light, when the scientist had appeared, injecting civilians with a mithril serum that had turned them into monsters.

With one strike of a blade, Sareniya had dealt two grievous wounds. For Aria, it was a wound that continued to bleed for years, leaving her hollow, a shell of the girl she'd once been.

And for the brother, it was a wound that cut deep, that festered and grew, consuming everything in its path.

His brother for the world.

As someone who bore no love for his own family, Jaeil didn't understand this all-consuming need for revenge.

He looked down to see that his feet had taken him to a familiar crossroads, one that he'd trodden countless times in his youth. If he took the path to the west, it would lead him to a meadow where a single zelkova tree grew among a field of wildflowers.

Instead, he turned east. The path took him beneath the shadows of the walls that surrounded the gardens. They were built to provide protection for the palace, but also acted as a boundary. Beyond the walls was the wind forest, and just beyond that, the edge. Many believed the forest was haunted, the wind sweeping through the trees sounding like the cries of restless spirits.

Jaeil shifted aside a veil of wisteria to find what he was searching for: a hole in the wall.

Crouching, he crawled through to the other side.

He'd been nine years old that fateful night ten years ago. His father had expressly forbidden him from visiting the eastern gardens, but Jaeil had wanted to see the performers.

Earlier, his father had beaten him, though the bruises weren't visible on his body, so he'd hidden them from Ren.

He knew that if he'd told her, she'd have insisted on healing him. It was a power they'd discovered when he'd fallen from the zelkova tree while trying to retrieve a kite she'd lost in its branches. Crying over him, guilty that she was the cause of his pain even though it had been *his* choice to climb, she'd laid her small cheek to his ankle. At first, he'd thought it was her tears that had healed him, but later he'd realized it was her Light, transferred through her touch. Afterward, whenever he was hurt, whether because of accidents during his training or his father's rage, she would heal him.

Even then, when all he'd wanted was his father's approval, he'd known to keep Ren's powers a secret from his father.

He'd known, even though his father never expressed such intentions, that he would hurt Ren if he knew the truth, that he'd find her *dangerous*.

On the night of the Festival of Light, after Ren had left for the forest in search of her mother, Jaeil had gone to the zelkova tree to wait for her. But then he'd remembered how his father had forbidden him from visiting the gardens, and he knew something terrible was about to happen. Jaeil had fled the meadow in search of Ren, finding the white feather just as his father's soldiers stepped out of the woods.

Later, when the general had claimed that both Ren and the queen had perished in the storm, Jaeil had known the truth: His father had killed them. At least, that's what he'd believed until several weeks ago, when he'd seen the Light appear in the east.

In a way, Jaeil could understand how a single moment could change the course of a person's life. After that night, he no longer cared to earn his father's approval. And the storybooks he'd treasured lost all the wonder they'd once held. He'd even stopped seeking out other forms of storytelling; he hadn't seen a troupe performance or a puppet show in years.

A branch snapped behind him. He whirled around, spotting a figure moving slowly through the trees.

His heart raced, recalling the rumors of lost spirits of those who had wandered too close to the edge . . .

He frowned; the figure wasn't a ghost at all, but a girl.

Ren.

What was she doing? He narrowed his eyes, trying to make out her expression in the dark.

She must have spotted him by now—he was in her direct line of sight. He opened his mouth to make some irreverent comment about her choice of nocturnal excursion, when he caught sight of her eyes.

They were blank, empty of expression. Open, but unseeing.

She was walking straight toward him, would *collide* with him if one of them didn't move out of the way. He stepped aside at the last minute.

She passed by him without a glance.

Unease settled in his gut. Was she . . . sleepwalking?

"Princess," he called out to her. She didn't react, only continued to walk forward.

He realized, with acute panic, that she was headed toward the edge.

"Ren!" he shouted, this time grabbing her shoulder and turning her toward him.

His heart pounded as she gazed up at him with those blank eyes, then she blinked, and he could see the moonlight reflected in them.

"What are you—?" she started, then stopped. She sounded confused. "Where am I?" She peered around at the forest.

"You were walking in your sleep," Jaeil explained carefully as he let go of her. "It was like you were in some sort of trance."

She shook her head. "I heard a voice . . ."

A chill swept over Jaeil, recalling once more the stories he'd heard as a child. He eyed the shadows beneath the trees. When he returned his gaze to Ren, she was studying him.

She must have regained her senses, because a small smile appeared on her lips. "Don't tell me you *still* believe in ghosts?"

A flush crept up Jaeil's neck. "I'm cautious," he averred. "Demons exist, don't they?"

As he said the words, he regretted them. Ren's expression shuttered.

He'd avoided returning to the Floating World for many reasons, but the feeling of living in a world of magic troubled him the most. There was a scientific explanation for demons. They were a byproduct of mithril. Even if mithril itself had magical components, it was still an ore mined from rock. On the Floating World, ghosts existed—in theory—and at least one celestial maiden with untold powers.

"Your arm," Ren said.

It took Jaeil a moment to realize what she was referring to. She gestured at the arm he was pressing to his chest, and reached out her hand. On instinct, he drew back.

She stepped forward, persistent. "Let me see it."

"I'm fine," Jaeil said. "It'll heal."

"Jaeil."

He went still. It wasn't often that others called him by his name, without his title. Even Sana and the commander referred to him as "Captain."

If anyone else had called him by his name, he would have reprimanded them severely.

But this was Ren. For the first quarter of his life, the only times he'd heard his name spoken with affection were from her lips.

"Commander Su told me about the attack in the square during the Festival of Light," Ren said softly. She reached again for his arm, and this time he let her take it. "That's where you broke your arm, isn't it?"

Re-broke it, but he didn't correct her.

He closed his eyes at the first hint of her magic. It wasn't painful; it felt like a warm river sweeping up his arm.

"Commander Su said that you were investigating murders in the Under World," Ren said. "That you concluded they were the work of demons." He opened his eyes, waiting for her to finish her thought. "I want you to be in charge of investigating more about the demons, about why they're appearing *now*, and for what purpose. And . . ."

She drew in a breath, meeting his gaze. "I *will* need your counsel. The war with Volmar . . . it needs to end."

"You saved my life," Jaeil said. "I'm yours to command."

She wrinkled her nose. "That's not why I did it, so that you'd feel indebted to me."

He raised a brow with the unspoken question.

"I . . ." She appeared to struggle with her answer. "I only hoped that you'd support me, that you'd help me. You know this world better than I do."

"Not really," he said. "I left the Floating World shortly after your . . ." He didn't finish the sentence.

Her disappearance. Her murder. Her death.

He studied her, wondering if there was more to the answer she'd given him. "You would trust me?" he asked. "I kidnapped you." His eyes strayed to her shoulder, where his dagger had bitten into her skin. "I hurt you."

She didn't answer for some time. Finally, she said, "You were my closest friend."

"I was your only friend."

"That's not true. I had Doona."

"I was your only friend who wasn't an elderly woman," he amended.

"I want to trust you, like before. I *need* to trust you. That makes me vulnerable, doesn't it? My uncle would say I'd be foolish to."

"Your uncle would be wise." Not because he didn't think she could trust his loyalty, but because he didn't know if his counsel would be enough to help her with everything she hoped to accomplish. If *he* would be enough.

"I forgive you," Ren said softly, "for what happened in the Under World. Will you forgive me?"

He frowned, unsure what she was referring to.

"I never kept my promise to meet you by the zelkova tree."

Jaeil felt as if the breath had been knocked from his body. Then he turned his face away. "It was a promise between children. Nothing more."

After regaining his composure, he said, "You're not alone in this.

I, too, want to stop the spread of demons, and I want to end the war." Enough lives had been lost.

"It's not just the war," Ren said. "I want to bring an end to Sareniya's rule altogether, give autonomy back to the people of the Under World and the Occupied Territories."

Jaeil raised a brow. "Your intentions are good," he said, "but Sareniya and Volmar are in an active war. To cut off Sareniya's support now would be to condemn the country to defeat, and possible invasion. Sareniya might be rich, but it doesn't have a large population. Outside the capital, there are maybe twenty villages of a few hundred people each. The bulk of its soldiers come from its territories."

"I have my powers," Ren said quietly.

"So you would use them to force Volmar to surrender? How is that any different from threatening them with the combined military might of Sareniya, the Under World, and the Occupied Territories?"

"See, *this* is why I need you," Ren said, fervent. "Even now, you're helping me find the right path."

He shook his head. "I don't know about right or wrong. I'm a soldier, not a strategist."

"Don't underestimate yourself. If it wasn't for you sending Sunho after me, I wouldn't be here."

"Don't remind me," Jaeil drawled.

"The morning at Bright Moon Temple, you stopped the assassins before they could kill me. Your father wanted me dead, but you gave me the chance to face him on my own. You said that you couldn't save me, that I could save myself. You believed I could defeat him, didn't you?"

"Believing in you isn't strategy." It went against all logic, and Jaeil had a logical mind. He hadn't known that morning if Ren could defeat his father—her chances were slim to none—but he had . . . hoped. A dangerous emotion.

"It's late," he said, weary of the subject. "You should go back to your room. Rest. Your aunt and great-uncle will have their own trials for you to face."

"They will, won't they?" Ren heaved a sigh. "I wish I had a loving family who welcomed me with food and warm hugs."

Jaeil observed Ren carefully. "You did have that, didn't you?" As a child, it was what she had wished for the most. A family that loved her.

"I did," she said. "I do."

"I'm happy for you," Jaeil said.

This time it was Ren's turn to blush, and for a moment, it appeared as if she glowed. Light radiated from her skin.

"My uncle is here with me, you know," she said. "My adoptive uncle. It's a long story. I want you to meet him."

Jaeil wondered if she meant the boy he'd seen with her in the hall, the one with curly hair.

"Good night, Jaeil."

He bowed as she left, watching her walk slowly back in the direction of the Queen's Palace.

He thought of the scientist who'd chosen to destroy the world for his brother. He didn't think there was anything he hated, *or* loved, enough to make the same choice.

And yet, as he watched Ren walk away, he had the fleeting thought that he might try to save the world for her.

CHAPTER 11

SUNHO

The Floating World
Training Grounds, Western Gardens

YURHEE AND TAG were eager to return to Wolryudang, and so, the morning after the trial, Sunho accompanied them to where they'd left the *Sparrow* on the white stone walkway outside the palace. In the hours they'd been gone, several doves had landed upon the deck and wings, roosting like kings.

"It's too . . . sterile here," Yurhee said with a shudder, wrinkling her nose at the tranquil fountain pool and the manicured lawns beside the flawless, paved footpaths. "I haven't seen a speck of dust or a clump of trash. It's unnatural."

"The gardens are nice," Tag said.

Wook, Ren's uncle, had shown them the western gardens the previous night, before bringing them to the guesthouse. Yurhee hadn't complained about the extravagant network of attached bathing pools *there*.

"Will you be all right?" Yurhee asked Sunho, her brow furrowed with concern. "They were whispering about you in the hall last night. They know you arrived with Ren. There'll be rumors."

Yurhee and Tag had received some curious looks, but it was Sunho who'd drawn the most attention. He had picked up on a few of the whispers. Most he'd dismissed, though one had caught his interest.

She's just like her mother.

"Give me a black-market weapons dealer over gossiping nobles any day." Yurhee shuddered again, more heavily this time.

Tag, who'd coaxed the doves from the aircraft with crumbs from his pocket, nodded his agreement. White tufts of feathers stuck out of his hair.

"Some advice from an older, wiser person . . . ," Yurhee began.

Tag looked over his shoulder, as if to see if someone else had joined the three of them.

"Don't give them a reason to hurt Ren through you. They'll ask less questions if you have a clear purpose for being here."

Sunho considered Yurhee's words—he did believe she was wiser than him. "Like a job?"

"That's right. People like us need purpose in our lives. We can't just lounge around on silk cushions eating sweetmeats all day."

"Sounds like purpose enough for me," Tag said.

"Ren will worry less, too," Yurhee said softly. "She has to find her way in this world. So do you." She stepped back. "If it ever gets to be too much, you know where to find us."

As he gazed at Yurhee, he felt an overwhelming sense of gratitude. He couldn't ever have imagined that, from working together on jobs in the Under World, she'd grow to become someone he'd trust. Both of them had become invaluable friends.

Yurhee didn't linger on a goodbye, giving him a two-finger salute before leaping onto the aircraft.

Sunho turned to Tag. "Tell Haru—" he started, then stopped, unable to find the words. "Tell Haru I'm sorry for not coming back."

"You will," Tag said. "Just not today. We're going back to the Under World, but that doesn't mean we're not a part of this, whatever

Ren has planned. If you ever need *anything*, Sunho, send for me. I'll come."

Sunho watched the *Sparrow* until it was only a speck on the horizon.

Afterward, he went in search of Wook, cornering him outside the guesthouse.

Though Ren had told him, he'd still been surprised how young her uncle was, only a year older than him. Sunho studied him for signs of mithril poisoning, but he seemed entirely healthy. His sun-kissed cheeks were rosy, his eyes bright. His open face reminded Sunho of Ren. If he hadn't already known the truth, he might have thought they were biological siblings.

"You want to be a guard?" Wook asked in disbelief, after Sunho had told him of his plan. He'd come up with it after Yurhee had left, taking her advice. "*Why?* You could just follow Ren around as part of her retinue. That's what *I'm* going to do."

If there were rumors circulating about his relationship with Ren, then his role as a guard would put them to rest. But more than that, he needed . . . a distraction. He felt the Demon stir within him, like a dark tide rising against the shore. "Please."

Wook tugged the collar of his robe aside, scratching the side of his neck. "I'll let Head Maid Eun know. She's the one who oversees the comings and goings of everyone in the palace."

He then mumbled under his breath, "I hope no one expects *me* to be a guard."

SUNHO DIDN'T HAVE to wait long before Head Maid Eun sent a servant to direct him to the western training grounds.

Members of the Sareniyan guard who weren't on patrol spent their days practicing drills on a great field. After reading the missive Head Maid Eun sent with the servant, the officer at the guardhouse assigned Sunho to archery practice.

He snagged a bow and arrows from the armory before joining the others.

He was strapping an armguard to his forearm when he was approached by one of the younger guards. "Is it true you arrived with the princess?"

Sunho glanced at the boy; he'd forgotten that training with the palace guards meant they would *speak* to him. "Where *was* she this whole time?" he prodded.

"They say she was living in some backwater village far from here," snickered a girl with gold earrings. She turned, and Sunho squinted as the sunlight glinted off the bright metal. "Is that where you're from, too?"

"He's from the Under World," said a third guard, a smirk on his face. He was medium height, stocky, with narrow eyes and a sharp nose.

"Don't be mean, Jinok," the girl chastised, though her tone was playful.

"It's true. You can tell by the pallor of his skin." Jinok's smirk turned cruel. "They say most Under Worlders never even see the sun."

The girl with the earrings wrinkled her nose. "That's disturbing."

"From the Under World, like . . . ?" began the first guard who'd spoken, trailing off.

The whole group fell silent. They exchanged glances, as if having a secret conversation.

"He *is* rather handsome." The girl slid her eyes up Sunho's body.

Jinok's eyes darted to her, his lips turning downward in a frown. He took a step toward Sunho, his hand curling into a fist. "We've been training our whole lives to be a part of the Sareniyan guard. What makes you worthy of a position? Because the princess favors you?" He scowled defiantly. "How do we even know she's who she says she is? She could be a pretender, like the general claimed."

Sunho tensed as the Demon writhed beneath his skin, seeking escape.

"That's enough, Jinok!" Another guard stepped between them. Jinok retorted, but Sunho had stopped listening.

He drew in a breath, then released it slowly as the Demon subsided.

A gentle hand pressed his shoulder. "Are you all right?"

Sunho caught his breath. "Ro-Rohoon?" Sunho said, and his voice broke on the name.

A soft hand, a figure that was large and intimidating but cast the gentlest of shadows . . .

"That's Chulsoo." The girl who'd risen to his defense stood before him, indicating the boy beside her. He saw that the boy he'd mistaken for his friend was tall, with broad shoulders and a youthful face. *Not Rohoon.*

"My name's Hwani," the girl continued. She was around his own age, her hair braided and pinned behind her head. "Sorry we didn't speak up sooner." She scowled in the direction of Jinok and the others. "They're just jealous that you know the princess."

"Are you all right?" Chulsoo repeated.

"Yeah," Sunho said. The Demon appeared to be under control. For now.

"They're such cowards." Hwani shook her head, as if disappointed in her fellow guards.

"Hwani's the strongest warrior among us," Chulsoo said, clearly proud of his friend. "There's no one more gifted with either a bow or a spear."

Hwani laughed, and the sound reminded him fiercely of Heetae—for a moment, it was as if he was with them again, his best friends, protecting one another, laughing together.

Then Hwani shook her head. "Come on. Let's actually start the training we're *meant* to be doing."

For the rest of the morning, Sunho kept away from Jinok's group, practicing archery alongside Hwani and Chulsoo.

He kept his mind focused, concentrating on loosing arrow after arrow. When he was focused on a task, he could forget the Demon, could forget that it felt *closer* than before.

He'd first noticed it when they'd arrived at the Floating World, when the archer at the tower had released his arrow. In the seconds it had flown through the air, Sunho had felt his control over the Demon slip. If Ren hadn't dodged out of the way, if it had *struck* her, Sunho didn't think he'd have been able to hold the Demon back.

It was as if, because it had been released before, it was waiting for him to lose concentration. It would only take a moment, a single lapse in thought. It . . . terrified him.

Sunho loosed an arrow and it veered to the left, missing the target entirely.

"You're clumsier than you look," Hwani said, her tone sympathetic.

Sunho scratched the back of his head with his hand, smiling sheepishly.

"I'd be careful if I were you, Hwani," the guard with the earrings called over, laughing. "The princess might not take kindly to you encroaching upon her territory."

Hwani rolled her eyes.

Sunho looked between the two guards. "What does she mean by that?" he asked.

Hwani hesitated, exchanging a glance with Chulsoo. After appearing to consider her words, she said bluntly, "There's a rumor that you're the princess's lover."

Sunho's cheeks flushed with surprise, then embarrassment. He felt foolish that he hadn't seen that coming. He wasn't Ren's family, like Wook. He couldn't even claim to be a friend from her childhood.

Hwani shrugged. "Most would have probably dismissed it as a rumor, except that the queen . . ."

"What about the queen?" Sunho asked sharply. He recalled the whisper he'd heard in the hall. *She's just like her mother.*

"We're not supposed to talk about it," Hwani said. "When her mother was a little older than the princess's age now, she fell in love with a soldier from the Under World. Lord Muyeol . . . the Floating Council . . . they killed him."

"Just like they'll kill you," Jinok sneered from where he'd been eavesdropping.

Sunho didn't react to his taunt; neither he nor the Demon were threatened so easily.

Jinok scowled, seeing his barb had missed its mark. "Well, what's the truth, then? How is it that you know the princess?"

"I protected her," Sunho said, hoping the truth would ease any rumors, "when the general sent assassins to kill her."

"*You?*" Jinok appeared unimpressed, likely having observed Sunho's skill with a bow, or lack thereof. "I doubt that. No, I think she brought you here for an entirely different reason."

Sunho knew Jinok was trying to get a reaction from him, that the other boy wouldn't stop. He wouldn't give him the satisfaction. Deliberately, Sunho turned his back.

"Like daughter, like mother," Jinok said, his voice smug. "What do you think? Would the princess welcome *me* into her bed?"

Sunho launched himself at Jinok.

He couldn't even blame the Demon. They were *his hands* wrapped around Jinok's neck, *his knee* grinding his stomach into the dirt.

"Say that again," Sunho growled. "I dare you."

He heard shouts behind him, hands pulling at his arms, but he didn't loosen his hold. Jinok was scrambling for air, his arms flailing.

Then he saw it—his fingers had lengthened, his nails growing into talons that dug into the side of Jinok's neck.

He let go of Jinok in horror, stumbling backward.

"You're bleeding!" cried another guard.

Jinok pressed his hand to his neck. "He must have had a knife on him."

Sunho looked down at his hands. They'd returned to normal. But he hadn't imagined it. He'd transformed, if only for a second. Turning, he fled.

CHAPTER 12

REN

The Floating World
The Celestial Palace

REN WALKED SWIFTLY across the courtyard outside the Celestial Palace, tightly gripping her skirt, careful to keep the hem above the ground to avoid tripping. She'd have preferred to wear the trousers and jacket she'd arrived in, but she understood that if she wished to be *perceived* as the celestial maiden, she must look the part. She'd selected her dress from one of the ornate chests in her room; it was light blue and woven of the finest silk, the cape inlaid with pearls. The bodice was unique in that it went over the silken jacket, while the long sleeves were left to tumble from her wrists to the ground.

She hadn't braided her hair, but instead left it to fall loose over her shoulders and down her back, as was traditional for royal women. She wore a single hair ornament, a thin silver band that circled her brow. From the tip dangled a sapphire the shape of a teardrop, the color reminding her of mithril, but paler.

As she made her way up the steps of the palace, she gazed at the glittering facade, wrought entirely of crystal and glass. Inside was the main throne hall, where she would face the Floating Council for the first time. She wasn't even certain if her mother had been allowed to sit in on council meetings, or if she was only paraded about during ceremonies and festivals.

Lady Maya was waiting for her in the antechamber. Like Ren and her mother, her aunt shared the same black hair characteristic of celestial maidens, though she wore hers in a tight bun. She had beautiful—if severe—features, a straight back, and assessing eyes.

"Aunt Maya," Ren said, inclining her head in a bow.

If her aunt was surprised that Ren had addressed her so familiarly, she gave no indication.

"You look lovely," she said, sweeping a critical eye over Ren. "I hope you were able to sleep well enough last night."

"I did, thank you," Ren replied, though it was far from the truth. After leaving Jaeil, Ren had returned to her room, but hadn't managed to sleep for more than an hour, tossing and turning upon the massive bed.

She wondered if her aunt would bring up what had occurred at the trial the evening before, when Ren had spoken out against her, but she only turned toward the entrance to the hall.

"Wait!" Ren called out. "There's a matter I wish to discuss with you." She felt suddenly uncomfortable, her cheeks reddening. "Sunho, the boy who came with me . . . I want him to be my personal guard."

She didn't know why she should feel so embarrassed. It was a reasonable request. Sunho had experience working as a bodyguard; he'd done so when he'd been a sword-for-hire in the Under World. More than that, he'd already protected her, on their journey to Seorawon, and many times after.

Lady Maya scrutinized Ren for what felt like ages. "I don't think that would be wise," she said finally.

Ren straightened her back, mirroring her aunt's posture. "It's my choice."

Lady Maya was already shaking her head. "He was seen arriving with you. There are already rumors. He is young, handsome. An unsuitable companion for an unmarried princess."

"He's my friend," Ren said, not caring that her aunt might think her childish.

"Think of your mother. If you were ever caught in, gods forbid, a compromising situation, history could repeat itself."

Ren's whole face flushed. "That isn't— That's not—" Ren drew in a slow breath. "What do you suggest?"

"He's already taken it upon himself to train with the royal guards. If he proves himself worthy, he could put himself forward as a candidate for your personal guard. He will have to *earn* that position, however. If it is given to him, that will only lead to scorn—not just for you, but for him."

Ren was surprised at the logic and wisdom of her aunt's suggestion. As princess, Ren could order that Sunho fill the role as her personal guard, but that left them open to criticism. Her aunt's way, no one would question Sunho's place at her side once he proved he belonged there.

"He'll earn it," Ren declared, and Lady Maya's eyebrows rose slightly, as if amused at her confidence.

Ren cleared her throat. "There's another matter I wish to discuss with you. About my own training."

Lady Maya tilted her head, studying her. "What do you mean?"

"I wish to train my powers."

Ren knew that her mother hadn't had powers, nor had her mother before her, but that didn't mean knowledge of the magic in her bloodline hadn't been preserved somewhere. There must be historical records, detailed annals of the reigns of past rulers.

Lady Maya nodded. "I will have someone escort you to the Temple of the Goddess after the council meeting. Is there anything else?"

Ren sagged with relief. "No, that's all. Thank you."

Turning from her, Lady Maya signaled the guards standing outside the doors of the throne hall, who then proceeded to draw them open, the clamor of dozens of voices spilling into the antechamber.

Her aunt stepped into the hall and a herald announced her arrival: "The Lady Maya, scion of the royal house of Sareniya."

As Ren waited for her turn, sharp movement to her right caught her attention.

There was no one in the antechamber other than her except the guards. The walls, she'd noticed when she'd entered earlier, were made of mirrors. As she turned toward her reflection, the sounds coming from the hall dimmed, and all she could hear was her own heartbeat, pounding thickly in her chest. A woman gazed back at her. She had hair as deep as the night, and a face like the moon. Though the chamber was windless, a voluminous black robe fluttered around her shoulders. *Mother?*

"Her Royal Highness, Princess Sareniya!"

She turned, startled at the herald's booming voice. When she looked back to the reflection, the woman was gone, replaced by a girl with wan cheeks and wide eyes. She was herself again.

Shaken, she turned from her reflection and stepped into the hall.

The evening before, the nobles had stood in a crowd before the dais. Now they assembled on either side of a long, carpeted aisle.

Whispers followed as she walked toward the dais, and she was glad for her billowing sleeves that hid her clasped hands.

"Princess."

"Sareniya."

And then: "Aria."

Ren looked toward the woman who'd spoken. She was perhaps in her sixties, with cool gray eyes.

"Forgive me," the woman said. "With the way you're dressed, you looked so much like your mother, I thought I'd seen a ghost."

Ren shivered, thinking of the reflection in the mirror and the specter on the airship. What was happening to her? Why was she seeing someone who wasn't there?

Though she'd teased Jaeil the evening before, ghosts didn't exist. At least, not in the physical sense. And yet, she'd seen the spirit, had heard her voice . . .

Bowing, the woman stepped back into the crowd. Ren proceeded down the aisle.

She'd half expected to see Lord Muyeol seated on the throne, as he had been the evening before, but he stood to the side, his head lowered as she passed.

Ren gazed up at the dais. Above it was a stained-glass window depicting a mural of outstretched wings. A wave of dizziness gripped her, and she clutched the banister as a memory veiled her mind—one of her mother seated on the throne as the sunlight pierced the glass behind her.

As she came out of the memory, Ren fought to get her breath under control. She needed to be more vigilant. Occurrences like this would happen more frequently the longer she walked in her mother's footsteps.

"Princess?" She heard Lord Muyeol call out from over her shoulder. "Do you need assistance?" He didn't sound concerned so much as smug, as if her weakness was expected.

"No, thank you," she said, keeping her voice steady. She climbed the steps without further interruption before turning to sit on the throne, her hands gripping the arms on both sides.

The crowd that had struck up whispered conversations when she'd stumbled quieted as Lord Muyeol addressed the room. "We have a few important matters to discuss. First, the princess's personal guard must be selected as soon as possible. As tradition follows, one will be chosen from the royal guards, at a trial to take place tomorrow morning on the training grounds outside the western gardens."

Ren met the gaze of Lady Maya, who stood with the group to the right of the aisle, behind Lord Muyeol. This group was larger in number than those who stood to the left—at least twice the size. Ren surmised that these were the two factions, those who supported her aunt and great-uncle to the right, and those who were more independent-minded to the left. She would need the support of *both* if she was to make any meaningful changes.

"We must also discuss the matter of the princess's attendants," Lord Muyeol continued. "All of whom, of course, will be selected from the heirs of the nine clans." This pleased the right-side group, who tittered in response. "Lastly, there is the matter of choosing a prince consort—"

"I would like to discuss a more *important* matter," Ren interrupted, not liking the direction of the meeting, or that point in particular.

Lord Muyeol's expression was cool as he met her gaze.

Refusing to be rattled, she raised her chin. "I wish to negotiate a truce with Volmar," she declared.

Startled cries erupted across the hall. Lord Muyeol quieted them with a raised hand. He lifted a brow. "What do you propose?"

Ren stared at him, surprised that he hadn't argued with her.

"I'm—I'm not sure," she said, and winced at the scornful looks she received, "only that I wish for this war to end." Her palms were sweaty. She felt as if she was playacting a role she hadn't prepared for, which was close to the truth. She might have the blood of the celestials, but she felt like an imposter.

"I know you have sympathies for the Volmarans—" Lord Muyeol began.

"What do you mean?" a noble asked sharply.

"She was seen saving a Volmaran soldier," answered a man standing among Lord Muyeol's supporters. "During the most recent attack."

This news was met with outrage. Gazes that had once appeared curious and open turned hostile and cold.

"He was only a boy—" Ren started to protest, remembering how the soldier had reminded her of Wook, how he'd bled in her arms, how he'd begged for his life.

"You dishonor the memories of *our* soldiers," one noble shouted. "Do you know how many of our people the Volmarans have killed in this war?"

"That's why the war must end," she insisted, "for the sake of everyone!"

"It's gone too far for that," said the same noble. "Something you'd know, had you returned sooner."

Ren gaped, unable to speak. She'd witnessed the murder of her mother, had fled from assassins. She'd been *a child*.

Lord Muyeol raised his hand again and the hall quieted. "I think these are matters the council members should discuss privately. We will reconvene in a few days' time to hear possible solutions. Was there anything else bothering you, Princess?"

Ren gripped the arms of the chair even tighter; she wanted to shout in frustration. It was clear her great-uncle meant to undermine her in front of the council. And yelling at him would only help further that cause.

"The evening before the Festival of Light—" she began, keeping her voice calm, a monumental task. "There was a demon attack in the Under World. I wish to know what is being done to protect the people there."

The word *demon* elicited another powerful response from the council members, gasps and cries of outrage.

A deep furrow appeared between Lord Muyeol's brows. "That was weeks ago. There haven't been any further instances. There are witnesses who saw Juwon flee the city. Posters bearing his likeness have been distributed throughout the territories. If he's seen again, he'll be apprehended."

Juwon. So that was the name of the scientist she had met in the labs. She still remembered his fingers digging into her skin as he grabbed her wrist, his words when she'd drawn her hand back: *I am cursed.*

"I think he's continuing to develop his research," Ren said. He'd taken a vial of her blood that night for some unknown purpose, and even if she hadn't seen him at the mountain laboratory, she knew he was involved. "Something awful might happen if he's not stopped."

"You speak of the Mithril Enhancement Project," Lord Muyeol said.

Ren drew back in her seat. "You know of the project?"

"I was the one who ordered it."

Before she could respond, Lord Muyeol turned toward the hall. "We were losing ground in the war, and so I came up with a solution. The project was to create an enhanced type of soldier using mithril. Unfortunately, it was a colossal failure. The majority of the subjects who were injected with mithril died upon receiving the serum. The few who survived were . . . transformed. Their blood turned blue. They lost all rational thought. They became demons, *monsters*."

Lord Muyeol's gaze returned to her, and she shivered. "They're abominations," he said, "regardless of whether they were once humans. If any of them are found to have survived, they will be destroyed, immediately and without exception."

REN WAS EXHAUSTED by the time the council meeting was over. The nobles had spoken at length about topics that seemed trivial compared to an ongoing war. They didn't wish to discuss the increasing number of migrant camps outside the Wall or the reports of sick crops in the Outer Territories, saying those were matters for the Under World. Ren could only watch in deepening dismay as her great-uncle guided the conversation so that, by the end, any solutions that were agreed upon were ones *he* desired.

At least Lady Maya had remembered her promise, sending a guard to escort Ren to the Temple of the Goddess. As she entered the grand foyer, she was struck by the silence. After the dissonant noise of the throne hall, it was like a gentle oasis. Acolytes in long, flowing robes walked slowly across the marbled floors. As Ren made her way down the aisle of the main area, she gazed up at the vaulted ceilings. At the front of the temple was the altar where supplicants prayed beneath a statue of the original celestial maiden.

It was odd to think that the maiden, a goddess, was her ancestor. The sculptor had depicted her as a young woman with a gentle face. Her eyes were downcast, her hands clasped together. Her white wings weren't outspread but wrapped around her like a cloak.

A soft rustling drew her attention to where a priestess emerged from another chamber. "Princess, you honor us with your presence," she said, greeting Ren with a low bow. "The head priestess has been waiting for you." The woman gestured Ren back toward the chamber she'd entered from. "Please follow me."

Ren nodded at her guard, indicating that she was to wait for her in the main area, before following the priestess. The woman led Ren through a small courtyard, then a larger one, before entering a stone building that contained only a single set of stairs that appeared to lead into darkness. A dozen or so steps down, however, a faint light began to emanate from below. It wasn't warm, like the glow from lanterns, but cooler. The staircase ended at a large underground cavern.

Before her was a garden. Untidy rows of large, fluffy cabbages grew beside turnip heads and rich, green cucumbers. The light came from stones buried in the earth. It had a bluish tint to it and appeared to originate from streaks of a blue mineral in the stone's surface. Ren moved closer, mesmerized by the light, her hand moving toward the stone.

A woman poked her head up from where she'd been crouched among the vegetables. "It's beautiful, isn't it? Mithril."

Ren snatched her hand back. "Isn't it poisonous?"

"Yes," the woman said, and Ren recoiled. "But not always. When it's in its natural state, it's not harmful at all. Its presence helps the plants grow. These rocks shouldn't cause you any harm." Reaching out her gloved hand, she patted the stone before withdrawing and rising to her feet.

The head priestess was of middling height, dressed in breeches, with her gardening gloves hoisted to her elbows. "Mithril itself isn't poisonous when left alone," she said. "It's when it's *taken* that it becomes so."

Ren nodded slowly. She remembered how when she'd visited the mines, she hadn't felt sick, though she'd been surrounded by mithril.

Ren followed the head priestess into another chamber, where the air was warm and thick. At the center of the room was a pool; lazy whorls of steam rose from the surface.

A white set of clothing had been laid out on one of the large rocks that surrounded the pool.

"Places like these are sacred," the priestess said, her voice echoing in the chamber. "Your ancestors would come here to cleanse their spirits and seek wisdom in the water. Hopefully you'll find answers to the questions you might have."

The priestess then bowed, leaving Ren alone in the chamber.

She quickly changed before stepping into the water. The pool was shallow, and she crouched, submerging her body up to her neck. As the heat relaxed her muscles, she moved to lie on her back, closing her eyes. She wondered what exactly she was supposed to be doing. She never was particularly skilled at meditation, much to Auntie's dismay. Whenever she and Little Uncle were given a task as part of their training, they could never sit still. Auntie would come back to find them tussling in the grass, or in the middle of a contest of who could climb to the highest branch of a tree.

With a sigh, Ren opened her eyes.

She was no longer in the chamber.

She sat up abruptly, her heart racing. Long grass swayed on either side of her, tickling her bare feet. She drew in her legs to stand, gaping at her surroundings as a warm breeze swept back the strands of hair that had fallen across her face. She was in a meadow.

She *knew* this meadow, had visited it many times before. She recognized the pond that always harbored at least two ducks, and the small river that wound along the eastern edge, and the zelkova tree . . .

It wasn't there. That didn't make sense; the tree had *always* been in the meadow, ever since she'd first discovered it when she was five years old.

Movement to her right caught her attention. A young girl was wading into the river. The water was up to her knees. Her hair, cut short at the neck, was damp, as if she'd already taken a dunking before Ren's arrival.

"Rina, come back from there! It's dangerous."

Ren followed the voice to where an elderly woman sat on a rock beside the pond. She seemed to notice Ren at the same time because she said, "Oh, hello."

Ren quickly tried to make sense of what was happening. "Where am I?" she asked. It didn't appear to be winter at all, but summer. "*When* am I?"

"What an odd question! Rina, why aren't you listening to me? Come out from there!"

The girl slogged from the river, trudging across the grass toward them. As Rina came closer, Ren saw that she was pretty, with a brown, sun-kissed face, and cheeks flushed from the sun, even if she was sulking.

"You're a celestial maiden," Ren said—she made the connection from having appeared in this meadow, after submerging into the pool, and the girl's name. "Rina is a diminutive of Sareniya, isn't it?"

The girl ignored her, plopping to the ground and taking off her boots. She upended one and a goldfish flopped out. Picking up the goldfish by the tail, she dropped it into the pond.

"Excuse my granddaughter," the elderly woman said. "She's had a poor upbringing."

"*You* raised me," Rina said.

Ren jerked her head up, gazing at the woman. That meant *she* was a celestial maiden as well.

Ren had hoped to find records of the maidens' powers; she'd never imagined she could learn directly from the source.

"What is your name?" Ren asked.

"You can call me Grandmother."

"I'm Ren. I think you're my ancestor." She drew in a breath. "I've come here to learn from you."

"Oh?" Grandmother raised a brow. "Did you hear that, Rina? She wishes to learn from me. You should do well to heed this wise older sister."

Rina wrinkled her nose.

Ren glanced at the girl. "I guess she's my ancestor as well." An odd thought. "Maybe both of you could teach me?"

Grandmother laughed, slapping her knee. "What would she be able to teach you? She's nine years old!"

"I don't understand," Ren said, frowning. Rina may have appeared nine years old in this place, but if she was Ren's ancestor, then she must have grown up and had a daughter of her own, otherwise Ren wouldn't exist.

"The Ancestral Realm," Grandmother said, gesturing to the meadow. "That's what we call this place. Here, Rina is only a young girl. She doesn't know of her future."

"I see . . . ," Ren said slowly. "Then why is she here?"

"I can hear you, you know," Rina grumbled. She'd finished pouring water out of her boots and sat cross-legged in the grass. "What is it that you want my grandmother to teach you, anyway?"

"Magic."

"Oh." Grandmother frowned. "I'm afraid I haven't an ounce of that."

Ren's heart sank. She gazed once more around the meadow. "How do I get out of here?"

"I don't know how it works," Grandmother said. "You might have to learn a lesson before you're able to go back." She studied Ren with a thoughtful expression. "I might not have magic, but I can still teach you.

"Across the river, there's a mulberry bush. Pick a basketful of fruit and bring it back to me."

Ren sighed. It wasn't like she had any better ideas on how to get back to the temple. Approaching the river, she dipped her toes into the icy water before swimming across, the current threatening to upend her. She didn't have a basket, so she bundled the berries in her skirt, holding it together with one hand while swimming across with the other. She was soaked and shivering by the time she returned.

Grandmother and Rina ate the fruit, then Grandmother made her run ten circles around the meadow carrying Rina on her back.

When she was finished, she collapsed, with Rina tumbling onto the grass beside her.

"I might not look it," Ren grumbled, "but I'm used to such tasks. My aunt had me do the same training."

"Your aunt is wise," Grandmother said. "She must be, since she's one of my descendants."

"She's not one," Ren said bluntly. "I was adopted."

Grandmother stared at Ren as if she'd sprouted a second head.

"What happened to your mother?" Rina asked, flopping over.

"It's a long story, but there was a betrayal on the Floating World.

Because of it, I was gone for ten years. I came back, but now there's a war, and a darkness in the form of demons spreading over the land."

"That sounds very serious," Grandmother said sympathetically. "It doesn't concern us, though, does it?"

Ren scowled, while Rina drew her knees to her chest.

By the time Ren had finished completing the rest of Grandmother's tasks—which included constructing a tower out of rocks the height of Rina and weaving a cushion of grass for Grandmother to sit on—it was dusk, and Ren had reached her limit. "I don't know how any of this is helping me," she complained loudly.

"Growth doesn't occur overnight," Grandmother chided. "You can only grow stronger through discipline and hard work, and you *need* to be strong if you wish to fend off demons."

"Yes, but how does that help me with *magic*?"

"If you haven't figured that out yet, then you haven't really learned a thing, have you?"

Ren wanted to scream in frustration. "You've never had any magic," she said harshly, "so you don't know what it's like to carry this responsibility."

A short silence followed her outburst, then Grandmother said quietly, "I think it's time for Ren to go back." Rina nodded in agreement.

Ren's stomach dropped. "Wait, I didn't mean—"

She was suddenly underwater. Flailing, she found her footing, gasping as she broke the surface of the pool.

All around her, mithril shone from the walls of the caverns. She was once again beneath the Temple of the Goddess.

CHAPTER 13

REN

The Floating World
Training Grounds, Western Gardens

REN WOKE THE next morning in a foul mood. After returning to the palace exhausted and sore—though time passed slower in the Ancestral Realm, she still bore the physical effects of her training—she'd slept fitfully. She rose only when Head Maid Eun knocked at her door, informing her that the test to choose her bodyguard would soon begin.

Little Uncle met her in the main courtyard outside the Celestial Palace.

"You look lovely . . . ," Wook began, frowning when Ren delivered him a baleful glare. ". . . Or not?"

Ren sighed. "You look nice yourself," she said. She'd noticed it before, but he appeared very handsome and grown-up in his silken robes and gentleman's hat, though even that couldn't tame his unruly curls, some of which slipped out from beneath his forehead band. "The life of a nobleman suits you."

"Not really." He scratched at his neck, flushing with embarrassment, though he couldn't hide a small, pleased smile. "I'm just that good of an actor." Wook's grin faltered as he studied her. "There are dark circles beneath your eyes. Aren't you sleeping?"

"I'm fine." Ren turned her face away. She didn't want him to worry, which he undoubtedly would if he knew she was having nightmares again, like the ones she used to have when she was a child, of demons chasing her through a dark forest. And also, that she feared her mother's ghost was haunting her.

The test was to take place in the western gardens, on a field where the palace guards drilled when not on active duty. Ren was surprised to find a great number of people when she arrived. Large red tents had been arranged around the grassy area. Beneath them, groups of nobles lounged on silk pillows, partaking liberally from tables laden with bright confections and succulent fruits cut into the shapes of flowers and stars.

A ripple went through the field at Ren's arrival. She felt a hundred gazes as she made her way toward the covered dais where she was to view the test.

The participating guards had also taken notice of her, bowing as she passed.

She searched for Sunho among them, but he wasn't on the field, at least not yet. More guards were arriving by the minute from the wooded area surrounding the barracks.

She felt a churning sensation in her stomach, which she attributed to nerves. She'd spoken to her aunt with confidence, but she hadn't any idea what to expect at today's trials. She *needed* Sunho to succeed. Then no one could question his place at her side.

They'd only been separated for little more than a day, yet she yearned to see him. She wondered if he felt the same.

An admiring crowd had gathered around an archery area where a strong-looking boy wielding a large bow was shooting arrows aggressively into the center of a target.

"That's Jinok," Wook said, following Ren's gaze. "Apparently, he's Lady Maya's nephew on her husband's side. Everyone in the palace believes he'll be the one with the highest marks in the test."

Ren worried at her lip as she stared at the young man, who looked every inch a warrior with his muscular stature and fierce gaze.

She then turned to Wook with a frown. "Wait, how do you know that?" Wook had known about the test as long as she had, possibly even less.

"Yesterday while you were gallivanting at the temple," Wook droned, "*I* was out gathering information I thought might be useful. The other candidate to pay attention to, at least according to the nobles at the card tables, is a guard named Hwani."

"You were *gambling*?" Ren admonished, though she was secretly impressed.

"Buying someone a drink is the best way to loosen a tongue," Wook said, adding with a grin, "and to take all their money."

"I'll have to remember that the next time I'm in need of coin," drawled a voice from close by.

Wook startled, his eyes widening. Jaeil stood behind them, having apparently stepped from one of the large tents. Ren was relieved to see how much better he looked than he had two nights before. He'd tidied up his appearance, shaved the stubble on his jawline, and tamed and cut short his dark hair. He wasn't wearing a hat like the other nobles, and his features were stark beneath the winter sunlight.

It was difficult for her to parse the steely warrior he was now to the boy she'd known, who'd been quiet and bookish.

"How's your arm?" She raised her hand on instinct, wanting to check the extent of her magic. From the corner of her eye, she saw the nobles beneath the tent titter in response.

She returned her attention to Jaeil. He hadn't moved, as if waiting to see what she'd do next. "It's good as new," he said, "thanks to you."

Clearing her throat, she withdrew her hand. "This is my uncle," she said, "the one who I'd spoken of before. Wook, this is Jaeil."

She anticipated Wook's witty remark, but he remained uncharacteristically quiet. She glanced at him to see that color had risen in his cheeks. She smiled to herself, realizing he must be embarrassed about what Jaeil had overheard.

"Stay behind the lines during the test," Jaeil warned, flicking his gaze briefly to Wook before returning to her. "There will be a lot of arrows flying about. The wind could blow one off course."

She grinned. "That shouldn't be a problem."

Jaeil's expression softened; he was likely remembering how she'd sent the wind to knock the cup of poison from his hand. With a brisk bow, he strode back toward the tents.

"I've been meaning to ask . . ." Wook tugged at the sleeve of his jacket. "How is it that you know the captain?"

Ren realized that the two people who'd meant the most to her in her childhood had just met, however briefly. She'd never told Wook about Jaeil—after she'd left the Floating World, she'd put him out of her mind. She did feel guilty about that now. Jaeil had asked her not to forget him, and she had. It wasn't intentional—she'd pushed *everything* about her past from her mind.

"He was my childhood friend," she said, though that choice of words didn't seem adequate to explain what he'd meant to her. He was her companion, her solace, as she had been his. They'd had no one else.

"Oh," Wook said. Ren sighed, relieved that he understood her. "So he's in love with you."

"What? *No.* That's *not* what I meant by a childhood friend!" She looked around them to see if anyone had heard, but everyone appeared distracted by the guards who were lining up in groups for the test.

"Isn't that what it always means?" Wook said. His tone was teasing, but there was an odd look in his eye.

Before she could ask him what he meant by that, she was distracted by the arrival of a new group of guards. She immediately spotted Sunho. Warmth flooded her veins, and she felt her wings pulse against her back, though they didn't emerge.

He had changed from Tag's ill-fitting clothing and now wore the silver-and-crimson uniform of a guard. She resisted the urge to fly across the field to him, though the desire was overwhelming. It was then that she noticed he was walking closest to a girl in the group. She was around their age, pretty, her reddish-brown hair tucked into a crown of braids. The girl must have said something amusing because Sunho laughed, the sweet sound traveling the distance to her ears.

Ren felt as if she'd been struck in the chest. The feeling caught her so by surprise she almost staggered backward.

"Ren," Wook said, catching her shoulder. "They're starting the test soon. You have to take your seat."

She tore her gaze away, letting Wook guide her toward the dais. She tried to calm her heart. There was nothing to be upset about, to be *jealous* over. She should be pleased that Sunho was making friends. Of course others would gravitate toward him. He was naturally kind, and when he smiled, it felt like receiving a gift—she should know.

Approaching the dais, she held back a groan when she saw she'd be seated between both her aunt *and* great-uncle for the duration of the test. Little Uncle smiled at her sympathetically before leaving her to join the nobles in the tent. She climbed the steps and took her seat.

On the field, the guards had formed neat lines. Sunho was facing in her direction, yet he hadn't looked up to the dais. Not once.

He *must* know of her presence on the field. Everyone was watching her, some more openly than others. Since his arrival she could hardly tear her gaze away, so why was it so easy for him to ignore her? She felt consumed by her thoughts of him, her emotions like open wounds, yet he appeared completely unaffected.

"Princess," Lord Muyeol said. "Forgive me for not properly greeting you. I'd retired from the council shortly after General Iljin's rise, leaving my daughter to oversee matters. But now that he's been deposed, it seems it is my duty to return and guide the both of you."

"I am grateful for any wise counsel you might grant me, Great-Uncle," Ren said, and Lord Muyeol smiled, satisfied. "But perhaps my aunt would have more insight and interest in the current affairs of the world."

Lord Muyeol narrowed his eyes. Ren glanced at her aunt to see that she wore a remote expression, though her lips were puckered slightly.

Ren returned her gaze to the field, searching for Sunho. She found him kneeling on the grass a short distance away.

The feelings that rushed over her were like a sickness—her pulse raced, her breath quickened. It was the strength of her reaction that confused her. Before, she'd worried for him, had longed for him. But this felt different, more powerful. What had changed?

Slowly, he lifted his gaze and, for the first time since they'd been on the same field, he looked directly at her. It was as if the world crumbled away, and all she could see was him.

Is this how the celestial maiden felt when she saw the face of the woodcutter for the first time, the heat of his eyes upon her? I think I might have understood, then, why she'd chosen to leave the sky.

For you, my love, I'd forsake Heaven.

She was the first to break eye contact, her palms slick as she gripped the arms of the chair.

It wasn't just that he'd looked at her; it was the *way* he'd looked at her. As if he'd been aware of her all along, as if there was no one on this field, on the Floating World, more aware of her than him.

The official raised his voice to be heard across the field. "Let the test for the royal bodyguard begin!"

CHAPTER 14

SUNHO

The Floating World
Training Grounds, Western Gardens

SUNHO DUG HIS fingers into the ground, gripping his chest with the other. The Demon had been dormant ever since his fight with Jinok, but now it raged inside him, struggling for release.

"Sunho." He felt a soft pressure on his arm and turned slightly to find Hwani crouched beside him.

After he had fled the fight with Jinok, Hwani and Chulsoo had gone after him, insisting that Jinok had deserved it. They'd more or less adopted him, and he was grateful to them. "Is something the matter?" she asked.

Sunho shook his head. He thought back to just an hour earlier. He'd arrived at the training field with Hwani, Chulsoo, and a few others. After warming up, they'd retired to the shade.

Chulsoo had been regaling them with a story when the hairs on Sunho's arm stood up. Ren was nearby. He realized it was the Demon that was aware of Ren. What did it mean that it could *sense* her?

"We have to line up," Hwani said. "The test's about to start."

Sunho got to his feet, careful not to glance in Ren's direction. He didn't have to look at her to know exactly where she was; he could even sense her heartbeat, which quickened the moment their eyes finally met.

He followed Hwani dazedly, taking up a position behind her in one of the two lines forming on the field. Their captain, an older woman with silver hair, had explained the rules to them the evening before.

The test would be in two parts, with archery first followed by one-to-one combat with the candidates' weapon of choice. Scores of up to thirty points for each category would be awarded at the end of each round, with the position of bodyguard filled by the candidate with the highest total marks.

The two groups of candidates separated into parallel lines, each facing a target that stood forty yards away, shooting two at a time. After each round, the targets would be moved farther back until they were at one hundred yards for the final round.

"Good luck," Hwani said. "You'll need it with that bow." He still had the same training bow he'd borrowed from the armory.

Hwani stepped up to the white line, her back straight as she lifted her bow. She drew back, her lips parting slightly as she released the arrow. Sunho could almost hear it singing as it cut the air, before striking the center of the target.

The official raised his flag, his voice traveling across the distance. "Ten points!"

The nobles let out a great cheer. Turning, Hwani bowed in Ren's direction before moving to the back of the line.

One by one, the archers ahead of him took their turns.

"Nine points!"

"Six points!"

"Nine points!"

Sunho stepped up to the white line.

A smatter of jeers rippled through the crowd as he nocked an arrow.

"Can his bow even shoot that distance?" he heard someone comment.

He drew in a slow breath. His bow was half the size of the others, and there was wind on the field, making a straight shot almost impossible. Angling the bow slightly upward, he drew back the bowstring, and released. The arrow arced upward, like a wayward kite, before slowly descending toward the target, splitting the wood close to the center.

"Ten points!" the official shouted, raising his flag.

"Lucky bastard," Chulsoo whooped from the other line.

The officials moved back the targets to seventy yards as Sunho joined the end of the line.

"That was incredible!" Hwani said, and he rubbed the back of his head, embarrassed.

As he lowered his hand, he sensed eyes on him.

Jaeil. He was observing him from the sidelines, a frown on his face. He'd seen Ren standing with the captain earlier. Like before, the Demon stirred, like a flame curling within.

He closed his eyes, concentrating on calming his breathing.

"Sunho?" Hwani was speaking to him, her face pinched in concern. "Are you all right? It's your turn."

He shook his head, stepping up to the line. As he drew back the bowstring, a voice whispered in his mind.

We seek out the ones we love. But love in the heart of a demon is no different than hate. And so we seek out to destroy those whom we love the most.

It was Junho's voice.

He didn't understand. The voice belonged to his brother, but Junho was dead; Sunho had killed him; he'd never said those words.

He released the arrow. It landed with a thud outside the eight-point circle.

"Six points!"

Sunho broke from the line as the officials readied the targets for the final round. He stumbled inside a nearby tent.

What had just happened? That voice, those words . . . Could it be the Demon, tricking him? He grabbed a cup of water from a table and splashed it onto his face.

His senses stirred, alerting him moments before Ren followed him into the tent.

"Sunho, what's going on? Are you—what's wrong?"

Her presence overwhelmed him. The Demon struggled to rise to the surface, clawing for release.

A memory arose, from when he'd been the Demon. He'd flown without direction, lost in a maelstrom of pain and fear. He would have gone on like that for an eternity if it wasn't for a tugging at his soul. It felt like a ribbon of Light tied to his heart, drawing him east.

The memory broke, leaving him breathless, his head and heart pounding.

We seek out the ones we love. But love in the heart of a demon is no different than hate. And so we seek out to destroy those whom we love the most.

He'd *sought out* Ren on the commander's ship. The Demon had been drawn to her because of his feelings for her, his longing for her.

It wasn't the dark parts of Sunho—his anger, his fear, his pain—that tempted the Demon, it was Ren.

He needed to get out of here, he needed to get away. *From her.*

"There's nothing wrong," he said, struggling to keep his voice steady. "I just made a bad shot." A shudder went through him, and he drew in a jagged breath. "It's better this way. Hwani is a strong warrior. She can protect you."

He'd only spent a few hours with Hwani and Chulsoo, but he sensed they were kind and dependable—like Heetae and Rohoon had been.

Hwani would guard Ren. She'd keep her safe from anyone who might harm her. *From him.*

"I don't understand." Ren stepped closer to him. "What are you saying?" She reached out a hand.

"Don't."

"Hwani doesn't even *have* the top score." Ren drew back her hand, and he knew that he'd hurt her. "It's Jinok."

Sunho's heart stilled. "Jinok?"

The tent flap swung open and Wook barreled inside. "Ren, hurry up. They're ready to start the third round, but they can't without you."

Ren appeared as if she wished to say more, but then Wook continued hurriedly, "Lord Muyeol saw you enter this tent." Something about that particular detail made Ren's face turn pale.

She followed Wook from the tent, flinging one last look at Sunho. His heart ached at the confusion he saw on her face.

Sunho stumbled from the opposite end. His gaze immediately found the scoreboard, where colored flags denoted the participants.

He'd been so preoccupied with the Demon, he hadn't realized

Jinok had a score of twenty points. He searched for Hwani's flag and saw she had the second-highest score at nineteen.

It was possible that Jinok might lose points during the one-to-one combat portion of the test, but he was also a strong close combat fighter.

The officials had moved the targets one hundred yards out.

Hwani stepped to the white line. She released the bowstring, the arrow rippling in the air before striking just outside the ten-point ring.

"Nine points!" shouted the official.

Sunho saw Jinok smirk from the other line, readying his own bow. He'd shoot last, at the same time as Sunho.

Sunho nocked his final arrow.

Relaxing his shoulders, he focused on the target. He drew back the bowstring to its limit.

Tendrils of darkness spread from his hands, strengthening the bow, holding it together as he pulled the string back even farther, farther . . .

"Hey, watch it." He heard Chulsoo call out a warning. "It's going to break—"

Out of the corner of his eye, he saw Jinok release his arrow.

Sunho twisted his body at the last minute, loosing his own. At the same time, the limb of the bow cracked apart as the arrow whipped through the air, embedding itself in the direct center of the *other* target. Jinok's arrow shattered upon impact with Sunho's.

A hush fell over the field.

Then Jinok roared with fury, throwing down his bow. "He can't do that!" he shouted. "That's not allowed! I demand a reshoot, and *he* should be disqualified."

"Silence!" Lady Maya rose from her seat. "Normally such acts would warrant immediate disqualification, but since this candidate has shown previous loyalty to the princess, we'll leave the decision up to her." She turned her gaze to Ren. "Do you wish for this soldier to be disqualified?"

"No," Ren said softly.

Lady Maya nodded, as if she'd suspected such an answer. "Then, for a compromise, I suggest that the candidate duel my personal guard; if he should defeat him, then he'd be worthy of being yours. Does this satisfy you, niece?"

Sunho gazed at Ren, willing her to offer up a different solution. Ren appeared uncertain, her brows furrowed, but then she nodded.

Sunho closed his eyes. Then there was only one choice left to him.

He would have to lose. On purpose. He couldn't become Ren's bodyguard. He couldn't risk tempting the Demon further.

A man from Lady Maya's entourage stepped forward. He was middle-aged, tall, with bulging muscles.

"For this new test," the official said, "the fight will last until either party surrenders."

"No!" a voice rang out. "To first blood."

Sunho's eyes snapped open.

It was Lord Muyeol who'd spoken. "An enemy targeting the princess wouldn't *surrender*," he sneered.

Ren's eyes darted with panic to the older noble.

If the other guard pierced his skin, Sunho would be exposed as a demon, a mithril soldier.

"Wait, no . . . ," Ren started. "He can't—"

"Princess," Jaeil interrupted, his voice calm, controlled. "It would honor *me* to fight the candidate, as your champion."

A sense of dread rose in Sunho's chest. He could have held back fighting Lady Maya's champion, but he didn't think he could stop the Demon from craving Jaeil's blood; he wasn't sure if he even wanted to.

Jaeil leaned forward, whispering in Ren's ear.

With his heightened sense, Sunho just barely picked up his words. "*Trust me.*"

"Very well," Lady Maya said. "Captain Jaeil will duel the candidate to first blood."

CHAPTER 15

SUNHO

The Floating World
Training Grounds, Western Gardens

SUNHO FACED JAEIL across the arena. A cool wind swept down from the mountains to the south, rustling the trees surrounding the field, their spindly branches clicking and clacking. Over those same mountains he knew there was a meadow, overrun with late-blooming flowers. He'd made a promise to Ren in that meadow, to guard his life as if it were precious, worthy. But that was before he'd turned into a monster.

Before he'd known the truth.

He looked down at the sword gripped in his hand, another weapon he'd borrowed from the armory. It made him think of his own sword, and the red ornament Ren had given him, both lost. Dropped when the general had grabbed him by the neck and tossed him through the Sky Door.

General Iljin's son stood before him now. Sunho knew that Ren trusted the captain, that they'd been friends as children. But Jaeil had kidnapped her, had *hurt* her.

He felt a shadow of the anger he'd felt that night, a flame flickering to life.

"Begin!" the official shouted.

Sunho raised his sword, his eyes never leaving Jaeil.

The other boy had changed since Sunho had last seen him in the hall, and not just in his clothing and appearance. He held his sword in his left hand—yesterday, that arm had been broken. At some point between the trial's end and today, Ren had healed him.

Anxiety curled in his stomach. She'd been in danger, so close to the son of her enemy. Sunho imagined her reaching out her hand, placing it upon Jaeil's arm. The Demon stirred as another, darker emotion took hold, curdling his blood.

Sunho attacked, racing across the field and swinging his sword at Jaeil, who parried, skidding back on the grass. Sunho jumped back only to strike at Jaeil at a different angle. Jaeil twisted his arms, his elbows high, blocking the attack once more, although now there was an edge to his expression, as if Sunho had surprised him with the aggressiveness of his assault.

He'd fought Jaeil before, but had forgotten how fast the older boy was. He managed to block every one of Sunho's attacks, each clash of their swords ringing out across the field.

Jaeil was skilled—Sunho acknowledged him as a worthy opponent. Had Sunho been an ordinary swordsman, then the captain might have had a chance of defeating him. But Sunho had been part of the Forty-Fourth Regiment, given injections of mithril that had changed him, making him stronger and faster. Newfound skills that made them akin to gods, as Teacher had shouted with zealous rapture. *You've been given the gift of mithril.* But Sunho knew the truth: They'd been cursed.

The Demon roared within him, fed by the adrenaline of battle. His arm rippled as the power of mithril coursed through him, heating his blood and expanding his muscles. His next strike would cut clean through Jaeil's sword, would sever his arm.

Jaeil had threatened Ren, had hurt her, had *touched* her.

He felt a tremor slip down his back as his wings strained beneath his skin.

He staggered back in horror. What was he doing? Jaeil wasn't his enemy. Ren had *saved* him from execution.

This wasn't like Sunho, having these violent thoughts. He had to suppress them, or he'd lose control. If he transformed, he wouldn't be able to differentiate between friend and foe—what if Ren tried to stop him, and he lashed out at her?

He felt more than saw Jaeil moving fast toward him, the glint of sunlight on his raised blade.

Sunho lifted his sword at the last minute, the impact reverberating up his arm.

"Sunho," Jaeil hissed, panting, sweat slick against his brow. "Listen to me. Lord Muyeol knows about the mithril project. He'll kill you if he discovers what you are."

Jaeil released his attack and they leaped apart. Sunho registered Jaeil's words, his eyes darting to Lord Muyeol. Ren stood beside him, her hands clasped in front of her. Another tremor swept through him, and he had to fight to keep the Demon under control. He tore his gaze away.

Sunho waited until Jaeil attacked, the movement bringing them close enough where they could speak without being overheard. "What's your plan?"

"Let me win," Jaeil said. Sunho must have looked skeptical because he added, "If you can't trust me, then trust Ren. I'm going to come at you first from the left, then the right. Don't block me, and try not to make it obvious."

Jaeil feinted, swinging his sword toward Sunho's unguarded left side.

Sunho raised his sword, as if to block. Jaeil shifted abruptly, striking to the right.

It went against all Sunho's instincts not to defend himself. The Demon could heal most wounds, but not a blade through the heart.

Jaeil followed through with his attack, the movement bringing them close; he could hear the other boy's rapid heartbeats. There was a ripping sound and a rush of cool air against his skin. One of the nobles screamed. Sunho staggered backward, pressing his hand to his side. Jaeil's sword had torn through the armor.

"First blood has been drawn!" the official cried.

He lifted his palm away. It was coated in blood.

Red blood.

Sunho stared down at his hand, disoriented. Then he realized he didn't feel any pain; his skin beneath the blood was unbroken.

His eyes darted to Jaeil, who moved his hand behind his back, fingers curled in a fist.

"I think this spectacle has gone on long enough," Lady Maya said. "If it please you, Princess, the remaining candidates will continue with the test."

Before Ren could look at him, he quickly turned away.

"We should get you to a healer," Jaeil said loudly. Then quieter, for Sunho's ears only, "And away from this blasted field before they decide to take a closer look."

Sunho draped his arm around Jaeil's neck, placing more weight upon him than necessary. Jaeil grunted. They didn't enter the healer's tent but headed toward the woods that bordered the training grounds.

Once they'd reached the cover of the trees, he removed his arm. He stood silently as the older boy ripped a strip of cloth from his sleeve, wrapping it around his hand. Jaeil had moved so quickly, Sunho hadn't even seen the moment he'd sliced open his palm.

"I think you're the one who's in need of a healer," Sunho said, troubled.

"This arm was broken not ten hours ago." Jaeil shrugged. "A cut on the hand hardly registers."

A moment later, he had finished with the makeshift bandage. "Come on," he said. "Since I have you, there's something I think you should see."

From the woods, they traveled to the eastern gardens. When Jaeil pulled back a fall of wisteria to reveal a hole in the wall, Sunho raised a brow, though he didn't question him, crawling through.

They'd walked a fair distance when a branch snapped not far behind them.

"We're being followed," Sunho muttered.

Jaeil cursed, slipping behind a tree and pressing his back against the trunk. Sunho joined him, crouching on his heels.

A few moments later, Sunho heard the approach of footsteps. Their pursuer was quiet; had Sunho not had such a keen sense of hearing, he might not have known of their presence.

Something about the way they walked—their light-footedness—felt familiar.

Sunho realized who was following them just as Jaeil grabbed their pursuer. Before he could shout a warning, the older boy had jammed him against the tree by the collar.

Wook yelped, gazing at them with a wide-eyed expression.

"Jaeil," Sunho warned when Jaeil didn't let go, though he must have recognized Ren's uncle. His hand curled into a fist; if it came to it, he would protect Ren's family as if they were his own.

Finally, Jaeil let go of Wook, who slumped back against the tree. "Why are you following us?" he demanded.

Wook winced at Jaeil's frosty tone. "Ren sent me." His eyes darted to Sunho. "To make sure you weren't hurt. Though . . ." He lifted his chin, his gaze lingering on Jaeil's bandaged hand. "It seems we were mistaken as to whom we should have been concerned about."

Jaeil flicked his gaze away; a muscle in his jaw tensed. "You weren't mistaken. As you can see, we're both alive. Now you should head back. The princess might need you."

Wook jumped to his feet, clearly able to bounce back quickly. "Ren can take care of herself," he said cheerfully. "She's holding her own against her great-uncle. It's the two of you that she's worried about."

"Then tell her I'm investigating the *thing* she asked me to, that I might have found a lead, and I need *his* help." He jerked his head in Sunho's direction before turning and striding away.

That didn't seem to deter Wook, who joined Sunho in trailing after him.

Jaeil only sighed in resignation. Sunho was curious what Ren had asked Jaeil to investigate, but figured he'd find out soon enough.

As they walked, Sunho noticed that several of the trees were tied with white strings. Wook must have seen them, too, because he pointed to one as they passed. "What are those?"

"They indicate our proximity to the edge," Jaeil said. Sunho was surprised that the other boy had even answered him. "Some also believe they act as a warning of the presence of ghosts."

Wook stepped closer to Sunho, eyeing the dark shadows beneath the trees.

Sunho hadn't thought he believed in ghosts, except the voice at the training grounds had belonged to his brother. Yet he'd have remembered if Junho had ever spoken *those* words to him.

After a few more minutes, Sunho saw where Jaeil was leading them—a cave, its mouth about seven or eight feet high.

Jaeil tossed aside the large tree branch that had been blocking the entrance, causing Wook, who was standing nearby, to yelp and jump away. "I discovered this cave two nights ago," he said.

Sunho peered into the mouth. Jaeil and Wook would see only darkness ahead, but Sunho could make out a path that curved to the left after a few hundred feet.

"Where does it lead?" he asked.

"I'm not sure." Jaeil crouched by the cave entrance, rummaging through a bag he must have set there earlier. "I only went about a quarter mile before I turned back . . ." He trailed off, as if he had more to say, but then pressed his lips together.

From the satchel, he withdrew a lantern. Lighting it with a match, he held it up to the darkness. A chilling wind blew up from within.

Wook shivered. "You went down there *alone*?"

"I wanted to ascertain what lay on the other side of this cave; a hidden entrance could pose a risk to Sareniya's borders."

Sunho nodded. It was the logical response; he would have done the same.

Wook gaped at them both.

"Shall we?" Jaeil led the way into the darkness.

"You only have one lantern?" Wook asked, pressing closer to Jaeil, who held the light. Jaeil didn't move away, but seemed, subtly, to angle the lantern closer to Wook.

"I wasn't expecting company," he said.

"What about him?" Wook gestured at Sunho.

"I can see in the dark," Sunho said.

Wook's eyes widened, but Jaeil didn't express surprise, continuing to walk forward at a measured pace.

Sunho frowned at the back of Jaeil's head. Though Sunho's memories of when he was a Demon were muddled, he remembered that Jaeil had been the first to arrive at the meadow when he'd turned into the monster. The other soldiers hadn't witnessed his transformation—otherwise Sunho would have been executed the moment he set foot on the Floating World.

Not only did Jaeil know Sunho's secret, but he'd *kept* it. He had sliced open his own hand to hide the fact that Sunho's blood was blue. Which also meant that he knew that blue blood was the mark of a mithril soldier. What else did he know about the project?

"There's a reason why you wanted me to come with you, isn't there?" Sunho said.

Jaeil stopped walking, turning back toward him. Reaching into the pocket of his coat, he withdrew a syringe. Sunho recoiled at the instrument.

"I discovered this on that first night. I think whoever dropped it brought it from deeper inside." Jaeil gestured farther into the cave. "Before I was arrested, I was investigating murders in the Under World. I'd concluded they were the work of demons. The princess tasked me with furthering my investigation. I wanted to return to this cave as soon as possible in order to do so."

Which was why he'd left the bag of supplies, Sunho realized. He would have come back with or without Sunho.

"I hadn't planned on asking you to join me," Jaeil said, "but it occurred to me that you might be the one most equipped to help me, with your abilities, and . . . personal investment. Was I wrong?"

As Sunho stared at the syringe, he recalled another, wielded by Teacher. Since transforming back from the Demon, he'd been so busy grappling with his guilt of what he'd done—to his brother, to Ren—of what he *was*, that he'd forgotten: Someone had made him this way.

"You weren't wrong," Sunho said grimly. Jaeil nodded before continuing into the darkness.

THEY'D WALKED ABOUT a half hour before reaching a set of stairs that curved against the wall, trailing steeply downward.

"It's so dark," Wook whispered, shivering.

"You can hold on to me," Sunho offered, but it was Jaeil whom Wook grabbed on to when a piece of rock fell in the distance, resounding through the cavern like a gong.

Sunho waited for Jaeil to brush him off, but the captain took Wook's hand and placed it firmly on his shoulder. "Stay close," he said, to which Wook weakly nodded.

For several hours they descended; it would take them at least the same amount of time or more to make the return trip. Sunho thought of telling Jaeil to turn back when he felt a vibration in the air, like humming.

Mithril. He sensed its weighted presence all around him. Slowly, the cavern walls began to brighten, glowing with azure strands of ore.

"Wh-what is that?" Wook whispered.

"Mithril," Jaeil breathed, then, as if remembering himself, he pressed his hand to his mouth. "Damn it, I don't have a filtration mask."

Mithril was poisonous. It wouldn't affect Sunho, however. Though he recalled that the last time he'd been in the mines with Yurhee, Tag, and Ren, none of them had gotten sick.

"Should we turn back?" he asked.

Jaeil's gaze lingered on Wook, a grim expression on his face. "We've come this far. Let's see what's at the bottom of these stairs. If any of us shows signs of mithril poisoning, we're heading back immediately."

They traveled down until they reached another cavern, at the back of which was a massive cave-in, the remnants of a building beneath. Judging from the scorch marks, it had been caused by explosives.

Sunho recognized the building through the rubble; he'd been there before. The place where he'd fought Rohoon, where he'd *killed* him, where he'd last seen his brother and been injected with the serum that had turned him into a monster.

The mithril labs.

CHAPTER 16

JAEIL

The Floating World
The Mithril Mines

JAEIL STEPPED OVER rubble, pressing a handkerchief to his nose and mouth as he searched for access into the labs.

After reaching this point, Sunho had told him that on the night of the Festival of Light, he and Ren had accompanied a pair of rebels to this location, where the rebels had set off explosives around the facility. They had done a thorough job of it, much to Jaeil's vexation.

The exterior had caved inward, obstructing the entrance. He was pierced with a searing cold as a sibilant wind swept through the cavern from one of the massive tunnels high above them. There was little in the vast, hollow space to block the freezing air currents that emptied into the cavern like vicious, miniature tempests.

Wook shivered for the third time in as many minutes.

Jaeil frowned. He shouldn't have allowed Ren's adoptive uncle to accompany them—he wasn't a soldier like Jaeil and Sunho, who'd been trained to ignore discomforts to their bodies. He was soft, a civilian.

Jaeil rarely interacted with civilians. Sana would say that would be preferable for the civilians, too, standoffish and ill-humored as he was. His lieutenant was still recovering at Hagye's military hospital after she'd saved him from being gored by a monster—that had been *his* pleasant experience the night of the festival.

No, Ren had been unique in that regard, the one person in his life who'd expected softness from him. In his cold, militant childhood, surrounded by cruel men, she had been a solace to him.

Jaeil removed his outer robe, handing it to Wook. The smaller boy stared at him for a beat before taking the robe, wrapping it around his shoulders. "Thank you," he said softly.

"Jaeil." He looked over to where Sunho was crouched by the ruins. A part of the building had collapsed at an angle, leaving a narrow entrance. "I found a way in."

Jaeil peeked through the opening; darkness stretched an interminable distance forward. When he held up the lantern, the light barely penetrated.

He wouldn't have thought there'd be a path, but Sunho, with his keen eyesight, had seen a way through. As before, Jaeil studied the other boy. He was a conundrum, the only soldier from the Mithril Enhancement Project who'd survived—at least that they knew of.

"I'll go first," Sunho said. He didn't wait for Jaeil to answer, ducking into the hole.

Jaeil motioned for Wook to follow, then proceeded through with the lantern.

The space was tight, and they had to crouch to avoid debris from the explosion, climbing over concrete slabs and ducking beneath steel beams. Jaeil was surprised to note that Wook easily navigated the path before remembering that Ren had said her adoptive family had been professional acrobats.

A great groaning sound reverberated above them, and Jaeil's

unease heightened, unsure if it was the wind echoing in the cavern, or the ruined building about to collapse atop them. Soon the ground leveled out to a tunnel tall enough for them to stand.

"You said you'd been here before," Jaeil said, noticing Sunho had stopped, staring intently down the dark tunnel.

Sunho nodded slowly. He seemed to be going through some strong emotion since sighting the mithril labs.

"Twice," Sunho said. "It wasn't until I came here the second time that I remembered the first. My brother . . ." He turned to Jaeil. "You said you knew where to find him."

Jaeil's chest tightened. He realized what he was feeling was *guilt*. It was an unusual emotion for him, and he'd had it twice within the span of several minutes, the first time when Wook had trembled from the wind. He didn't particularly care for it.

"I did serve with Junho," Jaeil said. "For a year, we served together in the Eighth Regiment. My father called me away from the front lines for a time. When I returned, your brother was gone. I assumed he'd been transferred." He cleared his throat. "I have connections in the army. If he's in one of the other regiments, I'll find him—"

"He's dead."

Jaeil winced. A dull throbbing began at the back of his skull. "I'm sorry to hear that."

"I was the one who killed him," Sunho said. "It was an accident. It happened . . . here."

An accident . . . but that wouldn't take away the guilt Sunho must be feeling.

"You don't have to go farther than this," Jaeil heard himself say.

They were impulsive words, and likely he would come to regret them—he'd asked Sunho to accompany him because of his abilities and knowledge of the project—but Jaeil *would* go on alone, if Sunho decided to turn back.

"No," Sunho said. "I want to know why this happened to me."

Jaeil frowned, observing Sunho carefully. "But you *do* know, to some degree, don't you? I heard about the program you were a part of." He recalled Commander Su's words, parroting them. "The objective was to create a new type of soldier, using mithril, for the purpose of winning the war."

"That was Sareniya's objective," Sunho said.

Jaeil nodded. It's what he'd suspected, with the scientist's history and his actions in the square. He might have begun the project under the direction of Lord Muyeol and the Floating Council, but he'd clearly had his own agenda from the start.

"If Teacher is alive," Sunho said, and his voice held an edge to it, "I'm going to kill him."

Jaeil lifted a brow slightly, though Sunho was too lost in his thoughts to notice. Sunho was already a strong ally; motivated by revenge, he'd be lethal.

And easily manipulated. Jaeil had already done so before—he'd dangled the possibility of reuniting Sunho with his brother in order to get him to go after Ren. He could do it again.

Once more, he felt that tightening of guilt in his chest, and buried it deep.

"If by 'Teacher,' you mean the scientist in charge of the program," Jaeil said, "he's very much alive."

Sunho didn't react—Jaeil supposed that the other boy had known, or suspected, the truth already.

"Both of us could benefit from sharing what information we have with the other," Jaeil said.

"And with Ren," Wook interjected. Ren's uncle had been watching them carefully; Jaeil suspected he would relay what he'd seen and heard to Ren upon his return.

"Yes," Jaeil agreed, "with the princess most of all." They would gather the information, but only Ren could follow through with actions.

"But later," Jaeil said. "This lantern won't last, and I, for one, do not relish being stranded in the dark."

They continued traversing the tunnel. It ended at a cavernous room, the opposite end inaccessible due to a large crater in the ground.

Here, Sunho stopped. His skin, already pale, took on a sickly pallor. The air of the laboratory appeared to be weighing heavily on him.

"So, it's because of mithril that you can see in the dark," Wook remarked, his naturally cheerful voice bright in the gloom. "Also how you were able to make that shot with the bow and move so swiftly during the duel."

Sunho nodded. "While poisonous, mithril has magical properties. When humans are exposed to the element, it changes them. Most succumb to the poison before it can have other effects, however."

Wook seemed to consider this, his brow puckering. "*I* was exposed to mithril," he said. "When the demon that came to Gorye Village scratched me with its claws. Some of its blood must have mixed with mine, because I developed a fever and my blood turned blue. I would have died if it wasn't for Ren. She'd brought back an antidote, but it didn't work. It was her magic that healed me."

Jaeil considered Wook. He was the only known case of someone being cured of mithril poisoning. If he had been cured of the infection, then it was possible that such results could be replicated.

He would have to keep a careful eye on the boy.

"From what you've explained," Wook continued, "then you're saying everyone who was infected with mithril and *survived* developed powers, except for me."

Sunho's brow puckered. "I guess."

Wook sighed loudly. "Well, *that's* unfortunate. I would have liked to see in the dark, move really fast, and be incredibly good-looking."

Sunho's cheeks turned a curious shade of blue, and Jaeil realized he was blushing. Raising his shoulders to his ears, Sunho turned abruptly, heading toward another, darker tunnel that branched off from the room.

Wook's expression softened as he watched Sunho. Jaeil realized he'd *meant* to distract Sunho from the horrible memories of the labs.

He must have sensed Jaeil's gaze because his eyes met Jaeil's. Jaeil raised a brow, and for some reason, Wook blushed bright pink before hurrying in pursuit of Sunho. Jaeil followed at a more sedate pace.

The tunnel ended at another cave-like room. Unlike the others, this one remained mostly undamaged. As he stepped onto the obsidian floors of the large, echoing chamber, he felt as if he were treading over a dark lake.

While Wook and Sunho moved farther into the room, Jaeil trailed the wall until he found a curtain hanging over a crude opening.

As he stepped into a cramped space, he knew immediately he'd found where the scientist had been living. It had been cleared hastily; papers and scrolls were scattered haphazardly across the floor. Against the wall was a cot with a thin mattress; beside that was a chamber pot. Jaeil gave both a wide berth, moving toward the one other piece of furniture in the room: a desk. He shifted open one of the drawers, jerking it when it snagged on a nail. There was only a single small, side-stitched book inside.

Flipping through the pages, he found a list of shipments aboard an aircraft named the *Flying Serpent*.

"J-Jaeil."

He looked up to where Wook now stood in the opening, having pushed back the curtain.

"I mean, Captain—"

"'Jaeil' is fine," he said. "Did you find something?"

"I think you should take a look at this."

He followed Wook to the very back of the chamber, where Sunho stood beside what appeared to be the remnants of a large tank. It had shattered during the explosions. A puddle of viscous blue liquid spread like ink from beneath the base. Careful so that his boots didn't touch the foreign substance, he crouched to the floor.

The color of the liquid wasn't just blue—it was aquamarine, like the light of the brightest star. Liquid mithril.

Spotting an object in the liquid, he reached out with his gloved hand to pick it up, the mithril sluicing off it like oil. The object was long and tubular in shape, connected to a mechanism that was designed to fit over a mouth.

"What is that?" Wook said from behind his left shoulder.

"A breathing apparatus," Jaeil said. "I've seen them used in the medic tents; they're to help assist the patient with receiving airflow."

Carefully, he wrapped the breathing apparatus in a handkerchief pulled from his pocket, then placed it into his satchel. He would send it to Hagye by courier to have the scientists there conduct tests.

His gaze then landed on something that had caught on one of the broken shards—a long strand of black hair.

Someone or some*thing* had been kept inside the tank. But if there had been a creature inside, where was it now?

Jaeil suppressed a shudder, remembering the newly transformed demons the night of the festival, their fetid breath and gnashing teeth. What dark purpose did the scientist have for these experiments?

"Jaeil." Sunho now stood on the far side of the cave. "Take Wook and go back."

"What did you find?" Jaeil walked across the cavern to join Sunho.

"Another path." He followed Sunho's gaze upward. It wasn't a path, but a tunnel near the top of the cavern. The stones surrounding the entrance to the tunnel were smeared with the mithril substance, though it appeared almost silvery from a distance. "Whatever was inside that tank escaped through there," Sunho said.

"How—?" Jaeil started, then cut himself off. The creature that had been inside that tank wasn't human. It wouldn't be subject to human limitations.

"You shouldn't go alone," Jaeil said. It was too dangerous, and he hadn't had the foresight to bring weapons with them.

Sunho was already shaking his head. "It'll take us another day, maybe more, to come back. Whatever trail is left might be completely lost by then."

"Then I'll go with you," Jaeil insisted.

"You can't," Sunho said, and Jaeil knew he was right. That tunnel had a vertical incline; he wouldn't be able to scale it for long, let alone in the dark. "I'm not like you," Sunho continued softly. "That's why you wanted to bring me, wasn't it? Because of my abilities. Whatever that creature is, I'm the best equipped to fight it."

"Damn it," Jaeil cursed. "Then take this, at least." He withdrew a grappling gun from his satchel, then tossed it to Sunho.

He met the other boy's gaze. "Good luck."

He then turned to Wook, who was gazing at the dwindling candle in the lantern. Jaeil suspected it would go out long before they'd reached the surface.

"Let's go," Jaeil said grimly. "It's a long way back."

CHAPTER 17

REN

The Floating World
The Queen's Palace

REN PACED HER room all morning, waiting for Wook to bring news of Sunho. After the test, they'd gone into the woods and hadn't returned, even as shadows moved across the gardens of the Floating World. She didn't understand. Where could they have gone? It was as if all three of them had vanished.

She had been right to put her trust in Jaeil. He had moved so quickly, she hadn't realized he'd cut his hand until later; it had been his blood that ended the bout.

Yet it was Sunho who she worried for, who occupied her thoughts. When she'd followed him into the tent, there was something about the look in his eyes, as if he felt . . . cornered.

A gong sounded in the distance, reminding her that she was late to a meeting of the Floating Council. She slid open her door to find the lithe figure of Hwani, her new bodyguard, waiting in the hall. Lord Muyeol had been furious that Jinok had been disqualified following his outburst at the test. But, Lady Maya had insisted a guard needed to be coolheaded. Following the archery portion, Hwani had excelled in one-to-one combat, rightfully earning the position.

Her new bodyguard bowed. "Your Highness." She was around Ren's age, perhaps a year or two older, tall and strong-looking; her weapon of choice was the bow, though she also excelled with pole weapons. She'd introduced herself shortly after the test had concluded. When Ren had asked, shyly, how she knew Sunho, having recognized Hwani as the girl Sunho had laughed with earlier, she'd explained that she and another guard, Chulsoo, had befriended him on their first day.

Hwani had given Ren a wry look. "He's a handsome boy," she'd said in a dry, even tone. "I told my betrothed so, when I saw her later that evening."

Now, standing before her, Ren glanced down the hall. "Has there been any news for me?" she asked.

"I'm afraid not, Your Highness," Hwani said. She hesitated, as if unsure of her forwardness, then added, "Sunho is strong. I've never seen someone more skilled with a sword. Wherever he is, I'm sure he's all right."

Ren smiled, grateful. "Thank you." She gathered herself. "I'm late to the council meeting." They hurried together to the hall.

As before, the nobles stood on either side of the aisle, with Lord Muyeol and Lady Maya presiding at the front.

"We were just discussing your proposal for a truce with Volmar," Lord Muyeol said after Ren had taken her seat on the throne. "While it's admirable you seek a peaceful resolution to the conflict, I'm afraid it's a child's dream. To declare an end to it now would be to spit on the graves of all those who lost their lives in pursuit of Sareniya's glory. Our strategists believe that in ten more years, we can take the capital itself."

"Glory?" Ren repeated. She tensed, heat flushing through her body. "I will not condone a war over sore pride when lives are being destroyed. How many more graves will there be in ten years?"

"Perhaps that isn't the right word," Lord Muyeol said in a placating tone. "Regardless, this war is for the sake of the Floating World, *your* legacy."

He raised his strident voice to carry over the assembled nobles. "The Floating World is falling!" he bellowed. "We need to secure our position, or risk losing the peninsula to Volmar!"

Ren sat back on the throne. She hadn't known the Floating World was *falling*, but it made sense—mithril was what kept the landmass afloat, and they'd been mining mithril for the war for years. She had a fleeting memory of speaking with the head priestess. *Mithril itself isn't poisonous when left alone. It's when it's* taken *that it becomes so.*

"That's what the general believed, isn't it?" Ren said.

Lord Muyeol's gaze was steely as it met hers. "He was wrong to betray the council, but he was never wrong in his conviction. The war is necessary to keep our borders safe from invasion, to keep Sareniya safe. To keep *you* safe."

"I refuse to believe that. I won't be part of such a legacy."

"Foolish girl," Lord Muyeol seethed. "Kingdoms aren't sustained on the fanciful dreams of young girls."

"This isn't a *kingdom*," Ren said coldly.

Ten years ago, Lord Muyeol retired from the council, not out of sorrow for the loss of Ren's mother but because he couldn't control the general. He might have even supported him. But now that Ren had returned, her great-uncle wished to have total authority, intimidating her into doing his bidding just like he did her mother.

"It's a *world*," Ren said, holding Lord Muyeol's furious gaze, "and *I'm* it's heir."

"Insolent child," he hissed. "You'll be the ruin of Sareniya."

Turning on his heel, he stormed from the hall.

A weighted silence followed his departure. The nobles watched her, waiting for what she would do next.

"Does my great-uncle speak for all the council members?" Ren demanded. "Lady Maya, I would have your opinion."

She held her breath as she waited for her aunt to speak. If Lady Maya openly supported her father, turning her back on Ren, then it would be near impossible to get support from the others. Yet Ren had an inkling that her aunt had a mind of her own.

"There used to be a man in this court," Lady Maya said slowly. "A Volmaran."

"You speak of the Volmaran ambassador," Lady Go said, a woman in her late forties with gray-streaked hair. "He and his family were sent back to Volmar at the start of the war."

"I think if truce negotiations were to be extended to the Volmarans," Lady Maya said, "then perhaps he would be willing to lobby on our behalf."

Ren felt the tension in her muscles relax slightly. Finally they were making a *plan*. "What about the Sareniyan ambassador in the Volmaran court?" Ren asked.

"That was I, Your Highness." A soft-spoken woman stepped forward into the aisle. Her face was heavily lined, though she couldn't be older than forty. Ren guessed the ambassador had suffered due to her ties with the northern empire. "There is no excuse for Volmar's actions in the war . . ." The woman trailed off, hesitating.

"Speak freely," Ren said.

"The Volmaran empress, she is a matriarch. She has lost many members of her family to this war."

"You believe she would be amenable to a truce?"

"I believe she has personal reasons to consider one."

"Send a letter to the Volmaran ambassador," Ren ordered. "Tell them that if the empress offers terms, then I will consider them in good faith. Impress upon them that I am eager to end hostilities."

AFTER THE COUNCIL meeting, Ren made her way to the temple with Hwani in tow. As she submerged herself beneath the water, she had the fleeting thought that she might see Grandmother and Rina again. Oddly, she didn't find the prospect disappointing; despite the seemingly futile tasks they'd set, she'd enjoyed her time with them.

However, when she opened her eyes, she was in the main throne hall. The space appeared vaster without the presence of all the council members. The carpet stretched to the open doors, though there only appeared to be darkness beyond them, as if the world didn't exist outside this room.

"Who are you?" echoed a sonorous voice.

Ren whirled around. A woman sat on the throne. She was startlingly beautiful, with long black hair and straight, elegant shoulders.

"M-my name is Ren." She cleared her throat. "I'm your descendant."

"You?" The woman appeared doubtful, and Ren might have been offended had she not had the same thought.

The woman leaned forward, tapping long nails against the arms of the throne. "I guess you must be, to visit me here."

"Where *is* here?" Ren asked, thinking of the darkness behind the door. "Grandmother . . . another maiden called it the 'Ancestral Realm.' Do you . . . live here?"

"Of course not. If you are my descendant, far, far . . ." The woman paused, looking Ren up and down. "*Far* in the future, then I am long dead and gone. In this place, I exist only as I am. I have no knowledge of what's to come in the life I had lived. I can only teach you what this version of Saya knew in this moment of her life. I'm assuming you *have* come here for me to teach you?"

It took a moment for Ren to register her words. "You have magic?"

Saya scowled, as if Ren had said something deeply offensive. Rising from the throne, she approached Ren, grabbing her wrist. There was a dizzying moment as the world warped around her, and then suddenly they were in a different room entirely.

Ren staggered backward. "How did you do that? Is that another power?"

Saya scoffed. "Don't be ridiculous. The unique circumstances of this place allow me to change our location."

Ren gazed at the room. It was filled with all manner of weapons, more weapons than she'd ever seen in one place, glaives and spears and double-headed axes. "Where are we?"

"The celestial armory. Do they not have such a place in your time?"

If they did, she'd never heard of it.

Saya walked toward a stand that held a magnificent horn bow. She trailed her fingers down the fine wood. "This was mine. I was quite the archer. Are you . . . ?"

"I'm not," Ren said. In their family, Wook was the only one with any talent for a bow.

Saya sighed. "What weapon did you train with?"

"A paper fan," Ren said proudly, "and my umbrella."

Saya appeared disturbed. She walked to a wall where several swords of varying sizes were displayed. She took the smallest one from its stand. As she turned it in her hand, Ren was shocked to see that the blade was blue.

"It's made of mithril," Ren breathed.

"Mithril is the strongest ore to exist," Saya said, "nigh unbreakable in its solid form. Our magic can be channeled through the metal. By imbuing a weapon with Light, you can sustain it for longer."

"But I thought mithril was poisonous when disturbed," Ren said.

"Not to those who bear celestial magic." Light spread from Saya's hand, leaping to the blade where it shone bright, like a star.

Ren reached eagerly for the sword. "I want to try."

Saya passed it to her. The weapon felt awkward in her hands, heavy despite its diminutive size.

"Magic is ruled by the body, the mind, and the heart," Saya explained. "The body produces the Light, which is why you must train it. Your mind directs it, which is how you differentiate between your healing and attack powers, and how you produce your wings. Strength lies within the heart. The stronger your heart, your *will*, the stronger your power."

For the first time since meeting her, Saya's expression softened, as if calling to mind a bright memory. "No arrows flew as swift as mine, as straight and true."

Then her gaze focused once more on Ren, and she frowned. "Try imbuing your Light into the sword. Call it forth from your core, feel it spread through your arm to the hilt, then into the blade."

Ren held the sword out before her. She concentrated on Saya's instructions, but only managed to call upon a spark of Light that soon fizzled out. "It's not working."

Without warning, Saya reached out and pressed her fingers to

Ren's temple, quickly letting go with a curse. "You've been suppressing your powers. Why would you do such a thing?"

"I—I wasn't allowed to use them."

Saya reared back, her expression one of horror. "Who would dare keep you from your magic?" she demanded. "Your mother?"

"No, my . . . aunt." Auntie had always warned Ren to keep her powers a secret, so that she wouldn't be discovered. So that she'd be safe.

"A maiden?" Saya appeared incredulous. "No . . ." She scowled. "*A human.*"

"She was trying to protect me—" Ren said in a small voice.

"How is that protecting you? She left you vulnerable. Like the woodcutter, who stole our ancestor's wings, she stripped you of your magic. She was holding you back because she was afraid. Humans are always afraid of magic, even as they covet it for themselves."

No, Auntie had only wished to protect her, had told her to hide her magic for her own safety. But then she thought of Lord Muyeol and the general. *They* were afraid of her.

"If you are to become stronger, there's something you must remember. You are not human. Your ancestor was a daughter of Heaven. In order to become powerful, you must embrace who you truly are."

THE SUN WAS setting by the time Ren made her way down the long path toward the Queen's Palace, Hwani keeping watch from a short distance.

An attendant was pouring the last bucket of hot water into the tub when Ren arrived. The room held a draft, but the bathing area at least was protected by a large paper screen.

"Do you require assistance?" the attendant asked.

Ren shook her head, and the woman nodded, backing out of the room with her head bowed.

"I'll be in the gardens, patrolling the area, if you need me," Hwani said, before taking her leave as well.

Alone at last, Ren grabbed her mother's journal from the false compartment. Undressing hastily, she submerged herself up to her chest, careful to keep the pages above water.

She opened to the page she'd read previously.

Is this how the celestial maiden felt when she saw the face of the woodcutter for the first time, the heat of his eyes upon her? I think I might have understood, then, why she'd chosen to leave the sky.

For you, my love, I'd forsake Heaven.

She felt her skin, already warm from the water, flush with heat. She turned the pages, skimming until she found a passage that mentioned Juwon.

He is like a shadow, a sweet boy who follows Hyun with stars in his eyes.

I had feared his resentment—that because Hyun's light shone for me, Juwon would resent me. But it seems that I was mistaken.

Because Hyun cares for me, Juwon cares for me as well. He wishes to know me.

He has a brilliant mind. He wants my opinion on every new discovery. He even jests about what a proud uncle he will one day be, which, of course, embarrasses me greatly.

Though I like it when he makes these jests. I also like the way they bring color to Hyun's cheeks.

What sort of love is this?

I've never had siblings. Because of Hyun, I have gained a brother.

If anything, I am the one who is envious. Theirs is a special bond. Something unbreakable.

The next few passages were rather detailed accountings of Aria's meetings with Hyun, and so Ren skimmed those pages, until she found another mention of the scientist.

Juwon has been scarce the past few weeks.

I asked Hyun where his brother was, but he's as in the dark as I am. I know he worries. He says that Juwon has found something down in the dungeons.

She skipped ahead to another page.

Tomorrow the council will decide the matter of my consort. I know they mean for me to marry into my uncle's wife's family, as hers is one of affluence, but I will tell them the truth: Hyun is the one that I want. I love him. In my entire life, I have never asked for a single favor. How could they deny me? With just this one thing, they could secure my happiness forever.

Ren turned the next page to see that it was torn from the journal. *All* the pages had been torn but for the last.

He is gone.

There is no more light in the world for me.

Ren was startled by a low, scratching sound.

The bath was still warm, but she stood abruptly, bracing her body against the cold before grabbing a robe.

At first she thought she might have imagined the sound. But then it came again, followed by a loud bump from beneath the floorboards.

She thought of shouting. Hwani would hear her from outside. But what if it was nothing?

Just in case, Ren reached for the hair ornament she'd removed from her braid, wrapping her hand around the thin cylinder.

She kicked aside the carpet. Beneath it was a trapdoor.

There was another loud thump.

Raising the ornament, she threw it open.

Only to come face-to-face with Sunho.

CHAPTER 18

REN

The Floating World
The Queen's Palace

"SUNHO!" SHE REACHED for Sunho's hand, pulling him from the trapdoor. "Are you all right? Why were you—?"

His arms circled around her where she crouched, one gripping her shoulder, the other her waist. His heart beat fast against her own, his breaths ragged. She looked past him to see a dark tunnel running beneath the room. How long had he been wandering alone in that darkness?

His powers made it possible for him to see in the dark, but that didn't mean he wouldn't feel the oppressive weight of it, nor terror as the air began to thin.

His skin was like ice. A shudder racked his body.

Ren called upon her Light, the warmth spreading through her limbs to where they touched. She slipped her fingers beneath his hair, pressing them to the back of his neck.

They stayed like that for several minutes, until his shivers subsided. She released her magic, even the small use leaving her breathless.

Now that Sunho was out of immediate danger, she let herself feel the other emotions stirred up by his arrival—relief that he was unharmed, curiosity about what he'd been up to since they last parted, and joy that they were together again.

And something else, an awareness that came to her slowly, that grew in strength the longer he held her.

She realized how close their bodies were, and how little she was wearing; her robe clung to her damp skin.

He must have sensed the sudden tension in her because he withdrew, placing distance between them. She felt once more the coldness of the room and wrapped her arms around herself.

His gaze didn't meet hers, but shifted to take in their surroundings, passing the ornate furniture and lingering on the tub and the whorls of steam that rose up from the water's surface.

"Where are we?" he asked.

"We're at the Queen's Palace," Ren said. "This is my room. Sunho, what *happened* to you? How did you end up here?"

He winced, closing his eyes. "Jaeil found the entrance to a cave, outside the walls of the gardens."

He told her how the three of them had followed a staircase down to the same cavern that had held the mithril labs. She shivered, remembering that awful place, where she'd met Juwon for the first time.

"A trail of mithril marked a path. It was another tunnel, but one that led upward that the others wouldn't be able to reach, so I went alone. The tunnels were long and narrow. They would branch off in random directions. After a while, the mithril trail ended, but I was still . . . there." He shuddered. "There were moments when I thought I'd be stuck down there forever."

Ren shifted closer to him, lifting her hand to his cheek. He opened his eyes to gaze at her. They were lightless, haunted.

"You're here," she said firmly. "You're not in the dark any longer."

She saw the awareness of where he was return to him, his eyes focusing on her. It was the first time he'd truly looked at her since entering her chamber, and her heart beat faster.

But then he drew back from her touch, and she felt it like a punch to the gut.

He rose to his feet. "I should go."

She stood with him. "Wait! It must have been freezing in the tunnels." She gestured at the tub. "Take a bath first. The water is still warm. You'll feel better afterward."

She thought he might refuse, but he nodded hesitantly.

"I'll find you something clean to wear," she said quickly, before he could change his mind. She hurried to the clothing chests, digging through the piles until she found a robe that would fit his broader frame.

She hurried back, stepping around the screen only to stop short. He was in the middle of removing his shirt—revealing his wide, straight shoulders, his tattoo inked across the right side of his chest, the taut lines of his stomach—before dropping it to the floor.

Ren snapped her gaze away, her pulse racing. She quickly dumped the robe onto the nearest table and fled to the other side of the room. Crouching in the corner, she wrapped her arms around her knees.

Her heart thumped painfully in her chest. She'd seen others undressed before—the people in the caravan weren't shy when it came to bathing. She'd even undressed Sunho when she'd needed to tend his wound. Yet something was different now. *She* felt different, as if her bones were made of glass, her skin of petals. She buried her face in her knees.

She didn't have to wait long—Sunho's use of the tub was more functional than hers had been. She heard the floorboard creak, then the smooth glide of fabric.

She waited long enough for him to dress before standing and turning to face him. The robe fit him well. She'd thought it a simple one of dark blue fabric, but she could see now that it was far more elegant, threaded through with a silver design of a dragon. It must have belonged to a consort of one of her ancestors.

"Thank you," Sunho said softly. "I do feel better." His eyes caught hers, and he smiled. She felt as if her heart might burst. Then he lowered his gaze. "It's late."

"Won't you stay a little longer?" Ren winced at the pleading in her voice.

"Wook will tell you everything you need to know," Sunho said, "about what we found in the labs. He and Jaeil should have come back by now."

"It's not that." She *did* want to know what they'd discovered, and to share her own knowledge, but that could wait until they were all together. "I want to talk with you. Just the two of us."

Sunho's eyes sparked mithril blue, a warning. "I *can't*."

"It's because of the Demon, isn't it? Because you don't think you can control it."

He hesitated, then nodded.

She took a deep breath, stepping closer to him. "You can learn to control it. I have so much to tell you—I've been meeting with my ancestors to learn more about my magic. How you describe your powers, they sound similar to mine. We could learn to control them together."

She felt a buoying sensation at the thought of training with Sunho, spending time together.

Sunho shook his head. "Our powers aren't the same. Yours is goodness and light. Mine is darkness and death."

"It's not!" She thought of the darkness she had at times sensed from him. It was never hostile or cruel, but gentle and calm.

"You don't know what the Demon is like," he whispered.

"Then *tell* me." Why wouldn't he talk to her? He appeared so closed off, while she felt as if she were splintering inside. "It's like you've given up. You're not even *trying*."

"That just *it*, Ren," Sunho said, and his voice broke. Her breath caught at the pain he was trying to hide, as if he was as torn up as she was. "I'm *always* trying when I'm with you. The Demon . . . it wants you. *Only* you. It wants to consume you.

"I can control it, but not when I'm with you. Even now . . ." He sucked in a harsh breath. "I don't want it to hurt you, Ren. *I* don't want to hurt you."

"You won't! I promise. You wouldn't—"

His eyes met hers, then slowly they lowered. He raised his hand, slipping his fingers beneath the collar of her robe. She sucked in a breath as he traced the scar there, the scar that *he'd* put there.

The skin around the scar was sensitive, and she shivered beneath his touch.

Her pulse raced. She met his eyes, and she could see the mithril glowing in the irises, a vibrant blue. His gaze flicked to her lips.

She wanted him to kiss her. She felt as if she'd never wanted anything more, his breath on her breath, his darkness enveloping her, until all she could feel was his embrace.

But then cool air washed over her.

He'd stepped back, his hand returned to his side. "I won't hurt you again."

Hot tears sprang to her eyes. "If this is how you felt, then why did you agree to come to the Floating World?"

He frowned. "To protect you."

"I can protect myself. And even if I couldn't, I have Hwani now. And Jaeil."

A pained expression swept over his face. "What are you saying?"

"I'm saying that if you don't want to be here, then you should leave."

Sunho winced.

She regretted the words as soon as she said them—she'd never spoken so harshly to him before.

Or did she mean them? She *wanted* him to hurt as much as she was hurting.

"Maybe it would be better that way," he said, so soft she almost didn't hear his words.

He then turned, striding across the room toward the door. Panic seized her.

"Wait, Sunho!" she cried, but he was already gone.

She sank to the floor. What had she done? She felt sick. Tears flowed down her cheeks.

Back at the cottage, she'd told him she loved him. At the time, she'd convinced herself she wasn't sure how she meant it—he was her *friend*—but deep down, she was afraid that she did know, that she'd always known.

She wasn't certain what had changed, if reading her mother's journal had revealed her own heart to her, but she knew—it wasn't solely friendship she felt for him.

It was so much more.

But he didn't feel the same. If he did, he wouldn't have given up on her so easily. On them.

What if he never came back? Before, he'd fled because he'd been lost to the Demon. But if he left now, it would be his choice.

She loved Sunho, but it wasn't enough.

"Don't cry, sweet darling. Let me take the pain away."

It was the voice again. Her mother's voice.

She stood slowly, moving in the direction of the gardens, where the voice had come from. Logically, she knew ghosts didn't exist, and yet . . . She hadn't known about the temple pool, that there was such a place, where she could go to speak with her ancestors.

Her mother had never protected Ren while she was alive, but maybe her regrets had brought her back.

The grass was cold beneath her bare feet, yet she didn't feel a chill. She could see her breath in the air, forming into crystals. She took a step, then another. Her mother's voice had come from farther away, toward the cliffs.

"Princess!" she heard a voice call, as if from a distance.

Then suddenly, from right in front of her. "Princess!" Hwani was grasping her shoulders, though she hadn't felt her guard grab hold. "What are you doing out here? You're freezing. You need to go inside."

She felt the cold then, like a thousand knives. It came upon her suddenly, and she gasped from the pain. Hwani quickly removed her jacket, placing it around Ren's shoulders as she led her, shivering, back inside. Hwani's voice was loud as she shouted for attendants to bring more braziers into the room.

Ren looked toward the garden, but the presence had disappeared. Her mother—if she'd been there at all—was gone.

CHAPTER 19

JAEIL

The Floating World
Training Grounds, Western Gardens

IN THE WEEK since returning from the mithril mines, an experience he wished never to repeat, Jaeil noticed a growing distance between Ren and Sunho. He'd thought them devoted to one another. Sunho had tried to relieve him of his head when Jaeil had kidnapped Ren, though he'd argue he was trying to *save* her from her own poor decisions. And Ren had abandoned her duties as princess to go on a harebrained quest to restore Sunho to his original form, information he'd learned from Wook during their never-to-be-repeated climb. But none of that seemed to matter now—the princess and her soldier were avoiding one another, even when they were so clearly suffering being apart.

Jaeil found the whole situation excruciating to witness.

As Ren's adviser, *he* couldn't avoid her. Neither could he escape Sunho, who had taken up training with Jaeil's soldiers, the few who hadn't returned to Hagye after his father's attempted coup.

He'd been observing their drills all morning from his vantage beneath a tent. A cold, punishing rain had started an hour ago and hadn't let up. That hadn't stopped his soldiers, nor Sunho, who'd moved from exercise drills to one-to-one combat, their practice armor streaked with mud.

Sunho moved fluidly across the grass, blocking attacks from both his left and right. After Jaeil's soldiers had realized Sunho's uncanny skill with a sword, they'd started challenging him in pairs.

Even without his mithril-enhanced senses, Sunho was an exceptional fighter. It appeared that while his mithril enhancements resulted in innate abilities—heightened senses, strength, and agility—others he needed to "activate," similar to Ren's Light. But from what Jaeil could tell, Sunho never reached for that source of power, which he called the Demon.

Jaeil didn't condone the military's experiments. He found them inhumane, and was disgusted that his father had signed off on them initially, even if he had moved to shut them down later.

However . . . since Sunho had already been subjected to experimentation *anyway*, Jaeil found it wasteful not to ascertain his potential use as a weapon. No one had ever accused Jaeil of not being pragmatic.

His attention was drawn to the squelching footsteps of a noblewoman and her retinue approaching across the field. Since his return to royal favor, he'd been visited more often by nobles wishing to influence Ren through him. Normally he'd be dismissive and rude—he disliked nobles even more than he disliked commoners—but he didn't wish for his actions to reflect poorly on Ren.

Reaching him, the noblewoman stepped beneath the tent, leaving her attendants standing in the rain. She was young, though older than his nineteen years.

"Captain," she said, delicately licking her red-painted lips. "I'm disappointed. I'd have liked to see *you* out there."

"In the rain and the mud? I think not. I much prefer my position."

"Oh?" the noblewoman intoned, her voice dropping an octave. "I think there are much more preferable positions."

Jaeil slid his gaze to the noblewoman, not missing her innuendo.

He knew he inspired affection in both men and women. Ever since he'd turned fifteen—his severe, sullen features more suited to a youth than a child—he'd been the focus of many a desirous eye, much to Sana's amusement. Jaeil didn't pursue encounters of that particular nature unless it was advantageous to him, which it rarely was. Also, romantic affairs were inconvenient, often stirring up unpleasant emotions. For the other party, at least.

"I've brought you a gift." The noblewoman gestured at one of her rain-soaked attendants, who lifted a cloth-covered basket. Taking the basket from the sodden girl, the noblewoman placed it on the table that held the practice weapons, knocking over a glaive. Lifting the cloth from the top of the basket, she revealed several pastries tucked within. "It's so cold. I thought it might warm you up a bit."

"You have my gratitude," Jaeil murmured.

"Only gratitude, Captain?"

He tired of this. Ren would just have to deal with the repercussions of choosing an ill-mannered military adviser.

"It appears," he said in his most scathing tone, which Sana had once told him could make grown men weep, "that in spite of your less than subtle attempts for more, it's the only emotion I'm inspired to have."

The noblewoman sucked in a sharp breath before storming away in a huff, her attendants rushing after her to keep an umbrella above her head.

As she left, she passed Wook, who was running in the opposite direction. Jaeil frowned; the other boy hadn't bothered with an umbrella. Rain had plastered to his curls, soaking his shoulders and arms. Catching sight of the noblewoman, Wook attempted to bow, only to trip, falling headfirst toward the mud.

Jaeil caught him before Wook could hit the ground. He'd stepped into the rain to do so; the rainwater that slid down his neck was cold.

"You're quite clumsy for an acrobat," Jaeil said mildly as he pulled Wook to his feet and led him beneath the tent.

Wook scratched the back of his head. "Who was that?" he asked, his eyes following the noblewoman and her retinue.

"I'm not sure. Hopefully no one the princess holds in high regard," Jaeil said dryly. "She brought pastries." He gestured toward the basket before picking the glaive from off the ground, balancing it once more against the table. "You're welcome to partake."

Jaeil paused, a smirk playing along his lips, amused despite himself. "Hopefully they're not laced with aphrodisiacs."

He meant the words as a jest, but Wook turned an alarming shade of pink.

Jaeil sighed; he really should refrain from jesting. It wasn't his strong suit. "Did you need something from me?"

"Oh!" Wook grinned sheepishly. "Ren asked if you'd meet her at the entrance to the dungeons. She says there's something she wishes to look for." He then shuddered. "Not sure why she'd want to go *underground*, or where the dungeons even are."

"They're south of the training grounds," Jaeil said. "My father is being kept there." He didn't know what compelled him to add that last part. It wasn't relevant information.

Wook's eyes widened. "I'll go with her!" he said hurriedly. "You stay here, and I'll—"

"No," Jaeil said. Prisons were dark. He wouldn't subject Wook to another bout of darkness so soon after their first. The candle had been at the end of its wick by the time they'd made it halfway up the stairs; they'd had to navigate the rest of the way blind. To distract Wook, Jaeil had asked the other boy to tell him a story. At first his voice had wobbled, but after a while, he'd grown in confidence. His voice had echoed across the cavern, rich and bright, leading them both out of the darkness.

"Yes," Wook said with a heavy sigh, and Jaeil frowned, unable to determine why the other boy sounded so sullen. "You'd probably want to be the one to take Ren."

Not particularly. He didn't relish the thought of comforting Ren as she pined over Sunho. But he *did* need to speak with her. He'd discovered something from the ledger he'd taken from the mithril labs that he thought might be important.

"Does she wish to meet with me now?" Jaeil asked.

Wook appeared somehow more distraught than before. "Aren't you going to eat something first?" he blurted.

Jaeil glanced at the basket, having forgotten about it. Wook grabbed a pastry from the top without looking, ripping off a large chunk of it with his teeth and chewing.

Jaeil watched Wook's jaw as it worked to chew the bread before he swallowed, coughing slightly. "It's perfectly safe, see?"

Before Wook could take another bite, Jaeil reached out and extracted the pastry from his hand. He brought it to his lips and took a bite from the same side that Wook had bitten. "Are you certain about that?" he asked.

Wook gaped at him.

Turning, he left the other boy, stepping out from beneath the tent.

The rain had abated, but Jaeil could sense the stirrings of a storm, the tent flaps rippling in the wind. In the east, black clouds gathered.

Sunho was standing with two of his soldiers. They stared at the pastry in his hand. In all likelihood, they had probably never seen him eat before.

"You did well today," he told the soldiers. "You're dismissed." They quickly bowed, leaving him alone with Sunho.

"Do you hold back when you fight the others?" Jaeil asked.

The other boy eyed him warily. "Yes."

"If you had to estimate the percentage of how much of your strength you were using just now, what would it be?"

Sunho seemed to consider his question. "Thirty percent," he finally said.

Jaeil raised a brow. He wondered if that had been the output Sunho had used to fight *him*. "If you accessed the Demon, how much percentage stronger would you be, at your highest capacity?"

Sunho held his gaze. "One hundred."

Extraordinary. Just by tapping into the Demon, he'd have more than twice the strength. If he transformed, he'd likely have even more. If only they could tap into that potential . . .

"I'm on my way to meet with the princess," Jaeil said. "She wishes to search for something in the dungeons; they connect to tunnels that run beneath the castle. Would you care to join us?" Jaeil studied Sunho carefully, then added, "We'll be quite alone."

He waited for Sunho to react, but the soldier's expression remained carefully blank.

Jaeil felt a tick of annoyance. He didn't understand this boy. If Sunho was as much in love with Ren as Jaeil believed him to be, then why wasn't he doing everything in his power to stay by her side?

With a shake of his head, he left Sunho, taking a bite of the pastry as he went.

REN WAS ALREADY outside the entrance to the dungeons when Jaeil arrived, accompanied by Hwani, now a familiar sight beside her. Jaeil knew little about Ren's bodyguard, only that she belonged to a minor vassal family of a noble clan. The guard was tall, even taller than him. Jaeil stood a little straighter.

"Hwani," Ren said, "will you wait outside? I'll be quite safe with the captain."

"Yes, Princess," Hwani said, her eyes narrowing on Jaeil as he passed.

The guards at the entrance handed Jaeil a lantern, which he accepted with a grimace, resigned to his fate of venturing down dark stairwells. It was odd—he'd spent most of his life in the Under World, and yet a week in the sun, and it was as if he'd lost all resistance to the darkness.

He'd been afraid of the dark when he was a child, and yet he'd later chosen to live in the Under World. He thought it would make him stronger. Braver. He wanted to separate himself from the boy he'd once been. Who'd been afraid of his father. Who'd lost Ren to the forest. That boy had been weak, his head filled with fairy tales. No one would ever accuse Jaeil, a captain in the Sareniyan army, of being weak or soft.

The stairwell was damp, and Ren suppressed a shudder.

"Here—" Jaeil began to remove his overcoat.

"No, it's all right. I'm not cold. It's just . . . dark."

He reached into an inner pocket of his coat and pulled out the ledger he'd found in the mithril lab, thinking to distract her. "I wanted to show you this," he said. "I marked the page that I thought might interest you."

Ren took the ledger, and he held up the lantern for her to read, her brow furrowing as she studied the writing—an accounting of the money the lab had spent on mithril obtained from the ninth ward mithril factory.

"This ledger shows a shipment of mithril aboard an aircraft called the *Flying Serpent*," Jaeil explained. "I searched records for an airship with that name, but I couldn't find one."

"Maybe it's a code?"

"I thought that at first, too, but then I realized I was searching in the wrong place.

"It's not an airship," Jaeil continued, unable to hide his excitement. "It's a boat."

Ren frowned. "I don't understand. The Floating World doesn't have rivers. Or at least, rivers that lead anywhere."

"Yes, but the Under World *does*. I think there was another laboratory, a second location in the Under World. A few weeks ago, when I was investigating the murders in the city, I hadn't realized they were the work of transformed humans. The first body was found by fishermen in the Outer Ring. The second outside the Wall, near a sewer exit. If I had to make a calculated guess, the second laboratory must be either near or *in* the sewers."

Ren returned the ledger to him, and he placed it back inside his coat. "Do I have your permission to pursue this lead?" He wanted to leave as soon as possible, recalling the storm clouds he'd spotted earlier. It would be a big one, if the size and darkness of the clouds was any indication. And storms on the Floating World were fierce, often lasting for days.

Something in his gut told him that they were running out of time, that the scientist was close to achieving whatever he'd been planning. If Jaeil could discover what that plan was, he might be able to stop it.

"You'd have to leave," Ren said quietly.

Jaeil felt like he'd been punched in the gut. He'd never heard Ren sound so . . . forlorn. What was Sunho *doing*? He wanted to shake some sense into the other boy for having this effect on her.

"I should be gone for two days at the most," he said. "Is something the matter?"

"I'm fine. I haven't been sleeping well . . ." There was a look in her eyes that made Jaeil feel uneasy. "What's down that way?"

Jaeil let her change the subject, following her gaze to where the path split in two. To the left was . . .

"The prison."

"Do you wish to visit him?" Ren said softly.

"No."

They took the right path. "Why did you want to come here?" Jaeil asked. "Wook mentioned you were looking for something."

"I've been reading my mother's journal. *He's* mentioned in her journal—Juwon, the scientist. He was the younger brother of . . . He found something," she finished. "Down here."

They continued walking deeper through the warren of tunnels, occasionally opening doors that led into abandoned cellars. They'd been wandering for an hour when they entered a chamber that was unlike the others. It appeared to be a storage room, filled with oddities and old relics.

Jaeil picked up a celadon cosmetic box, its color worn from age, studying the fine craftsmanship. He turned to see that Ren had gone very still, staring at the pieces of an old bow that was missing its bowstring. It was massive; when intact, it must have been twice the size of the standard-issue shortbows.

"A fine weapon," he said. "It's a shame it wasn't properly cared for."

"How old do you think it is?" Ren asked, and there was a hint of wonder in her voice.

Jaeil noted the warped wood and thick coating of dust. "I'd guess a couple of centuries."

"Centuries . . . ," Ren breathed.

Jaeil studied her carefully. "Why?"

She swallowed, shaking her head. "It's nothing."

As Ren perused the far side of the room, Jaeil moved to the back, where a tapestry hung on the wall of an alcove. It depicted three celestial maidens bathing in a pool beside a waterfall, steam rising to cover their naked bodies. On the bough of a pine tree hung their robe-like wings.

Beneath the tapestry was a chest, and he lifted it open to find it empty.

"What do you think was inside it?" Ren asked, coming up behind him.

"Clothing," he guessed. "Blankets. Maybe even this tapestry."

Ren huffed, clearly frustrated. "The diary said Juwon found *something*. I just wish I knew what it was."

"Maybe it was a celadon cosmetic box," Jaeil quipped.

"Maybe." Her lips quirked briefly. "They were close," she said softly. "My mother and Juwon."

"That makes sense," Jaeil said. "They shared a common interest. They loved the same person most in the world.

"That is," Jaeil amended, "before you were born."

"You of all people know that's not true."

Neither spoke for several minutes. Finally, he asked, "Do you resent her?"

"How could I? My mother never had a chance to love me."

Jaeil didn't think that was true. He didn't believe Ren did, either. Her mother had been grief-stricken, but she was still *her mother*. She could have chosen to love Ren.

"Jaeil, I have a favor to ask." Ren turned bodily toward him, lifting her chin. "It's about Sunho."

Jaeil eyed her warily. "What about him?"

"Will you watch over him for me?"

His chest tightened with that unwelcome feeling again—guilt. Earlier, he'd been wondering how to *use* the other boy. "He and I aren't exactly friends," Jaeil hedged. Though they'd acted civil enough with each other in the mithril mines.

"Please," Ren insisted.

"You're my sovereign," Jaeil said. "You can command me." When she didn't say anything, continuing to look melancholy, he sighed. "Does he really need looking after? He's stronger than a dozen of my best soldiers. He's stronger than *me*."

"Just . . . ," she whispered. "Promise me."

Jaeil should have known better—there was little he wouldn't do for her. "I promise."

LATER THAT EVENING, Jaeil was making last-minute preparations when he heard a knock on his office door, and was surprised to see Sunho enter.

The wind howled behind him and he had to shut the door to be heard. "Take me with you," he said. "I've been in the sewers before. And I have a contact who can navigate them."

Sunho must have divined his destination from Wook, who'd extrapolated it from Ren. Logically, he *should* take Sunho with him; the younger boy would be an asset in the sewers, just as he was in the mines. But then he thought of Ren's face, how miserable she had looked. *You'd have to leave.*

He cursed his softness. "No, you need to stay here. Give me your contact's name," he said, turning his back to Sunho. "I'll send a message to them."

"I *need* to leave," Sunho said.

And something in Sunho's voice made Jaeil turn. The other boy sounded . . . tortured. He didn't know what was going on between Sunho and Ren, but maybe time apart would help them both figure out what it was they wanted.

"All right," Jaeil said finally. "But tell Ren you're leaving first. More importantly, let her know you're coming back."

THEY ENTERED THE hall a half hour later. Jaeil frowned at the sheer amount of people—more than were at his trial.

He spotted Ren atop the dais. Her expression was cold, distant, and for a moment it appeared as if it was Aria staring out at the crowd.

Then his gaze was drawn to a delegation of people dressed in black with the emblem of a rising tiger on their shoulder guards. Volmarans.

"I speak on behalf of Jindeok, empress of Volmar," a woman was saying, her voice carrying across the chamber. "The empress will accept the treaty proposed by the council on one condition: that the princess of Sareniya agree to marry her grandson, Jinpyeong, prince of Volmar."

A resounding silence filled the hall, before all chaos broke loose.

"Damn it." Jaeil stepped back as the crowd surged. They wouldn't be able to speak with Ren, not with this many people. And they were out of time—no aircraft would take off once the storm set in.

Jaeil made a split-second decision. He turned to Sunho, whose face was shuttered. "Let's go."

The aircraft was finishing launch preparations by the time they arrived.

"Captain!" the pilot shouted over the howling wind, gripping Jaeil's forearm and pulling him aboard. He reached back to help Sunho. "You made it just in time. A few minutes later, and we wouldn't have been able to launch!"

"Jaeil!" a voice shouted behind them. He whipped around to see Wook racing up the gangplank as it was in the middle of retracting.

"What are you doing?" Jaeil grabbed Wook before he could tumble off the ship.

"I was trying to"—Wook's eyes widened as the ground fell out beneath them—"stop you." He must have realized what had happened because his face turned pale.

An uneasy feeling lodged in Jaeil's stomach. He was taking not just Sunho but Wook from the Floating World, two of Ren's main supporters.

"We won't be gone long," he said aloud, as if to reassure himself.

Sunho had sank to the floor, his back pressed to the wall of the aircraft, his head in his hands.

Jaeil wasn't worried about Ren's safety. Hwani had a reputation as a capable warrior. There was no one better suited to look after Ren.

It was just that he hadn't liked that look in Ren's eyes, down in the dungeons, as if she were being haunted.

Or *hunted.*

CHAPTER 20

SUNHO

The Under World
Fourth Ward, the Outer Ring

SUNHO PRESSED THE back of his head against the plush interior of the horse-drawn carriage. Outside the curtained window, the buildings passed by in a blur.

Had he made a mistake by leaving? Standing on that dais, Ren had appeared fragile, alone. He'd wanted to go to her but hadn't dared. She was a princess. He might not understand all the rules, but he couldn't act on impulse.

And then there was the Demon.

In the week since that awful night, nothing had changed; he was still afraid of hurting her.

He had hoped that he could control it, but that night proved that he was *losing* control. He knew the Demon's strength was tied to his emotions.

And there was no one he felt more strongly for than Ren.

He knew what he had to do, but he couldn't bring himself to do it.

He had to leave the Floating World, far enough away that he wouldn't be tempted to return.

The thought made it difficult to breathe, but he would do it, to keep her safe. He had almost convinced himself it was the right decision when he'd found out about Jaeil's mission. Sunho had begged the older boy to take him along, hoping the distance would dull his longing for Ren, but it was worse.

He yearned for her, somehow even more than before.

Beside him, Wook craned his neck out the carriage window. "I didn't know what to expect coming here. Honestly, I thought it might be frightening. But it's really quite beautiful. The lanterns make the city glow."

Jaeil looked up from the ledger he'd been flipping through. "I think it's beautiful, too."

Wook must have been surprised by Jaeil's response because his lips parted, then he smiled tentatively.

Earlier, they had passed the checkpoints from the Core into Mid City, and the Outer Ring, heading toward the docks of the fourth ward. When the stench of the river began wafting through the windows, Sunho knew they had arrived. The coachman pulled on the reins and the carriage ground to a stop.

A soldier, a young woman with bright eyes and short hair, was waiting outside to greet them.

"Yumi," Jaeil said, stepping down from the carriage. "We need to meet under less malodorous circumstances."

Yumi's eyes widened, as if she hadn't expected Jaeil to tease. "Y-Yes, Captain. That would be—" She broke off, started again. "Yes, Captain."

Wook gave her a sympathetic smile.

Yumi cleared her throat. "I received your missive and came here directly. I questioned the dockmaster, but he said he hasn't seen the *Flying Serpent* for a few weeks now."

"I figured as much," Jaeil said. "Is there an entrance to the sewer here?"

"Yes, sir. Follow me."

"I'd given some thought on the best place to look for a secret laboratory," Jaeil explained as they left the dockyard, stepping off the wooden planks onto the muddy banks of the river. "An obvious place would be the sewers located beneath the ninth ward mithril factory, as that was the main supplier of mithril to the labs. But I find it hard to believe that's where the scientist, Juwon, would have hidden one.

"In any case, I sent a team to search there. The factory is in the northwestern quadrant of the city. The other two bodies were found in the south and eastern quadrants. If we travel the path from the docks where the first body was found to the Wall, where the second was discovered, we might find a clue to the laboratory's location."

They reached the sewer entrance, a large pipe that spewed blackened water into the river. Jaeil held up the lantern, shining it toward the dark entrance. The light barely penetrated a few feet in.

He turned to Wook. "You don't have to go in there. You can wait out here with Yumi."

Yumi, standing to the side, waved good-naturedly.

Wook patted the bow he'd slung across his shoulder. He'd taken it, and a quiver of arrows, from the armory at Hagye. "If you *do* encounter any demons, you'll need some cover. Believe it or not, I'm quite a skilled archer. And finding this scientist is personal to me. He created the demon that destroyed my family."

Jaeil studied Wook a few seconds longer, but when the other boy didn't drop his gaze, he nodded. "Don't stray too far from me, or Sunho."

"I'll go first," Sunho said, entering the pipe ahead of the others.

He only had to walk with his head ducked a few steps before the narrow tunnel opened into a larger one. He kept his senses alert for the presence of demons, but the only sounds he heard, besides the gurgle of sewage water, were the rats skittering along the walls and his companions' heartbeats: Jaeil's was slow and steady, Wook's a bit faster. Something squelched beneath his boot, but he didn't look down.

They'd gone a short distance when Sunho spotted a lone figure standing by the wall.

"Tag," he called out, more to alert the others to Tag's presence than for his friend's benefit—he'd likely seen their lanterns from a distance.

Tag raised his hand at their approach. As they came closer, his silver hair caught the light of their lanterns.

"You could have waited for us outside," Sunho said warmly. He was glad to see his friend.

"I wanted to check that I had the right map." Sunho noticed then that Tag was holding a large scroll in the glove of his left hand. "Don't worry," he said. "I've been in the sewers before." He winked, and Sunho was reminded of when Tag had led him through the sewers the first time.

Wook frowned. "But why were you waiting in the dark?"

"I wanted to conserve my light," Tag said reasonably.

"Yes, but . . ." Wook struggled to speak. "Never mind." He gestured to the captain. "Have you met Jaeil?"

"Yes," Tag replied flatly. "He ransacked my home, kidnapped my guest, and terrified my grandmother."

". . . Oh."

"Grandma Jin is your grandmother?" Sunho asked. He hadn't

thought Wolryudang's proprietress was related to either Yurhee or Tag.

"She's everyone's grandmother," Tag answered.

"Technically," Jaeil cut in, "*you* weren't there at the time. So, we haven't met."

"*Jaeil*," Wook groaned.

Crouching, Tag picked up the lantern at his feet, lighting the wick with a match he then flicked into the murky water. Sunho saw that Tag had brought a crossbow with him, slung over his shoulder.

"This tunnel system is old," Tag said, "built at the same time as the city. Yurhee got this map from an engineer who helped do some repairs a few years back." He handed the map to Sunho, who was the only one who could see it clearly in the dark. The map showed a labyrinth of tunnels and passageways branching off in seemingly random directions.

"This way," Tag said.

They'd walked a half hour when Tag stopped, pointing down a tunnel that was wider than the one they were currently walking down. "That way leads to the Madang District. Those tunnels are well-traveled, by maintenance workers, mostly. If there was anything to be found there, we'd know."

Tag stepped through a wall that had crumbled, and Sunho and the others followed him into a narrower tunnel than the one before. There was less sewage, but the air was thicker, mustier. Tag checked the map before heading north.

"Why are none of you afraid?" Wook exclaimed.

"I'm afraid," Tag deadpanned.

Wook gave him a doubtful look.

The tunnel was too narrow for them to walk more than two apace. Sunho stepped forward to join Tag, who'd taken the lead.

Wook caught a rock in his shoe, yelping. While Jaeil stayed behind to help him, the other two boys walked ahead.

Tag pulled the collar of his jacket down. "I never apologized for shooting you when you were a demon," he said. The piercing in his lip shone in the lantern light. "I'm sorry."

It took Sunho a few seconds to pinpoint what Tag was referring to. Then he remembered the airship, when he'd crashed belowdecks in his monster form. Tag had shot him with his crossbow. Sunho wondered how long the other boy had been carrying the guilt of that choice. To others, Tag might appear unfeeling, but his emotions had always been clearer to Sunho.

"I would have rather died than hurt Ren," Sunho said.

Tag slumped, as if a weight had been newly lifted from his shoulders.

After a few minutes of walking in silence, he stood a little straighter. "How are you?" Tag asked.

If it was anyone else, Sunho might have brushed off the question, but this was Tag.

"Ever since I've come to the Floating World," he said truthfully, "I feel as if I'm constantly fighting to keep the Demon under control, so that it won't break free and hurt anyone. So that *I* won't hurt anyone."

"You call what you become 'the Demon'?" Tag asked. His tone was neutral, curious.

Sunho nodded, closing his eyes. "I know it's not the Floating World that the Demon is reacting to. It's Ren. It's . . . affected by her, more than anyone else."

"That makes sense," Tag said, and Sunho opened his eyes to look at his friend. "The Demon is a part of your soul. You are one and the same. The Demon is affected by her because you are."

"Which is why I have to *leave*," Sunho said, despairing. If there was anything else that he could have changed to stay, he would have done it. But it was hopeless. The one thing that he would never change was his feelings for Ren.

"Not necessarily. The first time you met Ren as the Demon, you lashed out at her. You couldn't control it—"

Sunho winced.

"—but the second time, you protected her.

"In the Volmaran laboratory," Tag explained. "The explosions caused the roof to cave in. You broke the chain to protect her."

Had he done that? His memories of that time were all jumbled.

"And then the third time, you transformed back, because your soul recognized hers."

Tag's voice was soft but firm. "The feelings you have for Ren, they're the same when you're the Demon. You say you'd rather die than hurt her. I think the Demon would do the same."

A buoyant feeling stirred in Sunho's chest—hope. But to know for certain, he'd have to get close to Ren again. He would have to risk hurting her.

A startled cry echoed down the tunnel.

Wook.

He raced back the way they'd come. He ran into Jaeil and Wook sprinting in the opposite direction. "What's happened?"

"There's something down here with us," Jaeil said, breathing harshly.

A low growl reverberated through the tunnel, echoing off the walls.

"My neighbor, Haru," Sunho said. "He told me there was a rumor of a bear in the sewer."

"I'd heard it as well," Jaeil said. "I sent soldiers to investigate. They never found anything."

Another cry echoed down the tunnel, but this time it was high-pitched. Sunho peered into the darkness, unsheathing his sword. The tunnel stretched a few hundred feet before swinging to the right.

A woman appeared around the corner, skidding in the sewage before jerking upright. Matted hair covered her face. Slowly, she began to lope toward them, then faster, reaching out with nails that had extended into claws. *Demon.*

"Tag, aim right above my shoulder," Sunho instructed. "I'll tell you when to shoot." Only he could make out the demon in the darkness; the others wouldn't be able to see her until she was almost upon them.

Sunho felt the weight of the crossbow as Tag rested the barrel on his shoulder.

Sunho waited until the demon drew closer, her cries getting louder as she spotted them.

"Now!"

He winced at the sharp recoil as the bolt released from the chamber. It struck the demon in the throat and she fell, gurgling in her death throes.

More shrieks reverberated down the tunnel.

"How many are there?" Jaeil peered into the darkness, stepping forward.

"Four," Sunho said, counting them as they careened around the corner.

"We'll wait for them to draw closer," Jaeil said. "Don't go for a killing shot," he told Wook, who was nocking an arrow, his expression grim but focused. "It's too difficult in the dark, and we can't waste arrows. Aim to wound." Tag nodded, indicating that he'd also understood. Jaeil's eyes locked with Sunho's. "We'll take care of the rest."

Sunho returned his attention to the approaching demons.

Wook released an arrow that embedded into the shoulder of the closest demon. Tag's bolt found another's thigh, and it dropped to the ground.

Jaeil was swift with his sword, decapitating it quickly, then moving forward to block the snarled attack of another.

Sunho thrust his blade into the chest of a demon, withdrawing in time to see the one grappling with Jaeil lunge for his neck. Sunho threw his sword. It impaled the monster, pinning it to the wall.

Wook shouted, and Sunho twisted around to see a demon had escaped past Sunho and Jaeil, its claws extended toward Wook.

Tag threw his crossbow aside. Grabbing a bolt by the shaft, he jammed the bolthead into the side of the demon's neck. It screamed, swiping at Tag, but he twisted the bolt. It ceased moving, flopping lifeless to the ground.

"Is everyone all right?" Jaeil asked in the aftermath, his gaze sweeping toward Wook.

"Tag!" Wook shouted.

Sunho's heart lurched. The silver-haired boy was cradling his arm. That last demon must have caught him with its claws.

"Let me see." Sunho reached for him.

"It's just a scratch," Tag said, drawing back his arm, but Sunho insisted. The wound was shallow, but not insignificant.

"We have to get back to the Floating World," Wook said. "Ren will heal you."

"I'm fine," Tag said.

"But what if you're infected?" Wook pressed. "When I was clawed by a demon, I became ill. I would have died if it weren't for Ren."

A thought seemed to have struck him, because he reared back in horror. "What if *they* could have been cured?" He gestured to the demons, who'd all transformed back into humans following their deaths. "Did we just kill human beings— Did I—?"

"Demons can't be cured after they've been injected," Sunho said. He had no proof of his claim, but he knew it to be the truth. Ren had tried to cure him, and it had felt like fire ripping through his soul. "You became ill after you were infected by the demon's blood, but you didn't transform. The transformation is induced by the serum. The effect is . . . anatomical; it cannot be reversed."

"We'll have to monitor you for signs of mithril poisoning," Jaeil informed Tag. "Are you all right to go on?"

Tag nodded.

"How can you be so coldhearted?" Wook shouted at Jaeil's back, moving to Tag's side.

Jaeil glanced at Wook before averting his gaze. He forged ahead. Sunho picked up Tag's crossbow. Then, wresting his sword from the wall, he followed Jaeil.

The demons had left a trail. They raced down one narrow tunnel after another, until they entered a passage that was brighter than the others. Jaeil held up a hand, approaching slowly.

At the end of the hall was a large, hollow chamber, at the back of which stood a massive floodgate. Electricity crackled from the lights strung up along the ceiling, illuminating a space that had recently been abandoned, with overturned worktables and instruments smashed across the ground, dripping blue ink.

As Jaeil headed to the back of the room, Wook helped Tag to a chair, pulling bandages from one of the worktables and wrapping the other boy's arm.

Sunho ventured farther into the laboratory. Like the one in the mines, cages lined the walls, where the demons that had attacked them must have been held. Catching sight of something on the floor, he leaned forward to pick it up.

It was a padlock, the key still wedged inside.

Someone had opened these cages intentionally.

He whipped around. "Jaeil," he warned.

A loud groan reverberated across the chamber as the floodgate opened and a massive demon stepped through.

This must be the "bear," Sunho thought. It was the height of two full-grown men, barrel-chested, with gigantic paws and incisors the length of swords. Unlike the feathers that had sprouted from Rohoon and Sunho, it had huge clumps of bloodied fur.

It swung its arm, flinging Jaeil across the room, where he slammed into a wall, stunned.

"Jaeil!" Wook cried, charging forward.

"Stay back!" Sunho shouted. This monster wasn't like the others. It couldn't be killed, not by a human.

Sunho called forth the Demon, letting it rise up with a fury. With a roar, the bear-demon lunged at Sunho, but he was faster, twisting out of the way. He plunged his sword into the demon's side, using his weight to jam it halfway up the blade before leaping back. The demon howled. Grabbing the hilt with its teeth, it wrenched the sword from its body, snapping it in half.

Blood gushed from the wound, dropping sapphire puddles onto the floor. Sunho didn't wait for it to recover. His claws burst from his fingers, and he slashed them across the demon's neck. It staggered backward, falling onto one knee. Then it began to shift.

As Sunho watched the agonizing reversal, he wondered if, beneath the monster, there'd be someone he knew—one of the soldiers he'd fought alongside—but the man was older, dressed in tattered black robes.

He coughed up blue, brackish blood. "He warned us about you," he hissed.

"Who?" Sunho grabbed him by the collar. "Teacher?"

The man sneered, blood oozing from his cracked lips. "The one with the black wings."

He reared back. *Rohoon?* But no, Rohoon was gone.

Sunho was desperate to ask more, but the man's eyes were glazing over. He was running out of time.

Sunho jerked him forward. "What is Teacher planning?"

"He wants what we all want. An end to Sareniya."

"How does he plan on accomplishing such a goal?" Jaeil demanded, coming up beside Sunho. Blood dripped from a nasty cut over his left eye. "Is he allied with the Volmarans?"

The man's eyes rolled to the ceiling, and he started to babble, "Keep your eyes down, Servant of Sareniya. You are unworthy of the light.

"You cannot save her," the man howled. "*She's* there, on the Floating World. She, who all of this has been for. It'll be over soon."

"Who's there?" Sunho cried. "Can't save who?"

But he knew.

Ren. Ren was in danger.

He dropped the man, scrambling to his feet.

Jaeil caught his arm. "What are you doing?"

"I have to get to Ren."

"He might be bluffing."

Sunho stared down at the man, who'd gone silent, though his eyes remained open; a blue teardrop slid down his cheek. "I don't think so." He had no reason to lie. Sunho didn't imagine he had any loyalty, just pain and fear. "And even if he is, I can't risk it."

"We're deep underground, without an aircraft." Tag had stumbled over, supporting his left arm with his right hand. "You'll never make it in time."

Tag was right. Even if he discovered a faster way out of the sewer, it would take hours to find a transport vessel that could carry him through the storm, even longer to reach the Floating World.

His heartbeat thrashed in his ears. He shouldn't have left her. If anything happened to Ren, he would never forgive himself.

"Sunho," he heard Wook call from behind him.

He turned and the others stepped back. He knew what they saw, the mithril glowing in his eyes.

Blue blood dripped from his hand where he'd pierced the demon, his hand that had returned to normal.

He could save Ren. There was a chance of reaching her in time, but only if he transformed.

Only if he became the Demon.

CHAPTER 21

REN

The Floating World
The Queen's Palace

THE STORM WAS raging outside by the time Ren returned to her room in the Queen's Palace. She quickly dismissed her attendants, wishing to be alone, while Hwani took up her usual position outside her door. Toeing off her slippers, she staggered to the bed, falling face down onto the blankets.

The day had started off badly and had only gotten worse. After the Volmaran ambassador had declared the empress's terms, Ren had been ushered into a private chamber with Lord Muyeol, Lady Maya, and other senior members of the council.

She hadn't agreed to the terms, but neither had she rejected them outright. What she *had* agreed to was a meeting with the prince.

Since Sareniya and Volmar were still at war—though hostilities had ceased since Commander Su's arrival at the border of Volmar—the meeting would be held on more neutral ground.

It was Lady Maya who'd proposed the Under World. Not exactly a favorable meeting place for the Volmarans, but the ambassador had agreed that Ren, as Sareniya's sole heir and the last celestial maiden, should not leave its vicinity. To ensure fairness, the Sareniyans would allow a large party of Volmarans to enter the city, up to fifty soldiers, not including the prince's personal retinue. Ren had let Lady Maya take control of the negotiations from there.

She'd been distracted. Her mind had kept straying to earlier in the hall, when she'd seen Sunho enter with Jaeil, her traitorous heart leaping at the sight of him. She'd still been frustrated with how they'd parted, but that didn't mean she didn't long for him.

She didn't know what it was she wanted from Sunho. Only that there was a crack in her heart, and even though he was the one who put it there, she also knew only he could mend it.

When the ambassador had announced the terms of the treaty, the betrothal, she'd looked for Sunho, panicking when she couldn't find him. It wasn't until later that she discovered that he'd left with Jaeil, and that Wook had followed them.

All week, she'd felt as if she was losing him. What if he never came back? What if she'd lost him for good?

"Sareniya . . ."

The doors that led to the gardens banged open, letting in wind and rain.

She climbed from the bed, hurrying across the room. She stumbled into the biting wind, pressed forward until she passed through the arch that separated the queen's private gardens from the eastern ones.

Guards with umbrellas patrolled the grounds, but she swept by them as if she herself were a ghost, close enough to see their breaths misting the air. She didn't question how this was possible; her mind felt cloudy, hazy.

"Sareniya . . ."

She reached the wisteria tree that covered the hole in the wall, ducking through and entering the wind forest. She stepped over the thick white rope that stretched between the trees, strung with paper charms—wards to deter ghosts and other malevolent spirits. In the distance, far off to the south, she heard the roar of the waterfall.

At the edge of the cliff stood a figure.

Hair spilled down her back, its own dark waterfall. She wore a cloak of night. Unlike on the airship, the fabric fluttered in the wind. It was real. *She* was real.

She turned toward her, and Ren looked into a face so much like her own.

"Mother," Ren breathed.

It was *her*. Aria. Ren might not have seen her since she was seven years old, but she would never have forgotten her face. It had haunted her for the past ten years.

Ren stumbled forward. "I don't understand," she said. "How are you here?"

"I've come to warn you," Aria said, and Ren gasped at the strength of her voice; before, it had hardly been a whisper. "You're in danger."

Warmth radiated throughout Ren's body. She'd been right. Her mother *had* returned to protect her.

"Muyeol means to seize power and take control of the Floating Council," her mother insisted. "He's in alliance with Iljin."

Ren frowned. That couldn't be right. Her uncle had almost executed the general. And if he had such a plan, her aunt would have told her—wouldn't she?

"You can't let them take from you what they took from me," Aria said. "You're all that's left of the celestial maiden's legacy—*my* legacy. Promise me you'll heed my warning, that you'll guard yourself against them."

Ren still had doubts, but she nodded. "I promise."

"I can't stay long. Come to me." Her mother held out her hands and Ren took them. Her fingers were icy.

"Are you . . . Are you a ghost?" Ren asked.

Aria's eyes softened. "In a way. I am the remnants of my soul, left upon this world to safeguard you. Now tell me, what do you wish to ask me?"

Ren choked back a sob. There were so many questions she wanted to ask her mother, but one mattered the most. "Why did you leave me?"

"I was weak. I should have stayed. I failed as a mother; I should have protected you. Forgive me, dear Ren. I love you."

Her mother's arms wrapped around her. Her arms were delicate, soft. She smelled like the rain that fell gently all around them. The storm raged across the floating island, but not here. It was as if they were cocooned, separated from the rest of the world. Tears slipped down Ren's cheeks. This was all she'd ever wanted: to hear those words from her mother. *Forgive me. I love you.* That was her greatest wish.

And yet, in all her memories, her mother had never embraced her.

She felt warm, she felt safe, she felt *loved*, and that's how she knew . . . *she knew* . . .

It wasn't her.

The specter must have sensed the tension in Ren's body because its arms tightened around her. Ren tried to break away, but it held fast to her, its fingernails digging into her arms.

"Darling girl, why do you struggle?"

Ren could see now the bluish cast to the specter's skin, smell the metallic scent that coated the air.

"It'll all be over soon," the specter crooned as she turned with Ren in her arms, backing her toward the cliff's edge. Ren's heart pounded like a drum; she felt a sharp, tugging sensation, as if the breaths were being pulled from her body. Her magic, like a constant flame, *flickered*, and Ren realized with horror that the specter was draining her of Light.

With painstaking slowness, Ren reached for the knife tucked in her belt. Snatching it, she swiped it across the specter's face. It connected with flesh, and the specter screamed, letting go of her.

Ren stumbled backward.

And then she was falling off the edge of the world.

Terror gripped her as she plummeted into an abyss-like darkness. The pressure was overwhelming; she felt crushed by air, the wind battering all around her. The storm, which had been held back by the specter's magic, raged in a fearsome tempest, the rain lashing at her face. She couldn't spread her wings to save herself. She had no more magic left; the creature had drained her entirely of Light.

She realized these had been her mother's—her real mother's—final moments, and she screamed with fury and despair.

Something large swept toward her in the sky. She didn't have time to shout before familiar arms circled around her, one hand sliding against her back, the other beneath her legs.

She felt the soft brush of a feather against her cheek.

She lifted her eyes, her breath catching to find Sunho gazing back at her. His face wasn't that of a monster, but *his*.

"Are you all right?" he asked, his voice unsteady. She didn't understand. She was no longer falling. "Wrap your arms around me."

She obeyed, sliding her arms around his neck. Her eyes widened at the sight of his wings arching from his back.

They were large, the length spanning at least twice that of hers.

Dark feathers swept past her, and she flinched, remembering the slicing pain of his feathers, but the ones that brushed her skin were soft, passing like petals.

She felt his chest expand with a breath, his hands tightening around her, then they were soaring through the air.

She'd thought she'd known what it was like to fly, but it was different to be carried. Her stomach dropped as they descended, and she held tightly to Sunho, pressing her face into his neck.

He swept them south, around the rim of the world. Soon, she became aware of a great roaring sound, and realized it was the waterfall. They flew so close that she felt its cool spray upon her face. And then he was flying behind the falling rapids, winging them lower and lower to the streambed below.

He landed on his feet, staggering a few steps, though he didn't drop her. With an almost aching tenderness, he placed her on a large, flat rock before stumbling back from her toward the water. She started to climb down.

"Stay back," he croaked, dropping to his knees in the streambed. His fingers dug into the gravel as he started to transform, his wings appearing to retract into him. And then he was Sunho again, his clothing torn at the back, but otherwise completely human.

Shakily, he stood. She was already off the rock, racing toward him before he'd fully turned to face her. She collided with him, her arms wrapping around his waist. He'd raised his own arms instinctively to catch her.

She was sobbing, soaking his already wet shirt. All the emotions she'd felt in the past hour, the days since arriving on the Floating World, crashed down upon her. She'd been so afraid, and confused, and *lonely.*

"Don't cry," Sunho said. "You're safe now. I'm sorry I didn't come sooner."

Fisting her hand against his chest, she pushed him, gently at first, then harder. He didn't move to avoid her, letting her fists thump harmlessly against his chest.

She was relieved he was here, but also *so upset.*

"You *left* me!" she cried.

"I'm sorry," he repeated. "I—I hurt the people I care about the most."

She knew he was thinking of his brother—and the other boy, the one he'd fought in the mithril labs.

"I was afraid of hurting you, like them."

Yet he'd come. He'd risked using his powers; he'd transformed into the Demon, at least partially, to save her.

"What changed?" she asked.

"I couldn't bear the thought of losing you. I would do anything to be with you. It kills me, to think that I could hurt you, but . . . I'll fight every day, endure whatever I must, if it means I can be where you are. Ren . . . I never want to leave your side again."

The storm had abated, revealing the moon for a short time, only for it to be swept behind a cluster of clouds. She groaned in frustration, glancing up at the sky as the light dimmed. Why couldn't the clouds cooperate when she needed them to the most?

"I can't see you," she lamented.

"I can see you." Sunho's voice was low and warm and close.

She inhaled sharply as his thumb traced the curve of her cheek. Gently, he lifted her face upward. She felt his breath against her lips.

"Wait," she whispered. "Last time, in the meadow . . ." She blushed.

"What if my Light hurts you? I don't know how to control it." She might have laughed at the irony of the situation, but she felt fragile, and a little desperate.

"You won't hurt me," he said, echoing her words from the other night back to her. "And even if you do, it'd be worth it."

She laughed nervously. "What are you saying? You—"

The moon slipped from behind the clouds.

She drew in a sharp breath.

He was gazing at her, his eyes intent upon hers. He was looking at her as if she was all that occupied his thoughts, his heart.

A shiver of trepidation swept through her. But it was a different sort of fear than earlier. It made her skin feel alight, her limbs soft and tender. She might have fallen if he wasn't holding her up.

Slowly, he lowered his head, his gaze never straying from hers. When they were inches apart, he asked, "Can I?"

"Yes," she breathed.

He closed the distance between them, pressing his lips to hers.

It was a gentle kiss, soft. She felt a sigh go through her.

When he leaned back, opening his eyes to look at her again, she lifted her face to his, seeking more.

His eyes widened slightly—the blue in his irises darkening—but he didn't draw back.

With a soft moan, he kissed her again, stronger than before.

When she felt his mouth open against hers, she melted, pressing closer to him.

Heat rose in her chest. It started in her core and curled outward, spreading down her limbs and the arch of her back.

Sunho let go of her, his breaths ragged.

"What?" she gasped. "What's wrong? Did I hurt you?"

"No, you're—"

She saw a bright light reflected in his eyes, and realized it was *her*.

She was glowing.

CHAPTER 22

SUNHO

The Under World
Outside the Wall

SUNHO KEPT HIS gaze on Ren as her Light spilled out onto the rocks beneath the waterfall, bathing him in its incandescence. He gasped as it swept over him, like stars alighting on his skin.

Ren closed her eyes, her brows furrowing as she focused. The Light began to retract until it was emanating from a single point on her body, the palm of her hand. It then rose like a drop of water, forming into a perfect sphere. Ren opened her eyes, blinking as she and Sunho stared at the sphere floating in the air like a tiny moon.

"I didn't know I could do that," she said.

Sunho lifted his hand to the Light.

"Wait—!" Ren started.

His fingers passed through it. The sphere was like her wings, emitting Light without heat.

"Incredible," he breathed. Ren had said that she thought their magic was the same, and he'd doubted that, but maybe there were aspects that were similar. Their magic seemed to grow and change based on their intentions, their emotions.

Before, when he'd transformed fully into the Demon, he'd been filled with grief and rage, and when he'd fought the greater demon, he'd transformed with the intention to kill, but this time when he'd transformed, he'd only wanted to protect, and just his wings had manifested.

"We should find the others," he said. "They'll be worried."

"Little Uncle!" Ren exclaimed. "And Jaeil. Where are they?"

He scratched his cheek. "I sort of . . . left them in the sewer. They should almost be at the north exit by the Wall, though, if they continued that way. We could meet up with them."

Before they started walking, Sunho ripped pieces from his clothing to wrap Ren's bare feet; he would have given her his boots, except they were more likely to hinder her than help. Afterward, he reached for Ren's hand. She took it, and together they headed in the direction of the Wall, the sphere trailing after them.

They'd landed near the waterfall, which meant they were miles from the Wall. He'd forgotten how much *bigger* the Floating World was than the Under World. Sunho was contemplating turning into the Demon again, if only to carry Ren, when he spotted carriages approaching from a distance. He tensed, curling his hand into a fist, his fingers primed to become claws, when he saw Yumi poke her head from one of the carriage windows, waving vigorously. The carriages pulled up beside them, releasing Wook, Jaeil, and Tag.

"Ren!" Wook cried, rushing forward and sweeping her into his arms. "Yumi spotted the light from the Wall, and I just *knew* it was you." As if pleased by his words, the ball of Light bobbed in the air before winking out.

Sunho studied Tag for signs of mithril poisoning. He'd had his arm properly bandaged by Yumi. "I'm fine," the younger boy said. "It doesn't look like the wound's infected."

Sunho worried his lip. "We'll have Ren look at it just to be safe." He then turned to Jaeil. "Were there any more?"

"No, but I marked the location of the laboratory on the map. I'm going to send a team from Hagye to sweep the area." Jaeil took the spare coat that Yumi must have brought for him, placing it around Ren's shoulders. "You're freezing. We have to get you back before the council realizes you're missing."

Sunho inserted himself between Jaeil and Ren. "I'll go with her," he said firmly. "In this carriage." He nodded to the first one.

Ren blushed, pressing her hands to her cheeks.

Jaeil lifted a brow. "It doesn't matter to me," he drawled. "I'll ride with Yumi."

Turning his back on them, Jaeil headed to the second carriage.

Tag looked between the carriages, then joined Jaeil.

Wook plopped into the seat opposite Ren and Sunho, his gaze darting between them. "Something happened between you two, didn't it?"

Ren scoffed loudly. "What are you talking about? He saved me and then we came here. I don't know about you, but I have bigger priorities than—" She cut herself off.

Wook's eyes narrowed. "Than what? Romance?"

"I'm tired." Ren closed her eyes. Leaning against the window, she pretended to sleep.

Wook's gaze went to Sunho, who just shrugged. *He* didn't have to explain himself; Wook wasn't *his* uncle.

AFTER REACHING HAGYE, Ren, Jaeil, and Wook boarded an aircraft, while Sunho took Tag aside. Ren had closed his wound when they'd arrived at the base, and his friend was admiring his freshly healed arm.

"I might contact you in the next week or so." Now that they'd identified a threat, they'd need to act quickly. "We'll need your help. Yours and Yurhee's."

Tag nodded. "We'll be ready."

Back on the Floating World, Sunho guided Ren to her room, careful to keep out of sight of the rotating guards. Once inside, he checked the crawlspace beneath the trapdoor, moving the tub over it to block the entrance.

The only exits from the room were the door to the hall where Hwani kept watch and the one to the eastern gardens. Patrols made rounds of the gardens throughout the night. Ren had managed to slip out in between one under the specter's influence. He made a mental note to tell Jaeil to increase the number.

"This is reminding me of when we were in the Under World the first time," Ren said. Sunho turned to where she was standing in the middle of the room, observing him with a small smile on her face. "You were so protective then, too."

She leaned forward playfully, her hands behind her back. "I don't think whatever attacked me will come back, now that it knows I'm aware of it."

"Still . . ." Sunho moved to the back door, sliding it on its track and jiggling it to test its sturdiness. "It's better to be cautious." He pointed to the latch. "Make sure you close and lock this every night."

"I will," she promised, though she couldn't mask the smile in her voice. "You could stay," she said. He glanced at her to see she was blushing. "It's almost morning."

"There are some other things I want to check," he said. She looked disappointed, so he added, "But I'll see you later tonight."

He hesitated, then opened his arms, and she came to him, pressing her face to his chest. He waited for the Demon to react, but it remained dormant, perhaps sated from its earlier appearances.

After a few moments, she let go with a sigh.

He stepped back. "Tonight," he repeated, then slipped out the door.

He waited until Ren had closed it behind him, listening for the jangle of the lock, before heading east. He jumped over the wall of the gardens, jogging through the forest toward the cliff.

The ground was scuffed where Ren had grappled with the specter. It must have been the *she* that the greater demon had spoken of with such awe and fear.

Sunho shuddered, remembering the moment he'd seen Ren fall from the cliff. He'd glimpsed the dark shadow that had pushed her, but hadn't hesitated, diving after Ren as fast as his wings could carry him.

Something glinted off the ground. He crouched down to find traces of blood—Ren must have broken the creature's skin during their struggle.

The blood was silver with streaks of crystalline blue.

Mithril.

THAT EVENING, SUNHO met with Ren, Jaeil, and Wook in the library of the Queen's Palace. Ren sat at the head of the table, while Sunho had chosen to stand by one of the bookshelves to have a better view of the room's exits. Wook sauntered in last, commandeering the seat across from Jaeil.

"We need to pool our information," Jaeil began. "Sunho, can you tell us everything you know about the project you were a part of?"

"My regiment, the Forty-Fourth, were the main subjects of the project," Sunho said grimly. "Most of us were born in the Under World, and therefore had a natural resistance to mithril's poisonous effects—"

He told them about the injections; about the changes they wrought in their bodies; about those who'd perished, succumbing to the poison; and then, lastly, about that fateful day when he received the injection that turned him into the Demon. He kept his voice steady, devoid of emotion. "They called their organization the Black Robes, and we called their leader 'Teacher.'"

"*He's* the monster," Wook seethed.

"I have noticed, more recently," Sunho said, "that the serum seemed to have worked differently depending on the person. The majority of those injected become mindless, like the demons we faced in the sewers. But a few exist in a half-transformed state. These demons are stronger than the others. They retain some of their faculties, and they can speak. I've been calling them 'greater demons' in my head."

"And then there's you," Jaeil said. "Someone who can transform from a human to a demon and back again."

Sunho nodded. As of yet, they hadn't met anyone else who could do the same.

"We know the Black Robes had at least two laboratories," Jaeil said slowly, and it was as if Sunho could see the other boy's mind working. "One in the mithril mines, and another in the sewers beneath the Under World."

"There's another," Ren said, perking up. "A facility hidden in the mountains across the border of Volmar. It was well-guarded. They were conducting experiments there, too. There was a man . . ." She tilted her head to the side, pursing her lips. "It wasn't Teacher. This man was taller. I couldn't see his face. He wore a mask. Do you have any idea who that might be?" she asked Sunho.

His memory was hazy. In it, he saw the face of the masked man, and a voice, but the words were hard to make out, muffled.

"I don't know," he said, frustrated with himself.

"It's all right," Ren said gently. "You were in a lot of pain."

"If there's a facility in Volmar," Wook said, "then doesn't that mean the Volmarans are working with Teacher?"

Jaeil shook his head. "It's unlikely. Juwon wants to destroy Sareniya. The Volmaran empress wouldn't want to give him the means to destroy empires. Far better for her to marry one of her grandchildren into the celestial family. Then her bloodline will inherit not only the Floating World but the power of the celestial maidens."

Sunho shifted on his feet. The thought of Ren marrying anyone, let alone a Volmaran prince in an unloving political alliance, made him feel uneasy.

"We haven't yet talked about the biggest mystery," Ren said. "The specter." She shuddered, and Sunho took a step toward her before she caught his gaze, smiling weakly to reassure him. "I first saw it on the airship on the way here. And then on the Floating World, I could hear its voice . . ."

"That night I saw you in the forest," Jaeil said, "you were following it, weren't you?"

Ren nodded. "When I hear its call, something comes over me; it's as if I'm in a dream. I can't resist it. But also . . . I don't *want* to."

She drew in another brave breath. "I thought it was the ghost of my mother. I—I wanted it to be." Her gaze turned fierce. "I think it *knew* that. It preyed upon that weakness in order to draw me out, in order to steal my magic." She placed her hand over her heart.

Ren's magic would replenish with time and rest—it had already begun to—but the terror of what she'd experienced would take longer to recover from.

"I found something when I went to the cliff to look for clues," Sunho said. "There was blood on the ground, but it was silver, streaked with strands of mithril. I'd seen remnants of it before, though I hadn't known what it was at the time. In the mithril laboratory."

Wook sat up in his chair. "That's where the tank was. The specter must have been held there."

"I think you're right," Ren said. "I *saw* it there, the first time I met Juwon. He'd taken my blood—I didn't know for what purpose at the time, but it was for that *thing*."

Jaeil, who'd been quiet, leaned forward in his chair. "What you're describing . . . ," he said, "mind manipulation, magic harvesting, these aren't powers attributed to demons."

Sunho shook his head slowly. "Mithril enhances what's already inside you; it wouldn't give you magic, not like the powers Ren is describing."

A silence fell over them as they each considered the possibilities.

"Whatever it is," Jaeil said, "something about it is pivotal to Juwon's plans—the greater demon in the sewers revealed as much. And even if Juwon fled after the Festival of Light, the specter remained here because . . ."

"Because of me," uttered Ren. "Because my blood wasn't enough.

It needs my Light for some reason. It *still* needs it. It hadn't finished when I scratched it with my knife."

"Which means it'll be back for more eventually," Jaeil said.

"But not on the Floating World," said Sunho, "now that it knows we're aware of it." They'd taken precautions beyond more guard patrols and locks on Ren's doors—Ren had ordered the hole in the wall beneath the wisteria tree sealed and filled the passage beneath her rooms with dirt.

"The meeting with the Volmaran prince," Jaeil said. "That's when they'll make their move. Juwon will want to act quickly now that we're onto him. The specter would stick out, which means *he'll* be the one to try something, perhaps by kidnapping you, and the best time to do it is when you're away from the Floating World. He'll likely either bribe or threaten his way into joining the delegation."

"If that's the case, then Ren can't be there to greet them," Wook insisted. "It's too dangerous."

"Juwon won't show up unless Ren is at the meeting place."

"You want her to act as bait?" Sunho growled.

Jaeil's expression was shuttered. "It's her choice."

"I'll do it," Ren said. "I have to meet the delegation regardless. Juwon won't know that we're expecting him. We can catch him unaware and stop whatever he's planning."

Sunho grimaced, but he didn't argue further. He'd known that would be Ren's answer.

"Should we not warn the Volmarans from the empress's household that Juwon might try to infiltrate their group?" Wook asked.

"We can't be certain that they're not working with the Black Robes," Jaeil said.

Ren nodded grimly in agreement.

"Teacher won't come unprotected," Sunho said. "He'll bring . . . contingencies."

"You mean demons," Jaeil said bluntly. "Or more specifically, vials of serum to *turn* people into demons. That's a strong possibility. That's why you'll join Hwani in protecting Ren. You'll stay close to her the whole time."

Sunho nodded curtly as the plan fell into place. They would catch Teacher, Sunho thought darkly. And if not catch him, then *he* would kill him.

"What if Teacher doesn't show up after all?" Wook asked, scratching his chin. "Does Ren need to become engaged to the Volmaran prince?"

Ren quirked a brow. "I have an idea about *that*."

AFTER THE OTHERS had left, Sunho met with Hwani in the gardens outside Ren's room.

"Thanks, Hwani," Sunho said, lifting his hand in greeting. "The meeting just finished."

She pulled the string of her chin strap and removed her guard's hat. With a sigh, she raised her face to the clear night sky. Sunho knew she was still feeling guilty that Ren had been attacked under her watch.

Ren didn't hold Hwani responsible, of course—the specter's powers were *supernatural*—but that didn't stop Hwani from blaming herself.

"You should rest," Sunho said. The other guard hadn't left her post since Ren's return. "I'll watch over the princess tonight."

Hwani tilted her head, eyeing Sunho from the side. "Oh?"

Heat crept up Sunho's cheeks. "That is, I'll guard her. From *outside*."

"Right." She grinned, and Sunho relaxed at her teasing. "I'll see you in the morning."

After Hwani had left, he approached the door to Ren's room, hesitating before crouching and knocking gently on the papered wood.

It opened seconds later, revealing Ren's surprised face. She drew the door back farther, ushering him inside.

"I told Hwani to get some rest," he said, then stood. He surveyed the dim interior of the room. A single lantern sat on a writing desk. "What were you doing?"

"I was writing a letter. I'm going to give it to the Volmaran prince with instructions to deliver it to the empress. I told her that I would give back the lands Sareniya had taken in the war. That is, if the people who live there even want that. And . . .

"That I don't wish to marry." Color had risen in her cheeks. "Not yet, at least."

Pressing her back against the door, she slid to the floor. Sunho joined her, stretching out his longer legs.

"How did we even get here?" she said with a sigh. "I wanted to be a nobody. A nobody can live a long, happy life. A nobody can keep their loved ones safe."

He thought of the conversation they'd had on the rooftop outside his apartment all those weeks ago. He'd wanted to be a nobody too, if that meant they could stay together.

"Whether you're nobody or a celestial maiden, I'll stay by your side," Sunho said. "I'll protect you, Ren."

She shook her head, resting it against his shoulder and whispering sleepily as her eyes fluttered closed, "We'll protect each other."

CHAPTER 23

REN

The Floating World
The Celestial Palace

REN CALLED A council meeting the following morning to discuss the arrival of the Volmaran delegation. She remembered falling asleep on Sunho's shoulder the night before. She'd woken alone on her bed, the blankets tucked neatly around her. Since arriving on the Floating World, it was the first time she'd felt rested.

She walked into the hall with her shoulders back, Hwani flanking her.

As she took her seat on the throne, Lord Pyo—a nobleman belonging to her great-uncle's faction—stepped forward. "Princess, before we begin the meeting, I'd like to address a startling rumor that has been circulating the palace."

Ren kept her head raised so that only her eyes looked down at the minister. "What rumor?"

"Is it true that you left the Floating World in secret the night before last, and only returned early the next morning? You were seen in company with Captain Jaeil, your uncle, and another, a young man of dubious origin."

Ren could see her great-uncle's hand in this, though he'd relinquished his honored position at the foot of the dais, instead standing far to the right of the aisle. Since his outburst in the hall a week ago, he attended the meetings yet hardly spoke, as if withholding his counsel was some great punishment for her. Ren imagined that he was biding his time until an opportunity arose to regain control over the council. She hadn't believed the specter's warning, that her great-uncle was conspiring with the general, but she had asked Jaeil to keep an eye on her uncle's whereabouts, just to be certain.

"The rumor is untrue," Ren said, voice clipped. "Now." She turned toward the left side of the aisle, which had grown in number in the week and a half since her arrival. "Have we chosen a meeting place in which to greet the Volmaran delegation?"

Lady Go stepped into the aisle, bowing low. "The Volmaran prince is said to be a patron of the arts. Might I suggest the Kumwhan Opera House as a meeting place?"

The name elicited images of a grand stage surrounded by a hundred glowing lanterns. At the center of the stage, performers in silks and painted masks would leap and twirl as the theater rumbled from the beat of drums.

"Is the opera house not in the eighth ward?" Lord Pyo drawled. "Your sister is the eighth ward minister, is she not?"

"She is, which is why I suggested it as the meeting place," Lady Go said smoothly. "My sister is a great lady. Our clan would be honored to make the necessary arrangements to receive a royal delegation."

Ren needed to consult with Jaeil, but she thought it an ideal setting. A play would provide distraction for the Volmarans, and a storied theater vantage points for archers, as well as clear exits. If they could get Juwon inside the theater, he'd be unable to escape.

"Yes, I think that would work perfectly," Ren said. "Thank you."

When the meeting was over, Ren waited for Lord Muyeol to take his leave before approaching her aunt.

"May I speak with you?" she asked.

Lady Maya tilted her head in a questioning manner but didn't object, following Ren into the small chamber behind the throne room.

"I wanted to share with you a . . . suspicion I have," Ren began. She'd thought long on whether to share her misgivings with her aunt. If she brought them up during one of the council meetings, she knew Lord Muyeol would only dismiss her, as he had before. "I believe Juwon, the scientist behind the attacks in the Under World, will attempt another one during the meeting with Volmar."

Lady Maya seemed to consider her words, her brow furrowing. "I understand your concern," she said slowly, "but it's unlikely he will make an appearance. His facility was destroyed."

"But what if he comes back?" Ren insisted.

"His likeness has been spread throughout the Under World," Lady Maya said. "Once he sets foot past the Wall, he will be recognized immediately. Why would he risk returning?"

"Because of what was done to his brother."

Lady Maya lowered her gaze. "That was a long time ago."

Ren was surprised to hear a hint of melancholy in her aunt's voice. Her breath caught as she was struck by a thought. "Did you know him?"

"Not personally, but . . ." Lady Maya closed her eyes, as if reliving painful memories. "Your mother and I were cousins, but we rarely spoke. Your father, however . . . he was my friend, ever since we were children. We grew up together. He was as much a prisoner of this world as your mother was—trapped by bloodlines, the never-ending struggle for power, for wealth.

"He is no longer of this world," Lady Maya said softly. "His family, too—the general saw to that. What I'm trying to say is that I understand how pain can . . . linger, how it can make you act in ways you might regret . . ." She trailed off and Ren wondered if her aunt was regretting how she'd treated *her*. "But the past is the past," she said firmly. "Juwon won't return. He *can't*. We—*you* should look toward the future. Your main concern should be the Volmaran prince, on securing the alliance and ending this war. *That* is your role in all this. Do you understand?"

Ren turned away, unable to meet her aunt's gaze as she nodded. "I understand."

THE NIGHT BEFORE the delegation was set to arrive, Ren paced her room. Everything appeared to be going to plan—Lady Go's sister had agreed to host the delegation at the opera house—yet still, she felt nervous.

She didn't know if the specter would return. Its purpose had been to lure her out to the edge, but why? It had the ability to take on her mother's appearance, and it had stolen her Light, if only temporarily . . . If it was a new kind of demon, it was the most dangerous they'd ever encountered.

Her only reassurance was that once they captured Teacher, they'd have answers. And whatever the specter was, they would hunt it down and destroy it.

The door to the back garden slid open. She whirled around as Sunho slipped inside, shutting the door silently behind him. "I told you to lock this at night," he chided, though there was warmth in his voice.

Ren rushed toward him, colliding with his chest. "I didn't think I'd see you before tomorrow." She leaned back to look at him. He'd trimmed his hair, and he looked so handsome, it made her stomach flutter.

"Jaeil's arranged it so that I'll be a part of your main guard, along with Hwani. I'll be with you the whole time."

Her heart soared. She trusted Hwani to protect her, but she'd feel more reassured with Sunho there.

They were standing so close. She could feel his heartbeat through his chest, hard and fast against her own. She hadn't been alone with him since the night they'd returned from the Under World.

She saw the familiar spark of blue in his eyes before he pulled away from her. "Give me a minute."

She nodded, wrapping her arms around herself. She knew that he drew back not because he was rejecting her but because he wanted to stay. Though she couldn't help wishing he would hold her a little longer.

After a few minutes, he seemed to get the Demon back under control, because his eyes were clear when he looked up at her.

"What does it feel like?" she said quietly. "The Demon?"

"Like I'm running a fever. My pulse quickens and my blood feels hotter. My senses become more heightened, too. What does it feel like for you?" he asked. "Your Light?"

She closed her eyes, trying to put the sensation into words. "Like a warm embrace, but from the inside."

As she said the words, she felt a twinge of guilt. He'd just told her the Demon's power felt uncontrollable, like a sickness, but when she glanced up at him, he was smiling softly. "That sounds nice," he said.

They stared at each other a while longer. Warmth infused Ren's body; she felt happy, blissfully so.

"I should go," Sunho said.

Her stomach plummeted. "But you just got here!"

"I wasn't supposed to come. Jaeil warned me not to, with the rumors . . ." She knew he spoke of the rumors Lord Pyo had mentioned. She'd wanted to laugh at his phrase, "of dubious origins." They *knew* Sunho had arrived with her, and that he was from the Under World. If Lord Pyo had meant to shame her for her conduct and the company she kept, he'd misjudged her sorely. "But I wanted to tell you about tomorrow, and . . . I wanted to make sure you were all right.

"We don't know exactly what will happen tomorrow," he said, his voice wary. "Teacher might not even make an appearance. But if he does . . . there's a possibility you'll have to speak to him."

Ren shuddered, remembering the eerie chamber, the syringe he'd used to take her blood. He was even more of a threat to her now, if Jaeil was right and he was planning on kidnapping her.

"And if the Volmarans are aware of Teacher's plan, and are helping him . . ." Sunho frowned. "There could be a fight. You'd be in the thick of it."

"I wouldn't be alone," she said, remembering their promise last night. *We'll protect each other.*

He smiled at her words, though even his smile couldn't hide that he was worried.

Ren was worried, too, but she had faith in Sunho. In Jaeil, Hwani, and Wook. And in herself. She wasn't without her own means of defending herself, though she wished she'd had more time to visit Saya, or her other ancestors, to learn more about her powers.

Tomorrow they would capture Juwon and secure a truce with Volmar, ending the war.

Tomorrow it would all be over.

Her eyes strayed to Sunho, lingering. And maybe, just maybe, the two of them could leave all this behind. Once he had full control of the Demon and she was free of the Floating World, there would be nothing to stop them.

It felt like a fantasy, but she would hold on to it for as long as it would last.

CHAPTER 24

SUNHO

The Under World
Kumwhan Opera House, the Eighth Ward, the Core

THE KUMWHAN OPERA House took up a whole city block of the eighth ward. Unlike the palaces of the Floating World, made of crystal and glass, the theater was composed primarily of rich, ruby wood imported from the Occupied Territories. Dozens of paper lanterns cast a burnished glow over the building, making it appear almost gilded.

A great crowd had gathered outside to await the arrival of the celestial maiden. From his position across the street, Sunho searched among them for glints of steel, evidencing concealed weapons. A dark-haired woman wearing a silken black dress embroidered with purple flowers was directing ushers into the crowd to make a path for Ren's arrival.

"Well, if it isn't Sunho." He turned toward the voice lilting from the alleyway behind him. "You've come a long way from the emotionally closed-off mercenary we met outside the ninth ward mithril factory."

"Yurhee," he said, greeting her with a warm smile. "It's good to see you."

“See, Tag? Would the Sunho of a month ago have greeted me with such sublime affection?”

Tag quirked his lips, amused.

“*Tag*,” Yurhee breathed. “Is that a smile I see on your face?”

Tag turned his back entirely to Yurhee. “We’ve been watching the opera house for the past two days,” he informed Sunho, “ever since we got your missive.

“Most of the performers and stagehands are from companies that regularly work with the theater,” Tag said. “Only a few were hired at the last minute to fill smaller roles. We followed them after rehearsals, asked around about their backgrounds. There’s nothing to indicate any of the people contracted by the theater have ill intentions.”

“There are two exits to the building,” Yurhee added. “The main entrance, and another at the back for the workers. Everyone entering and exiting the theater who are not part of the Sareniyan court are vetted by the eighth ward minister.” Yurhee pointed to the woman in black Sunho had spotted earlier.

“Thank you,” he said, returning his gaze to his friends. “You’ve been a great help.”

“Good luck,” Tag said. “We’ll keep a lookout from here.”

A HALF HOUR later, Jaeil arrived, accompanied by a contingent of soldiers from Hagye Military Base. Sunho repeated Tag and Yurhee’s report as they entered the theater through the main entrance. The interior was just as opulent as the opera house’s exterior facade; hundreds of lanterns with low-burning candles gave the room a mysterious, dreamy ambiance.

The most significant feature of the room was a square stage that took up the entirety of the middle, surrounded by silk cushions from which patrons would view the performance.

The wood of the stage appeared almost black. It gleamed in the candlelight like water, reminding him of the cavern floor of the mithril labs. The likeness settled uneasily upon him.

"There's been a change of plans," Jaeil said as they walked around the stage toward the back of the theater where Ren would sit with the Volmaran prince. A short, elevated dais had been erected at the north side, where someone had placed two elegant cushions side by side, one embroidered with the double wings of Sareniya, the other with the rising tiger of Volmar. "Hwani will guard Ren alone, at least on the dais itself.

"Teacher will recognize you." Jaeil cut off Sunho before he could protest. "He won't reveal himself if your presence is known. You'll be close, but out of sight." He nodded toward the thick red curtains behind the dais. "Humans pose little threat to him, but he'll at least fear you, the successful results of his own experiments."

Sunho didn't like the association with Teacher, but Jaeil was right. Teacher valued his own work enough to fear Sunho the most.

Which was why Sunho had to be the one to kill him. He tightened his hand on the strap of his bag, which held his sword.

"We'll puncture holes through the curtain, from which you'll be able to view Ren and the stage. Assuming you can't also see *through* physical objects."

Sunho watched Jaeil unconsciously raise his arm to cover his chest.

"I can't," Sunho drawled.

Jaeil dropped his arm. "Right."

They continued up a flight of stairs to a second-floor balcony, where Jaeil directed archers to stand two paces apart, leaving room for the Volmaran archers to take their positions.

Once that was finished, he rejoined Sunho by the balustrade. From their vantage, they could observe the entirety of the theater except directly below them. Minister Go stood near the entrance, directing a team of workers in setting up small individual tables for each of the patrons. The tables were inlaid with mother-of-pearl, each with a porcelain tea set and plate layered with flower-shaped cookies.

"To tell you the truth," Sunho said, "I never would have imagined that you and I would work together."

"Yes," Jaeil said slowly, "it's . . . quite unfathomable. Although, technically, we had been working together from the start, when I hired you back at Bo Dan's. You just betrayed me."

Sunho scowled.

"But I acknowledge we had a rough start, especially when you crashed through my skylight with the intention of killing me."

Sunho sighed. He should have known better than to attempt civil dialogue with Jaeil.

Jaeil's gaze moved upward, to the vaulted ceiling of the opera house. "I should put archers on the roof, shouldn't I?"

"Yes," Sunho said dryly.

THE THIRD PARTY to arrive at the opera house was Ren, in the company of Lady Maya, Lord Muyeol, and the rest of the Floating Council. They were greeted by Minister Go, who led Ren to the dais. Hwani immediately spotted Sunho and Jaeil on the second-floor balcony, nodding subtly in their direction before returning her gaze to Ren.

Ren took her seat, bowing to the minister, who then left to see to the comforts of the other guests. Also in attendance were the other seven ministers of the Under World—excluding Minister Jo, who had been revealed as a traitor.

Time seemed to slow now that they had only to wait for the Volmarans to arrive. Sunho shifted his feet, his mind going through one possible scenario after another.

They'd taken every precaution. Jaeil, barring his unfortunate personality, was competent. It came as a surprise, but Sunho *trusted* the captain. Jaeil wanted Ren's safety almost as much as he did.

He could see Ren clearly from where he stood. Her gaze was fixed on the side of the stage where a group of costumed performers had gathered, and he knew she was likely thinking of her own troupe, the one she shared with Wook and her aunt.

Since this was a grander production, there was a team of twenty performers, two of whom were costumed already as trees, tottering onto the stage to plant themselves at the northeast and southwest corners.

A fanfare of trumpets signaled the arrival of the Volmaran delegation.

With a nod to Jaeil, Sunho climbed back down the steps. He took up his place behind the curtains, peering through the crude slits in the fabric. His field of vision was limited by the curtains, and he noted with dry amusement that the power to see through physical objects would have been helpful. Still, he had a clear view of the Volmaran prince as he approached the dais.

He appeared to be in his late twenties, slender, with a graceful walk.

"Your Highness." He lowered himself at the waist in an elegant bow before lifting his head. "The rumors are true. You are a great beauty, just as your mother was."

Sunho felt his jaw twitch and the beginnings of a headache, but he kept himself focused. The prince wasn't *wrong*. Ren was stunning, dressed in a white flowing robe, the long, wide sleeves trailing almost to the floor.

"Had you ever met my mother?" she asked, and there was a hint of yearning in her voice.

"No, but my grandmother held her in high esteem. She was great friends with your grandmother. She never believed the general's claims about the circumstances of the celestial maiden's passing. The war began shortly afterward, otherwise she would have properly mourned your mother's loss."

Ren was quiet for a long moment, and Sunho had to resist the urge to go to her. Then she said softly, "You honor me. I hope our countries can return once more to the peaceful relationship we had in the past."

"Yes, that is also my greatest hope."

Climbing the steps of the dais, the Volmaran prince took the seat beside her. Sunho rolled his neck, easing some of the tension in his shoulders. His gaze caught on Jaeil, who had moved and now stood at the southern end of the balcony. He couldn't have *seen* Sunho, but the captain's eyes were narrowed in his direction regardless, as if to warn him off.

Sunho frowned. He wasn't so jealous that he'd interrupt a meeting to *end a war*.

"I'd like to introduce you to my adviser, Hannabi," the Volmaran prince was saying.

An icy sensation shot down Sunho's back, and he slid his hand toward the hilt of his sword. A cloaked figure stepped forward, removing his hood with gloved hands.

He looked much changed; his face was gaunter, his spectacles gone, but it was *him*.

Ren, for her part, didn't react. He was bold to show up without a disguise. He'd met Ren in the mithril labs; he must know she'd recognize him.

"It's a pleasure to meet you, Your Highness," Teacher said. His voice was soft, sibilant. It made Sunho want to grind his teeth.

"The pleasure is mine," Ren said smoothly.

Minister Go directed Teacher to a seat, far enough from the dais to let Sunho ease up on the handle of his sword.

His gaze went to the balcony to see Jaeil had disappeared. He spotted him a few seconds later on the ground floor, a few feet behind Teacher—he'd noticed him, too.

Loud booms echoed across the theater. They came from two performers pounding on barrel drums on the sides of the stage.

Bright lanterns were lowered from the rafters above as a young man wielding an axe walked to the center, his face painted in white clay with charcoal slashes for eyebrows. He was followed by a performer holding an empty straw basket. She wore a mask that depicted an elderly woman with grooved lines in the cheeks and a heavy scowl. She kicked him in the side with her foot, then gestured at the empty basket, as if to chastise him for not providing enough food for them to eat. Then a flute trilled as a deer leaped onto the stage.

Sunho had never seen this play acted out in person; nevertheless, he knew the story by heart. "The Woodcutter and the Celestial Maiden." He tore his gaze away, sweeping the audience for signs of danger, but each face appeared to be riveted to the performance.

The trees began to sway as the woodcutter, after sparing the deer's life, followed it into the forest. Reaching the pool with the waterfall, the woodcutter hid behind one of the trees.

A hush fell over the crowd as a lone zither denoted the arrival of the celestial maidens.

Sunho was so attuned to Ren that he heard her indrawn breath the moment she sighted them.

The maidens were dressed in robes of blue, yellow, and red. Stitched across the back of each of the robes were silver embroidered wings. An upbeat tempo began to play as the sisters removed their outer robes and frolicked in the pool, their joy infectious.

Distracted as they were, they didn't notice the woodcutter sneaking up from behind the tree to grab one of the robes from the lowest branch. It was the red robe, belonging to the youngest maiden.

Catching sight of the woodcutter, one of the sisters pointed. The music turned frantic, as the two older sisters gathered their clothing, leaping away. They turned back, beckoning for their youngest sister, but she was trapped, her wings stolen. As her sisters fled back to the heavens, she fell to the ground, weeping.

Until this moment the performers hadn't made any sounds, leaving their voices to the instruments, but now the young performer sobbed, her cries wrenching the otherwise silent theater.

Sunho's headache grew stronger, a throbbing at the back of his skull.

He swept his gaze toward Teacher, whose hand was in his pocket, drawing out an object.

Sunho burst from behind the curtain. At the same time, Jaeil grabbed Teacher's wrist, twisting. The object—a syringe—fell to the floor, where Jaeil crushed it beneath his boot.

Mutterings of concern rose up from the audience, and a few seconds later the electricity crackled, lighting up the entirety of the room.

"What's the meaning of this?" the prince demanded, having stood up from his seat. "Unhand my adviser."

"This man is a Sareniyan," Jaeil declared loudly. "A traitor."

From the ground, Teacher's shoulders started to shake, but not from fear. He was laughing. Sunho's stomach pooled with dread. He whipped his head toward the audience, many of whom were standing now.

A scream tore across the theater, followed by an awful cracking—the sound of bones breaking as they reshaped anew. A woman—one of the Volmaran delegates—was transforming, her back arched at an unnatural angle as her fingers extended into claws, her teeth into fangs.

Hysteria overtook the room, Sareniyans and Volmarans alike scrambling to escape. Sunho raced toward the demon but was stopped by the surge of the crowd.

He leaped onto the stage. Most of the performers had fled, although one of the trees had fallen over, the actor inside prone on the stage. He jumped over them, spotting the newly transformed demon attacking a noblewoman. Sprinting, he dropped to the ground, skidding along the floor of the stage. He let the momentum carry him into the air, landing with his sword embedded in the demon's chest.

Shouts erupted from the second floor, where another human had turned.

How many were there? How was this even happening? His gaze caught on an empty syringe near where the first woman had transformed.

She had injected *herself.*

He felt a burst of movement behind him, twisting around to see a demon race across the stage toward Ren. It sprang at her, claws extended.

Hwani pierced the demon with her spear. Behind her, the prince had drawn his sword, looking on with horror.

He hadn't known. How had Teacher wormed his way to the prince's side, and in such a short period of time? Nothing made sense. Sunho felt like there was a gaping hole that they'd all overlooked.

Where is Teacher?

Sunho spotted Jaeil fighting against another demon, its jaws snapping near his face as he held it back with his sword. An arrow whistled through the air, cleaving through the demon's neck from where Wook crouched on the balcony.

There. Teacher had almost reached the main entrance. Sunho called upon the Demon, using its strength to leap across the stage, slamming Teacher into the ground.

"Was this your plan?" Sunho growled.

"Oh, Sunho," Teacher said piteously. "You have much to learn."

A piercing sensation ripped through Sunho's skull. He released one hand to grip his head, his fingers digging into the side. The pressure was unbearable, like a vise slowly tightening its jaws. And Sunho suddenly realized the theater had gone silent; everyone had ceased their attempts to escape.

A figure garbed in a black cloak stood at the entrance.

Its face was grotesque, with a wide, gaping mouth and crooked horns.

Except . . . Rohoon had worn a cloak to disguise his transformed state. This demon had rounded fingers beneath its gloves and a body that appeared human. It was only its face that was monstrous.

Slowly the man lifted his hand, removing the mask.

Sunho felt his hands loosen their grip on Teacher, and he staggered backward.

"I killed you," Sunho whispered as he gazed upon his brother's face.

CHAPTER 25

REN

The Under World
Kumwhan Opera House, Eighth Ward, the Core

THE MAN IN the demon mask, who'd been present at the laboratory in the mountains, was Sunho's brother, Junho. The resemblance was undeniable. While his brother was thinner with long, straight hair, their coloring was the same, as were their eyes—their irises dark but for that spark of blue.

Sunho staggered backward, dropping to one knee.

Ren lunged forward only for Hwani to call out to her, "It's not safe, Princess!" Her guard's expression was grim as she tightly gripped the handle of her glaive.

Ren swept her gaze over the theater. They'd stopped Juwon, yet it didn't feel like a victory. Cries of pain echoed from the shadows surrounding the stage. At least three Volmarans had transformed into demons. She didn't know how many innocents were injured or killed in the onslaught.

Half the Sareniyan nobles had fled out the back door, including Lord Muyeol. She spotted Wook on the second floor, directing guards to help carry out the wounded, and her aunt assisting an elderly woman from where she'd fallen to the floor.

Ren rounded on the prince. "Were you an accomplice in this?"

"No!" he cried. "I don't know what's going on!"

Ren frowned. His horror appeared genuine, and his people had also been caught in the slaughter. "But you introduced Juwon as your adviser."

"Juwon?" He shook his head. "I've known Hannabi since I was a boy. He advised my mother before me. Even the empress called him friend in their youth. He's like a grandfather to me."

A pounding sensation began at the back of her skull as her gaze darted to Teacher, prone on the ground. That didn't make sense. Juwon was her mother's age, younger even. Had he somehow manipulated the prince into seeing someone different, with an illusion, perhaps? But how? No one could have the power to do that, not even with mithril. Sunho had explained it to them: *Mithril enhances what's already inside you.* It can't *give* someone magic.

Unless someone *else* had put an illusion over Teacher.

Her vision turned hazy as an odd, dreamlike sensation swept over her. She felt a person approaching; a black silk dress with purple peonies entered her line of vision.

"Come with me, darling," Minister Go crooned, "it's dangerous here."

She began to lead her down the steps of the dais, Ren's skull pounding even harder.

With great effort, she turned her face toward Hwani but her guard stood still, her eyes unfocused. She didn't protest as Minister Go guided Ren down the remainder of the steps and onto the stage.

The minister was stunning. How had she not noticed her beauty before? Her elegant updo had come undone, and her obsidian hair tumbled around her shoulders like tendrils of night.

She appeared to change the more Ren stared at her. Her features became more youthful, her cheeks plumping as her lips reddened. She seemed somehow to grow taller, her back straightening; Ren winced as her nails dug into her shoulders, leaving crescents in her skin.

Ren's heart beat wildly in her chest like a caged bird, though she didn't know why. Minister Go was helping her, wasn't she?

As if from a distance, she heard Jaeil shout her name.

"Ren!" she heard Sunho cry; his voice sounded panicked.

Ren raised her face. Minister Go truly was beautiful, stunningly so. *Like my mother*, she thought. Except Aria had never worn the expression on the minister's face—something about the curl of her lips seemed . . . cruel.

The wooden floorboards of the stage rattled beneath her.

Ren stumbled, falling as Jaeil swept his sword toward Minister Go. With a hiss, the minister sprang backward, moving quicker than Ren would have thought possible. Then Sunho was there, his attack fierce as he brought his sword against the woman's neck. She appeared to slip beneath it, gliding away.

Ren gaped at them from the floor. Both Jaeil and Sunho were viciously attacking Minister Go, were trying to *kill* her. She'd never seen Sunho so murderous, nor witnessed such a lethal look in Jaeil's eyes. They moved in tandem, attacking in turns, relentless. Jaeil lunged at Minister Go, shifting aside at the last minute as Sunho leaped from behind him, plunging his sword downward. Minister Go jerked backward with a shriek; Sunho's blade connected with the train of her gown, slicing through the fabric. Bolstered, they moved to either side of her, sweeping in for a joint attack.

The minister raised her hands. Ren screamed as a burst of wind erupted from her palms, flinging both Sunho and Jaeil backward.

Ren scrambled to her feet as Minister Go turned toward her, no longer attempting to hide the hatred twisting her face.

A roar echoed across the theater. *Sunho.* He was transforming, his features elongating as wings erupted from his back. With a furious cry, he launched himself at the minister.

He was almost upon her, teeth bared, claws extended, when something large slammed into him. *Another demon.* They skidded across the stage, clawing and snapping their teeth at each other's throats.

The other demon was larger than Sunho, stronger. It pinned him to the floor. Feathers sloughed from the demon's face, revealing Junho's beneath.

"Stay down, brother." Junho's voice was cold, devoid of emotion.

The fogginess over Ren's mind ceased as she faced the imposter.

"Who are you?" Ren demanded. But for the performer who'd fainted, prone inside the tree costume, she and the imposter were alone on the stage.

The woman had shed all vestiges of Minister Go. Whoever she was, Ren had never seen her before. Everything about her was lovely, from her long swanlike neck to her oval face and straight brows. Only her eyes were disconcerting: black, endless pools of night.

"I am Sareniya," the woman said, "the first in this world to bear such a name."

"I don't understand," Ren whispered, though she feared that wasn't true. From the beginning, the specter had been different from Juwon's other experiments; *she had magic.* But more than that, Ren knew she spoke the truth because of how strongly she resembled her mother.

"I've come back to destroy those who stole from me what I treasured the most," Sareniya said. "Even you, darling girl, the last of my descendants."

The first celestial maiden. Somehow Juwon had brought her back, using mithril. *Mithril and my blood.* She realized, with horror, that in the labs he'd taken blood from her for the purpose of reviving Sareniya. But she hadn't regained all her powers—that's why she'd lured Ren to the cliff. In order to be restored fully, she needed Ren's Light.

Ren reacted out of instinct. Drawing Light from her core, she flung it at Sareniya's chest.

It appeared to envelop her, only for the Maiden to sweep through it, catching her by the throat. A barrier of Light erupted around them—though this was different from Ren's, tinged with otherworldly blue—spreading to the outermost parts of the stage.

Ren cried out as the Maiden began to siphon Ren's magic; her chest tightened from the pain as her body weakened. She grabbed the Maiden's wrist, channeling her Light in an attempt to burn her.

"Don't resist," Sareniya soothed. "It'll be over soon."

Ren could hear Sunho roaring in the background. Arrows rained down upon the shield, but none could penetrate Sareniya's Light.

"This is the only way." Sareniya rested a hand on Ren's cheek. "How small you are, how young and weak. You remind me so much of myself, she who'd only known love before it was stolen from her. I am grateful for you, young one. Because of your magic, I will be restored. It is right that I should take your Light, as it was me you inherited it from. After all, we are family, you and I."

"No," Ren gasped. "My family would never hurt me. You're not my family. You're a *monster*."

Sareniya's eyes flashed. Ren screamed as Sareniya pulled the Light more forcefully from her than before. Ren felt her heart quickening, her vision dimming. She was draining her of Light, *of life*.

Suddenly, Sareniya screamed.

From behind the Maiden's shoulder, Ren saw a knife embedded in her back.

Thrown by the performer who'd been prone on the ground, the costume of the tree tossed aside.

"How dare you hurt *my* niece!" a strong, familiar voice shouted fiercely.

Ren's heart lurched. "Auntie!"

The Maiden slung a spear of Light at her, but Auntie was agile. She leaped away, then spun back. Grabbing Ren's arm, she wrenched her from the Maiden's grasp. Together they stumbled off the stage. Ren was quickly surrounded by guards; Hwani, released from the Maiden's influence, threw her glaive up before her. Jaeil, bleeding from the side of his head, directed archers to surround the stage, firing arrows at will.

Sareniya screamed, ripping the knife from her back, and released gusts of wind to destroy the arrows. Her body pulsed with Light; she rose into the air as great wings erupted from her back, shimmering silver and ethereal blue.

Auntie had saved Ren before Sareniya could drain her of Light entirely, but it didn't matter. She'd taken enough to complete the process that she'd started on the cliff.

She was restored to her original form, the most powerful maiden to have ever lived.

She released a stream of Light that shattered the ceiling of the opera house. Nobles screamed as pieces of wooden beams showered over them. Sweeping her wings downward, she launched into the air. The force sent a strong blast of wind outward, intercepting another wall of descending arrows. She then flew through the broken ceiling and into the black sky of the Under World.

Junho let go of Sunho. Winging through the theater, he grabbed Teacher in his talons before flying through the ceiling. Sunho rose to his feet, having transformed back into a human. He lifted his gaze skyward. The anguish on his face matched the devastation in her heart.

In one night, everything had changed. A new enemy had appeared, more powerful and frightening than she could have ever imagined. One who, if she couldn't gather the courage and strength to defeat, would destroy everything and everyone she loved.

ACT THREE

Celestial Maiden

CHAPTER 26

SUNHO

The Under World
Inner Courtyard, Hagye Military Base

SUNHO SAT ALONE in the inner courtyard of Hagye Military Base, on a raised platform that overlooked the yard where the soldiers carried out their morning drills. It was empty—those stationed at the base had been deployed across the nine wards with orders to quell the looting and riots that had erupted overnight. Hysteria had overtaken the city, many having witnessed Sareniya's flight from the opera house. She hadn't immediately fled but circled the city.

The people of the Under World might have welcomed her with awe and veneration, as they would have a goddess, if it weren't for the demon in her wake. It soared behind her, a black void against the dark sky.

The demon. A monster. *His brother.*

Junho was alive.

Sunho closed his eyes, reliving the moment in the opera house when he'd turned to find his brother standing there.

He'd been frozen, unable to comprehend the reality of what he was seeing. An enemy could have stabbed him through the heart, and he wouldn't have felt it, so great was his shock.

He didn't understand how Junho was alive; Sunho's hand had punched through his brother's chest.

Except he did: Before Teacher had injected Sunho with the serum, he had injected Junho. It must have taken hold, the mithril healing what should have been a fatal wound.

Sunho pressed the arch of his palm to his forehead, applying pressure to the throbbing ache that hadn't dissipated, even with Junho's departure. Junho had been human before his transformation—not like Rohoon, or the greater demon in the sewer—which meant he was like Sunho. He had the ability to transform into a demon and back again.

But if Junho was like him, why hadn't his brother searched for him? For more than two years now, Junho had let Sunho believe he was dead, that *he* had killed him.

"Sunho."

He lifted his head to see Tag approaching across the yard. There were dark circles beneath his eyes, and strands of his silver hair stuck up in various directions.

"Jaeil said I could find you here."

Sunho moved aside to make room for Tag on the platform. Jaeil had sent him to Hagye before Lord Muyeol could return from where he'd fled and demand his capture. There was no hiding what he was now.

Sunho had spoken to Ren first before leaving; she had agreed with Jaeil's assessment. They needed to let the events of the night settle before making any moves. Sunho, at least, was reassured by the presence of Ren's adoptive aunt. She'd been encircled in Auntie's embrace when he'd left the theater.

"Here," Tag said, and Sunho glanced over to see that he was

holding out a small scroll in the air between them. "Yurhee told me to give this to you."

Sunho unwound the string and unrolled the slip of paper.

Congratulations on finding your brother, she wrote in messy, bold characters. *The resemblance is uncanny.* She'd proceeded to draw a crude sketch of a demon with black feathers and overlarge fangs.

Beside him, Tag groaned, pressing his hand to his face. He must have read the message over Sunho's shoulder. "She promised she'd written something meaningful," he mumbled.

Sunho quirked his lips. Carefully rolling the scroll, he slipped it into the pocket of his jacket. "It's meaningful," he said.

For several minutes, neither of them spoke. Then Sunho leaned back with a sigh. "My brother was at the laboratory in Volmar."

"I know—he was wearing that same mask." Tag hesitated. "He let us go that night. He saw us, but he didn't alert anyone."

Sunho closed his eyes, concentrating on his memories, the confusion and longing he'd felt flying through the storm, the fury at being captured and shot with the tranquilizer.

Then, as if a veil had been lifted from his mind, he heard his brother's voice.

We seek out the ones we love. But love in the heart of a demon is no different than hate. And so we seek out to destroy those whom we love the most.

"He spoke to me," Sunho said. "That night." He repeated Junho's words.

"It's the same for you, isn't it?" Tag said quietly. "You wanted to protect Ren from the Demon, so you stayed away from her. What if your brother hadn't come back because he was afraid of hurting *you*?"

Sunho had wondered that, too. "But why is he helping Teacher?

He's the one who did this to us." Sunho wanted to tear Teacher apart for what he'd done. How could Junho not feel the same?

"Are you going to go after him?" Tag asked. "When we first met, that's what you wanted the most. To find your brother. You know that he's alive now."

That *was* what he'd wanted. For two years, that had been the reason behind every one of his decisions. But everything had changed that day in the reed field, when he'd woken up beneath a red umbrella.

He didn't know how to feel about Junho, but he did know one thing for certain.

"I'm not leaving Ren," Sunho said.

Tag nodded, as if he'd expected that answer. "You know, Yurhee's feeling pretty put out that she hadn't clocked Minister Go as an imposter."

"She shouldn't blame herself. If that creature truly is the original celestial maiden, then she'll have powers that we don't even know about."

"She'll be hard to beat," Tag said grimly. "There's only one person who has a chance."

The fear that had started with the appearance of the celestial maiden returned in force. Demons he understood—he would fight a hundred, a thousand of them, if it kept Ren safe—but a celestial maiden was different. He didn't know if he could protect Ren, and that terrified him.

Sunho jerked his head up at the sounds of dozens of pounding feet. Soldiers wearing the winged insignia of the royal guards stormed into the courtyard.

Sunho and Tag were quickly surrounded. Sunho considered resisting but let them bind his hands behind his back. They were outnumbered, and technically Sareniyans weren't his enemies, though they clearly disagreed.

He and Tag were ushered from the courtyard onto the parade grounds, where Lord Muyeol stood surrounded by his personal guards.

Jaeil was with him. The captain looked furious, his eyes narrowed, though he appeared to be showing restraint, for now.

Sunho was harshly pushed to the ground by his shoulder; his knees dug into the dirt.

Sunho had expected Lord Muyeol to order his capture, but not so fast. He'd underestimated the nobleman's determination, or his hatred.

"A soldier from the Under World," Lord Muyeol read aloud from a scroll in his hand, "indentured at eight to the army, served six years in a scouting unit before being reassigned to the Forty-Fourth." He closed the scroll in disgust. "I'm curious how you and my great-niece met, how she came to regard you with such . . . affection. Her mother had the same affliction. An Under Worlder and a Sareniyan. And she, not just a Sareniyan, but *Sareniya*. A queen. An empress. A goddess.

"*Your* queen. *Your* empress. *Your* goddess. She's so high up, a literal star, and you—you've always belonged in the darkness."

"I've heard quite enough."

Jaeil stepped in front of Sunho, facing the noble.

"You might have the means to carry out unlawful arrests on the Floating World," Jaeil said, his voice icy, "but this is the Under World, and Hagye Military Base is under *my* jurisdiction."

"You're no better than him," Lord Muyeol sneered, "though your family hides it behind wealth and rank. Your ancestors were from the Under World."

"The princess chose me as military adviser," Jaeil retorted, nonplussed. "To gainsay me is to betray her."

"She's a child," Lord Muyeol said dismissively. "Uncouth. She needs to be controlled. She relies on orphans." His eyes landed on Tag with a sneer. "Traitors." His gaze speared Jaeil. "And monsters." Sunho flinched. "She will be the destruction of us all."

"Or the only one with the power to save us," boomed a new voice.

The guards parted to allow an older man through.

"Commander Su." Jaeil bowed. "Your sense of timing is impeccable, as always."

"And you never disappoint in your ability to infuriate those who are meant to be your allies," Commander Su responded, but with undeniable affection.

He turned to one of the soldiers accompanying him. "Please escort Lord Muyeol to his aircraft. An accounting of his actions will be delivered to the princess upon her return."

"You'll regret this," the nobleman seethed as he was led away.

"Is it wise to antagonize such an *ally* as him?" Jaeil said mildly.

"Perhaps, but it appears we have bigger problems."

Jaeil immediately sobered. Sunho helped Tag to his feet, and together they waited for Commander Su to speak.

"There are sightings of demons to the north, over the border of Volmar. A new war is coming, and if we're not ready, it'll swallow both the Floating World and the Under World whole."

CHAPTER 27

REN

The Floating World
The Temple of the Goddess

REN OPENED HER eyes to see that she was in the meadow again. With a groan, she pitched backward onto the soft grass. In the temple, when she'd lowered herself into the pool, she'd hoped to wake up in Saya's time, or in a time where another maiden with powers had lived. The pool clearly had a different idea.

She gazed up at a bright, cloudless sky. A flash of deep blue caught the corner of her eye as a magpie winged overhead. She followed it to where it landed a short distance away, hopping and pecking the ground where one day the zelkova tree would grow. She wondered if that's how the seed for the tree would arrive in the meadow, as stolen treasure ferried in the beak of a magpie.

She sighed—this was how she was occupying her time, ruminating about the origins of a tree instead of thinking of ways to stop Sareniya. Last night, she'd immediately left the opera house, and the Under World, for her safety. And this morning, she was supposed to have conferred with the council on preparations for war, but instead she had come here. She rolled from her back onto her stomach, and when that was uncomfortable, rolled over onto her back once more.

"Stop that, you're squashing the flowers."

Grandmother sat on the same rock by the pond as she had the first time, a wooden fishing rod in hand.

With a sigh, Ren joined her, flopping onto the grass and pulling her knees to her chest.

The red buoy sank in the water, but the fish didn't take the bait; the buoy plopped back to the surface, continuing its lively bobbing motion.

Not for the first time, she wondered how far back Grandmother and Rina had lived, what the Floating World was like when they walked its gardens. Had Grandmother known a celestial maiden with powers in her lifetime? When was it that her ancestors had begun to lose their magic?

It was warm in the meadow, but Ren felt a shiver go through her. Losing her wings would be like losing a part of her soul.

Not wishing to dwell on it, she raised her gaze to sweep the meadow. "Where's Rina?" she asked.

Grandmother chuckled. "After your visit, she took it upon herself to start training. I think you inspired her."

Ren hadn't thought time passed here when she herself wasn't present—Saya had said as much. But perhaps it was different for Grandmother and Rina. Ren was still uncertain what it was she was supposed to learn from them.

"What are you two blabbering on about?" Rina appeared from beneath the trees at the edge of the meadow. "Shouldn't *she* be training?"

"You're right." Ren got to her feet. "What sort of exercises were you doing? Is it all right if I join you?"

Rina sniffed. "Well, since you asked so nicely . . ."

Rina had set up an obstacle course in the woods, which included making Ren run up a hill with a pile of sticks on her back and leaping over rolling logs of wood. Hours later, sweaty and exhausted, they splashed into the pond. At the same time, Grandmother nearly caught a fish, hollering in outrage when it escaped during the commotion. Ren threw water over Rina, who in turn splashed Grandmother. All three of them were soaked by the end, and Ren was breathless with laughter.

It felt like a rebellion, to laugh after what had happened in the opera house, to laugh when she knew what it was that she had to do.

As the sun sank from the sky, she found that she was reluctant to return to the temple.

"I'm sorry I can't help you with what it is you truly wish to learn," Grandmother said.

Rina scoffed. "One shouldn't attach so much importance to magic. Most people don't even have it. I think it's braver to have no magic at all and stand up to more powerful foes."

Ren smiled, thinking of Auntie. "Perhaps." She sighed. "But this foe is not just powerful, she's not of this world. She's our ancestor, the original celestial maiden."

Ren told them everything—how Sareniya had lured her out to the cliff, taking her mother's form so that Ren would believe it was her mother's ghost; how she'd begun to siphon Ren's Light and was stopped, only to finish the process at the opera house, regaining her full strength.

"She wants revenge for what was stolen from her. She wants to destroy the Floating World."

"Maybe you're right," Rina said grimly, "and going through training exercises like today won't be enough."

Grandmother shook her head. "There must be a way to defeat her."

"How did she even come . . . back?" Rina asked. Ren explained to them about Juwon and his experiments.

"He must have discovered something that belonged to her," Ren said, remembering the line she'd read in her mother's journal: *He says that Juwon has found something down in the dungeons.* "I saw an old tapestry in a room showing celestial maidens bathing in a pool. Beneath it was an empty chest. If he discovered something inside—her original robe, perhaps—then maybe he used that to bring her back." In combination with Ren's blood, and mithril.

"Remember this," Grandmother said grimly, "whatever she is, whether a reincarnation of Sareniya or a revenant, she's not a true celestial maiden; she's a monster brought back into this world using mithril. Even if she doesn't believe it, deep down she knows that there's only one. The last. *You.* Only you have the power to stop her."

Ren drew in a deep breath, a coldness sweeping through her. She'd already known, when she'd watched Sareniya transform into her winged form and take to the sky, that *she* would be the one to face her.

"That's also why she'd taken your mother's form, wasn't it?" Grandmother murmured. "To hurt you. To weaken you."

"Why would it hurt you to see your mother?" Rina asked with a frown.

Ren felt the coldness spread further.

"Am I wrong?" Grandmother asked softly.

"It's not her fault," Ren whispered. "My mother had a difficult life. I think I reminded her of everything that had been taken from her."

"Hmm," Grandmother said, careful not to bestow judgment.

"She sounds awful," Rina said flatly.

"No," Ren said, but she was oddly relieved that there was someone who was on her side.

"Your time with us is coming to an end," Grandmother said as the meadow pulsed around them, the skies darkening and the trees bending inward.

"So soon?" Rina said.

"I have to go back anyway." Ren sighed again. "Today's my coronation."

She recalled the conversation she'd had with Lady Maya, on returning to the Floating World.

She had stood together with her aunt on the deck of an imperial airship. From the railing, they'd gazed down upon Sora, dawn spreading over the city like the wings of a phoenix. "At a time like this, when we face a powerful foe," her aunt had begun, "it is paramount that we have a strong ruler who can unite the Floating World, the Under World, and the Outer Territories.

"My father will no longer be an opposition to you," her aunt had added, "once you're queen."

They had received news that Lord Muyeol had attempted to arrest Sunho, and had only been stopped by Commander Su's arrival.

"Will you accept this responsibility?"

Ren had felt the mantle of the celestial maiden settle on her shoulders. "I will."

"Your coronation is today?" Rina asked in disbelief. "And you came *here*?"

"I wasn't sure if I was ready. I am now." She was careful not to show them the fear she truly felt. "Thank you, Rina, Grandmother." She held their gazes. "I needed this."

"Visit us again soon," Rina said hurriedly. "I'll try to think of ways to help you."

By then, it might be too late.

"Take care, Ren!" she heard Rina shout before she was swept from the meadow.

Back in her rooms, she changed quickly from the clothes she'd worn at the temple into something more suitable for a coronation before reaching for the pack of food items she'd hidden away earlier. She rechecked the contents before placing the pack, and a sword she'd taken from the armory, out of sight behind the paper screen.

Her attendants slid back the doors as Head Maid Eun arrived to help her with the last of her attire, but it was Auntie who stepped over the threshold.

Before the opera house, she hadn't seen her for almost two months; at that time, Little Uncle had been in danger of succumbing to the mithril in his blood, and Ren had been preparing to leave without telling her.

She realized, with dismay, that she was about to do it again.

"You look beautiful," Auntie said. It was then that she noticed her aunt gripped a lacquer chest by the handles. "But you're missing one last piece."

She placed the chest on the floor, then withdrew from it the crimson robe.

As Ren peered closer, she saw that there were new images embroidered onto the back of the robe. A bamboo flute. A paper fan. A red umbrella. She'd thought the robe had belonged to her mother, but she could see now that she'd been mistaken.

It had always been meant for her.

"Did you know who I was when you saved me?" Ren asked as Auntie helped her tuck first her right arm, then her left, into the sleeves.

"No, but I knew who you *would* be." Auntie's voice had taken on a teasing lilt. She moved to face Ren. "My niece."

She smiled at Auntie's words, only for it to falter. "Your life would be so different if it wasn't for me."

Auntie would have left the Floating World and returned to her husband and brother, none the wiser. She would have been safe. They *all* would have been safe.

"That's true," Auntie said, wrinkling her nose. "I'd have fewer white hairs."

"I always loved your hair." The color reminded her of the warm bark of trees.

Reaching out, Auntie smoothed the collar of the robe with her fingers. "The truth is," she said, "I *did* know who you were. I had seen the general's soldiers searching for you in the woods."

Ren thought of how frightening that must have been, realizing that she had likely been the only witness to a treasonous act, how much courage she'd had to save Ren.

"When I took you from the Floating World, I was attempting to tangle threads that had been woven in the stars. I should have known the difficulties of tampering with destiny. Although I like to think that I bent them, just a little."

Ren laughed. "I think so, too."

"And maybe added a snarl or two."

"Little Uncle would warrant being called a sizable one."

Auntie winked. "Oh, he would take offense to that, wouldn't he?" Finished with her efforts, she stepped back. "For years I tried to protect you, perhaps hindering you at times, when I wouldn't allow you to use your magic—"

"No," Ren said adamantly. She refused to let Auntie believe, even for a moment, that she'd ever held Ren back.

"—I was afraid. Not just of what might happen to you if you were discovered, but also . . . I was afraid of losing you." Auntie's expression was gentle. "We are acrobats and actors, meant to pry and tease, on the outside of history, never the ones changing it. But you weren't a troupe performer to begin with, were you?"

"I'll always be a troupe performer," Ren said fiercely.

"I didn't save you because of who you were, or what you would become to me." Ren choked back a sob as Auntie's eyes glimmered. "How could I know that you would become my whole world?"

THE DOORS TO the great throne hall opened with a groan and Ren walked down the aisle, the crimson robe trailing out behind her.

"Her Royal Highness, Princess of Sareniya," the herald announced, her voice echoing through the vast hall.

She'd been given a crystal scepter for the occasion, and she held it tightly. The hall was more crowded than the day of the general's trial. It wasn't just council members present, but their families, and other nobles from Sora. The Volmaran prince stood with Lady Go's family, who had been cleared of all suspicion of treason. She even spotted the head priestess from the temple, accompanied by a few of her acolytes. Though it was a group of pale, darkly clothed people who snagged her attention—Under Worlders.

She turned her gaze back to the throne, holding her head high.

To the right of the dais, in the place of honor Lord Muyeol once occupied, stood Commander Su.

"My queen," he said, bowing low at the waist.

"Commander," she returned fondly. She was relieved that he appeared uninjured, and unchanged but for a few more lines on his venerable face.

Lady Maya stood at the foot of the steps, holding a crown in her gloved hands. The crown was composed of crystals, the tines like the spires of the castle. Ren lowered her head and her aunt placed it above her brow.

She then climbed the steps of the dais, turning to face the hall.

Her stomach fluttered uneasily. She had never been one to suffer from stage fright, but there were so many people she didn't know, faces she'd never seen before. Then she spotted Little Uncle standing with Auntie, whose expression was serious. But Wook had a smile for her, as he always did.

Jaeil had taken his place beside the commander, a steadying presence. When they'd been children, he had watched over her. It seemed he would continue to do so, for as long as she needed him.

Finally, her eyes landed on Sunho standing at the back of the hall, between Yurhee and Tag. If Sunho had been gazing at her before, she'd caught him in a moment when his thoughts had turned inward. She knew he was thinking about his brother, how he was alive, how he was allied with Juwon.

Ren yearned to go to him, offering him comfort just as she sought her own. But she knew that if he looked into her eyes, he'd see the truth of what she planned.

When his eyes lifted to hers, she looked away in guilt.

Lady Maya's raised voice rang out across the hall. "All hail Sareniya, Queen of the Floating World."

LATER THAT EVENING, Ren smiled reassuringly at her attendants. "I've had an exhausting day. Could you please tell Head Maid Eun that I wish not to be disturbed?"

"Yes, Your Majesty," the attendants murmured, sliding her door shut.

She waited until they'd blown out most of the lanterns in the hall before quietly slipping the robe from her shoulders; it would only slow her down. She grabbed the satchel she'd packed earlier, and the sword.

The difficult part would be sneaking past Hwani, but her guard was expecting intruders breaking *into* the palace, not out of it. And anyway, Ren only needed to climb onto the roof. She'd always been agile, and she made it to the top without making a sound, her boots balanced lightly on the curved tiles.

She waited until a cloud covered the moon, then, spreading her wings, leaped into the sky.

CHAPTER 28

JAEIL

The Floating World
Royal Guesthouse, the Celestial Palace

A NIGHT AFTER the attack at the opera house, Jaeil found himself faced with the most excruciating task—he had to visit his father.

When Iljin was general, he'd had three commanders, one of whom was Commander Su. The others, Habin and Naksol, hadn't yet declared for Ren. They both hailed from the Under World, proud and fiercely loyal soldiers. Admirable traits in one's allies; infinitely frustrating now that Jaeil needed them to cooperate. Their enemies would be back—he needed to convince the other two commanders, who led the right and left wings of the army, to return to fight for Ren. In order to do that, however, he needed his father to first release them of their oaths.

He knew what he had to do, and yet . . . he found himself putting it off, looking over reports on the new ordinance that banned children fifteen and under from being conscripted into the army, as well as correspondence from Sana's physician, who complained of her complete lack of regard for his professional and highly lauded opinion.

His return letter to the doctor was sympathetic; to Sana, he admonished her with affection, pressing upon her his desire for her full recovery so that she might return to him. He missed his lieutenant, even if she was infinitely annoying.

Somehow, he eventually ended up near the royal guest chambers, where honored family members or guests of the queen were housed when they visited the palace. It was on the opposite side of the dungeons entirely.

He was loitering in the courtyard, admiring the gardeners' particular choice of floral arrangements, when a door slid open and Wook stepped out from his room.

Catching sight of him, Wook stumbled. "J-Jaeil. I mean, Captain. What are you—why are you here?"

Jaeil studied the smaller boy. He appeared to be in a hurry, his curls slipping from beneath his headband; oddly, he was carrying an assortment of weapons, but without their blades—sword handles and wooden poles.

"What are those for?" he asked, ignoring Wook's question.

Wook glanced down at the weapons, as if he'd forgotten he'd been carrying them. "You know how Ren's been visiting her ancestors?" he said. "One of them told her that long ago, celestial maidens used to wield weapons made of mithril. I thought I could make her a weapon, something to help channel her Light."

"That's a brilliant idea."

A pinkish color rose in Wook's cheeks.

Jaeil felt a lightness in his chest—satisfaction that he'd pleased him.

"Were you waiting for someone?" Wook asked. "Um, I'm the only one staying here at the moment . . ."

"No," Jaeil said. When Wook waited for him to elaborate, he admitted, "I'm supposed to meet my father."

Wook's eyes widened. "I'll go with you!" he shouted.

The tension eased from Jaeil's shoulders.

"Aren't you busy?" he asked, nodding at the pile of half-made weapons.

"No, I mean— It's all right." Wook dumped the pile, albeit gently, onto the floor. "I have some time now. I'll go with you," he repeated, more calmly.

"All right," Jaeil said, acknowledging to himself that it wasn't chance that had brought him to the guesthouse.

Wook filled the walk to the dungeons with chatter. "We realized that mithril doesn't affect Ren, like it does humans. It also doesn't affect *me*, not after I was ill, and I'm guessing Sunho, as well." He had a pleasant voice, soothing. "Mithril is stronger than iron, than steel. With Sunho's enhanced strength, it stands to reason he'd need a stronger weapon, *the strongest.* And Ren would need something that could withstand her Light, though I don't think a sword is suitable for her. Too unwieldy . . .

"Sorry." Wook laughed, pressing his hand to the back of his head in a self-conscious gesture. "I'm blabbering. I . . . I always enjoyed smithing. If I wasn't an acrobat, I might have been a weapon maker."

"Don't be sorry," Jaeil said. "I'm keen to see these weapons. I hope you'll think of me, as well, in your list of beneficiaries. Though perhaps not the mithril part. I am human, after all."

His words seemed to have the opposite of the intended effect because Wook went completely silent. In any case, they'd reached the entrance to the dungeons.

They were greeted by the same guards from his sojourn with Ren, who handed him another lantern. The dungeons were damp and cold, not unlike the mines, though they were significantly darker without the presence of mithril.

Jaeil had been a guest here himself for the duration of the trial, and he shuddered at the unpleasant memories. His father's cell was at the very end of the corridor.

Gesturing for Wook to stay back, he approached the bars.

The cell was sparsely furnished with a cot and a desk. It reminded him of Juwon's room in the mithril mines. A lantern had been placed on the desk, though the candle within had almost dwindled to the nub.

His father sat on the cot, his boots on the floor of the cell. He didn't look up with Jaeil's approach.

"I wondered if you'd ever lower yourself to visit me." The general's deep, cold voice penetrated even the shadows of the cell.

For anyone else, Jaeil might have had a quick rejoinder, but this was his father. He'd learned a long time ago not to defy him. Already he felt fatigued. Jaeil thought of Sareniya sucking the Light from Ren, and wondered if this was but a fraction of what she'd felt.

He removed a scroll from his coat. "I have a document here I want you to sign," he said, not wasting time. "I've brought your seal."

For the entirety of his childhood, he'd seen it on his father's great oak desk, the emblem of their clan etched into the body—a white horse on a black field. He held it between the bars.

His father rose from his seat. He took both the scroll and the seal. Jaeil watched as he slowly unrolled the vellum, reading the statement Jaeil had written in bold, dark ink.

I, Iljin, former general of the Sareniyan army, relinquish all claims and forfeit the oaths of my commanders.

"Perhaps it wasn't such a hardship to lower yourself to visit me," his father said, "when you've already debased yourself serving her."

"The difference between Ren and me," Jaeil said softly, "is she would spare your life for my sake. While I would never ask her to."

Fury swept over his father's features, quickly stifled. "My entire life, nothing has disappointed me more than you. You covet nothing, and so squander your potential. My inheritance, the Floating World, would have gone to *you*.

"It was my gift," he spat. "You threw it away."

"Your gift to me was war and bloodshed," Jaeil said, and he didn't try to hide the pain in his voice, as he might have a month ago. "*Her* gift to me was peace." For a few soft, stolen moments in the meadow, he'd had that. "You can save someone with a simple act of kindness; not once did you save me."

The general affixed his insignia to the scroll, throwing both back through the bars. The seal hit the far wall, clattering across the stones. Jaeil leaned down to pick up the scroll. The seal was an heirloom, passed down from father to son; he left it there.

"You are weak," the general said as Jaeil walked away, his voice echoing down the long corridor, "and no son of mine."

Jaeil exited the dungeons with Wook, gripping the scroll tightly in his hands.

He closed his eyes. All he needed to do now was speak with the commanders, but he found he'd lost all sense of urgency. He'd never spoken in such a way to his father before. He waited for the crash of emotions one might expect to feel following such a fraught confrontation, but oddly, his mind was quiet. His hand trembled, but only slightly.

"Is there anything I can do?" Wook asked. Jaeil felt a gentle pressure on his shoulder—Wook's hand. He thought of the words he'd spoken to his father: *You can save someone with a simple act of kindness.*

"No," Jaeil said. With his eyes still closed, he lifted his face toward the sky. In this moment, beneath the sunlight, with Wook beside him, he felt at peace. "Just this will do."

Walking with Wook back to the guest quarters, he noticed guards running toward the main palace. Following behind, they discovered the courtyard filled with royal guards and soldiers. Jaeil shouldered his way to the center, where Commander Su stood with Sunho, and—

"Hwani," Jaeil said, alarmed. "What are you doing here? Where's the queen?"

The bodyguard appeared shaken. "The queen is missing," she said. "Since this morning, possibly earlier."

Jaeil's mind raced with possibilities. "Were there signs of a break-in?"

"She wasn't taken." All eyes turned to Ren's adoptive aunt. "She's going after Sareniya," Auntie said grimly. "She's going to face her alone."

"I should have known she'd do this," Wook said, cursing himself. "She left Gorye Village alone to save me. I should have stayed with her after the coronation. I should have—"

"It's not your fault." Jaeil grabbed Wook's hand to steady him. "You mustn't blame yourself."

A commotion behind him snagged his attention, and he turned to see Sunho parting the crowd, soldiers scuttling out of his way.

Jaeil let go of Wook, who'd gone still at his touch. Rushing after

Sunho, he grabbed his shoulder. Twisting the other boy toward him, he lurched back as shadows leaped off him.

"I'm going after her." Sunho had begun to transform, his voice shredded and guttural.

Jaeil shook his head. "We need you here." When they inevitably confronted Sareniya, Junho would be with her. Jaeil was a skilled swordsman, but he had no illusions that he'd be able to hold his own against Junho's Demon form. They needed Sunho to fight him.

"*She* needs me," Sunho cried, and Jaeil's expression softened, seeing the fear and desperation in the other boy's eyes.

"We have to be smart about this," he said slowly. "We don't know where she's gone."

"The Demon can sense her. When I transform, *I* can sense her."

Jaeil held his breath as the shadows behind Sunho grew, taking the shape of the Demon within.

"Can you control it?" Jaeil demanded. "Are you certain you won't hurt her, that you'll be able to tell her and your enemies apart?"

Sunho closed his eyes, his brow furrowed, as if even now he struggled to control the Demon.

"I can guess where she's gone," called out a new voice. The crowd stepped aside for Yurhee and Tag. "During the airship battle, when the Volmarans attacked," Yurhee said quickly, "another aircraft took advantage of the commotion and captured Sunho. Ren, Tag, and I followed it to a hidden laboratory on the Volmaran side of the Haebaek Mountains.

"There was a large board there tacked with diagrams, drawings," Yurhee continued. "One in particular seemed to catch Ren's eye. It was an illustration of a feather. It looked exactly like *this*."

From her pocket, she pulled out a feather, its edges limned in mithril.

"The Maiden, Sareniya, whoever she is, dropped it that night in the opera house. I don't know if the laboratory is where Ren's headed, but if I was going after *her*, that's where I'd look first."

"That's enough to convince me," Commander Su said, and began calling out orders to his soldiers, who dispersed. "We don't have time to gather a great force, so we'll take our three fastest ships," he informed Jaeil. "We'll resupply and pick up soldiers in the valley."

The valley. Jaeil felt as if he'd been struck in the chest.

Commander Su grasped Sunho by the shoulder, oblivious to Jaeil's turmoil. "Have patience." To the others, he shouted, "You have your orders. We leave within the hour!"

Hwani followed behind the commander, along with Sunho, Yurhee, and Tag, leaving Jaeil and Wook alone in the courtyard.

The Valley of the Rise and the Fall. It was located in Gaya Pass, the only pass that led through the Haebaek Mountains. As one of the few access points from Sareniya into Volmar, it held a strategic position, making it one of the most fought-over territories in the war.

Two months ago, before the light appeared in the east, before he'd sent Sunho after Ren and discovered the existence of demons, he'd fought in a battle in that valley. Only by some miracle, and Sana's intervention, had he survived.

A part of him wondered if it was his destiny to go back, that having eluded Fate once, they hungered for his blood.

"Jaeil." He turned toward Wook, who stood beside him. His lips were trembling, his eyes young and fearful. "Bring her back safe," he beseeched Jaeil softly.

The blow he'd felt earlier had dissipated, leaving only a feeling of rightness, of his destiny aligning—for all his past mistakes, *for being his father's son*, it was always his fate to save her.

"I'll her bring her back," Jaeil promised, "whatever it takes."

Wook's eyes widened. "Jaeil—" he started.

But Jaeil was already walking away, his gaze on the future. Or maybe it was on the past—he could no longer tell the difference.

CHAPTER 29

REN

The Haebaek Mountains
Occupied Territories

REN FLEW AS fast as her wings could carry her, gripping her satchel and the sword tightly to her chest. She flew in a northeasterly direction toward the Volmaran border, where she knew, somewhere within the Haebaek Mountains, lay Juwon's hidden laboratory.

She knew it wouldn't be long before she was discovered missing. She just hoped that Jaeil could convince Sunho not to follow her.

Sareniya was too powerful; she'd flung Sunho and Jaeil aside like they were chaffs of rice in a field.

She believed Sareniya was arrogant enough to face Ren on her own, but if Sunho had come with her, then Junho would defend his mistress.

Ren wouldn't force Sunho to fight his brother.

No, it was her responsibility to defeat Sareniya; she'd known it the moment Sareniya had fled through the ceiling of the opera house. Perhaps even before then. When she'd taken Ren into her arms, and Ren's heart had swelled only to break into a thousand pieces.

A clash of thunder ripped through the sky. She screamed as a lightning bolt seared the air above her, sending her into a tumble. The sky broke open, inundating her with a deluge of icy rain. With great effort, she righted herself, flying recklessly through the downpour. It was like swimming through an ocean storm, the wavelike winds crashing over her. The Haebaek Mountains loomed ahead of her, large and forbidding. Warily, she lurched in their direction.

The ground was far below. She didn't think she'd have enough energy to gain altitude should she seek shelter on land, and so she searched for an outcropping. She spotted one beneath a pine tree jutting out from the face of the mountain. She flew toward it, landing roughly on the small ledge. Rocks crumbled beneath her, and she pressed her chest to the cliff face, holding her breath. When the ledge didn't collapse entirely, she sank to her knees.

She quickly drew back against the wall. She didn't release her wings but wrapped them around herself as she brought her knees to her chest.

Her thoughts strayed to Sunho, who was likely panic-stricken by now. She wished she could reassure him. *Be patient a little longer. I'll defeat Sareniya and then I'll come back to you, and then we'll go home, together.*

Though where was home? It wasn't the Floating World with its pristine halls, nor was it the valley, which she could no longer see clearly—even when she closed her eyes, as she did now—the images blurry and fading, like a memory that was slowly being erased.

She didn't know how she could sleep; she was battered and exhausted and the pine tree offered little in the way of shelter. Still, she found herself floundering into oblivion.

She woke in the meadow to the far-off rumble of thunder.

"Ren, what's wrong? Are you all right?" She turned to where Grandmother approached through the swaying grass, Rina beside her.

Rina's eyes narrowed. "Where are you?" she asked sharply.

Ren then noticed what Rina had; she was soaked, though it wasn't raining in the meadow.

"I'm somewhere in the Haebaek Mountains, near the border of Volmar."

"Why would you—?" Grandmother started.

"You're going after *her*, aren't you?" Rina accused.

Ren winced at the harshness of her words. She turned to Grandmother, beseeching. "It's like you said, isn't it? Only I have the power to stop her."

With a huff, Rina stomped away across the grass.

"That's right," Grandmother said, taking Ren's hands. "She's not a true celestial maiden, but you are. You're stronger than her. Remember that, Ren."

"How can you be sure?"

"Because you're my descendant. 'Cause you're descended from *all of us*."

After bidding Grandmother farewell with an embrace, Ren went in search of Rina. She found her crouched in the dirt, in the same place where one day the zelkova tree would grow.

She had a stick in her hand and was scrawling in the dirt. "You can still go back. It's not too late. To the Floating World. To the people who care about you."

"I can't," Ren said. "I'm so close." She hesitated. "Grandmother has faith in me."

Rina threw down the stick, turning to face her. Ren had seen the younger girl sulking and vexed, but never furious. "She doesn't know what she's saying. Maybe she wants to believe that there's magic in her blood, enough to pass down to you. That there's magic in us, too."

Rina wiped her arms against her eyes, dislodging tears. "I want to believe that, but not at a risk to *your* life."

"If I can defeat her. If I can—" Ren swallowed. "If I can kill her, then this will all be over."

"You're being a fool! You're not ready to fight her. What have you learned here? How to carry sticks up a hill? She has *magic*, stronger than yours, you said it yourself."

"I have to try," Ren whispered.

Rina turned around, crouching in the dirt once more.

"Rina . . ." She didn't want to part like this.

"If you die, you won't visit us anymore," Rina said in a small voice.

"I promise I won't die."

"You can't make that promise," Rina said in a voice so soft Ren had to strain to hear it. "No one can make that promise."

THE STORM WAS raging still when she awoke, the rain cold and punishing. With a groan, she staggered to her feet, unfolding her wings. Gathering her belongings, she slipped once more into the sky.

Rina's words echoed in her head; she knew the younger girl was only concerned for her, but all of this was *Ren's fault*. If she had only suspected something was wrong sooner, had told someone, then they might have prevented Sareniya from regaining her full strength. Except that she hadn't, because she'd wanted to believe that the specter had been her mother's ghost. It was because of her weakness that Sareniya was allowed to return.

She focused on Grandmother's words, letting them lift her spirits. *She* was the last celestial maiden. Ren would channel her guilt and her anger and destroy the imposter, and if Rina's warnings tugged at her conscience, she pushed them to the back of her mind.

A lightning bolt seared close by her, and she tumbled from the sky.

CHAPTER 30

JAEIL

The Haebaek Mountains
The Valley of the Rise and the Fall, Gaya Pass

JAEIL DREAMED ABOUT the valley. He'd been knocked off his horse and dragged in the mud, his boot caught in the saddle strap, cradling his arm, which had been shattered from the impact of his fall. Sana had saved him, throwing his good arm around her shoulder as together they'd stumbled behind the walls of the fortress.

He shouldn't have come back here. The valley was a death trap, a grave, *his grave—*

He woke with sweat on his brow, his cheat heaving. It was still dark, though the storm had passed. Reaching for his coat, he dressed quickly.

The three ships from the Floating World had arrived only a few hours before. The commander had left them on the plains below, while a small group made their way up the Fall, the first of two steep inclines. It leveled out where the garrison fortress was located in a small valley, before the incline resumed, somehow even steeper: Sareniyans called this the Rise. On the other side of it lay Volmar.

That evening they began the process of moving soldiers from the garrison onto the ships, with plans to enter Volmar at first light. They had the Volmaran prince with them, who was anxious to return to his people and warn the empress of the threat of Juwon and the Maiden. The prince also acted as a surety against an assault from Volmar's many-numbered and ferocious army, whose general—a hard-hearted, bloodthirsty woman—was his beloved aunt.

The purpose of gathering more soldiers, however, wasn't to fight Volmarans, but to *increase* their numbers. They weren't yet certain what enemies they might face at Juwon's compound. Jaeil had gone over its layout in great detail with Yurhee and Tag. Yurhee had even sketched him a map, which incorporated some eccentric drawings.

There were two factors that set alarm bells ringing inside Jaeil. The first was that the compound, from Yurhee's descriptions, didn't appear to host a great number of soldiers. The Maiden was powerful, but she was one entity; she couldn't stand alone against the Sareniyan army, even if supplemented by transformed humans. The second was that, according to reports from the ninth ward mithril factory, Juwon had a finite amount of mithril at his disposal, enough to make serums for those who'd transformed in the opera house, but not much more than that.

Jaeil had learned by now not to underestimate Juwon. He had a plan; Jaeil just couldn't figure out what it could *be*.

Stepping from his chamber in the fortress, Jaeil braced against a chill wind. He'd forgotten how much colder it was in the north. He glanced down the Fall to the plains below, where dozens of campfires surrounded the *Blue Tortoise* and the other two airships. While Jaeil, Sunho, Yurhee, and Tag had decided to stay the night at the fortress, Commander Su had returned to the *Blue Tortoise*, along with Prince Jinpyeong and Hwani, who'd agreed to guard the prince until Ren's return.

Not for the first time, he searched the sky for signs of Ren. It unnerved him that they hadn't seen any. They should have caught up to her; she had wings, but the ships had rotors. From the Floating World, Gaya Pass was the easiest route through the mountains. Unless she was waylaid by the storm . . .

Climbing the stone steps of the fortress wall, he approached the guards stationed there.

The soldier on duty raised her hand to her forehead in salute. "Captain."

"What's the status of the signal fires?" Jaeil asked. He gazed across the valley, toward the Rise where beacons had been positioned on the lower ridges of the mountains.

"No changes in the night, sir," the soldier said. "Even with the storm."

Jaeil frowned, pressing his hand to the cold stone of the battlements. The sentries attending the fires would put them out if something was amiss. Still . . . Jaeil couldn't shake the uneasy feeling that had rooted in his gut since waking—he blamed it on his dream and being back in this accursed place.

"Signal the sentries."

The soldier picked up a large, flat shield, sweeping it down over the signal fire. From a distance, it would appear as if the fire had disappeared, only to reappear.

He waited for the sentries to return the signal. One minute passed . . . then three . . . five . . .

The fires continued to burn on both ridges.

"Do it again," Jaeil said. The soldier repeated the action. The fires blazed brightly in the distance. "Keep signaling the sentries," he ordered, heading back down the stone steps to the courtyard below.

Someone had anticipated his next move and had brought him a horse. He grabbed the reins, mounting it in one leap.

"Wake the fortress commander!" he shouted to the guards manning the gate, who winched open the great wooden doors. "Tell her that I've gone to check on the signal fires."

A whinnying sound alerted him to another horse being saddled, and he turned to find Sunho seated atop a white gelding.

"You might need me," the other boy said, and Jaeil noted the dark shadows beneath his eyes. If he was feeling uneasy about Ren's whereabouts, Sunho must be fully on edge.

"Let's go."

They tore from the camp, galloping up the Rise.

They reached the mountains in less than fifteen minutes. The sentries' horses were at their post, and Jaeil and Sunho tied their own horses beside them, proceeding up the ridge on foot. They took a circuitous path to avoid being spotted before reaching a position where they could see the fire blazing on the ridge.

"No sign of the sentries," Sunho said, his eyes glowing eerily in the dark.

"Let's wait a couple of minutes," Jaeil said. If the sentries had been compromised, then it was possible whoever had killed them was still in the vicinity.

When there didn't appear to be any movement, he motioned Sunho ahead of him. "I'll take the left side."

They sprinted from behind the boulder the last few feet to the fire. Jaeil rounded the beacon, meeting up with Sunho, who'd come around the opposite side.

"Nothing," Jaeil said. "You?"

Sunho's expression was grim. "I found the sentries."

Jaeil swore.

Halfway down the ridge on the other side of the cliff were the crumpled bodies of two soldiers.

"I don't understand. They would have seen an enemy approach up the path." Jaeil shook his head. "Come on. We have to report this."

He unhooked the latch keeping the logs in place, letting them tumble over the ridge, before extinguishing the fire. In the distance, the first drums boomed—the warning for an attack. The fortress had seen their signal.

"*Jaeil*," Sunho said.

He stilled at the strain in Sunho's voice, turning slowly to see the other boy standing at the northernmost point of the ridge, where the Rise looked out onto the Volmaran plains.

As he walked over to join him, his heart drummed painfully in his ears.

At first, he couldn't make sense of the undulating mass, even as the disturbing sounds—guttural cries and cracking jaws—rose up from below. Then, on the ripped and shredded uniform of one of the creatures, he spotted the emblem of a rising tiger, and he realized, with horror, that he was gazing upon what was the once the Volmaran army.

They'd been transformed.

JAEIL AND SUNHO swept on horseback through the gate, trailing the scouts' ponies behind them.

The fortress commander, a grizzled woman who had outlived more battles than the years Jaeil had been alive, awaited them in the courtyard. Torches blazed all around her, illuminating in a harsh glow the grim faces of the remaining two hundred garrison soldiers.

"Tell me what you saw," she demanded.

"The Volmaran army, just outside the Rise. They've transformed." He grimaced. "All of them."

Her eyes narrowed. "How many?"

"*Thousands.*" Though Jaeil didn't understand how there could *be* so many of them; Juwon would have needed a mountain of mithril.

"We could take a stand at the fortress," said Yurhee, who was dressed in her flying gear, her goggles dangling from her neck, "use the walls to repel the brunt of the attack."

"There are too many of them," Jaeil said. "We'd be overwhelmed quickly."

"No, she's right," the commander growled. "We'll make our stand here; hold the fortress long enough for those on the plains to board the airships. I've already sent a dispatch rider to Commander Su." She signaled to another, who immediately leaped onto a horse, bounding toward the plains with the updated orders.

"If they get past the fortress, we'll hold them in the pass. From there, we'll head to the ships and retreat. We'll lose the fortress, but at this point, we have bigger things to worry about."

While the commander relayed her directives to the rest of the officers, Jaeil took Yurhee aside. "I need you to do something for me."

Not long after, he joined Sunho standing with Tag at the battlements, shoulder to shoulder with the soldiers at the garrison. Two hundred versus ten thousand—it would be a massacre.

The sun rose over the Rise; its rays speared the valley. Jaeil raised his hand, squinting into the piercing light. On his right, Tag withdrew an arrow from his quiver, while Sunho unsheathed his sword.

A great rumbling shook the valley as a horde of demons streamed over the Rise. The sheer number made it appear as if a giant wave were about to crash down upon them, threatening to drown them in gore and death.

Jaeil raised his voice above the wall of approaching sound. "They're demons, but they *can* be killed!" he bellowed. "Aim for the heart, or the neck!"

The first wave reached the walls of the fortress. Tag released an arrow. It struck a demon between the eyes that went down with a scream. Arrows rained from the walls, piercing skulls and chests. One monster fell, only to be replaced by three more scrambling atop one another. They clawed their way up the fortress, leaping onto the battlements. Soldiers stumbled back in fear. Jaeil stepped over a fallen soldier to stab a demon through the chest. He heard a gurgling death cry, whipping around to see another demon dragging a soldier over the wall. *Damn it.* There were too many of them; the soldiers wouldn't hold back the horde, let alone buy time for Commander Su and the rest of the army to escape.

Then Sunho swept down the battlements, demons falling beneath his blade like reeds of grass.

His assault galvanized the soldiers. They yelled out battle cries, hacking at the demons with new ferocity.

From outside the fortress erupted a deafening roar. A greater demon had appeared among the teeming horde, massive, boar-like, with tusks protruding from its gaping snout. It began charging toward the fortress at a breakneck speed.

Jaeil whipped around. "Get back from the wall!" he shouted. "Get—"

An unholy boom shook the fortress, as if a detonation had gone off. The stones crumpled beneath his feet, and he fell through.

He came to seconds later, surrounded by broken stone. He was lying on his back, a sharp ringing in his ear. His blurred gaze focused in time to see demons flooding through a giant hole in the wall.

Using his sword as a brace, he lurched to his feet. The greater demon was swinging its head from side to side, goring soldiers who came within distance of its mighty tusks.

"Hey!" Jaeil called out.

He knew now from the greater demon in the sewers that they retained some of their human faculties, even while in their transformed state. So Jaeil did what he usually did when trying to distract his opponent—tried to get under its skin.

Jaeil noticed the insignia affixed to the demon's torn uniform. "You were once a Volmaran captain, weren't you? Your smell may be worse but at least your looks are an improvement."

With a roar, the demon lunged at him, but Jaeil was prepared. He shifted backward, one hand gripping his sword while the other grabbed for the dagger at the small of his back. He flung it at the demon's eye. It struck, and the monster screamed. Jaeil quickly leaped forward, gripping the hilt of his sword with both hands as he plunged it into the demon's chest.

Blood splattered across his neck and face. Like in the sewer, the demon transformed back into his human state. He was a man no older than Jaeil's own father.

"It's not their fault," the Volmaran captain said, blood bubbling forth from his mouth.

"What happened?" Jaeil seethed. "How did you become like this?"

"It was *her*."

"Who—?"

"She appeared in the sky, spreading her wings. I'd never seen anything like it, *so beautiful*. But then they began to glow, blinding and *blue*. When it was over, all that was left was pain and darkness."

"What are you saying?" Jaeil grabbed the man by the collar. "The Maiden has the power to transform humans?" But the captain pitched forward, having succumbed to his wounds.

With a curse, he dropped the dead man, turning toward the courtyard.

He took a few steps, then staggered, hit with a wave of dizziness. He pressed his hand to the back of his head only for it to come away red.

"Retreat to the Fall!" the fortress commander shouted before she disappeared beneath a mountain of demons.

All around him soldiers were dying. They went stumbling down the Fall, as even more demons appeared on the Rise.

It was a never-ending torrent of death.

A great cry erupted from the center of the fortress.

Sunho. He was transforming. His body grew until he was twice the size he'd been the other times; if he'd been a crow before, he was a raptor now, tearing into demons with his claws, his teeth, batting them away with huge, bladed wings.

The remaining garrison soldiers retreated as the demons converged upon Sunho.

Jaeil grabbed the reins of a horse that had lost its rider, swinging onto its back. He turned to flee, only to look behind him.

Sunho was fighting the demons, but the amount was too great. He saw Sunho go under. Jaeil waited a beat. He didn't emerge.

Cursing, Jaeil turned back, hacking at demons as he drew closer to Sunho. He saw the moment Sunho lost consciousness, transforming back into a boy as he fell. With a lunge, Jaeil grabbed him before he could hit the ground, pulling him onto the horse in front of him.

"You can't give up now." Jaeil gritted his teeth. "Ren needs you."

He raged through the crush of monsters, hacking and chopping at any that got too close. The beast he rode was just as fierce, kicking and rearing with hooves rimmed in steel.

They broke through the horde, racing down the mountainside.

"Jaeil!" Tag was waiting for them halfway down the Fall.

Jaeil pulled on the reins, then, with a grunt, shifted Sunho to Tag's horse.

"What are you going to do?" Tag shouted.

"I have to block the pass," Jaeil said, fighting back another bout of dizziness. He couldn't lose consciousness. Not yet.

Tag must have realized what Jaeil planned because he nodded grimly. "Good luck," he said, before turning and fleeing down the mountain with Sunho.

Jaeil headed in the opposite direction, breaking off onto a short incline path.

He found what he was searching for a few leagues up the path. He sent a silent thanks to Yurhee for carrying out his request. Perched on a ledge was a small scouting aircraft.

After sending his horse in the direction Tag had fled, he climbed aboard the aircraft, unhooking the anchor. As it took to the air, he directed it toward the mountain, dialing the rotors to their maximum speed and shifting the controls forward. If the impact was strong enough, it could start an avalanche.

He'd known the moment he'd spotted the Volmaran army that this was his only course of action. With this, he'd make it so everyone still alive made it out, and he'd keep his promise to Ren: Sunho would be safe. Unfortunately, he couldn't keep his promise to Wook, but he had to believe he was giving the others a chance to find her, to bring her home. The face of the mountain loomed closer as he leaned forward on the controls; his vision flickered, blackening at the edges, and he wondered if he'd pass out before the collision.

This had been his fate from the beginning, the story that had been written for him, the son of a despot, his inheritance one of darkness and cruelty.

He thought of Wook, and that moment of peace, a feeling he'd been chasing his whole life. He regretted not grasping on to that moment a little longer.

His heart lurched oddly, and tears scalded the backs of his eyes—if this was his fate, then why did it feel wrong? Why did he want to find another way, to break from this path, *to live*?

Something knocked into the aircraft, pushing it from his flight path. He whipped around to see it was another aircraft, piloted by a wild-haired woman with a patch over one eye. *Sana.*

A great shadow fell over him. His aircraft rattled as something huge sailed overhead.

It was the *Blue Tortoise*, flying straight toward the mountain.

"Commander!" Jaeil shouted just as the massive airship rammed into the side of the mountain.

A boom rocked the pass, the impact causing an avalanche of rocks to plummet toward the Fall. The screams of demons cut off as they were buried beneath.

The commander had blocked the pass. He'd accomplished the impossible, had sacrificed his life, had saved them, *had saved Jaeil* . . .

Jaeil's aircraft skidded onto a ledge. Trapped inside, he was unable to move, even as rocks fell all around him. As he began to lose consciousness, he thought he heard Sana's voice, calling his name.

She was close, and so he could rest; he let oblivion take him at last.

CHAPTER 31

SUNHO

The Haebaek Mountains
The Valley of the Rise and the Fall, Gaya Pass

SUNHO WOKE WITH a start as the ground jolted beneath him. He was slung over the back of a horse, galloping full tilt down the Fall. Grabbing a sword strapped to the saddlebags, he fell backward, hitting the ground and tumbling across the dirt. Struggling to his feet, he pressed his hand to his stomach, where blood dripped from a slash of claws across his abdomen.

He heard the skid of the horse as Tag pulled on its reins, but he didn't wait for him, releasing his wings. They erupted from his back and he took to the air, pumping them downward in great sweeping motions.

He flew back toward the valley. The *Blue Tortoise* was embedded into the side of the mountain. Gigantic boulders tumbled down the slope, dislodged by the impact of the airship.

The avalanche had blocked off the pass entirely, and the demons screamed as they tried and failed to scrabble over the boulders.

In the valley, the fortress was overrun, its courtyard in shambles. He recognized the fallen bodies of the fortress soldiers, but also Volmarans, who had transformed after death, their faces stretched in horror.

Shuddering, he turned his gaze away, squinting against the sun's powerful rays as he swept the mountainside.

Junho was here. He'd sensed him earlier, when he'd been in his Demon form.

A figure in black robes stood at the edge of a cliff, his cloak rippling in the wind.

Sunho landed on the cliff several feet away, gripping the sword as he faced his brother.

Before, he'd been too shocked at Junho's sudden appearance to see the changes two years had wrought upon him. Junho's long hair hung lank around his shoulders, and dark circles shadowed his blue-rimmed eyes. His face was gaunt; he looked far older than his twenty years.

"I don't want to fight you, brother," Junho said. Even his voice was different, lacking the joy it once held.

The rage that had been simmering inside Sunho exploded.

"Why are you doing this?" Sunho shouted. "Why are you helping him? You've been helping him for years, haven't you?" The night the soldiers of the Forty-Fourth had been injected with pure, unprocessed mithril—inducing the last and final stage of experimentation—Sunho had arrived at the laboratory only to discover Junho already there; he'd been wearing the same black robes as the scientists. "When did you join them?"

"About six months after we parted."

Sunho had suspected as much, but the betrayal still felt like a lash to the heart.

"Teacher's goal was to bring an end to the war," Junho continued, insistent, "to bring an end to Sareniya's rule. I believed in Teacher, the project. I wanted to create a world where children like us didn't have to fight." He closed his eyes as if his next words pained him. "Even if it meant sacrificing a few for the good of the future."

When he opened his eyes, Sunho could see the mithril flickering deep in his brother's irises. "In exchange for my help, I was promised that you would be kept out of the project. When you showed up at the laboratory that night, I was horrified. You weren't supposed to be there. It was *never* supposed to be you."

"And Rohoon and Heetae?" Sunho asked, his heart breaking.

Junho winced. "I'll never forgive myself for what happened to them."

Even while angry and confused, he knew why Junho had made his choices. His brother had always protected him. It was his role, ever since they were younger. At the orphanage, when there wasn't enough food, Junho would give Sunho his share. In the army, he took punishments that were meant for Sunho. By all logic, Sunho's childhood should have been filled with nothing but despair and suffering, but there had been moments of hope and lightness, even joy, because of his brother. He'd survived because of Junho.

"It's not too late to stop this," Sunho whispered.

"I can't come back to you, brother. My hands are red."

Sunho drew in a deep breath. "So you'll continue to protect Teacher, after everything. Do you still believe what he's doing is right? He's created an army of demons, resurrected a goddess who will stop at nothing until she has her revenge."

"He didn't create that army," Junho said. "*She* did."

"I don't understand—" Sunho started. But he realized Teacher couldn't have transformed that many humans into demons, not all at once.

"The Maiden is powerful. She not only has the power to turn

humans into demons, but she also has the power to turn them *back*. She can cure us. She can cure *you*, Sunho."

So this was why Junho was helping Teacher. Because he believed the Maiden would cure him.

"I know you've suffered. I know how the Demon makes it difficult to control your own body, your impulses. How it drives you to hurt the people you love the most."

Sunho lowered his gaze. Junho wasn't saying anything he hadn't already thought himself.

And yet . . . even if what Junho said was true, he didn't trust Sareniya. After destroying the Floating World and the Under World, she wouldn't turn them back, if she even had that power. She'd further use her army to destroy the Outer Territories and Volmar; she'd destroy *everything*.

No, there was no coming back from being a monster.

Sunho lifted his sword. "I don't need a cure. I *am* the cure."

He surged forward.

Junho threw back his robes; beneath, he held a silver sword, raising it to block Sunho's attack. Wings exploded from Junho's shoulder blades as he swept backward off the ledge.

Sunho followed, winging up with him in a vortex, the clash of their swords like crashes of thunder.

Mithril roared in his veins, his wings lengthening, the feathers turning to shards of mithril. He was faster than Junho, his wings powerful behind him as they hurtled him through the air. He was stronger, his attacks fiercer—Junho was weakening beneath his relentless assault. He would save Junho, even if it meant killing him.

The thought was cruel, it belonged to the Demon, except . . . he was in control. The Demon had answered *his* call.

He had a feeling then, like a rock dropped into a still pool. As if the Demon were weeping for him.

He raced toward Junho, his sword raised for a killing blow.

Junho closed his eyes, letting go of his own weapon.

Light bloomed across the sky over the valley. Sunho veered aside at the last moment as a beam of Light speared downward, demons screaming as they were incinerated.

Floating above the canyon, her wings aglow with mithril, was the Maiden.

CHAPTER 32

REN

The Haebaek Mountains
The Valley of the Rise and the Fall, Gaya Pass

SHE WAS HERE. Sareniya hovered over the valley with outspread wings, her feathers long and sleek, her wingtips as bright as the stars. Ren's own tufted wings were huddled around her where she'd landed on an outcropping.

After the lightning strike, she'd tumbled from the sky. She'd woken hours later, tangled in the branches of a tree. Though scratched and battered, she'd flung herself north, sensing, at last, the faint presence of the Maiden's Light. She'd lost her satchel in the fall, but had managed to keep her sword, gripping it tightly to her chest.

The valley below teemed with demons, screaming wretchedly as they tried to break through the massive wall of rock that had formed from the avalanche.

Even now, boulders tumbled down the mountainside from where the *Blue Tortoise* had crashed into its face. The front of the airship had been completely destroyed. The pilot who had stayed aboard had made the ultimate sacrifice. Ren knew who that hero was—the *Blue Tortoise* had only one commander.

The Maiden shrieked, the sound like breaking glass. Ren wrenched her head skyward, watching as the imposter dove over the valley and down the Fall. Leaping from the outcropping, Ren took off in pursuit.

The Maiden landed on the plains, where the last of the soldiers who'd been stationed at the fortress were scrambling onto the remaining two airships.

She lifted her hand, fingers splayed.

"No!" Ren screamed as Light erupted from Sareniya's palm, searing a path through the soldiers and cleaving through the side of the closest ship. Agony ripped through Ren, and she reached for a flurry of wind, flinging it toward Sareniya. It pummeled her in the back, and she stumbled. Whipping around with a shriek, she unleashed another beam, this one aimed straight toward Ren.

She released her wings, jumping out of the way and tumbling to the side just as Sareniya's Light seared the air, leaving scorch marks in the earth. As the fire dissipated, Ren gazed at the marks, tinged blue with Sareniya's Light. Grandmother's words slipped over her:

Remember this, whatever she is, whether a reincarnation of Sareniya or a revenant, she's not a true celestial maiden; she's a monster brought back into this world using mithril . . . Only you have the power to stop her.

This version of Sareniya might be powerful, but Ren could still defeat her.

Her magic must be finite, like Ren's. Even now, she could see Sareniya weakening, her chest heaving as she drew in shallow breaths. If Ren could hit her once, hard enough, she might be able to destroy her.

She needed to get closer. She'd only have one chance.

Sareniya threw spears of Light at Ren as she sprinted toward her, ducking and leaping to avoid getting hit. Ren had trained for this, with Grandmother and Rina. And before them, with Auntie, Big Uncle, and Wook. Her Light was a roiling storm inside her; she concentrated on what Saya had taught her, channeling it into the sword she still held, her hand viselike around the hilt. She was unused to such a weapon—it felt clumsy and heavy in her hand—but she held to it tightly. It would only take one swing, one arc of the blade.

"Ren."

Ren stumbled, her breath sawing in her chest. Her mother stood before her.

"Why are you doing this?" Aria's beautiful voice was confused, pained. It broke her heart. "I came back for you, so that we could be together. I thought that's what you wanted."

"You're not real," Ren said. The sword was shining now, imbued with her Light.

"It's the *Maiden* who isn't real," Aria insisted. "She took over my body. But I'm still here. My *soul* is still here."

A bead of sweat trickled down Ren's face, slipping down her cheek. It was possible. She'd thought Juwon had taken the celestial robe from the room in the dungeons, but he could have found her mother's body, after she'd fallen from the cliff . . .

That's what she wanted to believe. And it was because she wanted it so badly that she knew it couldn't be true.

"No more tricks," Ren whispered.

Aria's features twisted. "I never wanted you," she spat. "I had loved another, but they murdered him in front of my eyes, and forced me to marry someone else. In you, I saw the continuation of this accursed legacy.

"Do you want to know the truth?" Aria leaned forward, close enough for Ren to feel the icy puffs of her breath. "I never loved you."

In the corner of her eye, she saw Aria lift her hand slowly, blue Light pooling at the center of her palm.

For so long, all she'd wanted was her mother's love. She remembered holding the white feather in her hand, the key to unlocking her mother's heart, like the four-leaf clover and the countless talismans before.

She couldn't deny that she *still* wanted it, and yet . . .

She knew, deep down, what she had to do: She had to let her mother go. The ghost of her. The dream of her. Where she loved Ren, where Ren had forgiven her.

Only then could Aria be free.

Only then could *she* be free.

Ren's hand tightened on the grip of her sword.

She wouldn't be deceived. Even as Sareniya had drawn closer, so had she.

She lifted the sword, bracing against its bulky weight. Triumph sang through her as it arced toward Sareniya, the blade shining with Light.

She was stopped by an invisible force. She cried out, pushing against it, but her arms wouldn't move. It was as if her body was no longer her own.

"*Did you truly think you could defeat me?*" She recoiled at the dark, slithering voice, Sareniya's voice, speaking into her mind. "*So young and foolish. You never had a chance, and do you know why? Because your blood is diluted. You're too* human."

Sareniya had been toying with her. Why had she ever believed she had a chance of defeating her? Grandmother had been wrong; *she* was the original maiden, borne of the stars, the strongest and most powerful, while Ren was the last, the weakest, untrained and alone.

Sareniya placed her hand on the blade of Ren's sword and it shattered into a thousand pieces.

Ren dropped to her knees as the Maiden stood above her.

A roar rang down from the mountains.

Sunho. Ren twisted in his direction. He'd grown enormous in his Demon form, the largest she'd ever seen him, his fangs like curved blades, blue-black feathers covering him from his torso down to his taloned feet. The Maiden glided back, her wings extending as Sunho landed on the ground in front of Ren.

He roared again, readying to leap at Sareniya.

"Sunho, no!" Ren cried.

He sprang at the Maiden.

She speared him with a beam of Light that went straight through his chest.

CHAPTER 33

SUNHO

The Haebaek Mountains
Northern Plains, Gaya Pass

PITCHING FORWARD, SUNHO started to transform back into a human. Somehow, he was still alive, the Maiden's Light having missed all his vital organs. Already he could feel the mithril piecing him back together, knitting his skin, mending his bones, though it was agony to breathe, each inhalation like swallowing glass.

He knew, with devastating grief, that this was the end. The Maiden spread her wings, gliding toward him as she released a flare of Light.

His final thought was of Ren, how she'd looked standing on the rocks beneath the waterfall, the darkness revealing a sight only he could see, a precious sight, the face of his beloved.

The Light never reached him.

Junho had sprang in front of him, his wings outspread, blocking it with his body.

"Junho!" Sunho shouted.

The Light tore through him.

Sunho heard Ren scream in fury, then another blast appeared, silver and shining. *Ren's Light.* The Maiden leaped aside, but she wasn't fast enough; it seared the side of her chest. Dark blue blood gushed from the burn. With a scream, she leaped into the sky, winging back up the Fall.

Junho staggered, then fell to one knee, transforming into a human as he fell forward onto the grass.

"Junho!" Sunho screamed, crawling toward him. "*Junho!*"

Sunho cradled his brother to his chest. He was alive, breathing, though his body was covered in burns; the entire right side of his back was a mess of pulpy flesh.

"Sunho!" Tag and Yurhee raced up to him. He twisted his head in Ren's direction, where Hwani had sprinted from the airship to aid Ren. Tag tugged on his arm, his voice urgent. "We have to get out of here. That rock wall won't hold for long."

Sunho dragged himself to his feet before helping Yurhee and Tag lift Junho between them, and then together they stumbled toward the last remaining airship.

Screams and cries erupted from behind them as the demons broke through the rock wall.

The three of them managed to carry Junho up the ramp, piling aboard. Sunho was surprised, and relieved, to see Jaeil among those who'd made it on. Though he was unconscious, held in the arms of none other than his lieutenant, Sana.

The ship groaned, and there was a moment where it was unclear if it would even take off, with over a thousand passengers packed on a ship meant for three hundred. But then the mithril core kicked in, the ship clearing the earth just as the demons spilled onto the plains like a monstrous tide.

Sunho swayed from blood loss. It was as if his body, knowing that all his loved ones were out of danger, gave out. He collapsed, falling into unconsciousness.

* * *

HE WOKE TO the rumble of the airship beneath him. The door to his room opened and Tag entered carrying a bowl filled with water, a washcloth folded neatly on the rim.

"How are you feeling?" he asked.

Sunho started to sit up. "Where's Ren?"

Tag placed the bowl on a table before helping him. "She's safe," he said, once Sunho was properly upright. "Yurhee and Hwani are watching over her."

"My brother?"

Tag shifted his gaze, and Sunho twisted around to see Junho laid out on the cot behind him, the only other in the small room.

"It's a wonder you're both alive," Tag said. "Especially him. Even without Ren's magic, he managed to heal wounds that would have killed most anyone else. Yurhee did try her hand at suturing." Tag grimaced, as if he was disturbed by the memory.

An odd feeling stole over Sunho, a tingling warmth in his limbs. He'd thought the Demon was a curse, but he was alive because of it. It had saved him, had saved his brother.

Tag turned to go. "I'll leave you two alone."

"Tag . . ."

The other boy looked back. Other than a shallow cut beneath his right eye, he didn't appear to have suffered any injuries from the battle. Sunho thought he had much to be grateful for—his own personal losses from the night could have been much, much higher. He realized he'd never answered Tag's first question. "I'm okay."

Tag's lips quirked in a smile. "I'll let Ren know you're awake." He left the room, quietly shutting the door behind him.

The cot creaked as Sunho shifted his legs, placing them on the floor. He reached for a stool against the wall, moving it to Junho's bedside.

His brother looked peaceful, his long lashes dusting the dark circles beneath his eyes. He looked more his age when he slept, not weighed down by the burden of his choices.

As he gazed at Junho, he was struck with memories from their childhood with Heetae and Rohoon; although, in all his memories, Junho stood apart from the three of them, their self-appointed protector. Sunho couldn't recall his brother having friends his own age, to confide in and lean on. Until now, he'd never thought about how lonely his brother's life must have been.

Dark strands of hair were plastered to Junho's forehead. Sunho reached for the bowl that Tag had left on the table. Dipping the cloth into the water, he squeezed out the excess, then pressed it to Junho's brow.

His brother stirred. "Sunho?" he croaked groggily, wincing as he opened his eyes.

"I'm here."

Junho closed his eyes, easing back onto the cot. "I want to know . . . everything," he said. "Tell me about your life. What happened after we parted?"

Sunho wasn't much of a storyteller, but he'd learned a little from observing Ren. He spoke of his life as if it was a story, bringing his brother along with him on the journey. He told Junho about the missions he'd gone on with Heetae and Rohoon, about how it was Heetae and Sunho who managed to get them into trouble while Rohoon had to find ways of getting them out of it. Junho had chuckled at these tales, remembering their friends with fondness.

When Sunho spoke of the project, Junho covered his face with his hands, sharing in his grief.

"Afterward, I woke without memories in the Under World," Sunho said. "I hired out my sword for two years. That's when I met two rebels, Yurhee and Tag."

Junho listened carefully, laughing at Yurhee's and Tag's antics. He seemed to enjoy Yurhee in particular.

Finally, he spoke about Ren, about meeting her, about their journey together. He told him how she'd brought him back when he'd transformed into the Demon, and how for a long time he'd kept away from her because he'd been afraid of losing control. He didn't hold anything back; he wanted his brother to know how special Ren was to him. It was important to him that his brother understood.

By the time Sunho was finished, his voice was hoarse from speaking.

"You've found a home," Junho said. "I'm happy for you." Sunho knew that Junho didn't mean a place, but a person.

"I want to protect that home," Sunho said, "no matter what."

"Let me help you," Junho entreated. "I can never atone fully for what I've done. But for however long I have left, I will try. Though . . ." He smiled ruefully. "I don't know how much help I'll be. My wing. I can sense that it's gone."

While Ren and Junho's Demon had kept Junho alive, there were some wounds that couldn't be healed.

"I'm not upset about it," Junho said. "I'd have sacrificed more to save you."

"Why did you?" Sunho asked.

"I stayed away because I didn't think I could control the Demon. I thought the Maiden could cure me. I was afraid of hurting you.

But then you . . . defeated me." Junho laughed softly. "You've never beaten me before."

"I was always the weak one," Sunho acknowledged.

"Not anymore. Your strength reassures me. For once, I'm going to rely on you.

"Thank you, Sunho," his brother said quietly. "For being strong."

As if remaining awake even this long had been difficult for him, Junho let his eyelids flutter closed.

Just as his brother had protected him when they were children, Sunho kept watch over Junho through the night.

CHAPTER 34

REN

The Floating World
Aboard the Winged Zephyr, *Sora, Capital of Sareniya*

IT WAS MIDMORNING by the time they arrived at the Floating World. As Ren stood on the deck of the *Winged Zephyr*—the last of the Sareniyan battleships—a half dozen doves swooped over the bow, winging around her in a circle. She laughed at their antics, turning to Sunho to share in her wonder. But apart from Hwani, who stood a few steps back, this area of the deck was empty.

She sighed, returning her gaze to the sky. Sunho had remained belowdecks the entirety of the return journey, watching over his brother. She reminded herself to be patient; she would get the chance to speak with him soon enough.

From below, a great horn sounded from one of the watchtowers. The *Winged Zephyr* burst forth from a cloud. Beneath, Sora gleamed in the sunlight, alabaster white. Above the city, the crystal walls of the palace sparkled like jewels.

Auntie was waiting for her when she stepped off the airship. Her aunt was holding a red paper umbrella. She held it aloft, and Ren joined her beneath the shade.

"First, a runaway princess," Auntie chided, "now a runaway queen."

"I had help the first time," Ren said cheekily. "An accomplice, in fact." Auntie's features softened at the reminder.

"I'm not running anymore," Ren said.

Auntie wrapped an arm around her, the umbrella coming down lower to shelter them. "I know."

She would confront the Maiden, for what would likely be the final time, though she was afraid. Sareniya had already proven how much more powerful she was than Ren; she had no hope of winning against her.

With a sigh, Ren raised her face. "I'm sorry for leaving as I did. I worried you, didn't I?"

"I think you get it from me," Auntie said with a quirk of her lips. "Your reckless streak."

"Yes," Ren said fiercely. "I definitely get it from you."

Auntie stepped back, though she was careful to keep the umbrella above them both. "Now that you're here, there's someone who wishes to speak with you. Come—I promised to bring you to her as soon as you arrived."

Ren knew that Lady Maya and Lord Muyeol were waiting for her in the hall, that a council meeting must take place to address the threat of Juwon and the Maiden's demon army. Still, she followed Auntie without protest, signaling for Hwani to follow.

From the palace steps, they entered onto the main boulevard. It quickly became clear that Auntie was leading her to the Temple of the Goddess.

The head priestess greeted them in the vestibule. Ren hadn't spoken to the woman since she'd met her in the vegetable garden. "My queen," she said, after bowing deeply. "I'm relieved to see that you've returned unscathed."

"There were losses," Ren said quietly. They had yet to properly mourn Commander Su; his heroic act had slowed down the demon army in time for them to escape, saving countless lives.

"You must not blame yourself," the priestess said. Ren nodded, though she knew she would carry the weight of his loss, and the losses of those in the Valley of the Rise and the Fall, for a long time.

Ren gathered her breath. "Was it you who wished to speak with me?" she asked.

The head priestess nodded, her expression turning solemn. "I was disturbed when I heard what happened in the Under World. That Juwon, a mortal man, had somehow resurrected our goddess."

Her eyes flashed with outrage. "He has corrupted her beyond recognition. She does not belong here. You must send her back."

"Do you know how I can defeat her?" Ren asked, her chest fluttering with hope.

"I don't, but . . ." She pulled a thin scroll from the pocket of her robes. "I wrote to the Elder Priestess, the most long-lived and wisest of my order, and received a return message only this morning. She urges that you visit her. That you go as soon as possible."

"Where is she?" Ren asked, though she already knew.

"Bright Moon Temple."

REN WASN'T SURPRISED to find the council meeting already in session when she arrived. Lord Muyeol stood on the dais, spittle flying from his mouth. "The answer is clear! We will remain on the Floating World. The abominations cannot fly. As long as we remain here, we'll be safe."

“What of the people of the Under World?” cried a councillor. “We must shelter them from the coming horde.”

“They have the Wall,” Lord Muyeol said dismissively.

“We’ll have to make preparations to defend the city, then,” said Lady Go, “and appoint a new general.”

“No, the army will be stationed on the Floating World,” Lord Muyeol said. “The *entirety* of it. The safety of this city and its people is paramount.”

Ren strode into the hall. The councillors immediately bowed upon seeing her, though she noted her great-uncle kept his rigid stance.

“I reject such a plan,” Ren declared. “The bulk of the soldiers are from the Under World and the Occupied Territories,” she continued, “whose people we must offer to shelter behind the walls of the city. They’ll want to protect their families, their loved ones. I won’t ask them to fight for anything but their own homes.”

“From the beginning,” Lord Muyeol said, no longer trying to hide his contempt, “you’ve prioritized the welfare of everyone but the citizens of *this* world. Perhaps we should welcome the Maiden, if she is indeed the goddess reincarnated. At least then we might have a *true* queen.”

A shocked silence followed Lord Muyeol’s words.

Before he could spout further vitriol, Hwani held the curved blade of her weapon to his throat. “A threat against the queen is an act of treason.”

He attempted to move, but Hwani only pressed harder into his skin, drawing blood.

“How dare you,” Lord Muyeol seethed. “Your mother is vassal to my daughter’s husband’s clan. Your loyalty is to me.”

"By that logic, her loyalty is to *me*." It was Lady Maya who'd spoken. Until that moment, she had been observing the proceedings from her usual place to the right of the aisle. To Ren's surprise, her aunt moved to stand beside her for the first time. "But enough of inherited loyalties. It appears Hwani has a mind of her own, and she's made her choice."

Hwani signaled to two other guards, who tied Lord Muyeol's hands with rope, leading him away as he spewed foul curses.

When the room had quieted, Lady Maya cleared her throat. Only the slight shaking of her hand belied her feelings. Ren stepped closer to her aunt, who met her gaze, nodding briefly. Drawing in a slow breath, she addressed the council members. "My father might be . . . self-interested in his suggestions, but he's right on one aspect. We cannot leave the Floating World undefended. Until we know what they're planning—"

"They plan to destroy it," interrupted a new voice.

Junho stood at the back of the throne hall. He'd changed, no longer wearing the black robes of his order but a worn jacket and trousers. He'd cut his hair, and it fell loose around his shoulders.

Ren's stomach fluttered as she caught sight of Sunho, who'd entered behind him, though he appeared distracted. His brother's entrance had caused quite a stir. Many of the council members had also been present the night at the opera house.

"You were allied with Juwon," Lady Maya said sharply. "Why should we trust you?"

"I served Juwon, but I was never loyal to him. My desire has always been to protect my brother."

"What do you mean *destroy* the Floating World?" Lady Go asked. "I doubt even *she* has the power to destroy a whole landmass."

Ren had pondered the same question, after Sareniya had first made her intentions known at the opera house. She was clearly capable of *causing* destruction, with her mithril-enhanced Light and her army of demons, but to obliterate a world, as Junho suggested . . .

That was impossible, wasn't it?

"She doesn't," Junho said, and Ren felt a sigh go through her. "She means to sink the world by destroying the mithril mines beneath it. Without mithril, the Floating World will fall."

FROM THE THRONE hall, Ren hurried to the Queen's Palace to pack her belongings. She'd left Hwani behind, much to her guard's dismay—but she would better serve her by ensuring her orders were carried out here, while she was away. Flinging her ceremonial robes aside, she pulled on her trousers, buttoning her jacket over her undershirt.

Outside, the sky was darkening. The council meeting had gone on for hours, even after Sunho and his brother had departed the hall. Outriders had been sent to the villages and towns of the Floating World, with orders to evacuate to the Under World.

There wasn't enough time to flee farther; there also weren't enough ships.

All aircraft—military vessels, transport ships, even Sareniyan pleasure cruisers—had been sent to assist the evacuation efforts in the towns and cities that stood between Volmar and the Under World. Already there were reports that Seorawon had been overrun. Ren's heart ached to think of that once beautiful city in ruins, the clock tower effaced, the river swollen with the deceased. Refugees would start arriving within days, if they hadn't already.

As for the Under World, the Wall was their greatest defense against the coming horde; it was the safest place to shelter, even with the threat of the Maiden.

Ren would just have to stop Sareniya before she could destroy the mines.

She found Sunho on the western training grounds, in what appeared to be a deep conversation with his brother.

Ren wiped her sweaty palms on the front of her trousers. Junho was a demon, had allied with Juwon and Sareniya, had fought Sunho at Kumwhan Opera House and in the Valley of the Rise and the Fall. Yet still, she wanted him to approve of her.

Sunho spotted her first; he'd been listening carefully to Junho but at Ren's approach, he said something that caused Junho to turn toward her.

"You must be Ren," he said, once she had gotten near enough. "I wanted to thank you."

Ren smiled faintly, unsure of what he was referring to.

"For saving Sunho," he clarified, "in the reed field."

"He told you about that?" Ren stole a glance at Sunho.

"Among other things."

"Are you going somewhere?" Sunho asked with a frown. His gaze lifted from the satchel flung across her shoulder to her eyes.

"I . . . ," Ren began, then stopped and started again. "I'm going to Bright Moon Temple. It's a mountain temple south of here. There's someone there who might know of a way that I can defeat Sareniya. I wanted to ask if you'd go with me."

Though, seeing them together, she felt selfish for asking. Sunho had only just been reunited with his brother. He'd want to keep an eye on him, especially on the Floating World, where many would still believe him to be the enemy.

"Of course, if you wish to stay with your brother—"

"I'll go with you," Sunho said.

Junho was watching them, not bothering to hide his smile.

Ren felt suddenly embarrassed, though she didn't know why. "When will you be ready to leave?"

"I can leave now."

She blinked slowly. "You'll need supplies. A change of clothes, food . . ." She remembered when she'd first found him lying in the reed field—he'd had neither. She sighed.

Junho pressed his hand to his mouth and made a snorting sound. Ren realized he was *laughing*. "For how reliable he is," Junho said, "he's awful at planning, isn't he?"

Ren felt her shoulders relax, and her heart lightened. "He is."

"I'll pack Sunho's things," Junho said. "Meet me back here in fifteen minutes."

After they'd gone to the kitchens to collect a parcel of food items and retrieved his pack from Junho, they hurried to the port.

Leaning up against the hull of the *Sparrow* were Yurhee and Tag.

"Thought you'd be in need of a pilot," Yurhee said with a grin.

"We volunteered to be part of the teams going out to warn the villages," Tag explained. "We'll take you to Bright Moon Temple and then continue to the other settlements along the western rim."

"Thank you!" Ren effused.

THE JOURNEY WAS short, and they arrived at Bright Moon Temple by late evening. The priestesses greeted Ren and company at the gate, their lanterns glowing brightly in the darkness. They escorted them to a large wooden receiving hall, where a fire bloomed in a great brazier. An elderly woman sat before the fire. She had a wizened appearance, with more wrinkles than Ren had ever seen on a person's face. Tag had to nudge Yurhee, who couldn't stop staring.

When Ren told the Elder Priestess of the plans to evacuate, a younger priestess seated beside her answered, "We are staying. The Floating World is our home."

The others, who'd taken seats along the wall, nodded in unison.

"Elder," Ren said, aware that she was addressing a very old person, and therefore must speak with the utmost respect—at the same time, she was in a bit of a hurry. "The head priestess in Sora told me that you wished to speak with me, that you may know of a way to defeat the Maiden."

The priestess didn't answer her for so long that when she did, her voice booming across the hall, she startled Yurhee awake.

"Before you, many generations of maidens have come and gone who hadn't inherited the goddess's magic. The last recorded maiden to have powers that rivaled Sareniya was a warrior queen by the name of 'Saya.' She lived five hundred years ago."

Five hundred years . . . Ren had suspected Saya was further back in her line of ancestors, but not *five centuries.*

"And so, the place I'm about to speak of to you now has passed from memory a long time ago."

Ren sat forward, sensing the importance of the priestess's next words.

"Last night, one of my ancestors visited me in my dreams. It might seem impossible to believe—"

"I believe it," Ren said firmly. If the Ancestral Realm existed for her, then it must for others, as well.

"She spoke of a place deep in the mountains where the women in your line would go when in need of guidance. They called this place the Pond of the Daughters of Heaven. There, she said, you must take a test. If you should fail, you will forfeit your powers entirely. However, if you succeed, you'll receive a power even greater than the goddess's."

THE FOLLOWING MORNING, Ren and Sunho bade farewell to Yurhee and Tag before venturing into the mountains. The priestess had shown them the entrance the night before, a narrow path that led into a swirl of mist and snow.

It was like that first journey they'd taken to Seorawon. Sunho walked in front of her, forming a path in the snow for her with his boots. She found herself admiring the straight line of his back, the breadth of his shoulders.

She tripped on the root of a tree, one that Sunho had already uncovered. "Is something the matter?" he asked, helping her back to her feet. She brushed the snow from her knees. "You seem distracted."

She shook her head, hoping he didn't notice the flush in her cheeks. "Whatever test I'm to face, I don't know if you'll be able to come with me. You might have to wait. I don't know how long it will take."

"I'll wait for however long you need," he said, then added with a smirk, "I have a lot of food."

She rolled her eyes, though her stomach fluttered at his teasing.

"Weren't you angry with me?" she asked later that afternoon when they'd stopped to rest, their provisions boiling in a pot over a fire. "I left without telling you."

Sunho didn't answer for some time. "I wasn't . . . angry," he said finally. "I understood why you did it. I would have done the same to protect you. But that's not what we promised each other. In the meadow. We promised to work together. We promised to value our lives. Both of us broke our promises."

Ren nodded solemnly, knowing Sunho was thinking of his struggle with the Demon, though she blushed that he'd brought up the meadow.

They slept only for a few hours before journeying onward. They didn't have much time. Every hour, the demon army drew closer to the Under World.

Still, she found herself enjoying the journey, of being alone with Sunho, just the two of them.

While he'd wade across a stream, carrying his sword and their belongings over his head, she'd jump from rock to rock.

"Show-off," he chided.

They kept pace with one another, walking through sunlit meadows and dimly lit forests. He supported her in the darkness, and she guided him in the light.

They were like two halves of a whole. She just wondered what that meant.

He'd shown her through his actions how much he cared for her—he'd kissed her twice—so then why was she still unsure?

He was with her now; she should be satisfied. It was just that . . . she'd told him that she loved him. He'd been in his Demon form, but that had still been him.

And, well . . . *he* hadn't said the words.

It was evening by the time they heard the low drum of a waterfall, following the sound through twining vines of wisteria.

Ren knew immediately that they'd arrived at the pond the priestess had spoken of. The air here was warmer, softer.

A lush, forested area surrounded a pool shrouded in thick swirls of steam. At the far end, a small waterfall sent ripples through the pearlescent water, where it lapped at the rocks glistening on the shore. The urge to slip off her boots and submerge herself was palpable, as if the desire was written onto her soul.

"Oh, hello," said a voice.

Ren almost slipped off the rock she was standing on.

Sunho drew his sword, angling it toward the newcomer.

A young woman around their own age sat on a rock beside the pool. Ren would have sworn there was no one present when they'd arrived.

As Ren studied her appearance—she had black hair that fell to her waist and golden skin, as if she'd slipped from a star—Ren guessed her to be one of her ancestors. Though she wondered how one could appear before her now, while she was awake, and with Sunho present.

"You're here for the test, aren't you?" her ancestor said. "For that, you must enter the pool."

It made sense that a test here would involve going into the pond. She started to step over the rocks, making her way to the shore.

"Wait!" her ancestor called out. "You must leave your magic behind first." She pointed to a pine tree with a bough that hung over the water. "You must take off your wings, so to speak, and hang them on that tree."

Ren changed course, heading in that direction. Beneath the tree, she removed her clothing, her jacket and pants. Gathering them in her arms, she tossed them over the branch. She was left in only her undergarments. A strange feeling rushed over her then, and she gasped, doubling over. It felt as if a wind had swept through her body, leaving her hollow inside.

"Ren!" she heard Sunho cry out.

"You cannot interfere!" her ancestor shouted in warning. "If you interfere, she fails before she can even begin."

Ren drew in a deep breath before standing upright. She reached for her Light, but it was gone.

Her ancestor nodded encouragingly as Ren stepped into the pool, wading up to her waist. The water was warm, sluicing over her ankles. As her feet trod over smooth pebbles, she wondered how deep the pond went.

She walked farther, sinking beneath its surface.

CHAPTER 35

SUNHO

The Floating World
The Pond of the Daughters of Heaven

SUNHO WATCHED REN wade into the pool, submerging first up to her waist, then her chest and neck, until she was immersed entirely, the water closing over her head.

He held his breath for a minute, then two. When she didn't resurface, he took a step toward the water.

"I wouldn't do that if I were you." The young woman hadn't moved from her spot atop the largest of the boulders. "You must not enter the pool," she said. "Until the test is over, you must remain on the shore."

Sunho drew back, though his gut knotted in worry. The surface of the pool was smooth, not even a ripple or a bubble to indicate Ren was below.

"If at any point you wish to stop the test," the young woman continued, "you only need to take the maiden's clothing from the branch and leave."

He recoiled at the thought. He knew that Ren had left her magic behind when she'd stepped into the water, that like the story of "The Woodcutter and the Celestial Maiden," her clothes were tied to her magic. He would *never* take Ren's wings. To show the young woman his intentions, he crossed his arms defiantly.

She only raised a single eyebrow. "If you do leave, not only will her powers as a celestial maiden be lifted, but . . ." Her eyes were cool, assessing. "*Yours* as well."

Sunho went very still. "Do you mean the Demon?" he asked.

The young woman nodded. "The burdens that you carry, that both of you carry, will be lifted, and you'll be free to live as humans do."

She stood up from the rock. "You have until the trial is over to decide."

She then jumped from the rock and vanished. It was as if she'd slipped through a pocket in the air. Sunho might have been more shocked if she hadn't also appeared so suddenly.

He slumped backward; when his head hit the boulder behind him, he turned around, climbing atop it until he was seated cross-legged in the middle.

He closed his eyes, taking in a long, deep breath, then drawing it out slowly. He couldn't help it—he felt tempted. To be free of the Demon . . . he didn't think it was possible, had never even hoped for such a reality. Without it, he wouldn't have to worry about hurting the people he loved the most. Without it, he wouldn't feel as if he had a second skin, a second soul. And Ren . . .

Without her powers, she wouldn't be expected to fight Sareniya. Her powers tied her to a legacy she'd never wanted to be a part of. If she didn't have them, then she could leave. They could catch an airship and fly somewhere far away. Together.

He didn't think anything could tempt him into stealing her magic, but he hadn't known that by taking it, he could *save* her.

He felt a breeze stir the air and he opened his eyes, gaping at the two people who had joined him on the rocks by the pond.

"Sunho, it's been a while," Heetae said, grinning as he leaned casually on the rocks, one foot dipped in the pool. Strands of unruly hair stuck out from beneath his black headband.

His friend's appearance was the same as the last time he'd seen him—not the age he'd be if he had continued to live on in years, but sixteen, the age he'd been when he'd passed.

"Are you a spirit?" Sunho asked.

Heetae guffawed loudly, and Sunho's heart lurched. It was a sound he'd never thought to hear again, bright and filled with warmth. Heetae's eyes crinkled at the corners. "What are you talking about? You think *I* would stick around in this world? Think again!"

"We're just visitors," said Rohoon. If his heart had lurched hearing Heetae's voice, it broke at Rohoon's. Unlike Heetae, Rohoon was older, seventeen. Sunho had only seen his face at this age briefly, when he'd transformed from a demon into a human. Then he'd been covered in blood, on the brink of death. Perched atop the rock, he was healthy again, his face full. His eyes were soft as they beheld Sunho.

"We went to a pool like this one once," Heetae said, drawing Sunho's attention. "Remember? It was after one of our first scouting missions. I fell into the pool, but I couldn't swim. I thought I was going to drown."

"I remember," Sunho said. "I jumped in after you, even though I wasn't a strong swimmer myself. And then we both were struggling to stay above the water."

"That's right. And then Rohoon jumped in, only Rohoon started berating us, and we didn't know why he was so annoyed, until we realized that all three of us were standing. The water was only five feet deep!"

Heetae laughed so hard that he almost fell off the rock. Rohoon reached out to grab his arm, steadying him. Sunho was laughing, too, at first, but then he felt a sharp ache in his chest and his eyes filled with tears.

"Sunho, what's wrong?" Heetae asked, alarmed. "Why are you crying?"

"I'm sorry," Sunho said. "I'm so sorry."

Rohoon frowned. "What do you have to be sorry for?"

"Because if it wasn't for me, neither of you would be dead. You only volunteered for the mithril program because of me. Because I wanted to leave the army and find Junho."

"That wasn't your fault," Rohoon said firmly. "We chose to take the serum."

Heetae nodded in agreement.

When Sunho continued to cry, Heetae's expression softened.

"When you put that burden on yourself, you're taking away the choices we made, you know?" Heetae said gently. "We didn't have much control of our lives, did we? But we still made choices, to stay together, to watch out for each other. I'm proud of that. I'm proud of my life."

"I didn't know you were so wise, Heetae," Rohoon said, squinting as he smiled.

"I'm surprising myself!"

Sunho sniffed.

"Close your eyes, Sunho," Rohoon said.

He obeyed, and felt a finger gently brush away his tears. Then arms circled around him—first Heetae's wiry arms, then Rohoon's strong, solid embrace.

He somehow knew that if he opened his eyes, they'd be gone. So he kept them shut. As tight as he could.

"We have to leave soon," Heetae said. "We could only visit because of the magic of this place."

"You already carry a heavy burden, Sunho," Rohoon said. "Don't make us another one. You know we wouldn't have wanted that."

He had so much he wanted to tell them, that in his dark childhood, they'd given him moments of light, that he'd experienced happiness because of them. None of them had parents, and so they'd raised each other, taught each other what was right and what was wrong. When they were little, they'd imagined their souls as tiny balls of flames—Heetae's yellow, Rohoon's green, and Sunho's blue. They'd taken turns protecting and shielding those flames, making sure they never dimmed.

It was because of them, he knew that his soul was intact, that it was good.

"Thank you," Sunho said. "Thank you for being my friends."

He felt the soft pressure of their arms, and then they were gone. When he opened his eyes, he was alone.

With infinite care, he tugged Ren's clothing from the branch. As the jacket and pants fell, they transformed into a silvery robe, tumbling into his arms like a river of starlight. He was holding her magic in his hands—her wings, her Light, her soul. He knew that if he left with the robe, she'd be safe. She'd never have to suffer like Heetae and Rohoon, but he also knew that if he left, he'd be taking the choice from her.

He thought of his soul, a blue, indomitable flame. *Mithril blue.*

And he made his choice.

CHAPTER 36

REN

The Floating World
The Pond of the Daughters of Heaven

REN'S BODY FELT warm and languorous as she sank down into the pond. She wasn't afraid. Her visits to the temple had prepared her. She kept her eyes closed as she sank deeper until her toes hit the silty ground at the bottom. She opened her eyes.

She was beside the pool again, sprawled on her back on a large boulder, as if she'd never entered the water in the first place. Flailing, she sat upright, only to see that the young woman from before was perched a few feet away from her.

Immediately she could sense they were in the Ancestral Realm. For one, Sunho was nowhere in sight, the reality of which made her heart ache. To be in the same place, but separated by magic, made her feel ill at ease. Secondly, the light had changed; even though the moon remained in the sky, it had dimmed, and the objects around the pool—the waterfall, the trees, and the rocks—no longer appeared as vivid. It was as if she were viewing the world through a dream. In a way, they were.

"I used to come here with my mother," the young woman said. She'd drawn her knees to her chest. The gesture struck Ren as familiar—she'd seen Rina do the same. She herself had taken comfort in that pose countless times before.

"Sareniya was your mother, wasn't she?" Ren asked softly.

"They called me Nia," the young woman said, "to differentiate me from her. She was beautiful, and powerful, the first of her kind to live on this world, until me.

"I know why you've come." Nia shifted forward on the rock, her gaze intent upon Ren. "Unlike the others of our bloodline, I'm aware of what's going on in your present, that my mother's spirit has been resurrected, that she means to destroy the world."

"Yes," Ren said, meeting Nia's gaze squarely. "I'm going to stop her."

Nia nodded, as if she'd expected Ren to say as much. "I will help you to defend against her powers."

Reaching out, she pressed her fingers to Ren's forehead. Light bloomed from her fingertips, forming a band that settled around Ren's forehead like a crown. The Light was warm against Ren's skin. After a few seconds it dissipated, leaving only a tingling sensation.

Nia withdrew her hand. Ren noticed sweat upon the other girl's brow. "I've put a shield around your mind," Nia said. "She won't be able to control you. That should at least give you a chance."

"Thank you," Ren said, lifting her hand to her temple.

She then drew in a deep breath. "I think I'm ready now."

Nia blinked. "Ready?"

"For the test," Ren said.

"You have everything you need to fight the Maiden within you. The pool is restorative—the strength that you lost while fighting her has been returned to you."

"I don't understand," Ren said, shaking her head. "The priestess at the temple said my ancestors traveled here, that if I succeeded in a test, I would receive a great power. You said that in order for the test to begin, I had to enter the pool."

"Oh," Nia said, "*You're* not the one being tested. It is the boy."

Ren stood up abruptly. "What are you doing to Sunho?" she demanded. "Are you hurting him?" She'd jump into the pool and wake up from this place if she thought she could spare him a moment's pain.

"Of course not." Nia wrinkled her nose. "It's a simple test, really. It's the same that was given to the woodcutter. He can either leave your clothing where you put it, on the branch of the tree, after which you'll both return to the Floating World and face the Maiden. Or he can take it."

Ren went very still. "What happens if he takes my clothing?"

"You'll lose your powers, and so will he. You'll be free to leave and go wherever you wish. Return to the valley, perhaps, or even farther. There are other lands beyond this one."

Sunho would lose his powers. He'd lose the Demon. If the roles were reversed, what would she choose, if she thought she could save him?

"Do you wish to see?" Nia tilted her head to the side. "What choice your woodcutter will make?"

"He's not a woodcutter, he's . . ."

She was distracted by the scene before her. A boy and girl had appeared at the edge of the pool. The girl emerged from the water, droplets cascading off her shoulders, her black hair plastered to her chest and back.

It was *her*, except that it wasn't her because she was here on the rock.

"Sunho!" Ren shouted. "Don't be tricked. That's not me!" But of course, he couldn't hear her. He was in another realm, another world.

She turned frantically toward the bough of the tree, but it was empty. He'd stolen her clothing, hidden them. He approached the Ren in the water, removing his cloak and placing it around her shoulders. She turned her face up toward him, her lashes wet from the pool. He seemed arrested by the sight of her, his lips parting. Then, slowly, he leaned down, toward her.

She turned away before she could see him kiss the other Ren.

"It seems he's failed the test," Nia said. There wasn't any judgment in her voice.

"No," Ren said. "He hasn't." She raised her face. "Because that's not him. Sunho would never take my clothing because he knows it holds my magic, *my wings*. He would *never* steal my wings."

Ren raised her chin defiantly. "He knows me, he respects me, and he . . ."

Loves me.

"He's not a woodcutter, he's—" Ren struggled for the right words to encapsulate Sunho, saying the first ones that popped into her head. "He's a sword dancer!"

For a few long seconds, Nia stared at her, and then she laughed, throwing her head back. "Oh, I haven't laughed so in a long time," she said after a minute in which Ren turned a shade of crimson, wiping at her eyes. "I think I like you, great-great-great-great—oh you know what I mean—granddaughter of mine.

"Look," she said, directing Ren to the pool again.

The illusion had broken. It was no longer Sunho and Ren in the pool, but a different boy and girl. The boy was leading the girl out of the water, and as they passed, Ren recognized Sareniya. She was so much younger—just a girl, no older than eighteen. Her eyes were tearful, yet as she looked at the boy, there was a glimmer of curiosity in her gaze, and wonder.

"The woodcutter and the maiden," Nia said. "My father and my mother."

"Is this how it really was?" Ren said. "They look . . . happy."

"This is how I choose to believe it happened," Nia said. "Sometimes, that's all that matters."

Ren wondered at that, but perhaps that was the case for hundreds of versions of "The Woodcutter and the Celestial Maiden," told by countless storytellers. They could all be true, or none at all.

"The path you've chosen is a difficult one," Nia said. "But you must remember—my mother was never evil. Revenge was never what she desired. To return to her home, *freedom*, was what she wanted."

"I understand," Ren said. "Thank you, Nia."

SHE EMERGED MUCH less elegantly than Sareniya had, splashing in the water like a carp on land.

At first glance, the rocks surrounding the pond appeared empty. Her gaze swept toward the branch, but her clothing was gone. Yet doubt never crept into her heart.

"Sunho?" she called softly.

He appeared from behind the pine tree. In his hands, he held her clothes, yet they had transformed into a single garment. A beautiful silver robe. He held it carefully. Reverently.

She started to wade toward the shore, only to discover that she was naked, her undergarments having vanished while she was in the pool.

“Wait,” Sunho called out to her. “I’ll come to you.”

He stepped into the water, slowly making his way toward her.

As he approached, she overlaid the image of the woodcutter walking toward Sareniya, but quickly dismissed the memory. That was Sareniya and the woodcutter’s story. This was theirs.

When he reached her, he placed the robe around her shoulders.

She felt the robe transform into her wings, stretching out behind her on the water, shining and silver. She could see them reflected in Sunho’s eyes, his mithril-blue eyes, that telltale gleam that only showed when he was feeling strong emotions. That shone brightest for her.

“You didn’t steal my wings,” Ren breathed. “You didn’t reject the Demon.”

“The Demon is a part of me,” he said, “just as the Light is a part of you.”

Her heart soared to hear him speak those words. “The Demon was always beautiful to me,” she said. “Quiet. Still. Like a lake beneath the stars.”

She felt his darkness reaching toward her, sweeping around her. She wondered if it was the same for him, her Light surrounding him, alighting against his skin.

Then his hands were lifting her face to his, caressing her jaw, her neck.

“I love you, Ren,” he said.

Her Light burst forth from her, gilding the water in starlight and bathing the waterfall and the trees with a silver glow. The pool was illuminated. She was incandescent, but so was he, though his was a swirling shadow. She’d never felt safer than in the embrace of his darkness.

She pressed her mouth to his, and he returned her kiss, his lips soft and urgent against hers. She shivered as he slipped his hand beneath her robe, caressing her bare skin, her stomach and chest. She swept her hands through his thick hair, breaking their kiss only to press soft, feathery kisses to his temple and cheek, until he drew her back down, and then they were kissing again, more fiercely than before.

She didn't know what the days ahead would bring, but she wasn't afraid. Because Sunho would be there, fighting by her side. There was no one who made her feel stronger, braver. She believed in him. She loved him.

She filled every one of her kisses with her Light, her love. She felt his echoed back to her, the darkness striated with sparks of blue. She gasped as it swirled around her, the most beautiful sight she'd ever seen. Mithril was his love, she realized, just as the silver in her Light was hers, growing brighter and brighter until their radiance rivaled even the stars.

ACT FOUR

Toward the Mithril Sky

CHAPTER 37

JAEIL

Outside the Under World,
North of the Wall Infirmary, Yongin Military Base

JAEIL REGAINED CONSCIOUSNESS slowly as his surroundings came into focus. He was in the infirmary at Yongin Military Base; he recognized it by the astringent scent of alcohol and the hideous painting of an airship that sat on the wall at a degree slightly off from 180. All around him were his subordinates, who wore expressions of varying degrees of devastation, as if he were on his deathbed—which he very well might have been.

Jaeil felt a stirring in his chest that could only be annoyance. If they were here in this room, then they were neglecting their posts.

He sat up in the cot.

"Captain!" shouted Yumi, her eyes wide and alarmingly watery. "You're awake!"

Another soldier had the great intelligence to exclaim, "You're alive!"

"You shouldn't be moving," said Zeno, one of his lieutenants who'd been stationed at Yongin for the past three weeks. "Please, Captain."

"Where's Wook?" Jaeil said. There had been moments, while he was in and out of consciousness, when he'd heard the other boy's voice. He'd told him stories, conjuring images that had shaped Jaeil's dreams.

"Who . . . ?" Zeno puckered his brows in a frown.

They all stared at him blankly. For several seconds, he thought he'd damaged his head so irrevocably that he'd imagined the whole thing.

"I sent him out," said a new voice from the doorway. He turned to see Sana leaning against the frame, her arms crossed. "These brutes were intimidating him, and he needed rest. He hadn't left your bedside since you arrived."

Jaeil didn't react to this last comment. Pulling back the blankets, he placed his feet to the cold floor, working his shoulder.

His arm wasn't broken. That was a relief.

He pressed his hand to his side and winced. Stitches. He was wearing a white cotton shirt over his bandaged chest, and pants. It was the exact same uniform he'd worn as a prisoner, he thought dryly. Grabbing his coat from the upright rack, he made his way toward the door. Which was blocked by more of his soldiers, dawdling like hens.

He scowled heavily. "If you're not going to be useful," he said between gritted teeth, "get out of my way."

"Yes, Captain!" they shouted in unison, seemingly delighted at his orneriness.

Sana slipped away from the doorframe as he passed, catching up to him with a few quick strides.

"Might I ask where you're off to minutes after waking up from near-fatal injuries?" she said sweetly.

"The war room," Jaeil answered. "I need to see to the Wall's defenses." How long had he been unconscious? Two, maybe three days?

The demon army would arrive within the next two, if his calculations were correct.

"Of course," Sana said, gesturing in an insouciant manner for him to walk forward. "Carry on."

He eyed her. "How are you?" Besides a patch she wore over her left eye, she looked the same.

"Better than you," Sana answered cheerily.

"Thank you," he said, "for—"

"Saving your neck?" Sana finished with a grin.

"Yes, that." He scowled. "How did you know what I was planning? How were you even *there*?"

"I have a sixth sense when it comes to your particular brand of foolish behavior," she drawled. Then she said, more plainly, "I found out you were returning to that godsforsaken pass, so I stole an aircraft and pursued you. When I saw that the soldiers weren't going to make it out of that valley, it wasn't difficult to guess what you'd do next. You have a noble streak. It's annoying, honestly."

A noble streak . . .

He thought of Commander Su, and a wave of grief swept over him. It was because of the commander that so many of them made it back alive.

"I almost didn't make it in time," she said. "Losing you would have been catastrophic for me."

His gaze landed on Sana, and he lifted a brow. Was she being . . . sentimental?

"Who else would sign my payment slips?" she deadpanned.

"I'm glad you're feeling better."

Yongin's war room was a large tent near the center of the base. Both of his father's former commanders, Habin and Naksol, were present when he entered, standing around a large table laid with a model of the Under World and its surrounding terrain. He was surprised to find Sunho's brother, Junho, was with them, as well as Prince Jinpyeong of Volmar. They'd been in the middle of discussing the city's defenses when he'd arrived.

"The Wall is the greatest barrier against the horde," Habin was saying. Of the three commanders, he was the youngest, leader of the right wing, the second-largest fighting division apart from the main army. "The gates are the most vulnerable points."

"I've already sent teams to shore up the sewers, the river gates, and the train tunnel," said Naksol, commander of the small but fierce left wing.

"Reports have come in that not only Seorawon, but Haein has been overrun," a city captain added. "According to the refugees, the demon army has doubled in size."

"How is that possible?" Naksol hissed.

Jaeil remembered the Volmaran captain's words before he'd passed: *When it was over, all that was left was pain and darkness.*

"Sareniya has the power to transform humans into demons, doesn't she?" He directed the question at Junho.

"It's called the blood veil," Junho said grimly. "I've only seen her do it once before." He closed his eyes, as if reliving the terrible memory. "Sareniya appeared in the sky over the Volmaran army, her wings outspread. At first, they glowed with Light, then blue spores began emanating from them, drifting like snow to the earth. It only took contact with skin to induce transformation. By the time the Volmarans realized what was happening, it was too late."

A bleak silence followed Junho's recounting of what he'd seen.

"There are at least thirty towns between Haein and the Under

World," Habin said, "with populations ranging from hundreds to *thousands*."

That was a lot of potential victims for Sareniya's army.

"Can they be turned back?" asked Prince Jinpyeong, his voice strained.

"I'm not sure," Junho said. "I had believed so . . . Unlike the serum used on Juwon's test subjects," he explained, "the Maiden induced transformation through spores of her blood. It's possible that eliminating her will break the hold she has over them, and initiate a reverse transformation."

"Then we must put all our efforts into killing her!" Jinpyeong cried.

"We can't defeat Sareniya—only the queen can," Jaeil said. Her powers were too great; only someone of equal power could stand a chance against her. "Which is why our army must confront the Maiden's army on the battlefield, so that Ren can concentrate on fighting *her*."

"Captain Jaeil's right," Naksol agreed, "but we're overlooking a vital part in this endeavor, one that will dictate its success." Her steely gaze swept the room. "We need a general to lead us."

Jaeil felt the others' eyes upon him. He wasn't the obvious choice in age or experience, but he was the queen's chosen adviser. Still, he felt uneasy claiming a role that had so recently belonged to his father. Commander Su would have been the clear option, if . . .

Muffled shouts and raised voices shifted their attention to a disturbance outside the tent.

"What's going on?" Habin demanded.

One of his soldiers left the tent, only to return shortly. "Someone's trying to get inside," she reported. "A civilian."

Habin scowled. "Remove them immediately."

"Jaeil!"

Jaeil's heart jolted, and he whipped his head in the direction of the entrance. He strode from the tent, pushing back the flap.

Outside, one of Naksol's soldiers was dragging Wook away by the arm.

Jaeil didn't think. He grabbed the soldier's shoulder, jerking him back. "Release him," he growled.

The soldier, jumping at the sight of Jaeil, immediately obeyed. "My apologies, Captain," he said, bowing profusely. "I had orders not to let anyone disturb the officers."

Jaeil drew in a deep breath, letting his anger wash over him. It wasn't the soldier's fault. Though he had to resist the urge to punish him. Severely.

"Jaeil?" Wook said timidly from beside him. "I'm sorry. I shouldn't have tried to interrupt."

"Walk with me," Jaeil said. Turning abruptly, he headed in a direction away from the officers' tent.

"Where are we going?" Wook asked, keeping pace beside him. "Are you all right?"

"Sorry," Jaeil said. "I needed to leave or else I'd have to explain to Commander Naksol why I murdered one of her soldiers."

Wook's breath hitched, but then he nodded. They made their way toward the southern edge of the base, where a camp had been set up. Tens of thousands of tents ranged across the great plains outside the Wall. The entire army had assembled in one place—all eighty-eight regiments, except for the disbanded Forty-Fourth.

The battle to come would be the largest in scale that Jaeil had ever fought, with potential for astronomical loss of life on both sides.

"I wish I learned how to properly fight," Wook said, kicking a rock. Jaeil watched as it skittered into a mare's hoof, after which she stomped it into the ground. "Not just learn to shoot arrows on a stage."

"Not everyone needs to be a soldier," Jaeil said.

"But there's going to be a battle. And Ren needs to know that I can take care of myself, that I can fight. I want to be of use to her."

"You have other uses," Jaeil said, thinking of Wook's skill at crafting weapons. He wondered if Wook had finished the weapons he'd shown him.

"That's true," Wook said. "I'm very pretty to look at."

He clearly meant the words as a jest, but when Jaeil didn't immediately respond, his ears turned bright red. "I was joking. I know you meant my smithing skills—"

"Motivation," Jaeil said slowly, "is useful." His eyes roved over Wook's slender build and bobbing throat, his eyes that always seemed to regard Jaeil with an expression of alarm. And . . . wonder. Jaeil had been looked at with fear and admiration, hatred, and respect, but rarely hope, and never wonder. It made him feel odd, warm, even in winter.

"As for not worrying Ren," he said, "that's best accomplished by staying off the battlefield." He paused, then added, "That'll be preferable for me as well. I'll be better able to concentrate, if I know that you're safe."

His words seemed to have unleashed something in Wook because the other boy blurted, "When I saw you lying on that cot, I thought I was going to throw up. I've never been so afraid in my life, even when I was attacked by that demon. If you didn't wake up, I thought *I* might die." His hand flew to cover his mouth. "I'm sorry, I—I don't know why I said all that."

“Don’t be sorry,” Jaeil said softly. He closed his eyes. “At the end, when I thought it was all over . . .”

It wasn’t the circumstances in which he’d found himself that had surprised him—he’d made the choice to sacrifice himself so that the others could escape. That was his fate, his penance. No, what had surprised him was the feeling that had stolen over him—his desire to live.

He opened his eyes, holding Wook’s gaze with his own. “I only had one regret. That I hadn’t had more time, with you.”

Wook looked unbalanced—actually, he appeared as if he might faint.

“Captain!” Sana called out, jogging over. Her keen eyes trailed from Wook to Jaeil, though she didn’t remark upon Wook’s flushed face or how close the two of them were standing.

“The queen has just returned,” she said, her voice crisp, official.

He hadn’t known Ren was gone.

“She’s at the Wall, and she’s asking for you.”

JAEIL SHOULD HAVE known that when Sana had said Ren was “at the Wall,” she’d meant she was on top of it. He took the north gate lift, the air thinning as it gained altitude. It ground to a halt at the top and he exited onto the stone battlements, bracing against a piercingly cold wind. From this vantage, he could see the entirety of the encampment, stretching for miles from beneath the shadow of the Wall to Yongin Military Base, right outside the rim of the world.

The sun was setting, and Jaeil watched as one by one campfires were lit below, glowing like beacons in the darkness.

“Jaeil.”

He'd been concentrating so hard on the view before him, he hadn't noticed Ren's approach. She was dressed in a simple jacket and trousers, yet there was a regalness to her bearing. He'd first noticed it more prominently at her coronation, where he had gazed upon her, pride and awe filling his chest.

As children, he'd been afraid of the mantle of the celestial maiden that she would one day inherit. He'd thought it meant he would lose her—her friendship—but he could see now that he'd been wrong to think that.

She had come into her power, a celestial maiden who wielded Light and had wings, but *he* had also become someone she could depend on. He was still her friend.

She stopped before him, and he bowed. "My queen," he said.

"Walk with me. I have something I'd like to ask you."

As they made their way down the battlements, she began to shed her regal bearing. It was gradual, not noticeable unless one was observing her closely. She had always walked with grace, but there was a natural playfulness to her movements, her arms hanging loosely by her sides.

"Where's Sunho?" Jaeil asked.

He knew wherever Ren was, the other boy couldn't be far.

A soft blush rose to Ren's cheeks, and Jaeil wondered what memories Sunho's name had stirred up.

She gestured farther down the Wall, where he was sitting, his legs dangling over the ledge. Hwani was with him, though two large steps away from the fifty-yard drop. They were engaged in a heated conversion. Jaeil wondered what the two of them had to talk about—probably debating who was more skilled with a sword.

"For so long I pushed any memories of my childhood from my

mind," Ren said, drawing his gaze back to her. "So much of it was shrouded in sorrow, except for when I was with you." Her eyes were soft as they met his. "I relied on you so much when we were children. You were my companion. You were family to me even before I knew what family was."

He knew what she meant. Family had always signified pain to him, fear and disappointment. But if family was meant to bring peace, joy, and belonging, then she had been his true family.

"They're out there somewhere, Sareniya and Juwon, coming closer every minute, every second. I'll face her, but I can't do it alone."

Jaeil knew, with a keen sense of clarity, why she had wanted to see him.

"Forgive me, but can I rely on you a little longer?"

"Ask me," he said.

"Will you be my general?"

She was asking him to take on a great burden. Ten thousand lives beneath his command, and hundreds of thousands more in the city, to live or die by the decisions he made. He let the weight settle on his shoulders. He wouldn't dishonor her by asking why she'd chosen him over more experienced commanders. *He* was Ren's choice, and so he would serve her to the best of his abilities.

He lowered himself to his knee before her. "I would be honored to serve you as your general."

She pressed her hand softly to his shoulder. Then the warmth of her Light flooded him, heady and powerful, before it dissipated, leaving his senses tingling. She was gazing out at the plains when he stood.

Drumbeats echoed from below, where a great bonfire had been built at the center of the camp, its flames blazing against the darkness.

"I think it's a performance," Ren said. "Should we go look?"

Before he could answer, she jumped from the Wall, her wings spreading out behind her. Immediately Sunho joined her, launching into the air, his black wings sweeping downward. Jaeil stared in wonder. They were a beautiful sight, a girl and a boy with wings.

Then he met Hwani's distraught gaze, and together they sighed. They took the longer route.

SANA WAS WAITING for Jaeil at the edge of camp, flipping a dagger in her hand.

"Sorry about breaking up your moment earlier, Captain," she said with a grin, not appearing the least bit apologetic. "He's quite pretty."

"Stay away from him," Jaeil growled, "and it's 'General.'"

She immediately fell to one knee. "Forgive me, General."

He held out his hand, and she took it, rising to her feet. "I need a strong captain." In his new role, he would be responsible for the entirety of the army, which meant his own regiment needed someone to lead them.

"I understand that," Sana said slowly, "but I'd rather stay by your side, if that's all right with you."

It was the response he'd expected from her, and so he nodded. "I wouldn't want to fight beside anyone else," he said. As they walked toward the bonfire at the center of the camp, he added, "But really, stay away from Wook."

Someone had erected a small puppet stage by the fire. Spotting him, Ren rushed over. "Remember how we used to watch the puppeteers perform at the Festival of Light?" She was aglow with excitement—in fact, she was radiating, quite literally.

He settled her with Sunho in front of the gathered crowd before moving to a more tactical position on the sidelines. He was amused to find himself standing opposite Junho, who was also keeping an eye on their surroundings, though his gaze strayed most often to his brother.

As his attention shifted back to the stage, Jaeil was shocked to discover that the performer was none other than Wook, wielding a puppet deftly in either hand.

A hush fell over the crowd as Wook began his performance, weaving a story about a girl who travels to a mythical underworld to save a boy stuck in an enchanted sleep. It was Ren and Wook's story, cast as a fairy tale.

The audience laughed and cried, their attention riveted to the stage.

As for Jaeil, his gaze wasn't on the puppets, but on the boy above them, his fingers playful and quick, as if he was telling a story only Jaeil could hear.

CHAPTER 38

REN

The Floating World
The Temple of the Goddess

REN WANDERED THE wide boulevards and smooth stone avenues of Sora alone—or, as alone as she could be with Hwani keeping watch from a distance. She peeked into empty teahouses, where elegant celadon cups sat abandoned on tea trays, and through the flung-open doors of great mansions, the disarray of their inner courtyards evidencing a hasty retreat. Even the temple was deserted, the head priestess having sent the younger priestesses and acolytes to accompany the rest of the fleeing Sareniyans to the Under World.

Though not all the Sareniyans had chosen to escape to the Under World. A great many had joined Lord Muyeol to leave the vicinity of the Floating World entirely, declaring they would return once it was no longer under threat. Lady Maya and the remaining council members had urged Ren to intercede—they had taken the largest of the airships, including the *Winged Zephyr*—but Ren had let them go.

She refused to prohibit those who wished to leave from doing so, and she didn't need the airships—there weren't enough to evacuate the people of the Under World anyway.

They had made their choice, and she had made hers: To stay. To fight. Lady Maya had made the same choice, as had Jaeil, and so many others.

She came across a fountain in one of the city's squares. It had three tiers, like the fountain in Seorawon. Clear water spilled from one basin into the next in an endless cascade. She sat on the rim and pulled her satchel onto her lap. Inside were items she'd taken from the Queen's Palace. The first a book from Head Maid Eun, who'd left on the *Winged Zephyr*. She felt no ill will toward the maidservant—the woman valued rank and order, to which Ren had a natural aversion. The book had the names of every queen who'd ever lived in the Queen's Palace. She continued to pull items from the satchel, including the brow pendant in the shape of a teardrop that she'd worn at her first council meeting, as well as a camellia flower she'd plucked from the garden.

The last item she pulled from the satchel was her mother's diary.

She began to read, though it wasn't mentions of Juwon that grabbed her attention this time, but the small pleasures of Aria's day-to-day life.

She'd kept a kitten from a litter had by one of the groundskeepers' cats, and he had attached himself to her, following her around wherever she went.

She'd enjoyed gardening. She'd nurtured so many of the plants that still thrived today, including the camellia tree.

It had been while she was gardening that she'd met Hyun. Her kitten, now a rascally cat, had climbed a tree and gotten stuck on the highest branch. It was Hyun who'd retrieved him for her. *He is insufferable*, Aria wrote. *What's worse is that he's the most handsome boy I've ever met!*

Ren didn't know how long she sat on the rim of the fountain

reading her mother's thoughts, which ranged from melancholy and moody to silly and effervescent. Ren laughed and cried and laughed again. At last, she came to the final entry.

He is gone.

There is no more light in the world for me.

As she lifted her hand to close the book, she noticed that the thick sheet attached to the back cover wasn't fully glued down, and the corner of a piece of paper stuck out from the hidden compartment. It was a letter. Aria had addressed it to someone she called "Grandmother."

Meet me in the meadow, her mother had written. *There's something I want to show you.* At the bottom of the letter was a signed name.

THE LAST TIME she'd visited the Ancestral Realm, there'd been a storm on the horizon. Now, although the sky over the meadow was overcast, there was only a faint breeze in the air.

She spotted Rina crouched in the dirt a short distance away, her back to Ren.

As Ren approached, great tears began to fall from her eyes, down her cheeks and over her chin.

Though Rina must have heard her footsteps, she didn't turn.

Rina—a special name, one shared only between her and her grandmother.

She reached her, only to see what it was her body had been blocking from view. A zelkova sapling.

"It'll grow," Rina said. "Do you think it'll be as big as you one day?"

Tears slipped down Ren's face as she gazed at Aria.

Her mother.

This was what she looked like when she was nine years old, long before the heartbreak. How could she have never seen it before? She was beautiful.

"I know what ha-happens to you," Ren said, her voice breaking. After Grandmother passes, she'd experience loneliness and isolation.

"Don't tell me," Aria said.

Her expression was solemn as she gazed at Ren's face, at the tears that wouldn't seem to stop. "Not everything is sad, is it?"

Ren thought of the small joys she'd written of in her diary, and then of the boy her mother would one day love. Ren shook her head.

"I'll live those moments," Aria said quietly, "the happy ones, and the sad ones. And then . . . I'll meet you one day."

She knew. *She knew.*

Ren couldn't breathe. She was sobbing now, great hiccuping cries.

"I don't—" she cried. "I don't bring you any happiness."

Her mother had resented her; she'd never wanted her. Ren had represented everything that had been stolen from her. She would bring so much pain to this girl that she loved, who would one day become the mother that she'd loved *so much*. She couldn't bear it.

She felt a soft pressure against her cheek. Aria's small hand.

"I don't believe that," she said. "You bring me happiness now."

Ren sank to her knees as Aria's arms wrapped around her. It wasn't the love she'd sought from her mother while she'd been alive, but it was enough. It was enough.

After some time, Aria let go.

Ren wiped the tears from her eyes. "I—I found a letter you wrote," she said. "To Grandmother. You said you wanted to meet her here. To show her something."

"Oh, yes." Aria blushed. "I think I know. Come, look."

Aria crouched once more in front of the zelkova sapling. Ren watched in wonder as she raised her palms out before her. A spark of Light emanated from her hands, brief but bright before dissipating. The sapling shivered, only to sprout up by several centimeters, releasing a few sturdy leaves.

"A simple magic," Aria said bashfully, using her sleeve to wipe the sweat that had gathered on her brow. "Nothing grand or very useful."

"It's extraordinary," Ren said passionately, and Aria smiled.

"This is the last time you'll be visiting me, isn't?" she asked softly.

Ren started to cry anew.

"No, that's a good thing, I think," Aria said. She embraced Ren, one final time. "I'm sorry I couldn't help you more."

Ren shook her head. "I am strong because of you, because of Grandmother."

With a searing clarity, she understood that to be the truth. Her heritage wasn't a curse—it was a gift handed down to her by the women of her family. To give her strength, but most of all, to make her believe that she was capable of wonders.

Gently, Aria pushed Ren away. "That's enough crying. You're ruining my best jacket."

And with that, Aria was Rina again, surly and peevish, just nine years old.

"Now hurry up and go save the world."

"I will," Ren promised.

LITTLE UNCLE AND Auntie were waiting for her when she stepped off the aircraft outside Yongin Military Base. Overnight, the camp had cleared as the soldiers prepared for battle. A large trench that Jaeil had ordered dug the day before stretched across almost the entirety of the north Wall.

"I have a gift for you," Wook said, drawing her gaze. He held a long cloth-wrapped package in his arms. "It's the scepter from your coronation," he explained hurriedly as she took the package, unwrapping it carefully. "Apparently, it's been held by every one of your ancestors, you mother included. I replaced the crystal with a shard of mithril. I thought it might help you channel your Light. It's also the size and weight of Big Uncle's umbrella, and so I thought—"

Holding the scepter in one hand, she threw her arms around Wook. "It's perfect, thank you!" She remembered how unwieldy the sword had been; this was much more suitable as a weapon.

"And this, too," Auntie said, when Ren had released Little Uncle. She held up a paper fan. "These always come in handy."

"They do!" Ren tucked it into the waistband of her pants.

She was surprised to find Sana waiting for her just inside the main gate of the base. She bowed. "Your Highness."

Ren remembered how frightening Sana had been at Wolryudang, when she'd orchestrated her kidnapping. The lieutenant was on her side now, but that didn't make her any less intimidating. Her eye patch also accentuated her already piratical appearance.

Movement behind Sana caught Ren's attention as soldiers ran in varying directions across the base.

"What's happening?" Ren asked, her heart beginning to pound in her chest. "Has it already begun?"

Sana shook her head. "Not yet. A group of refugees from the Outer Territories were spotted on the north road, pursued by at least a half dozen demons. The general is leading a few volunteers to aid in their escape . . ." Sana paused. "He ordered me to stay behind to inform you personally."

Ren couldn't be sure, but she thought Sana was *pouting*.

"Sunho is with them," she added.

Ren didn't wait to hear more. Releasing her wings, she flew over the base. Below her, soldiers gasped, a few of them pointing.

She spotted Sunho alongside Tag in the middle of the group of soldiers heading toward the north exit. A blue sword shone from the scabbard strapped across his back—another gift from Wook. He turned at the shouts to see her flying toward him.

His eyes widened at the sight of her as she careened in his direction. He didn't hesitate, lifting his hands. He caught her by the waist as she flew into his arms. She released her wings, her full weight landing on his chest as she wrapped her arms around his neck.

"How could you?" she cried.

"I'm sorry," he said at once, and her traitorous heart skipped in amusement. He likely had no idea why she was upset.

"You were going to leave without telling me, weren't you?" It was her turn to pout.

She knew the whole of the army was staring. She was a celestial maiden, and their queen. But she didn't care. The boy she loved was leaving for battle and he hadn't *told* her first.

"I'm sorry," he said again. His voice was soothing.

She pushed away from him, lifting her face. "Prove it," she said recklessly.

His brows furrowed slightly, then, with a determined expression, he pulled her close and kissed her. She melted against him, the ground rumbling as cheers rose up all around them.

CHAPTER 39

SUNHO

The Under World
Yongin Military Base

HWANI WAS QUICK to retrieve Ren, arriving within minutes of her queen, with a team of swift horses and a carriage. It wasn't until the carriage was out of sight that Sunho rejoined Tag and the others.

They'd walked a few steps before Tag said, "You're embarrassed, aren't you?"

Sunho ducked his flushed face into his collar.

He hadn't meant to kiss Ren in front of so many people—in the moment, he'd simply forgotten where they were.

As they walked, Sunho noticed the stares he was receiving. Even if he didn't have a keen sense of hearing, he'd still have likely picked up on the whispers.

That's him, *the one the queen favors.*

Sunho braced himself, remembering Jinok's cruel remarks his first day on the Floating World.

Then she's not marrying the Volmaran prince?

Not after that kiss.

But he's . . . one of us!

He'd forgotten. Most of the soldiers were from the Under World.

They weren't disgusted, but awed that their queen would choose someone like him.

Still, the attention made his cheeks flame.

"Sunho!"

Chulsoo came jogging up to him, along with several others dressed in the silver-and-red livery of Sareniyan royal guards. While many of them had fled with Lord Muyeol and the other nobles, a large number had remained to defend the Under World.

He hadn't seen Chulsoo since the test—after that day, Sunho had trained exclusively with Jaeil's soldiers.

"All of you volunteered?" Sunho asked, his gaze sweeping the entirety of the group. There were fifteen of them.

"We couldn't let Hwani keep getting all the glory," Chulsoo said with a grin.

Together, they joined the rest of the rescue party gathering by the base's north exit.

Jaeil was already seated upon his mount, a pitch-black destrier with a white star on its forehead. He had changed from the night before and wore clothing that befitted his rank, black armor beneath a crimson-and-silver cloak.

He was flanked by a standard-bearer whose banner depicted the double wings of Sareniya, though the wings were connected at the bottom by a perfect sphere. Not a symbol of oppression as they once were, but of freedom. The queen's symbol. Ren's symbol.

"We'll ride out to meet the group in distress," Jaeil said. "The wagons are for the injured, children, and elderly." He motioned to carriages pulled by teams of four riders each.

Sunho mounted the horse that was brought to him, bringing it alongside Jaeil's stallion.

"Should you be riding out with us?" Sunho said. "You might be needed at the base."

"We haven't had a scout return since this morning, not even the aircraft."

Tag frowned. "You suspect something's wrong?"

"I don't know, but . . . These refugees are the first people we've seen in hours. I need to know what they know, what they've seen."

"Then we should hurry up and save them," Sunho said.

Jaeil eyed him, lifting a brow. "You make it sound easy."

"It is, for me," Sunho said. Maybe it was because of what had occurred at the Pond of the Daughters of Heaven, but he no longer felt as if there were two souls warring within him. Jaeil had once asked him how much stronger he would be if he had full access to the Demon—not only did he have that strength now, but he could call upon it *without* transforming.

"That kiss has gone to your head," Jaeil drawled.

It was Sunho's turn to eye Jaeil. "I want to test out my new sword on the demons," he said slowly. "Have you seen it? Wook made it *especially* for me."

"Maybe it's the demons' victory I should root for," Jaeil muttered.

Sunho grinned.

As he rode out with Jaeil, Tag, and the rest of the rescue party, he could sense his brother's gaze upon him, watching from atop the Wall. Junho had said he would rely on Sunho, but his brother remained a vigilant guardian. Sunho knew Junho wished to atone for his choices, but he couldn't help worrying for him. Sunho's soul had been saved; he hoped his brother would find a similar peace someday.

The rescue party thundered past towns that had been abandoned, its people having fled into the city.

They'd only gone a short distance before a burst of colored smoke hurtled through the air. The first had been yellow, a call for help. This smoke trail was red. Sunho urged his horse forward.

The group of refugees were racing down a bend in the road. There were at least six children among them, clinging to the backs of their guardians. They were pursued by double that number in demons.

"Secure the refugees!" Jaeil called to the others as the rescue party split apart around the fleeing group, meeting at a point to rush headlong into the crush of demons.

Tag whipped his crossbow in front of him, releasing a bolt that went hurtling into the chest of a demon.

"Sunho, now!" Jaeil shouted.

Throwing his mount's reins to Tag, Sunho leaped from the horse, skidding in the dirt.

From his back, he unsheathed Wook's sword.

The mithril in the blade sang to the mithril in his blood, and he flew across the dirt. The sword was an extension of his arm as he weaved between the monsters, dispatching them with quick, clean slashes. He didn't kill without remorse—these were lives he was taking, humans transformed against their will.

When the threat had been eliminated, he drew to a stop, panting.

He raised his head to check on the refugees when he felt the air shift behind him.

It was a demon, one he'd missed. He twisted around just as an arrow struck its neck.

He met the eyes of the bowman over his lowered weapon—one of the refugees, the bottom half of his face concealed from the dust beneath a cloth mask.

He nodded at Sunho, who returned the gesture.

They didn't linger out in the open but retreated swiftly back to the base.

A crowd met them upon their return. Junho separated from the group, coming toward Sunho. He scanned his brother's body for injuries. "Are you all right?"

"I'm fine," Sunho reassured him.

Yurhee, who had also stayed behind, grabbed Tag by the shoulders. He fended her off, his hand splayed against her cheek.

"Sunho," a new voice said. "I thought that was you."

Sunho stared as the bowman lowered his mask, revealing a proud, haughty face that Sunho recognized—Jinyoung, a member of the group of outlaws that had helped Ren and Sunho on their journey to Seorawon.

"It really is you." Binna stepped forward from the group. On her back she was carrying a small child, who popped her head over her shoulder to peer owlishly at him. "I must say, you're quite skilled for a sword dancer."

"What else was a lie?" Jinyoung scowled. "Were you and the princess really lovers?"

"*That* wasn't a lie," a soldier snickered, though it was said good-naturedly.

"No, I guess not," Jinyoung admitted grudgingly. "You can't fake that kind of devotion."

"Well, it's a good thing we helped you," Binna said, "otherwise you wouldn't have been here to come to our rescue."

"Where are the others?" Sunho asked. Besides Binna and Jinyoung, the cook and their leader had been part of the small band of outlaws.

Jinyoung's expression sobered. "They were turned," he said. "By that demon goddess."

"About that." Jaeil parted the crowd. Jinyoung and Binna bowed, catching sight of the standard-bearer.

"Thank you for coming to our aid," the archer said. "My name is Jinyoung, and this is Binna. We've come from Shima, a small village outside Seorawon."

"Shima . . . ," Jaeil said slowly, "I know of it. It's located west of Seorawon. You could have fled farther in that direction, but you came here instead, where you knew the demons were headed. Why?"

"We're outlaws," Jinyoung said, puffing out his chest. "We've been rebelling against the Sareniyan army for the past decade."

"And you're still alive," Jaeil acknowledged. "Which means you're survivors."

"That's right. We have a talent for staying out of sight. I've been keeping watch on the demon army. Last night, it was over a hundred thousand strong, maybe more. But when I looked this morning, there was only a quarter of that."

Unease settled in Sunho's gut. The army couldn't have disappeared overnight, but then where had they gone?

"I knew something wasn't right," Jinyoung said, "so I came to warn you. I would have come alone, but our group was spotted, and we had to escape together."

Jaeil closed his eyes, and Sunho knew the other boy was processing this new information and rapidly strategizing what to do next, had likely already deduced the reason for the army's disappearance. Sunho was surprised to realize that he trusted Jaeil completely. Whatever he decided, whatever path he chose to take, Sunho would follow him.

"What is he saying?" Chulsoo asked nervously. "What does that mean?"

"They're splitting the army," Jaeil said, looking up and toward the Wall. "They're not attacking from the north, as we thought, but—"

In the distance, the pounding of drums echoed first from the north side of the Wall, then from the east and west. Lastly, the south.

The Under World was surrounded.

CHAPTER 40

JAEIL

The Under World
Yongin Military Base

JAEIL THOUGHT BRIEFLY of what his father might have done before quickly dismissing the thought.

Jaeil wasn't his father. He never had been.

He rode out south from Yongin with Sunho and Tag. The refugees broke off from their group toward the north gate, where they'd harbor in the city for the duration of the battle.

Habin and Naksol had gathered the Sareniyan army on the plains beneath the Wall. All eighty-eight regiments awaited his orders. At his arrival, his commanders moved inward to meet him; their steeds, outfitted in bright armor, were like silver dragons converging upon him.

Naksol pulled on her reins, her charcoal-lined eyes flashing beneath her winged helm. "We've sealed off the entrances to the sewers, the river gates, and the train tunnel, which leaves only two access points into the city. The north and south gates." She grimaced, then added, "Only a small garrison defends the south gate."

Jaeil cursed himself for not seeing the possibility of this outcome, having believed that the demons, in their mindlessness, would strike the city to the north. He'd underestimated Sareniya's powers; she must be controlling them.

"Commander Habin," Jaeil said.

"Yes, General."

"Take command of the main army and meet the enemy here, at the north gate. I'll take control of the right wing and head east around the city."

"Splitting the forces." Naksol frowned. "Is that wise?"

"Our main objective is to keep the demon army out of the city and give enough time for the queen to challenge and defeat the Maiden," Jaeil said. "If we concentrate the forces here, we'll have a greater chance of defending the north side but will lose the Under World to the south."

He didn't like it—the enemy's numbers, even spread out, were significant—but this was their only chance to keep the people of the city safe for as long as they could.

"Understood," Naksol said. "Your orders, General?"

"Take the left wing and head west along the Wall to join me at the south gate. You'll meet resistance." Jaeil paused. "It will be difficult."

What he was asking her to accomplish was a nigh-impossible feat—her forces would be moving along the Wall as the demons converged upon them in multiple directions.

Naksol grinned recklessly. "I wouldn't have it any other way."

She left without further questions, calling her captains to her side.

"Commander Naksol and her soldiers are fierce," Habin said, "but the left wing is much smaller than the right wing. She won't make it."

Junho stepped forward. "I'll go with her."

"You're injured," Jaeil said. He hadn't seen Sareniya's Light sear through Sunho's brother, but he knew Junho had lost one of his wings as a result.

Junho extended his right arm. In the blink of an eye, it transformed into a massive wing, sprouting steel feathers, as if he held a bouquet of swords. With another flick of his arm, it transformed back into flesh, though his sleeve was now in tatters.

"I only have one wing." Junho rolled his shoulder. "But I think it's weapon enough."

Jaeil swallowed. "Indeed."

Junho rode to join Naksol, while Habin left to take command of the main army.

That left Jaeil with Sunho, Tag, and Yurhee. An odd assortment of allies, but none he trusted more with his life—a thought that would have seemed impossible a month ago.

He let the others ride ahead of him as he maneuvered his horse toward the right wing.

"Jaeil!"

He turned to find Wook racing toward him. His heart stumbled; they were about to be bombarded, what was he *thinking*—

He dismounted in time to grab the other boy by the shoulders.

"Wook," he said, shaking him slightly, "what are you doing here?"

"I wanted to give you this," Wook said, breathless.

It was a sword, exquisitely crafted, with a sturdy hilt and a sharp, double-edged blade.

"Thank you," Jaeil said, accepting it, "but you shouldn't have come. It's danger—"

"And this." Wook pressed up on his toes and placed a brief kiss on the corner of Jaeil's mouth.

Jaeil was rarely at a loss for words, but he found himself incapable of speech.

"Please, come back safe," he whispered. "I'll be waiting for you."

Turning, he then fled.

Jaeil allowed himself another minute of watching Wook, until he was certain he'd make it back through the gates of the city, before he mounted his horse once more.

Jaeil pulled his own sword from its scabbard, handing it off to a junior officer. He replaced it with the one Wook had given him. As he fought, it would remind him of all that he had to live for.

Sana was at the front of the cavalry when he rode up. If she'd seen his encounter with Wook, she didn't remark upon it, though her gaze lingered on the handle of his new sword.

"You're not a captain anymore," Sana said. "You should stay here and direct the main army."

"You know I couldn't ask anyone to take risks I wouldn't take myself."

"Hero complex," she coughed beneath her breath.

Jaeil maneuvered his steed so that he faced the cavalry. "You might have heard the rumors that the demons are transformed humans," Jaeil shouted, raising his voice so it could be heard over the snorting horses and the thunder of the demons in the distance. "The rumors are true. Fight with compassion, but not shame. We must reach the south gate in time to defend it from the horde. On me!"

With a shout, Jaeil urged his horse into a gallop, Sana on his right with his standard-bearer, and Sunho to his left, with Tag beside him. Yurhee had gone up to the top of the Wall with his runners, who carried orders for his artillery officers.

They rode southeast along the curve of the Wall. The ground rumbled with the hoofbeats of three thousand cavalry.

The demon army appeared in the distance, moving from light into shadow as they entered the plains beneath the Floating World.

He didn't slow down, urging his horse faster. It wasn't until the demons were within range of the artillery that Jaeil gave the signal to his standard-bearer, who raised her flag. Drums beat across the top of the Wall as catapults launched chunks of rubble into the horde. The demons screamed, slowing after each impact only to rush forward.

Jaeil spotted the entrance to the train tunnel up ahead, where engineers had detonated explosives near the entrance to block it. Habin's battalions were well-trained, and they quickly sprang into a defensive formation, raising their shields.

The demons reached them, colliding into their front line. They scratched and ripped at the soldiers, who held their positions, lunging with their spears through the gaps to pierce the demons. Sana fought fiercely beside him, expertly wielding a sword in each hand. Tag's arrows flew swiftly through the air, finding their marks, while Sunho's sword flashed like a bright star. Demons fell back, screeching in fear. Still, the sheer *number* of them made it impossible to push forward. As more arrived, they compounded against one another, generating an almost unbearable weight. If it continued like this, they'd never make it in time to meet Naksol and her soldiers.

"Sunho!" Jaeil shouted as he hacked at a demon that had managed to slip through the wall of shields. "I need an opening!"

Sunho leaped from his horse. Sweeping through the throng, he released his wings, piercing demons on either side.

He'd made a path big enough for the cavalry to rush through. As they raced forward, a great boom sounded behind them.

Jaeil whipped his head over his shoulder to see that the blockade sealing the tunnel had been destroyed, demons piling through the breach.

"Damn it! They'll get into the city that way."

"I'll go!" Sunho shouted. He launched himself into the sky before plummeting into the tunnel. A few seconds later, a great roar echoed from its depths, signifying that he'd transformed.

Jaeil pushed forward, reluctant to leave Sunho behind, but he had no other choice. The second half of the journey took twice as long as the first; demons swarmed all around them, snarling and snapping their teeth. Sana blocked a demon from tearing out his throat, while Tag shot arrow after arrow until he ran out, drawing a sword to hack and slash.

At last, Jaeil spotted the battle raging outside the south gate. By some miracle, the small garrison stationed there had managed to hold off the demons. A horn sounded in the distance—Naksol's battalions, coming around from the other side, with Junho at the front. Jaeil felt a pang in his chest; Naksol wasn't with them.

The soldiers of the left wing met up with Jaeil's group, and together they fought their way to the gate, barreling inside. Once everyone was through, they slammed them shut, and Jaeil shouted out orders to shore up the doors.

A roar shook the air. Jaeil skidded backward just as a creature flew over the gate. It was monstrous, with huge, reptilian wings, its armored chest scored with veins of mithril.

"Did you know about this?" he shouted at Junho. It was different than any demon they'd encountered, except for Sunho and Junho, which meant it was like them—a third-level demon.

"There *are* no others," Junho said. "Teacher only had one serum left . . ." Junho cut off. "It's *him*."

The monster was Juwon. He must have injected himself with the last serum, inducing a transformation. Juwon didn't land by the entrance but flew over them into the city.

"He's going after Sunho!" Tag shouted.

Jaeil cursed. "How do you know?"

"Because the only person who can defeat the Maiden is Ren," Tag said. "And if he kills Sunho, then that would be a blow she would never recover from."

Jaeil swore even more heavily. Sunho was strong, but Juwon's Demon form was massive—there was a chance he could kill him, especially if Sunho had been injured during the battle.

"Sana, take command."

She didn't hesitate. "Yes, General." She called the standard-bearer to her side.

Together with Tag and Junho, Jaeil climbed onto the south gate lift, ascending to the top of the Wall, where Yurhee had followed them in the *Sparrow*.

"I need a good pilot," he said without preamble.

"I wouldn't call myself *good*," Yurhee hedged.

"I'll settle for a reckless one."

She grinned. "Hop in."

Jaeil climbed aboard, immediately regretting his decision when the aircraft let out a heavy groan.

Junho stepped up beside Tag. "I'm coming with you."

"Can this thing fly with all of us?" Jaeil asked skeptically.

"Guess we'll find out!" Yurhee hollered.

Jaeil gritted his teeth as she cut the *Sparrow* loose and it lurched over the edge of the Wall.

It fell freely for several heart-stopping seconds before the mithril core kicked in and they soared east over the city.

They spotted Juwon flying ahead of them. His shape was long, serpentine, like a dragon pulled from the depths of the underworld.

"You were right," Jaeil said as he watched Juwon descend toward the train tracks that led to the tunnel. "He's trying to kill Sunho."

"He won't succeed," Junho seethed. "I won't let him." He launched himself off the side of the aircraft.

"Shit!" Jaeil cursed. Junho couldn't fly, he—

Except Junho had transformed, and with only one wing, was flying brokenly in pursuit, sweeping down toward the entrance.

"What should we do?" Yurhee shouted. "Should we turn back?"

"No," Jaeil said grimly. There was no turning back. They'd almost reached the end. Because if Juwon was here, then so was the Maiden.

CHAPTER 41

SUNHO

The Under World
The Tunnel

SUNHO WINGED THROUGH the tunnel as the demons cowered beneath him. Through his eyes, they appeared like black shadows limned in blue. Their appearance was different from Junho's Demon form; Junho had been aglow with mithril, lit up from within, its presence striated through his heart, his soul. Sunho knew it was the same for him. Which meant Sareniya's demons hadn't experienced a biological change—their transformation was temporary, reversible.

He landed heavily onto the tracks, releasing a powerful roar. The demons that had been racing down the tunnel fled back in terror.

None had reached the city.

Slowly he began to transform, the Demon leaving him like a cloak of shadow, dispersing into the darkness. He picked up his sword, which he'd clung to even as the Demon.

A rock skittered in the depths of the tunnel, and he turned to see a lone figure striding toward him.

Teacher.

Through the darkness, Sunho could see him clearly. Though something had changed. He no longer walked curled in on himself, facing the world as if it were a cruel hand, poised to strike. His spine was straight. Black, billowing robes fell from his shoulders, though Sunho noticed great tears in the fabric.

"It's curious, isn't it?" Teacher's voice echoed loudly down the cavernous tunnel. "Of all those who underwent the Mithril Enhancement Project, only two survived. Brothers. Is it in your blood, perhaps? Or is it your bond? That your will to save each other was strong enough to overcome the serum? Even death?"

Sunho approached slowly, keeping his sword in front of him.

"My brother was everything to me," Juwon said. "He raised me. When they took him from me, they shattered my heart."

Sunho's steps faltered. "It was the same for me," he said softly, Juwon's words echoing the grief he'd felt. He lowered his sword. "I understand the pain you went through. But . . . why did I have to suffer for your heartbreak? Why did my friends? I understand they shattered your heart when they killed him. But you broke mine, again and again."

"You're right, I was lost in my grief," Juwon said. "This cycle of pain and sorrow, let us end it here."

Juwon fell onto his hands and knees. His vertebrae elongated as the skin at his back broke open, revealing blue-black scales beneath. Veined wings erupted from his shoulder blades and a scream tore up his throat, bursting from his mouth in black bile.

Sunho slid back as he raised his sword.

Juwon's final form was dragonesque but warped, the Demon within him emphasizing his rage, his sorrow.

Sunho leaped to avoid a slash of his tail, skidding back as Juwon lunged at him, teeth snapping. He slammed into the wall of the tunnel, the great force causing pieces of the ceiling to crumble and fall. Sunho rolled aside as a boulder crashed to the ground where he'd been standing.

Then Sunho shot forward, mithril singing through his veins.

He didn't have to become the Demon to fight Teacher. He *was* the Demon.

He moved faster than he ever had before, his sword piercing Juwon's forearms, his hide, and his stomach.

The tunnel began to tremble as more rocks fell from the ceiling. Sunho vaulted onto a falling rock, leaping from it into the air, his sword angled downward. He stabbed Juwon in the chest, only to push back, landing once more on his feet.

Juwon roared, thrashing wildly as blood gushed from his many gaping wounds.

He was larger than Sunho, stronger, but his rage made him clumsy. He couldn't control the Demon. Not like Sunho, who didn't *seek* to control it, but accepted that it was a part of him, enhancing his fears but also his hope.

Yet if the Demon enhanced Sunho's emotions, it also strengthened his compassion. He wanted to punish Juwon for what he'd done, but he also ached for him, for the pain and loss that he'd endured.

Still, Sunho knew he had to end this vicious cycle.

Juwon reared back as Sunho lifted his sword for the final slash.

He was stopped by a loud *crunch*. Junho's wing had impaled Juwon from behind, the sharp ends having gone straight through his chest.

Junho released his wing, and Juwon transformed as he fell. Sunho caught him, lowering him to the ground.

His eyes, as they met Sunho's, were glazed; blood bubbled from between his lips. "I loved my brother," he choked out, his chest rattling with every word. "He was all I had in the world. He was like the sun. When they took him from me, it was as if they'd snuffed out the light. All I could see was darkness. It was all I could *feel.* I was alone.

"Do you know what that's like?" His eyes traveled from Sunho to Junho, who had come to stand beside him. "You do . . . you do . . . I'm sorry."

When his final breath passed his lips, Sunho placed Juwon on the floor.

Gradually he became aware of the scratching approach of demons. They were returning, undeterred by the collapsing tunnel. But he couldn't stay. Because if Juwon was here, then the Maiden . . .

"Go to her," Junho said.

"I don't want to leave you."

"I won't be alone." Junho nodded down the tunnel to where Jaeil was racing toward them, followed by Yurhee and Tag. "We'll defend the tunnel." He raised his voice so the others could hear. "But we won't be able to hold it for long. Hurry!"

Sunho sprinted past his friends, who ran to join Junho. His heart beat painfully in his chest. Juwon had been Sunho's age when his world was destroyed. Sunho might have shared the same fate, living with hatred in his heart, seeking only revenge, if it hadn't been for Ren.

She'd embraced the darkness within him, allowing him to accept the part of himself he'd wanted to hide from.

She hadn't saved him. She'd shown him how to save himself.

The world was filled with cruelties, some larger than others—he thought of his years at the orphanage, then in the army, what he'd endured in the mithril program, then the two years he'd spent in the Under World—but it was also filled with hope. For Sunho, there would always be hope, because of Ren.

She was waiting to challenge Sareniya. But she wouldn't be alone.

She'd never be alone, as long as he was breathing, as long as his heart was beating.

It beat for her.

He could feel the mithril responding to his emotions, coursing through his blood, his wings straining at his back as he burst from the tunnel.

He spiraled up toward the mithril sky, toward the Light, toward Ren.

CHAPTER 42

REN

The Under World
The Wall

REN FLEW SOUTH over the city to where her aunts were waiting for her on top of the Wall. It was odd to see Auntie and Lady Maya side by side, as different as a magpie was to a crane.

"Why are you both here?" Ren shouted, alighting atop the battlements. "You should have taken shelter with the others." The remaining Sareniyans had sought refuge at Hagye Military Base as they awaited the outcome of the battle.

"And leave our niece to fight the goddess alone?" Lady Maya wrinkled her nose. "I think not. It's my responsibility to stay," she added. "She's my ancestor, too, after all."

"I'm happy you're both here," Ren said, "but it'll be of more help to me if you leave, so that I can fight her without worrying for you."

"Then we'll go," Auntie said, "but not until she arrives. We'll wait with you until then."

Ren opened her mouth to argue some more, but *both* her aunts gave her stern looks, and she quickly shut it. She was outnumbered, though she couldn't help but be pleased about it.

She watched the battle from the Wall, gripping her scepter in one hand. She'd lost track of Sunho and the others when they'd circled east around the city.

She hoped everyone was safe—Jaeil, Yurhee, and Tag. Sunho would be all right. She had to believe that.

The air stirred as the world pulsed around her.

"She's here," Ren breathed. She turned to her aunts. "Aunt, Auntie . . . please . . ."

"Be strong, brave girl." Lady Maya took her free hand, pressing her fingers tightly before letting go. "I wish I had believed in you sooner."

"You believe in me now," Ren said. "That's all that matters."

She turned to Auntie. Her heart felt too big in her chest. There weren't words enough to express how much Auntie meant to her, how grateful she was, how much she admired and loved her.

"You were born to have wings," Auntie said. "Now fly!"

Ren took to the sky.

Sareniya approached fast, her wings trailing out behind her.

She flew to a stop above the Core, at the center of the city. As she spread her silver wings, they began to shine with blue Light. *The blood veil.* She was going to turn the whole city into demons.

Ren raised her hand and sent a spear of Light toward her. The goddess veered at the last second. With a scream, she whirled in Ren's direction.

An overwhelming pressure gripped her mind, as if drums were beating against her skull, but Nia's shield held.

"I see you've learned a new trick," Sareniya sneered. "But that won't help you."

She flew upward, toward the mines, releasing a beam of Light that struck the rocks with a massive blow.

"No!" Ren shouted as huge chunks of mithril fell from the sky onto the city.

She flung Light at Sareniya, who swerved out of the way.

With another scream, Sareniya threw a spear of Light that shattered the Sky Door. They spiraled up through the opening and into the sky above the Floating World.

Sareniya was relentless as she launched beams of Light at Ren, who managed to dodge them, nimbly weaving through the air.

Every beam that shot past her tore up the ground, leaving great swaths in the earth.

Lifting her scepter, she channeled her magic through the mithril shard. Her Light erupted from the stone toward Sareniya, who twisted around, releasing her own blast. Their powers collided, the energy causing the mountains to tremble.

"You've grown stronger in a short period of time," Sareniya shouted over the din. "How did you do it?"

"My ancestors taught me," Ren said proudly. She thought of Grandmother, Saya, and Nia. *Aria.*

With a furious scream, Sareniya launched more rays that Ren raised her scepter to block. They deflected off her weapon, spearing the buildings beneath them. They were above Sora now; Ren watched in horror as Light struck the boulevards, the temple and palace, the beautiful structures collapsing into pieces. "So your ancestors *gave* you their power?" Sareniya demanded.

"Most of them didn't have much power," Ren admitted.

Sareniya sneered. "So they were weak."

"No," Ren shot back fiercely. "I'm strong *because* of them."

She was empowered to know that the blood of the women who came before her ran in her veins—not because they were celestial maidens, but because they were her family.

She believed in herself because she believed in them. And because of Auntie, who raised her.

"Even you," Ren said. "I know I'm strong because of you."

She thought of Nia's words. *You must remember—my mother was never evil. Revenge was never what she desired. To return to her home,* freedom, *was what she wanted.*

Juwon had stolen Sareniya from the Ancestral Realm, had imbued her with his hatred, his malice. "Which is why I'm going to send you back. You don't belong here. This isn't your home."

Sareniya shrieked as Light erupted from her. Ren called forth her own Light to meet it.

As their combined magic filled the sky, a great pillar formed. The ground, the *world* began to crumble beneath them.

Ren's Light grew stronger, flashing as it overpowered Sareniya's. And then it engulfed her entirely. Ren had to look away from the brightness. When she turned back, Sareniya was no more, only a crimson robe falling to the earth.

But the pillar remained, powerful and all-consuming. It grew wider and wider, a tornado of Light, tearing up the ground, trees, and mountains. Great chunks of buildings were swept into the maelstrom, as were watchtowers and whole boats from the river.

The force of it was too strong; it started to pull Ren inward. She was about to be trapped, whisked away into its spiraling vortex.

"Ren!"

Sunho burst from around the pillar, scooping her up and into the sky.

All around them the landmass was breaking apart, separating into pieces. Sunho let go of her, only to grab her hand. Together they swerved through cascading rocks and toppling rubble, tumbling at last into a meadow.

Ren scrambled to her feet and raced to the edge. The pillar had dissipated, leaving behind a clear sky.

"Sunho, come look!" she shouted. The Floating World had split apart. Some of the smaller pieces rose to a higher altitude, no longer anchored to a greater weight.

Ren counted dozens of small floating isles, possibly more.

Below, sunlight spread over the Under World for the first time.

Something soft and cold touched her cheek. *Snow.*

"The demons," Sunho said in awe, having joined her at the edge. "They're changing back into humans."

Ren squinted, but she couldn't see. They were too far. "Describe it to me."

"It's like they're waking up from a slumber. They've stopped fighting. They're helping each other. Ren, it's incredible!"

Ren laughed and turned to embrace Sunho. He picked her up, spinning her in his arms.

"Look, the temple in the mountains remained intact!" She waved at the great mountain, on a piece of floating isle, though she couldn't see that far to know if anyone was waving back.

She wondered if the pond had remained, if Nia was watching from her ghostly perch. Ren imagined she was joined by her mother, that together they'd soon leave this world and journey home to the stars.

"What will happen now?" Sunho said. "There's no more Floating World."

"I'm not a queen anymore," Ren said, laughing shakily. "I wasn't a queen for very long, was I?"

Sunho frowned. "Does that disappoint you?"

"Not at all! But what do we do? I don't know if I can return to the valley."

She'd come too far, changed too much to go back.

"Well . . . ," Sunho said slowly. "We could stay here." They both peered around at the meadow. It was the same one they'd landed in weeks ago, where they'd shared their first kiss. It wasn't the largest of the pieces of the Floating World, but it was the perfect size for the two of them. "We could move the cottage in the reed field here, or we could make a new home."

"You mean . . . ," Ren said shyly, "you'd live here, with me?" She blushed at the thought. Just the two of them . . . it filled her heart with longing and joy. "We'd be so close to the sun," she said.

"And to the stars," he said.

"Then let's stay here, on this new world. A demon and a celestial maiden. What sort of life do you think we'll have?"

"I don't know," Sunho said, gazing at her with love in his eyes, "but I wouldn't want to spend it with anyone else but you."

EPILOGUE

Two Weeks Later

"CAPTAIN!" YUMI CALLED, running up to Jaeil outside the city hall council chamber.

"Sorry," she said when she reached him, rubbing the back of her head. "Habit."

Jaeil hadn't been a captain, nor a general, for several weeks, not since the Sareniyan army disbanded.

"It's governor now," Sana said, stepping from the council chamber to stand beside him.

Jaeil sighed. He was the interim governor for the time being, until the people of the city could properly elect a council, though he wasn't pleased about it.

"It's because you don't want the position that you're the best suited for it," Sana said, reading his thoughts, as usual.

Sareniya was no more. The Floating World had been destroyed. In its place were dozens of floating islands, some of which had already drifted from view. For the past two weeks, Jaeil had been working with the local government to restore order to the Under World and help acclimate the newly displaced Sareniyans.

"Governor . . . ," Yumi said, her eyes flitting between Jaeil and Sana, a small smile on her face. She'd been waiting patiently. "There's someone waiting for you," she said. "In the courtyard."

He found Wook by the circular fountain, gazing up at the sky. The sunlight brought out the traces of gold in his hair. Jaeil had the thought: *He is meant for the sunlight.*

"Oh!" Wook said, noticing him for the first time. "When did you arrive?"

"I just got here," Jaeil replied smoothly. "Was there something you wished to speak to me about?"

"My sister is leaving." Wook tugged at the bottom of his shirt in a nervous gesture. "She's going back to the valley."

"I see."

"I— She asked if I was going with her."

"What did you tell her?" Jaeil was careful to keep his voice neutral, though his stomach had dropped at Wook's words.

"I didn't answer her. I wanted to . . . talk to you first."

Jaeil tilted his head. "Do you want to go back?"

"No!" he said loudly. "I mean, I love my sister, of course, and I miss the people in the valley, but I—I want to stay."

"Then stay."

"You make it sound so simple. What would I even do here? I don't have a job. After my sister leaves, I won't have any family. I have nowhere to live."

"I have a house." Though he hadn't lived there properly for a year. "It's modest. But you're welcome to stay there."

"Live in your house?" Wook appeared shocked. "By myself?"

"No," Jaeil said slowly. "With me." He'd need to hire carpenters to renovate the estate. It was much too dark for Wook. He would need a shed for his smithing, and a garden.

"As for what you can do here," Jaeil continued, "you'll figure something out. You're resourceful. The Under World needs people like you.

Kind, good people." He paused, then added with a quirk of his lips, "To balance the people like me."

"You're kind," Wook said vehemently, taking a step toward him. "And good!"

"I was jesting," Jaeil said. "I can jest, you know."

Wook blushed. "I know."

"I didn't believe that I could be good, not until I met you." Jaeil removed his gloves and held out a hand to Wook. He took it, and Jaeil interlaced their fingers. "Stay with me, Wook. Help me build a better world."

Wook rested his head against Jaeil's shoulder. "*Yes.*"

THE COURTYARD OF Wolryudang was covered in snow. Sunho lifted his hand, catching a snowflake in his palm. He raised his face to the sky, where clouds drifted among the floating isles.

He had a memory of mithril clouds, but they were gone now. The factories had been shut down indefinitely.

He turned at the sound of footsteps. His brother descended the stairs of the teahouse, a satchel slung over his shoulder.

Junho looked different, dressed in the clothing Yurhee had procured for him, a soft yellow coat over a red jacket and pants. Her taste was . . . eclectic.

"Where will you go?" Sunho asked.

"I don't know," his brother replied. "I need time to figure out what it is I want to do with my life, to figure out who I even am." For so long, he'd been Sunho's protector; even when he served Juwon, it had been for Sunho's sake.

"There are also other demons out there," Junho said, "ones like us, who weren't transformed by Sareniya, but by Juwon. I want to find them, help them if I can."

"All right," Sunho said, struggling to hide his disappointment. They'd only just been reunited. But it would be selfish of him to ask his brother to stay with him. Junho needed to find his own way. "I'll be waiting for you."

"I'll come back." Junho smiled softly. "I'll always come back to you, brother."

IN THE MAIN room at Wolryudang, the morning after Junho had departed, Auntie informed Ren that she was leaving. Her traveler's pack hung from her back; her player's mask dangled from a string tied around her waist.

"So soon?" Ren said, sliding her seat back as she stood. "What about Wook?"

"What about that silly brother of mine?" Auntie scoffed. "He's decided to stay. Figures himself in love. Really I should disapprove of his choice, but when has he ever listened to me?"

"Jaeil is a wonderful person!" Ren protested.

"I know," Auntie said. Her smile was soft. "And what about you? Where will you go? Those floating islands look like they won't stay in one place."

"I hope not!" Ren said. "I want to see more of the world."

She and Sunho had decided to leave the cottage in the reed fields where it was—it could be a possible home for Junho, once he returned. Instead, they were building a house of their own. Yurhee and Tag were assisting them by ferrying the materials, while the head priestess—who was rebuilding her temple on the grounds of the old first ward mithril factory—had given Ren some of the seeds taken from her garden.

They had to hurry up, though. Their particular isle had begun to drift west.

"And you'll be with him," Auntie said.

Ren blushed. "Yes."

"Well, this is goodbye, then." Auntie's manner was brisk. "For now, at least."

Ren rushed into her arms. "Tell Hwi that I miss her, and that'll I'll visit soon, and—"

"Tell her yourself."

"—I love you."

"You must know," Auntie whispered, her breath warm against her hair, "how much I love you."

Six months later

FINISHED WITH THEIR chores for the day, Sunho and Ren lazed about in the meadow outside their cottage. Sunho was resting his head on Ren's lap while she held an umbrella over them both. Feeling the heat of the sun on his neck, he rolled over onto his side, murmuring, "Can you move the umbrella higher?"

"You're being very demanding," Ren teased, though she shifted the umbrella so it covered him entirely.

She felt the curve of his smile against her stomach before he sat up.

He took the umbrella from her hand, tossing it into the grass. "I can stand a little bit of sun."

She started laughing as he drew her into his lap. But when he kissed her, his soft lips pressing against her own, she sighed.

He was leaning toward her for a second kiss when they heard the sound of whirring propellers.

They scrambled to their feet in time to see the *Sparrow* appear over the edge of the island, bobbing in the wind.

Yurhee waved vigorously from the helm. She'd let go of the steering gear, and Tag was gripping the edge of the ship, his expression a mixture of horror and resignation.

"Poor Tag," Ren said, laughing.

Sunho grinned. "Should we go save him?"

Hand in hand, they ran to meet their friends.

ACKNOWLEDGMENTS

Thank you to my editor, Emily—your funny and warm notes always make me smile. And to Patricia—thank you for ten years of guidance and friendship; I'm so grateful to have you as my agent.

To the delightful team at Feiwel and Friends, thank you for everything that you do: publisher Jean Feiwel; designers Rich Deas, Beste Dogan, and Maria W. Jenson, and illustrator Guweiz, for another gorgeous book; copyeditor Starr Baer; proofreaders Jessica White and Jaime Herbeck; production manager Allene Cassagnol; associate production editor Kelly Markus, for the behind-the-scenes magic; and, of course, thank you to the marketing and publicity team at Macmillan and Fierce Reads, especially my lovely and fantastic publicist, Chantal Gersch, and the wonderful Teresa Ferraiolo.

To Hodderscape and the team: Molly Powell, Jo Dickinson, Sophie Judge, Kate Keehan, and more, thank you for providing the best home for my books in the UK; and thank you to Natalie Chen and Taylor Yinshi for the stunning cover design.

To Anissa and the team at FairyLoot, your support of my books has been life-changing, thank you.

To the incredibly talented and kind authors who offered early blurbs for *The Floating World*, thank you: Sue Lynn Tan and Judy I. Lin.

To my critique group, thank you for being the most supportive and loving group of friends: Janella Angeles, Ashley Burdin, Alexis Castellanos, Kat Cho, Madeleine Colis, Mara Fitzgerald, Amanda Foody, Amanda Haas, C.L. Herman, Katy Rose Pool, Akshaya Raman, Meg RK, Tara Sim, and Melody Simpson; and to my friends, thank you—I adore all of you: Nafiza Azad, Hannah Bahn, Veeda Bybee, Lauren Hennessy, Ashley Kim, Michelle Kim, Erin Rose Kim, Lyla Lee, Susan Lee, Cynthia Mun, Ellen Oh, Cindy Pon, Karuna Riazi, and Sarah Suk. And of course, thank you to my best companions, my pups, Toro and Leila.

Special shout-out to the incredible artists who worked with me on my preorder campaigns: Califlair, ZSJUN, and younyounsama, as well as all the artists who've worked on art for special editions of *The Girl Who Fell Beneath the Sea*, *The Floating World*, and *The Demon and the Light*.

Lastly, thank you to my family: aunts, uncles, cousins, nieces, and nephews, and, of course, Halmeoni, Mom, Dad, Camille, and Jason—I love you thiiiiiis much!

ABOUT THE AUTHOR

Axie Oh is the *New York Times* bestselling author of *The Girl Who Fell Beneath the Sea*, *XOXO* and *ASAP*, and the *Rebel Seoul* series. Born in New York City and raised in New Jersey, she studied Korean history and creative writing as an undergrad at the University of California San Diego and holds an MFA in Writing for Young People from Lesley University. Her passions include K-pop, anime, stationery supplies, and milk tea, and she currently resides in Las Vegas, Nevada, with her dogs, Toro and Leila.